The Adventures of
MYHR

P.N. ELROD

D0378189

THE ADVENTURES OF MYHR

A Baen Books Original

Baen Publishing Enterprises
P.O. Box 1403
Riverdale, NY 10471
www.baen.com

ISBN: 0-7434-3532-X

Cover art by Jamie Murray

First printing, June 2003

Distributed by Simon & Schuster
1230 Avenue of the Americas
New York, NY 10020

Production by Windhaven Press, Auburn, NH
Printed in the United States of America

To the *real* Myhr and Terrin,
Jamie Murray and Troy Rhodes.
This is a work of fiction,
Except for those bits that really happened.

CHAPTER ONE

Some place like Kansas, only not as hilly.

"I wish," I said, puffing hard because we were running flat out. "I really, really wish. You would. Develop your. People skills."

"Bite me," said Terrin, also puffing hard.

I'd have rolled my eyes, but needed to watch where we were going. It was midnight, with a lightning-shot sky dumping rain on us like daggers. Despite this, there were a number of very angry locals hot behind us, either a lynch mob or an *auto-da-fé*, which I think is Latin for barbeque. The crowd supplied themselves for either possibility, having brought along both torches *and* ropes.

No shoddy workmanship for Terrin, who is a wizard. When he decided to piss a person off he always put a two hundred percent effort into it. On this occasion, for reasons best known to himself, he caused a bouquet of purple daisies to sprout out of the bald head of the town's mayor. Bad enough, but they'd been infested with some kind of bugs that gave the man an attack of amazingly ugly hives.

Unfortunately for us, the mayor was popular and had an army of very large relatives all intent on avenging the family honor.

The thunder cracking overhead and the hiss of falling water kept me from hearing how close pursuit might be. As I had the better eyesight after dark, I led the way, hoping to find some spot where Terrin and I could go to ground for a minute so he could get us out. His traveling crystals had been charged up for weeks, but times had been pretty good on this stopover, so we'd put off leaving.

I had only a sketchy idea of the lay of the land here. We'd left the town in a random direction, striking off over ice rink-flat farm country. No matter where we went, we'd be seen.

"House," I said, pointing to a humped building with a thatched roof, the only thing in running range that might provide a temporary refuge.

"Okay." Terrin was shorter, but more than able to keep up as I tore over the ground, my boots making muddy salad of whatever crop the field held.

No lights showed ahead. At this hour any sensible farmer would be tucked away in bed having a good snooze through the storm, which is what I'd be doing now if Terrin hadn't wanted to make a spectacular magical point. Couldn't he have just given the mayor a little tummy ache instead? I hate those.

The house turned out to be a barn. Good. Then we wouldn't have to deal with yet another irate local trying to kill us. One mob was more than enough. We ripped around and found a door, dragging it open.

Inside, I curled my lip at the sudden stink of damp livestock, then violently shook water from my soaked mane. My rust-colored fur would either droop or be sticking out in clumpy spikes all over my head, but corrective grooming would have to wait. "How soon?"

Terrin was wheezing hard, but already shrugging off his oversize backpack. "Gimme a minute."

I knew the drill; it would take longer than that for him to set up. We needed something to block the door in case the mayor's relatives turned out to be marathon runners. Some bales of hay were stacked neatly against one wall. I grabbed one in each hand and hauled them over. A few mice got dislodged. My ears swiveled to track their scattered retreat, and I had to repress an urge to lunge. Not that I'm into chasing mice, much less eating them. The reaction was some deep instinct thing, nothing to get wound up about, put it down to my weird DNA mix.

I slammed the bales behind the door and went back for another two, then two more. But that wasn't the only entrance to the place. Another, larger door was at the far end. I didn't think there'd be time to take care of that one, too.

"Terrin?"

He was still rummaging in the backpack.

"What's the holdup?" I asked. "You didn't lose them? Tell me you didn't lose them."

He muttered something impolite as he dug. "Flashlight!" he snapped.

I took that to be a request, not an explicative, and shrugged my own pack from my shoulders. It was nearly pitch dark, for him, anyway, something I don't always remember. I prefer order over chaos and found my flashlight exactly where it was supposed to be. One click and its beam shone into Terrin's search area.

"Don't you throw anything out?" The inside of his bag looked like a Dumpster.

He snarled sudden triumph, having snagged up two perfectly formed clear quartz crystals. They were about

an inch in diameter and as long as my hand. Terrin gave
me one.

"Get ready," he said, dragging one heel along the floor
to make a rough circle around us.

I was ready ages ago. Outside, the first of the mob
had arrived and were pushing against the door. You'd have
thought the deluge would have put them off. The bales
would hold them for maybe . . . ahhh . . . no. The bales
weren't holding at all. The top one tumbled down in a
squashy crash as people on the other side applied muscle
against wood. Yells of unholy glee ensued as they inched
the door open against the rest of the barrier.

At the far end came energetic hammering on *that* door.
Until it burst open. A bunch of really big guys flooded
in, wearing even bigger grins. And I thought *I* had teeth.

"Get 'em!" several of them roared. They charged forward. Just then the group at the first door succeeded in
their assault, sending the last bales tumbling over into the
path of their friends. It was a wonderful pile-up, but not
enough to stop them.

"Now," said Terrin, in a strangely calm voice. His eyes
were shut as he held his crystal.

Against all sense, I shut my eyes as well, clutching my
crystal, and hoping my backpack was within the circle.

The yelling mob, the disturbed livestock, the splat of
rain on thatch, abruptly faded. I thought I felt the brush
of a hand grabbing my collar, but it seemed to pass right
through me before fading, too.

Then came the tough part. Well, it's not that tough,
and I should be used to it by now. It's the mental image
that gets to me. I don't know what Terrin felt during
the process, but to me it was always like being flushed
down a toilet. A rushing noise, a swirling, that sudden
twist, and the awful feeling that my guts were never
going to catch up with the rest of me, then the worse
feeling when they did.

Whoosh. Slam.

I held still, waiting for the next shoe to fall, but it never does. Once my consciousness figured it out I relaxed, sighing with relief.

Terrin said, "Why do you always groan like that? That was *fun!*"

"If you're an astronaut riding the vomit comet." I opened my eyes, squinting at a bright day. The barn and storm and riot were gone, left behind on yet another world. "Where are we? Is it home yet?"

"I don't think so. There wasn't time to pick a direction. Random chance again."

"Damn." The air didn't smell like home, though it was nice and soft. It had that fresh after-dawn tinge and felt like a late spring or early summer month. Grass, lots of brilliantly green, lush grass covered gentle hills, a living invitation to roll around and act silly.

Grass is coo-ool.

"Argh!" said Terrin, clapping a hand over his eyes against the daylight. He dropped and began hurriedly rooting in his pack again. "Sunglasses! Where are my shades?"

Mine were zipped in my jacket pocket. I put them on, then stowed away the flashlight in its designated pouch. My bag had been within Terrin's circle, thankfully. Some of the debris from the barn floor had traveled with us. I found my grooming comb with the wide teeth and started working on my still-wet mane. A quick run-through, another good head-shake and it would dry just fine in the open air.

The rest of me was still pretty damp, though. In silent common accord, Terrin and I put on dry clothes. He found his sunglasses and a purple fishing hat. "I don't like this place," he grumbled. "Something's not right here. Too damn much light." Under his short red hair he had naturally pale skin, so he had a right to complain. More than once I'd seen him lobster out after just an hour. Not a happy experience for either of us.

"You always say that, unless it's a night landing."

A grouchy snarl as he continued digging. "Gimme your crystal."

I gave it over. He put it in a small net bag along with his own quartz, safety-pinned it to the top of his hat, then pulled the hat down low over his brow. The crystals could start charging up with sun energy right away while we walked, an ingenious idea. Mine, as a matter of fact. He was a brilliant wizard, but I have my moments, too.

"So what happened?" I asked as he repacked all the junk he'd tossed around in his searches.

"What d'ya mean?" He pulled on a long-sleeved shirt and wrapped a bandana around his exposed neck to keep from burning. I never had to worry much about such things; my body-fur was better than sunblock-50.

"The mayor, the irate citizens, the mob, the chase scene. I just want to know why. We had a nice spot there."

"Mayor pissed me off."

"Obviously. How?"

"His attitude. Trying to act like he knew everything. Frigging amateurs. They do a little weather charm and think they've got the whole Multiverse in their hand when it's the other way around. I was *trying* to make him see what he was screwing around with; you can't just poke sticks at elementals for the fun of it. Unless you know what you're doing—and he didn't—all kinds of shit can happen."

"Weather? That storm . . . ?"

"Was his fault, not mine. Seemed to think he was helping out the farmers. I was trying to tell him he was sucking rain away from another area where it was *supposed* to be, upsetting balances, but he didn't want to hear that. Nothing pisses me off more than people who insist on being stupid. He wanted things to be growing in his *microscopic* piece of the planet—so I made some stuff grow to restore the balance."

"The purple daisies."

Terrin snickered. "Yeah. You should have heard everyone screaming when those sprouted out."

"I did. That's why I came downstairs with our packs." For the sake of survival I was forever prepared and alert to the signs that a hasty exit was at hand. Screaming people was one of them. At the little inn where we'd been staying the common room had overflowed with vocalized panic. "You spent good magic on that? It'd have been better to punch him in the nose; the same mob would have come after us."

"I didn't use *my* magic, I transferred some local energy in a different direction. There was more than enough off that storm for me to turn him into a Triffid if I wanted."

"Or maybe that giant carrot guy from *The Thing*?"

"Yeah, but the Howard Hawks version, not the other film—though *that* would have been fun."

Terrin had some really warped ideas of what constituted fun. Most did not bear thinking about.

"I had to transfer energy anyway, use up the surplus," he added. "That wannabe Oz dufus with his grandstanding was too busy floating his ego with all the applause to pay attention to his storm. He'd left things running, so it was building up to a good hail fall. Would have ruined all the crops. I took the edge off with that daisy gag."

"The bugs, too?" It hadn't been a pretty sight watching the mayor dancing around getting all bit up by the things. And it got downright revolting when he frantically started ripping his clothes off, the better to scratch at the hives.

"Those drained off the tornado that was coming."

"Really?"

"Yup. Nothing like spontaneous generation of life for using up excess power."

"Sure you didn't use some of yours? You look a little gaunt."

"I just played traffic cop, and it's this damn daylight that's messing with my looks."

He was touchy about his appearance, so I let it drop. "Will he ever get rid of the daisies and bugs?"

"Not anytime soon. He'll have to find another wizard to fix it back, and that will cost him. Maybe he'll learn a lesson or the other wizard can talk some sense into him. There's nothing worse than Talents who think they know everything about the Art. They're way more dangerous than those of us who do."

Terrin was an expert, and he did know a lot, but for the moment not enough to get us back home again. I kept quiet on that sensitive point and nodded toward a hill. "I think there's a road over there."

"What makes you think that?"

I shrugged. "It just seems the right way to go. You got your magic, I got my instinct."

"Okay. Let's go find out where we are. I'm starving."

We had traveling food in the packs, along with water, but those were for emergency only during stopovers in truly barren worlds. Whenever possible, we tried to live off the land. That usually meant taking odd jobs to earn our way. I'd do street-singing and story-telling, and when he had the energy, Terrin would trade minor magics for cash, but only in places where magic was accepted. Otherwise, he bartended.

Once upon a time, oh, a few dozen worlds ago, we lived on Earth—our Earth, the one you're on, not any of these other spots that called themselves by the same name. Terrin had a nice little metaphysical bookstore and coffee shop that afforded him the freedom to do what he liked. What he liked most after magic was getting laid—one of my favorites, too—and hardcore partying. The techno club raves he frequented in Deep Ellum in Dallas provided outlets for both. I'm more of a rock and roller. Techno is okay, just not for me. The rocker girls are just as cute.

I should really introduce myself, though. I'm Myhr—rhymes with *purr*—just Myhr, no other name that I can remember. What makes me more obviously different from most people are my cat features on a man's body. Just the face, I don't have a tail, though a lot of girls have enthusiastically assured me the tushy I do possess is very appealing.

And no, I am *not* related to the tunnel guy on that TV series. If that was true I'd have hit him up for an introduction to Linda Hamilton.

Where I came from is a mystery to me. Terrin thinks it was a magical experiment; I've speculated on genetics. I *do* have plenty of feline DNA making whoopee in my human-shaped bod—found that out when I saved enough cash working in Terrin's store to have a test made. So far no black-suited government types came banging on the door to make an issue of it. Terrin said he'd put up a protection spell around me to prevent that. Mighty altruistic of him, but I'm sure he did it for himself just to avoid dealing with the annoyance. Anything that keeps him away from parties and/or getting laid is an annoyance.

My lack of memory of where I was born and what I did before turning up on Terrin's doorstep never bothered me much. Not that I wouldn't like to know, but I don't stay up nights worrying about my origins. Lots of people might get bent out of shape over the big "Who am I?" question, but include me out. It's better to enjoy the moment and leave that angsty stuff to the heavy-duty thinkers. Bet if they got laid more often they wouldn't put so much time in on the topic.

How Terrin and I got bounced off our Earth and ended up ping-ponging from world to world is another story, which I'll get around to when I'm ready to tell it. In the meantime, we trudged up one green hill and down another and, sure enough, my instinct came through again, taking us to a thin dusty ribbon of a road.

"Which way?" asked Terrin. He stretched his back, making popping sounds. "Left, right, up, down, inside-out?"

"Left." I didn't know why, but that was the way. To what, I also did not know, though it usually meant people and food. That's how I found Terrin's shop after all. He'd fed me, so I stayed on.

"My left or yours?"

Mine, of course. He could have probably figured it out himself using his own internal compass, but the one in my subconscious worked faster and didn't cost any magical effort. Traveling spells and transferring weather energy around was exhausting, though he'd never admit it; better for him to conserve himself until we had a handle on this particular stop. He looked pretty pooped.

A couple of hours later we saw the signs of civilization, a slow and easy one, represented by a simple farmhouse, low tech again, with a penchant for thatched roofing. I'd have thought we were still back on the previous world but for the subtle differences in building design. Also, this house was washed in a dull brown color. The other place went in for bright primaries.

A waist-high wall marked the perimeter of the immediate yard and its vegetable gardens; the gate was unlocked, so we went in.

"Hello!" I called toward the house. Someone was home; smoke rose from the chimney.

We paused a short, respectful distance from the front porch so as not to make the owner nervous about our intentions. It was usually safer to assume people everywhere were paranoid. After a minute, a farmer-type in homespun, earth-colored clothes emerged from the dark interior to stare at us. Well, mostly at me.

"Hello," I said politely. "We're just passing through. Could you tell us how far it is to the next town?"

He stared some more. "Ikghop patuuny mafork?" he asked.

"I said, could you tell us how far to the next town?"

"Skidwhip humdish?"

"I almost got that," I said to Terrin.

"Keep him talking," he told me, his voice tight with strain.

"Hello, Mr. Farmer, the weather here is great, isn't it?"

"Red salad fork," said the farmer.

"Really? I can fix my alarm clock myself." I took off my sunglasses. My eyes made a hit with him, judging by how wide his own went in reaction. Vertical pupils are one of my best features.

He scowled. "Who are clipwiddles, anycrab?"

"Sorry, I didn't catch that."

He turned back toward the house. "Hey, Verna, I think there's a circus plading to fardibt."

"Got it!" said Terrin.

I glanced at him. He'd relaxed, but his face was still red from the effort. Language spells were also hard on him, but he only had to cast one once per world.

"I need a drink," he added, positively sagging.

"The well's over there," said the farmer affably, pointing. "Help yourself, the water's sweet. What was all that gobble-gobble? Your friend from another country?"

"He's from Barcelona." Terrin went to the well, lowering the bucket by means of a wooden crank.

"Oh." The farmer nodded, as though that explained everything. Maybe this world had such a place. "That where the circus come from?"

"There's no circus," I said. "We're just travelers."

"So you *can* speak English. Should have said so. Then why the get-up?"

"What get-up?" I asked, very innocently.

"The mask."

"Mask?"

He peered closer at me. I flared my lip whiskers and twitched my ears around so he could see it was all real. I'd been through this kind of interview a thousand times, but still found it amusing. "Well, I never seen the like! What kind of eyes are those? Gold as our old tabby's. Verna! You gotta come out here!"

"Yeah, Zack, what is it?"

Verna came out, did her turn at staring and asking the usual questions, and I did my turn at being charming. Unless they're allergic, most people like cats, so I played on it, enjoying myself. It eventually led to an invitation to lunch, and I traded stories of the road for food. The food was good, too, very close to that of the Earth I knew, so I didn't have to worry about its digestibility. Trust me, Terrin and I have been to places that really do have green eggs and ham. They taste about the way you'd expect from their looks, too, no offense to Dr. Seuss.

I helped with the post-lunch clean-up, which pleased Verna to no end, while Terrin got specific directions to the next town from Zack, along with some useful local information. As a first contact situation went, Captain Picard would have been proud of us.

We had about two hours of walking ahead, but with a full stomach I was in the mood for a little light exercise. Terrin wasn't pleased, but only because it was day. His pale skin was more suited for night rambles.

"Too damn bitching bright," he complained. "I don't like this place."

"Better than others we've been to."

"Something's not right here," he went on, sniffing the air suspiciously. "Too dry. Too . . . something."

I thought the weather was just fine. Terrin enjoyed complaining; he was good at it, but I wasn't in the mood to help him indulge. Verna's cooking was first-rate and its proper digestion deserved my undivided attention.

The walk in was easy, with a gradual traffic increase the farther we went. Much of it tended to be farmers with things to sell, but they'd give the way over to an occasional cart or passenger wagon, and a few times guys in uniforms would march or ride past. I checked these dudes out for weapons, since you can tell a lot about the level of a place's tech development by what kinds of things people used to kill each other. It's a sad comment on the human condition, but we're kind of stuck with it.

There were lots of swords—the skinny kind—bows, knives, lances, and a crossbow-type contraption. No firearms yet that I noticed, but maybe an ordinary soldier or town guard couldn't afford a pistol. I'd rather no one had to carry weapons at all, but people are people, and not everyone is as easy to get along with as I am. Not that I was above protecting myself, but I'm more of a lover than a fighter.

The town proved to be fairly large, sprawling beyond the confines of a high defense wall. That was good and bad. We could blend in better with a crowd, but unless they had a covered sewer system, things tended to get smelly in walled cities. I'd never fully appreciated the joys of modern sanitation until my first encounter with a genuine medieval-type settlement. True civilization—as I broadly defined it now—was any society with working indoor plumbing and real toilet paper.

More soldier types trooped past, not quick-marching, but not wasting time. Several of them stared at me, either puzzled or amused, and I heard speculations about circuses. That was good. No one was drawing back in abject terror, muttering about two-legged cat demons, or making signs against the evil eye. I'd experienced all of those in our travels, and being taken for a side-show exhibit is preferable.

Joining in with a knot of locals, we passed unchallenged through one of the many wide-open gates, which seemed a favorable sign of peaceful times. There were all different types of skin shades, costumes, and accents, lending a cosmopolitan air to the place, and everyone looked fairly healthy and well-fed. Hopefully, this would be just another quiet stopover until the travel crystals were charged up again with magical energy. Then we could take off for the next world under better circumstances than our last rapid launch. Maybe the next trip would even take us home.

Zack had recommended a place to stay that was cheap, clean, and served food that wouldn't kill you. He said to mention his name to the owner. After some asking around on the twisty cobbled streets we found it, a modest two-story structure, this time with a tile roof, not thatch. The ground floor was half-tavern, half-café. We didn't have any local money, but had learned to be inventive about making a living, and we're not shy about applying for work. The owner already had plenty of free help—his family—but after he got past the first shock over my looks I offered to sing and story-tell to bring in more customers, this in exchange for food, board, and tips. He was on the ball enough to see my face as a potential to draw in crowds.

"I run a family place," he said. "Has to be clean stories."

"All of them?" I was a little short on those.

"All of them."

"Okay, I think I can do that." So I wouldn't be able to share my stockpile of dirty jokes, I still had all the rest of Hollywood to draw on. He wanted a sample before taking me on, so I sang the Beatles' "When I'm 64," then rendered up a ten-minute medieval version of *Casablanca*, summarizing like crazy. I kept the Bogie impersonation intact, though, since I'm very good at it, and sang "As Time Goes By" in good voice. Instead of a plane, Ilsa left in a carriage. I try to avoid sad tales, but this one is always a winner with the women in the audience. When I got to the "beautiful friendship" line, the innkeeper's eavesdropping wife was streaming tears. I'd called it right again.

"Oh, that's the most *beautiful* story," she said, blowing her nose into her apron. "Clem, we keep him! He'll be better than that juggler who broke all the cups. And such a sweet face! And those gold eyes! Just like our old tabby!" She looked ready to scratch me behind the ears. I prefer belly rubs.

"Okay," said Clem, rounding on me. "You start today. Get outside and sing, and tell people to come by this afternoon for more stories."

"What about an evening show?"

"We'll just have the people staying here already—which would be you and your friend. There's a city curfew. Very strict. Everyone has to be off the streets by the sunset bell or the watch jails you."

That was useful to know. "Any reason behind this?"

"It's for our own good, so says Overduke Anton."

"Lots of crime?"

"Not since curfew started. There's less thievery with all the people in their own homes, so it makes sense to me. You want to be out and about at night you're either one of the overduke's watch or up to no good."

Nice black-and-white reasoning there, but it'd be tough on Terrin. The only time he liked being out was after dark. I'd have to make sure he knew the rules. He was presently talking to Clem's wife about soup recipes. In his checkered past he'd done some chef-type training at a restaurant and knew a thing or three about flavorings. He could charm people, too—when he was in the mood— and they were having a laugh about something or other. I beamed relief. It looked like we'd be comfy enough for the duration.

We took our packs up to the room; it was a small one,

of course, but being virtually rent-free I wasn't complaining. I mentioned the curfew to Terrin, but he said he was staying in anyway. He grabbed the cover off the bed, wrapped it around his shoulders, then sank cross-legged to the floor.

"See ya," he said, then his dark gray eyes rolled up so only the whites showed. He took long, slow breaths, in through the nose, out through the mouth. He'd be meditating for hours, which he usually did instead of sleeping. Just as well, for it meant I had the one bed to myself, and I liked to stretch out. I wanted to crash now, but had to go to work. Midnight on the last world, noon on this one. I'd be jet-lagged for a few days, or is that travel crystal-lagged? Oh, well, I could sleep tonight. With that curfew thing going on it would be quiet.

Changing into my show-time look, which consisted of a clean, pirate-style white shirt with some fancy black embroidery, polishing my boots, and fluffing my mane, I went downstairs to get started.

I was a hit in Rumpock, which happened to be the name of the city. The language spell usually translated names to a home-Earth equivalent, but not all the time. That often gave me a clue as to what songs to sing. What goes over well in Winnipeg can flop in L.A. You can't go wrong with the Beatles, though, so I shamelessly, and without paying royalties, sang one after another of those songs that lent themselves to *a capella* recitals. If I'd had a guitar, I could have done more, but hauling my backpack all over was as much luggage as I wanted to carry.

Into the afternoon and early evening I sang, answered questions about my looks with jokes, invited people inside, then sang some more and told stories. It was a good thing for me that back home I'd park myself in front of the TV and soak up countless old movies. Retelling all those tales saved me a lot of work making up my own. I'd spin them out with some reenactment, sometimes getting a member of the audience up there with me to help out. That always went over well, especially when I'd do *Romeo and Juliet*, because I'd try to pick out a cute, unattached girl for the other lead and feed her the lines. That was always good for a giggle. I was careful to improve the story by always giving it a happy ending. The one time I did it Shakespeare's way bombed totally. When it comes to dinner theater, people like a feel-good finish to go with their dessert.

That day's take was pretty good, and Clem let me keep half the tips. Tomorrow would be even better as word got around, he predicted. I hoped so. You can make a decent living telling stories—especially in a society without TV, computer games, radio, or a lot of books. From what I heard and observed, this town was definitely pre-Gutenberg, and I don't mean Steve. (I bet he spells his name different, anyway.)

Afterwards, while sharing the family's late meal, I played wide-eyed tourist with lots of questions, learning more about the ins and outs of Rumpock. Speculation about my cat's face led around to the topic of magic, just like I wanted. A few people in town were considered to be Talents. Whether it was of the stage show variety or the real deal like Terrin's remained to be seen. Clem and his wife, Greta, had only heard rumors of wonder-workings and were inclined to disbelieve them. I didn't press too hard for information.

Terrin and I had to be careful; some places were very anal about magic, so he usually kept a low profile. We'd hit more than one spot where wizards were the dish *du jour*. Those places weren't too healthy for me, either. Sometimes peoples' fears can be a real pain.

I trudged upstairs for a well-earned collapse, my brain pleasantly buzzed by exhaustion and Clem's own beer. As brews went, it would go over big-time in Dallas.

Terrin was still in the middle of the floor doing his

meditation thing, oblivious to my entrance. He hadn't moved a muscle since I'd left hours ago, but I was used to that. I prefer the old-fashioned kind of spacing out, which requires I fall into bed and check my eyelids for light leaks. Putting the candle I'd brought on a table by the bed, I gave in to a mighty stretch, loving the muscle-creaking agony. What a day, all umpteen hours of it.

We had a little square of a window covered with a wood shutter. I pulled it open for a last look outside and to get some air. The latter was none too good, being this deep in the city. Rumpock did have a sewer system, consisting of a series of open ditches that emptied into the Rumpock River. After learning that, I'd made a mental note to stick to hot tea or boiled water. And beer. Beer was gooo-oood.

The narrow street below was empty now, very quiet. I'd sleep like a log. If logs sleep. Now there was something to wonder about. Do logs sleep? Once in a while I come up with angsty questions that *do* bother me. Like why kamikaze pilots wear crash helmets.

Oh, yeah, the beer I'd had was *real* good . . . Clem had a winner fermenting in his basement barrels.

Down below I heard a soft sound like whispering. My ears sluggishly perked forward to pick up more. Probably someone who hadn't made the curfew. None of my business, but I snuffed the candle and peered out, my eyes fully dilated to take in the night view. Much of the color was washed away, a sacrifice to being able to see so well in the darkness, and boy, could I ever track movement.

Something was definitely on the move, too. I saw a rippling along the cobbles, like heat warping the air. The ripple grew more pronounced; the air thickened into a dark mist. Streaky at first, then growing more substantial the longer I stared. It covered the width of the street, flowing like a river. The only sound was that weird whispering, like thousands of secretive ghosts.

The fur on my nape went straight up.

Traveling with Terrin had brought me next to a lot of strange things, but nothing like this. It was huge. I angled my view to take in as much of the street as I could, coming and going. The whatever-it-was was everywhere, drifting along slow, but as though with purpose, with direction. Just as I began to wonder if it was intelligent or powered by intelligence, a tendril of the dark stuff oozed out from the main body and came creeping up the side of the building toward me.

I slammed the shutter into place and locked it, for all the good it would do. There were cracks around the closure, and that black misty stuff looked like it could just ease through. I backed away, staring hard at those small openings.

An inner sense told me the stuff was now level with the window, pausing just outside. Part of me wanted to open the shutter just a little bit for a look, but a much stronger part—one that had seen that particular *Twilight Zone* episode and what had been waiting for William Shatner on the other side of *his* window—kept me sensibly in place. Time to call the cavalry.

"Uh . . . Terrin? You might wanna see this. Terrin?" I shook his shoulder. "Come on, wake up."

He didn't snarl and wave me off, his usual way when being jolted from a meditative state. Eyes fast shut, his pale face was a sickly gray and slick with sweat. That wasn't right.

I half knelt and shook him again. "Terrin? Hey, buddy, don't do this, I'm scared enough."

Something audibly brushed against the window opening. I jumped, my heart trying to swim upstream to my throat.

I shook Terrin a lot harder now. No response.

He was absolutely rigid. Like a corpse.

Not right. *Not* right. Red alert. Battle stations.

The whispering grew more pronounced, stronger, almost seductive. Whatever was behind it wanted *in* and began bumping against the shutter—rattle-rattle . . . ting-tang . . . walla-walla-bing-bang.

Time to exit, stage left.

CHAPTER TWO

I tore off Terrin's blanket, slipped my hands under his arms, and hauled him backwards from the room. The hall was little more than shoulder wide, making it hard to maneuver, but I got us both clear, then kicked the door closed. The whispering faded slightly; the shutter racket remained strong. My heart banging a good counterpoint, I dragged Terrin downstairs, his rump catching on the steps, thudding all the way. Even *that* didn't wake him.

Clem heard the ruckus though, emerging from some back area of the inn, candle in hand. "What's going on?"

"There's *stuff*," I said, none too coherently as I pulled Terrin toward the common room, in too much of a hurry to pick him up. "Street, black mist, creeping, talking, wants inside real bad."

He stared down his long nose like I'd gone simple. "Uh-huh."

"Just look out and see—no! Don't look out and see! I mean, my friend won't wake up."

"Is he sick? I don't hold with sick boarders."

"It's some kind of nervous fit, nothing catching." *I*

hoped. "Help me get him on a table, bring that candle over. You got some smelling salts? What's that stuff crawling along the streets?"

"What stuff?"

"The black stuff trying to get inside." I glanced at the windows, but they were closed for the night.

"Nothing out on the streets this hour," Clem assured. "Just city watch."

"Is the city watch a bunch of black mist?"

Clem shot me a sideways "are you nuts" kind of look. I gave up to focus on Terrin. Clem's wife came out next and, having had several kids, was used to dealing with late emergencies. Greta had to admit this was a new one for her, but was willing to help. Clem and I got Terrin on one of the long serving tables and had to unfold him. He was still locked in his cross-legged position.

"Sure he ain't died?" asked Clem. He wasn't too alarmed at the prospect.

"Hush," said his wife, waving an open bottle of something under Terrin's nose. It smelled like cleaning fluid, heavy on the ammonia. I pinched my muzzle in reaction and fell away a few steps, ending up by a window. It had cracks around the edges like the one upstairs, but no signs of any black mist seeping through. Good, so far as it went.

Terrin suddenly mumbled, tried to move his head away from the bottle, then his face screwed up as though for a huge sneeze. It never happened, but his lids did finally peel apart. His eyes had gone from dark gray to ghost-pale silver.

"Argh! Agh! Foo!" he said, trying to wriggle away.

Clem held him down. "Easy there, son. Greta, I think he's had enough fumes."

Greta stoppered the bottle with a triumphant smirk. "Works every time."

I quit the window, along with its temptation to peek

out, and came over. "What the *hell* was that about?" I was scared, which translated as severe annoyance.

Terrin blinked at me, at all of us standing around the table gawking down at him. "You're not Auntie Em," he said to me with great certainty.

"I'm not Bert Lahr, either. 'Fess up. You weren't just asleep, were you?"

"Huh? What am I doing down here?" He shrugged off Clem's restraining hands and sat up, violently rubbing his nose. "Phew!"

"Were you dreaming?" Sometimes Terrin's dreams were more real to him than being awake. It took time for him to shake off the cobwebs.

"Dreaming? I was—why'd you interrupt my meditation?"

"Because there's this black misty stuff outside and it was coming in the window like the Marines landing."

"How much beer did you have?" asked Clem, conversationally.

"Not *that* much! Go see it for yourself." Now that Terrin was up and almost running I had more confidence about dealing with the heebie-jeebie fog river.

Clem shrugged and went to the door, the rest of us following. He unlocked and opened up.

The black mist still flowed strongly, but was retreating fast, beginning to shred into sooty wisps. "There! Just like I said."

"Where?" asked Clem. There was no way he could miss it, even with his normal eyesight.

I pointed. "There!"

Clem began to squint. "Sorry, friend, but I don't see nothing. You see anything, Greta?"

"Just a lot of dark street," she said. Neither of them struck me as faking; no one could be that oblivious.

Terrin tugged at my shirt sleeve. I looked. He shook his head once, lips pursed. I got the message and backed down, though it griped me. "Okay, maybe it was the beer.

Maybe I'm having an allergic reaction and hallucinating."
That was a total lie. I have a weird body chemistry.
Alcohol doesn't affect me as much as it does other people.
It takes a *lot* to get me drunk. I'd not had nearly enough
tonight for that.

"Sometimes the brewings don't set right with some
people," Clem said generously. "Now what about you, Mr.
Terrin? You were doing poorly for a bit there. Mr. Myhr
here was in a state about it, and I don't blame him. What's
your ailment?"

Terrin shrugged. "I'm just a really heavy sleeper. Sorry
if this dude got hyper about it. Sometimes he's jumpy as
a cat."

"Hey!" I said, miffed at the wholesale cliché.

The dig and my reaction to it did the job, distracting
Clem and Greta, letting them know that the situation
wasn't serious. I tendered apologies for the disruption,
then we all went back to our rooms; I hung behind so
Terrin walked in first.

"Is it clear?"

"Yeah, come on," he said.

"You saw that stuff outside. Tell me you saw that stuff."

"I saw that stuff."

"What was it? I didn't smell anything off it so it
couldn't have been river mist."

"You didn't smell anything because it's not wholly on
this plane of reality. That's why those two didn't see it.
You did, probably because of the cat in you, and I saw
because that's what I do."

"I was freaking out because it came up to our window and tried to get in. What is it?"

"Could be a lot of things." He opened the window.
"Street's clear now."

"Think that's why they have a curfew? To keep people
from running into that junk?"

"Maybe."

"So what are the lot of things it could be? A short list is fine."

He shrugged. "I don't want to commit until I know more. Could be restless souls, an astral river, a rip in the space-time continuum . . ."

"Don't soap me with the techno-babble, this ain't *Star Trek*!"

"I know. I'm serious."

That's what I didn't want to hear; I hate it when he's serious. It's the only thing worse than when he's kidding around. "What do we do? It might come back."

"I wouldn't worry. Nothing got in, did it?"

"Well, no . . ."

"And nothing will without me knowing. I put the usual wards up all around this place soon as we settled in. We're safe."

"Safe" is often a relative term with Terrin. He shifted away from the window and stooped to pick up his blanket. He straightened, halting in mid-motion, making a face. "Day-um! My ass hurts!"

"That happened when I took you downstairs."

"Next time wake me up."

"I tried. Clem thought rigor had set in. That was *not* your usual meditative state by a long shot."

"Huh. I'll have to find out about that. See if it has to do with the mist. Are there any other wizards in town? They might know something."

"I heard of a few at dinner. Don't know if they're real, though. People seem pretty neutral about magic here, but I wouldn't push it."

"We'll find out in the morning." He wrapped the blanket around his shoulders again and settled down, cross-legged.

"You're going to *sleep*?"

"Meditate. Do some astral-travel to see what's in the neighborhood. Chill out, don't sweat it. We're safe. Get some sleep yourself, and don't bother me until I wake up on my own."

I grumped—quietly—knowing more questions wouldn't get me anywhere. Between the leftover adrenaline and the fading beer buzz I was developing a headache. If I lay down now I might make myself conk out before it really kicked in. One last look outside, though. Terrin hadn't locked the window. He was way too trusting at times.

The street was empty. I had a bad feeling it was only temporary.

Morning came too soon. It always does. I almost wish it would tiptoe up, sweet and soft, and give me a gentle little warning of approach, but I'd have only beat it to a pulp.

This world didn't seem to have coffee, but Greta recognized the signs of sore need as I made my way gingerly to one of the common room tables. She brought a cup and poured in some kind of herbal tea alternative. Not the same as a triple espresso, but it was sweet and hot and helped restore me to life.

"No beer for you tonight," she said with a smile. "Perhaps some soft cider instead?"

"Yeah, that'd be great. Bet I need the vitamin C, anyway."

She smiled again; the language spell seemed to be translating my nonsense perfectly. I sometimes wondered how it was at translating the Beatles' songs, if those still rhymed or not. No matter, they were usually a big hit. If the crowd was up to it I might attempt a version of "Hey, Jude." It worked best with accompaniment, but sometimes I could get people to join in on the chorus part, clapping hands. Audience participation is a must in the business.

"Have you seen Terrin?" I asked. He'd left his blanket

on the floor. I'd caught my feet in it when I first staggered awake.

"Went out early. Didn't say when he'd be back."

He wouldn't.

"He didn't eat anything, either," Greta added. "He could use some fattening. Looks poorly, he does."

Terrin was short and his build on the spare side, a swimmer's bod. When we hit medieval-type worlds the well-fed locals took it as a sign of ill-health. He wasn't much for food unless he was doing supernatural stuff, then he sucked the chow down like a starving bear, so I was puzzled. He'd done a load of magic lately and should have been stuffing his face.

Revived by the hot tea, I charmed a sweet roll of some kind from Greta, then went out to explore a little before lunchtime when I'd have to be back for my act.

The inn's front door was wide open to a bright, sunny lane full of people. Not one sign of that black-fog river. I went around the building to check the window. The shutter was locked fast as I'd left it and seemed none the worse for last night's assault. No three-toed gouges, dents, leftover ectoplasm, or related supernatural junk had been left behind. I was almost disappointed, as any of that would have proved I wasn't a nutcase. Terrin believed me, at least. I think. I'd have to find him, and see what his astral trip turned up. Time to hit the streets.

My face is my fortune. Its impact on Rumpock's population was wonderfully flattering.

Those who had seen yesterday's show called and waved to me, telling their friends about the singing cat-guy at Clem's. I'd amble over and talk, asking questions of my own, making more jokes, gathering up a parade of kids as I went. Of course I'd have to stop and say hello to each of them as well. They were great, all wanting touch my fur and rub me behind the ears. I never got tired of it.

I love kids. Sometimes they had cute big sisters or single mommies.

After asking around I got directions to an apothecary, the usual place to go to pick up a trail that might lead to a Talent. I didn't have much interest in the magical arts, but did want to eventually get home again. Terrin and I always made the rounds hoping to find someone with a line on astral maps.

Those are really hard to come by. Our bad luck.

The way things work for Terrin is that he has *some* control over his travel spell. He can bounce us to physically compatible worlds, keeping clear of spots with poisonous air or all-ocean planets. Except for one place where everyone had these weird bumps all over their foreheads, the people looked like people, dogs looked like dogs, and cats looked like me.

What Terrin had no control over was direction. He'd explained the ins and outs of astral jumps or whatever it was we did, but tech stuff, even the magical kind, never stays in my head very long. I'm more of an artsy-fartsy kind of guy. Sing a song to me and I can remember it. Abstract concepts—and magic is full of those—usually put me into a state of "Hah? Whazzat?"

So we'd blip out of one place and pop into another, all of it fairly random. Terrin said we were more or less heading in the right direction for home. He'd also explained how he knew that, but I'd forget and ask him again. After the third or fourth time he'd only say "It's magic, okay?" to get me to lose interest. I had the idea our journey was like Columbus being more or less headed in the right direction for China. If all these other worlds weren't in the way we'd get there. A map would be a big help, the astral kind, which I took to mean it wouldn't be printed out on parchment like some medieval Mapsco.

Terrin said that once we had a map, he could figure how far we had to go and plot our jumps accordingly. It might take awhile since it was usually weeks before the quartz crystals charged back up again. Magical energy levels fluctuated from stop to stop.

Now if we really wanted a shortcut out, a fast exit before the crystals were ready, then gems were the medium to use. Precious gems. They carried a powerful charge naturally, and the bigger and more flawless the stone the farther we could go. But they vanished after the spell took effect. Terrin said they were completely consumed by the energy conversion, whatever that meant. Traveling first class is expensive. Quartz was more mundane, but had staying power.

The other problem with gems was coming by them. They're universally hard to find. Expensive.

A couple of times on worlds where magic was a cool thing Terrin would hire out as a wizard to some rich person. He'd take diamonds in payment, then off we'd go. The problem was finding a rich person willing to pay for services rendered. If they were rich enough to afford magic, then they usually had a Talent on call. I'd suggested to Terrin he stand on a corner and hold a sign: "Will Cast Spells for Gems."

His reply was creatively obscene.

He's a heck of a wizard, but doesn't know a damn thing about carving a niche in a competitive market. That, or he trusts in the Multiverse a lot more than I do to provide for us. I'd long ascertained the big M to be unfair, mostly crazed, and possessing of a very warped sense of humor.

It sure explains *my* existence.

Elsewhere in Rumpock, at Darmo House

Lady Filima Darmo sat in her Black Room, hovering over her scrying mirror, trying a little too hard to coax an image from it and getting a headache for her trouble.

She'd done all the right things, placing candles where their light wouldn't reflect in the mirror's surface, burning the special incense that made her nauseous, and focusing her will upon the Outside with the object of drawing it Inside. She had to find out what had happened last night with the Hell-river. The nightmare she'd had of being sucked into it had felt entirely too real, especially the part where she'd heard her dead husband laughing. Then there was that awful glimpse of Hell. Oddly, it was populated by dancing naked demons . . . females, with blue hair and bright orange skin. What were those about?

Filima's mirror remained innocuously blank, frustrating her. It was like trying to play a tune on her harp and not quite getting the last bit while everyone else played perfectly. And, of course, no one would dream of correcting her. That was the problem of having too much power. You reach a point where everyone says "yes" much too often, and find it's not as much fun as it should be. On the other hand, a mulish, inexplicable "no" was thoroughly infuriating.

And here was this damned magical (supposedly) mirror saying "no" to her on a regular basis. She'd have banged on it to force the issue, but the instructions strictly forbade rough handling of any kind.

As usual when she tried to scry, Filima felt the headache getting worse. It was that awful incense. And the mirror. And the whole bloody world trying to go wrong despite her best efforts to the contrary.

"Show me something helpful, dammit," she growled.

Before the throbbing in her head could crest into full-blown agony, an image finally surfaced. Rumpock's central bell tower appeared briefly. The landmark shimmered, replaced by a view of a tavern or inn of some kind. It had a sign with red lettering, but she couldn't make out the name. Emerging from the front door was a man . . . with a strange, improbable face, like a cat. He had to be wearing a mask of some sort, a very detailed one made of russet fur that covered the whole of his head. He waved in a friendly manner to someone, then moved out of sight.

The mirror went blank, seeming to suck the tiny moving pictures into itself. It would show no more.

Filima staggered out of the smoke-filled, stifling chamber before she got sick, pushing through thick layers of velvet curtains to gain the more breathable air of her Blue Room. The lighting here was normal, coming from several tall, slender windows. The fresh morning brightness hurt her eyes and not just from being in the Black Room. She preferred sleeping in late. It was the only sane thing to do most days.

Her maid stood ready with mint tea chilled with chips of winter ice. Expensive, but Filima could afford it. She drank the tea, which helped settle her stomach, and pressed the cold crystal of the goblet against her aching forehead.

What a pain, but it had been worth it, for scrying rarely worked for her; when it did, she always saw something truly important. Like the business with her dead husband. Before he'd gotten dead. That had been a near thing. She shuddered and made herself veer away from the memory. Best not to go there for now.

Despite the headache Filima wanted to celebrate this little success, but didn't dare. She had to carry on normally, even if she went crazy from it. She had no doubt that the maid would take her tray of cheer back to the kitchens, and by mysterious, circuitous routes a detailed description of this morning's goings on at Darmo House would find its way to the other clan houses within the hour, complete with Filima's every expression.

Another typical day in Rumpock. Tea and gossip. Little wonder she preferred to sleep them through.

Not typical, she thought. Something had changed. Something huge. She'd felt it last night when the Hell-river had been on the prowl through her dream. Whether it was connected to that man in the cat mask or her dead husband remained to be seen.

Damn Botello Darmo.

He'd been so nice at first. Why did he have to go stupid on her? Men, you can't live with them and you can't kill them. Not unless you're really, really careful, anyway.

An envelope imprinted with a familiar clan marking lay on the tea tray, catching her eye. That morning's mail, bearing another letter from Lord Cadmus Burkus. Either he'd be requesting she come to dine with him or begging permission to call on her. Good gawds, it had only been two weeks since her husband's funeral. It was indecent. How could such a handsome man be so damned thick? Didn't he see? She was not interested in him. Of course, his interest in her wasn't likely to be romantic. She was a rich young widow. Enough said.

Wearily and warily, she opened the envelope. Within the fold of heavy paper it held a single pressed flower. It sort of looked like a rose. Ugh. However beautiful it had been when in bloom it was a disaster now, all faded to gray and falling apart.

She sneezed mightily, turning the flower into dusty mulch. She brushed off her gown and told the maid to sweep up the mess. No, there would be no reply to the letter. Cadmus hadn't seen fit to include a note, after all— was she supposed to read his mind? Why did he think she'd enjoy some shriveled-up weed?

Unless it was a spell. That would be just like him to try casting a love spell on her. As if he had enough magical power to get through her protections. He really should know better. What a loser.

Filima finished her tea and sent for Captain Shankey,

the head of her house guard. A solid man, he'd been in Botello's family since his early youth, long before her own arrival. She liked him, but didn't trust him with information, only errands. He would die to protect clan Darmo, but like all the rest of the family she'd married into, Filima was forced to assume he had his own motives for doing so, and those did not necessarily include her best interests—especially if he ever got a clue about how his late master had passed on.

"Go into the city," she told Shankey. "Close to the bell tower there is an inn or tavern with red letters on its sign. You are to find a man in that area who wears a cat mask on his face. Bring him to me."

"A cat mask, my lady?"

"Just what I said. Ask around. There can't be many like him. Perhaps a circus has come and he's one of the clowns."

That explanation seemed to work. His mouth twitched slightly. Now *his* mind she could almost read. And he should be ashamed of himself. Just because she'd once been an oochie-coochie dancer in a side show was no reason to assume she was going to go back to it. Then again, if he assumed she was reestablishing contact with her old circus chums all the better to mislead the flow of gossip from her house.

Captain Shankey bowed deeply and left to carry out her orders.

Elsewhere in Rumpock, at Burkus House

Lord Cadmus Burkus sat in *his* Black Room, scrying through his own mirror, albeit with more success than Filima. He watched her stagger out, holding her head as usual, and clawing blindly for her cold drink. She sat for a time, apparently thinking, then spotted his envelope in the tray. *My, what a face she makes. You'd think it was a dose of the whistling runs instead of a token of my esteem.*

Cadmus pressed all his concentration on Filima's image, so as to not miss a single nuance of her expression as she opened the envelope. There, she had it in her hand now, the rose he'd sneaked from her hair at the Mid-Summer Festival last year. She'd caught him at it, though. Who would have thought the damned thing would have been so firmly pinned into place? What a yelp she'd given when he'd yanked too hard. He had to pretend to be swatting a bug . . . but he *had* palmed the flower.

Later that night he'd carefully pressed it in a book of love poetry in the hope that the verses within would travel via the rose to take root in her heart. Or something like that. Love spells were horribly tricky things, all sympathetic magic and fine print.

He stared in his mirror, his mouth dry. Would the love powder he'd sprinkled over the rose work?

He winced at the force of her sneeze. You could almost hear it.

Oh, dear. She didn't look in love, nor even the least bit wistful, only annoyed as she wiped her nose. Damn. Damn-damn-damn and darn. He had *so* wanted her to succumb this time. Maybe he should have used a book of lust poems instead. He'd read somewhere that lust spells were somewhat easier to achieve. She might be less allergic to a good healthy bout of pillow-pounding. Certainly she'd not had much of *that* in the latter months of her marriage. Botello had been far too preoccupied with other matters to bother with her. The fool.

Apparently unaware of her brush with True Love, Filima conducted a short audience with the captain of her house guard. What about? It had to be something to do with her scrying mirror. *What if she's been watching me watching her?* Cadmus bit his lip, fretting. That would be bad. Very, very bad. What could it have shown her?

Why was she even scrying at all? The mental demands always gave her a headache. Maybe that was why the love powder hadn't worked. Women with headaches were *never* in the mood.

Cadmus broke his link to his mirror and pushed from his own curtained sanctum into the outer room. It was rather plainer than Filima's fabulous Blue Room, the aged furnishings dating from a previous generation; Cadmus had scant money to spare for stylish household decor. If only one of his late near and dears had developed a talent for *making* money instead of spending it. True to his breeding, Cadmus suffered from the family affliction of squandering huge sums of cash, but he was quite proud that *his* expenditures were sensibly selective. No drinking himself to death with the finest and rarest of brandies like Uncle Tidmo, or collecting erotic pottery like Grand-pap Nuckle—though the estate sale of the pottery to other collectors had been rather profitable.

The proceeds allowed Cadmus to invest in himself.

Once he'd outlived his immediate relatives and got the money, Cadmus bought himself a first-rate gentleman's education. Of course, none of it was of much practical use in the world, though he was in great demand at parties for his wit, fashionable clothes, and beautiful body. He enjoyed himself, but it didn't improve his finances. That would only happen when he snagged a wealthy wife. He felt honor-bound to give her value for her money, so he kept himself fit, clever, and got as much practice in the arts of love as time and cash flow permitted.

It would be a double boon for him to actually *like* his future wife. And he did like Filima, quite a lot. She had money and a beautiful house; Cadmus saw to it that he possessed the good taste to be able to appreciate both fully. He could give her class, and she could give him . . . well, he'd spied on her bathing often enough. The goods were in mouthwateringly excellent condition despite

her retirement from the dancing stage. Botello Darmo
had chosen one hell of a woman to marry. How consid-
erate of him to leave her widowed while she was still in
her prime.

So far as Cadmus was concerned, Filima was perfect.
If only *she* would realize that.

Cadmus called in Debreban, the captain of his own
house guard, a tough young retainer pledged to duty, do-
or-die, so long as it was for the good of Clan Burkus. With
instructions to seek out and observe Lady Filima's captain to discover what he was up to, he also bowed low
and departed. Cadmus wondered if the fellow would
simply meet with Filima's man at a tavern to grumble over
a beer about working conditions.

One way to find out. He turned back into the Black
Room, closed the curtain, and hovered over his scrying
mirror. The image that came up was not, however, the
one he wanted. This one could speak, among other, less
pleasant, things.

He went very pale.

"Cadmus, you idiot," it said, highly irritated. "You've
been blocking me!"

Elsewhere in Rumpock, at the Overduke's Palace

Overduke Anton had not slept well at all. He struggled
against the wrinkled and tossed sheets of his big bed,
rousing his latest girlfriend awake.

"What is it, honey?" she mumbled sleepily.

"That damned Hell-river. Dreamed about it again."

"Aw, I'm sorry. Was it bad?"

"All my dreams about it are bad." This time Anton had
seen himself in the black mists, choking on their flow while
above him two demons laughed heartily as they pushed him
down. One of them looked like Lord Cadmus and the other
had a man's body with a face like a cat, which was

disturbing. Though somewhat fond of Cadmus, Anton rather liked cats. This one had been doing its almighty best to drown him and was succeeding despite his frantic fighting. The nightmare hadn't been too horrible compared to others he'd lately suffered, but was unnervingly real. How good it was to thrash himself conscious and encounter Velma's sane and comforting presence next to him. Much better than waking up screaming, which Anton sometimes did when he slept alone.

"You should see a doctor, then," said Velma. "C'mon, lemme give you a nice backrub."

Anton regarded the girl fondly. He prized her ability to state the obvious in as few words as possible and then forget the matter, so unlike the palace politicians who would worry a topic to shreds. Besides, none of them ever offered to give him a nice backrub. Not that he would have accepted. Anton rolled over and let Velma have her way with him until one thing led to another, with an enthusiastic conclusion that left them both in a happy, dozy state. It was his favorite way to start a day. Hell, it was his favorite way to end a night and fill all the hours in between.

But it was day, now, more's the pity. Time to go to work.

Clad in an expensive robe designed to awe the common people who would never see it, Anton strolled into his morning reception room to break his fast. A dozen of his retainers, councilors, and other payroll leeches bowed to him. And well they should, for he had a commanding physical presence, being taller than any of them, with a soldier's build and piercing blue eyes. It was rumored Overduke Anton could turn people to stone with a glance.

He found *that* wonderfully amusing. True, he could unnerve the most stoic types with his unblinking gaze, but they did it all themselves. Everyone felt guilty about something; all you had to do was watch and wait them out. You could get along quite well in life on a frown coupled with a glowering stare. Both came easily to Anton, who was not only blessed with an ingrained expression of perpetual annoyance but also was terrifically near-sighted. Any return stares were quite lost on him.

Anton grunted to acknowledge those present and went to the room's only table, seating himself on the room's only chair. Early in his rule he discovered that business sessions tended to run more quickly when everyone else had to stand. The table was just big enough to hold one sheet of paper. Once his morning cup of hot, very sweet tea had been placed on it, there was little room left for even half a sheet of paper.

No fool, Anton knew how to plan things.

He sipped gratefully at the tea, appreciative of its buffering qualities as he made the transition between bed and business. In the farthest-flung reaches of all the surrounding lands, in the meanest, most primitive of living conditions, he'd noticed a very important, very telling detail about people in general. They all had a morning cup of some flavored hot liquid before starting the day. That, or beer. Quite sensible of them, really. Kept them from cutting one another's throats.

His over-paid minions watched his every move. No one was allowed to speak until he said something first, and he never spoke until he was damned good and ready. Gawd knows how long they'd been out here, waiting. Not his problem if they had sore feet and aching legs from standing on the marble floor. They knew he was not an early riser.

His tea finished, he looked in the general direction of his chief minister, Lord Perdle. He was in his usual spot, a dark-clad blur with a thick chain of office draped on his shoulders. Anton spotted the gleam of its gold reflecting the late morning light.

"What's on for today, Perds?" Anton asked mildly, not squinting out of ingrained habit.

The others relaxed a trifle now that the business at hand was finally moving ahead. Anton waded through a number of surprisingly simple-to-solve problems very quickly. It made him uneasy. Were they hiding some disaster from him? He didn't like that. If only he could see their faces better. Unless they were within two paces of him they were all just pinkish, brownish or whitish blobs that talked too much. To find out what was going on under the surface meant he'd have to *listen* to them, and more often than not it was boring as hell.

Which reminds me . . .

Anton looked up to his right. "Perdle? Any changes with that Hell-river?"

"Changes, my lord?" Perdle had moved off to the left. He was supposed to stay in one spot so Anton knew where to turn when speaking to him.

"Yes. News. Alterations. Signs and portents. Had a bit of a vision about it." For some reason calling his nightmares "visions" held more weight with this lot.

"Indeed, my lord?"

"Indeed. Have someone look into it. Top priority, there's a good fellow."

The Perdle-blob leaned over to whisper to an underling-blob, who quickly vanished into the general blurs of the room. "It is done, my lord," Perdle announced.

Anton wanted to correct him. Obviously it wasn't done at all, only just begun, but it wasn't nice to correct people in front of an audience. "Right. Well and good. What's next?"

"The planning out of the Mid-Summer Festival, my lord."

"Oh, heavens, you can find someone else to deal with that. Next you'll have me arranging birthday parties for cats."

"For cats, my lord?"

Why on earth had he mentioned cats? Oh, that damned dream again. The only time he ever saw things clear and sharp was in dreams. Pity they tended to be bad ones. Who was that cat-demon, anyway? What did it represent? It had shoved him down into the black river with a human-shaped hand and quite inhuman strength. . . .

"Who did you wish to take charge of the festival arrangements, my lord?" asked Perdle.

Anton gratefully abandoned the dream memory. "See if Lady Filima Darmo is interested in having a go."

"But, my lord, she's still in official mourning. It's been less than two weeks since—"

"Then see her unofficially. Might do her good having something to take her mind off her grief." Anton hadn't noticed Filima being especially afflicted with suffering over the loss of her husband, but that could be her just showing a brave front to the world. She might welcome a diversion. "Must be terribly boring for her, all cooped up in Darmo House."

"But, my lord . . ." Perdle sounded helpless.

Anton hated that tone. "Out with it. *All* the objections."

"Lady Filima is under a bit of a cloud, socially. Lord Botello's death was . . . rather odd."

"People pop off all the time, Perdle, nothing odd about it at all. The posted notice was quite clear. Doesn't anyone bother reading the damn things? Did the whole city forget I conducted the inquiry myself? Botello died of natural causes. There wasn't a mark on his body. The physicians determined his heart stopped, died in his sleep. Never knew what hit him. We should all have so easy a passing. And the inquiry did cover the poison question, so forget about trotting that one out. If such a perfect, undetectable, and fast concoction existed, every apothecary would be rich."

"But, my lord, aside from the rumors, there's the

question of the other clan ladies. They might take it amiss that you never first considered any of them for the honor."

"I did consider them. That's why I hope Filima takes the job. The only time I ever really enjoyed myself at a party was at her house. She knows how to have a good time; the rest of them are too obsessed with protocol. Anything else?"

Perdle held silent.

"It's settled then. Ask Lady Filima if she'd like to play official hostess and plan the festival. My show of confidence in her should banish any rumors of foul play about the late Lord Botello. See to it, Perdle, there's a good fellow."

Perdle bowed low, then rose and murmured to another underling, who faded in the murky distance.

There were two aspects of his duties that Overduke Anton wholly treasured: being right and always having the last word.

Elsewhere, NOT in Rumpock, in Hell

Botello Darmo glared at his scrying mirror, which was on the wall, or something that looked like a wall. The handsome, if somewhat gullible, face of Cadmus Burkus peered out of its depths at him.

"Cadmus, you idiot," Botello snapped. "You've been blocking me!"

"I'm sorry, were you trying to get through?"

"Of course I have. What have you been doing all morning?"

"Oh, just keeping an eye on things."

"My wife, you mean."

Cadmus returned one of his more charming smiles. "Well, my dear old chap, she's your widow now, and you *did* give me permission to look after her."

"But not to slither into her bed!"

"I don't see what difference it makes to you. You're dead after all—"

"I'm not dead! I'm only bodily displaced!"

"Yes, and I'm terribly sorry about that. How are things today?"

Botello almost replied with a blistering flare of anger, but remembered to count to five instead. He didn't have the energy to waste on the likes of Cadmus. "Never mind that, something's happened on your side, and I want you to look into it for me."

"Certainly. Anything to help lighten your load," Cadmus said with the cheery confidence of one who knew he'd never be up to the task and therefore would not be blamed for his failure.

A lot you know, you idiot. "The Hell-river sensed something last night, something big."

"What might that be?"

"You're to find out."

Cadmus made a face. "I'll need more information."

"Go to an inn by the town bell tower, a two-story place with red lettering on the sign. There's a huge magical energy force in that area. Even you should be able to sense what's there."

"But there hasn't been anything like that around here since you—"

"Exactly."

"Just what sort of force is it? Person, place or thing?"

"Person," Botello said with certainty. He had no hard verification for what was only a feeling, but knew to trust his instincts when it came to magic. Cadmus remained skeptical. "You mean a Talent? There? I didn't think any were left in the town, not after you—"

"Never mind that. You find whoever it is and see to it he or she is on our side."

"We have a side?"

Botello snarled, forgot himself, and released a searing

flash of rage. In reaction, Cadmus cried out a pitiful wail of sudden agony and fell forward onto his mirror. His white, pain-distorted face pressed hard against it, presenting a flattened view to Botello.

"I'm deadly serious, you fool," Botello whispered through set teeth. "You want more, or have I made my point?"

Cadmus mumbled out something affirmative and apologetic.

The groveling pleased Botello. "Right, now pull yourself together and get moving. Before the day is out I want that person under your roof. Do whatever it takes. This is important."

"W-why?" Cadmus shakily pushed himself upright. "If I may ask?"

"You'll know when the time is right. Just do it. And stay off your damned mirror so I can get through to you."

With a wave of his arm, Botello severed contact, his own glass going foggy. It melted into the wall, which also melted, leaving him alone in a stark, dim landscape. He stood on one shore of the great black Hell-river, close to the great black Gates of Hell. So far as he was concerned, he was altogether on the wrong side of them. He shouldn't even *be* here, having not died in the normal sense of the word.

When he'd first arrived, Botello Darmo had been surprised at how *normal* the nether regions turned out to be, until it was explained to him that his perceptions were being purposely warped so as to preserve his usefulness. One of the demonic overlords gave him a peek at a small segment of Hell's reality for a second or two, to prove the truth of his assertion, which was more than enough for Botello. In that scant glimpse he understood that a tree was not really a tree, nor was a bird a bird. The actuality beneath was entirely awful, so he did his best to forget it when he was up and about on business, which was all the time. There is no sleep in Hell. It put everyone in a very foul state of mind.

"You'll have to hurry," a demon called over to him, the creature being Botello's own personal companion. Disturbingly like his Great Aunt Matilda, right down to the spiky moustache and bass voice, it was an unwelcome reminder of family. Sooner or later he was certain he'd run into a few deceased members of his clan in this place. The only thing worse than being in Hell was being stuck in Hell with a pack of relatives. "They want you to hurry. Or else."

It was doubtful that this particular demon had any clue as to what the overlords here wanted; the thing was just reverting to type. Its job was to torment souls, but for now it had orders to hold off and keep other creatures away. The most it was allowed to do was nag him, a distraction that could defeat the overlords' purpose.

Why couldn't they have given me a smarter guardian?

Probably didn't dare. What Botello had planned with the overlords would upset some very carefully laid out balances. They wouldn't want word of it to get around to the realm's general populace and thence to Outer Guardians. Botello had little worry for any of them, so long as the overlords down here remained ignorant of his very special private plans.

Botello strolled over and tapped the Gates of Hell. They seemed solid, as always. A formidable barrier they were, too, even if what he saw was just as warped to his scrutiny as everything else. This reality was all about symbolism. These gates looked the way *he* would expect gates to look; the overlords here saw something else again, and both versions were correct. The common symbol being that they were barrier and opening in one. Right now they were fulfilling the barrier role, and at any moment . . .

There. A heavy clank and clink as the lock tumblers fell into place, then that awesome yawning creak as the two halves parted, opening inward. Botello watched avidly, taking in every detail as another soul was about to enter Hell.

A naked man, borne up by some powerful invisible force, came hurtling through. He was screaming, but that was commonplace; they all made an appropriately unholy row once they realized where they were bound. The man was seized in midair by some flying demons who carried him away into the depths of Hell, indication that he'd been very bad, indeed, and soon his screams and their cackles of delight were lost in the distance.

Botello paid them no mind, his attention on the opening mechanisms involved. Most were not visible to ordinary sight, but he had enough magical training to see on other levels. He got a glimpse of Light beyond, but it vanished almost immediately. The Outer Guardians who delivered souls from one place or another were always too busy to linger. He'd several times tried to get one to pause and talk, but had been ignored.

The gates, vast metal-studded constructions a good (or bad) two yards thick, slammed decisively shut. The reverberating clang was truly impressive. The whole place shook from it, worse than being under Rumpock's bell tower. No wonder the overlords here wanted out; anything to escape that mind-numbing boom.

If that was what *they* heard. The gates were a perception. That fascinated Botello. All those demonic hordes kept confined to one spot by an *idea*.

Unaffected by any sound or action was the Hell-river. It flowed smoothly in under the gates, a thick black mist of negativity that circled the boundaries of the realm. If not exactly a tourist attraction, it was one of the more important landmarks here. But at night, much to the displeasure of the overlords, the river vanished altogether. It wasn't supposed to do that.

That was the *other* task given to him: to find out why

the river was behaving so strangely. They knew Botello had something to do with it, for the vanishing business began the same night as his arrival. He managed to convince the overlords of his own ignorance of the phenomenon, bartering himself out of torture with his willingness to solve the mystery, though in retrospect they gave in to his offer rather fast. He suspected they were afraid of the river. It was saturated with magical energy, and so far as he'd observed they never touched the stuff. He did not ask why, lest his revealed ignorance alter his situation for the worse.

He stood on the edge of the riverbank and looked down into the apparently bottomless depths of darkness.

"You better hurry," said the demon. It sounded bored.

Botello barely heard. He wore—or seemed to wear—the clothes he'd last been wearing while his soul still occupied his body. Under a heavy wizard's robe he was clad in an ordinary outfit, dark colored, a small rusty stain on the tunic, souvenir of his last solid meal. He was hungry now, but there was no food in Hell. Not the usual sort of nourishment, anyway.

He willed off his boots and socks, and part of his trouser legs vanished. Sitting, he dangled his bare feet in the black fog. He'd have splashed in it, had that been possible.

Through his soles he sensed a profound vibration, like the ground when a phalanx of horses charged past. He shut his eyes and opened up a few crucial internal shields. His feet ceased to be solid, merging with the river. He drew its dark energy into himself, quickly, before the demon noticed anything. Hunger fled from him.

Yes, there was a new force in this flow, strong and very intense. The river had sought it out for him, draining the source into itself, delivering it to one who knew how to feed on that magical power. Here was a feast indeed. He felt himself swelling like a leech, the stuff flickering through him like lightning, enough strength to challenge the demonic overlords themselves.

If this source lasted long enough he could push his plan forward in mere days instead of weeks.

There was a way out of Hell. Via the power in the river. Botello, who did not believe in coincidence, was certain an escape had been timely delivered to him.

So long as that idiot Cadmus didn't botch things.

CHAPTER THREE

Back in Rumpock, Near the Bell Tower

I found the neighborhood apothecary shop, "Ye Olde Frog's Eye," if that was the correct translation on the sign out front. The door was wide open, the same as all the other businesses up and down the street. It seemed to be the custom, reminding me of older sections of Toronto when the weather was nice. Well, the Toronto on about our fifth world. They had some decent tech there. I'd stocked up on the essentials of life: beef jerky, semi-sweet dark chocolate, and really warm socks.

The shop. A very intense olfactory experience. Even with the door open. The place was stuffed with all kinds of strange smelly things in bins, drawers, crockery pots, and blown glass vessels. Vinegar and garlic dominated, like some kind of twisted Italian eatery.

"May I render help . . . uh . . . sir?" A plump lady with a pleasant, full-cheeked face stared at me from her chair behind the counter.

"I'm looking for a friend of mine—short, red hair,

foreign clothes?" It was my usual description for Terrin. I didn't know what he had on today, but it was likely to be a T-shirt with a picture on it overlaid by a Hawaiian shirt, the louder the better. To compensate for my looks I usually tried to blend in with local costume, but Terrin never compromised. "He'll be wearing purple sneakers and sunglasses."

The lady took her time recovering. It helps them when I act like nothing's amiss. Eventually she snapped out of it. "Ye-esss. A young man like that came in. He was a little rude."

"That's the guy. Don't take it personal, he just gets preoccupied. Did he buy anything?"

"No, but he asked if I had any gems in stock. As if I could afford such things like Overduke Anton."

My ears perked at the sound of useful information. "So, this Anton dude is pretty well off?"

"More so than me, though I'm glad enough for what I have. Is there a circus in town?"

I disappointed her with my reply, but invited her to come enjoy the lunchtime show at Clem's later. "Think the overduke might be interested in auditioning a singing cat-guy? I'm great for birthdays, weddings, bar mitzvahs . . ."

"Oh, I wouldn't know. Mid-Summer Festival is coming up, lots of singers are in it. You could ask at his gate. He has the big palace on the east side of the city. Anyone will point you there."

"Then he's a party-hearty kind of dude?"

"Dear me, but he's not one for too much frivolity. Usually has someone else plan the festival. A very sober man is the overduke," she pronounced.

I hated him already. "Are there any less-sober types hanging around town?"

"The overduke has several clans under him. . . ."

That must tickle. I kept up with the questions, the ones

I couldn't ask at Clem's last night. I didn't want to give him the idea that I'd just pull out and take the act elsewhere for a better deal. Of course I'd give notice first.

I got a lot of names that might or might not be helpful, and a basic idea of local politics. The lady was careful not to give any personal opinions of the various clans in the city, merely repeating general knowledge. I didn't think it was from any fear of reprisal. As a businesswoman, she'd be aware of the importance of presenting a non-partisan face to the public.

And unless they're breathing down my neck with some inconvenient agenda, politics bore me. "Did you happen to notice which way my friend went?"

"Up the high street," she said, pointing.

"There any candle makers nearby?"

"Same way. On the left."

I thanked her and hurried on. Part of me was already getting used to the rhythms of the place. Since leaving the inn, I'd twice noticed the sounding of a huge bell in its high tower, marking the passage of the hours. Not much time left before I had to stand outside Clem's and persuade people to come in for the show.

Oh, yeah, no magic at the apothecary shop. Practitioners and herbalists probably went there for supplies, but I didn't pick up one whiff of the supernatural. I may not be interested in the stuff, but I am aware of it. Like being able to see that black fog last night.

I'd not discussed *that* with anyone. Until I checked with Terrin, it seemed wise to wait. People had enough fun dealing with my cat face; no need to give them cause to think I was certifiable, too.

The candle shop I found by smell. They sold all sorts of candles, lamps, and the oils to go in them. Many of the oils were stinky when burned, but they sold scents to mix in to offset that. Terrin was there, just winding up the purchase of a thick black candle half as long as his arm. I knew he didn't have any money, so he hit me up for some just as I walked in.

"My friend will pay," he said, hooking his thumb in my direction. His back was to me. He couldn't have seen my entrance.

It was pointless to ask how he knew I'd arrive at just the right moment to take care of the bill. Stuff like that always happened around him, especially if he was working on some magical project. I handed over a hard-won penny and shrugged it off.

"What's going on?" I asked once we were outside. "You only use black candles when you want to whip up some protection."

"I told you something was wrong with this world."

"What is it?"

"Don't know yet."

"You must have some idea."

He grimaced against the daylight and slipped his sunglasses on. His eyes were green today. Strangely, the color went well with his purple fishing cap. Our travel crystals were still in its netting, charging up in the sunshine. "I just know it has to do with the black mist."

Like I couldn't figure that out myself. "Find anything on your astral plane cruising?"

"Nope."

"What *did* you find?"

"Nothing."

"Nothing?"

"Zip. And *that* is weird."

"Finding nothing is weird?"

"Nothing *is* weird, as in there wasn't anything out there! Astral planes always have some kind of traffic. The one in this world is empty. No dreams, presences, elementals, projections, psychic tourists—nothing. Zip. O. La."

Even I knew that was extremely unusual. "Where'd everything go?"

He shrugged. "Sooner we leave here, the better. I gotta see about turning up a gem job. I want out a-s-a-p."

Toward that end I told him what I'd learned from the apothecary lady about the overduke. "He sounds like a stick in the mud, though. You better do more asking around before you offer magical services."

Terrin groaned and stretched. "I don't feel like offering today. Too damn tired. I need sleep, I've been tired since we got here."

He totally looked it, but I kept shut. No one likes to hear negative commentary on their appearance, especially Terrin. He wanted to visit an herb shop he'd heard about, so we strolled through the noisy swirl of a street that was half-shopping mall, half-flea market, half-conga line. People gaped at me, I waved back in a friendly way and collected another parade of kids. Terrin loved children too—on toast with a little Dijon mustard—so he moved on while I did more PR work. What can I say? I thrive on the attention and ear-scratching.

I invited people to come to Clem's for the show and some lunch, told a few jokes to whet their entertainment appetites and generally enjoyed myself. It lasted until I heard a good, loud scream.

Aw, come on—it was too *soon* for us to leave this place.

Elsewhere in Rumpock

Shankey, the head of the guards for House Darmo, paused before the red-lettered sign of an inn near the bell tower. Lady Filima had been specific about who and what to look for; she just hadn't mentioned that there were *several* inns and taverns in the area with red-lettered signs. This was his third stop, and he was hungry. That added to his annoyance. What inspired the annoyance in the first place was being followed by Debreban, his Burkus House counterpart.

The man was so incredibly bad at it.

Anyone skulking around in a cloak on so warm a day was bound to collect stares. Anyone skulking around in the purple-and-green colors of House Burkus could expect a helping of snide laughter as well. Shankey, anonymous out of his house uniform, almost felt sorry for the man but for the fact some of the amusement was spilling onto himself. He was so obviously the skulkee.

Before ducking inside to ask yet another wary proprietor about a guest who might be walking about in—oh, gawds—a cat mask, Shankey decided he'd had enough. He strode purposefully to a shop doorway where his skulker had attempted to conceal himself. People in the shop watched with interest.

"Hello, Debreban," he said, looking down.

Debreban attempted to appear casual, as though crouching in doorways was quite the normal thing to do. "Oh, uh, hi, Shankey. What are you doing here?"

"My lady sent me out to look for something."

"It's a good day for it. Nice seeing you."

Shankey made a face. "Cut the crap, Debreban. We both know a little of what's going on. Let's have a beer and swap stories."

After a moment's hesitation, Debreban stood up, brushing his knees. He was a well-built fellow, all blond hair and boyish charm, just a little short on talent in important areas, like following people who were neither blind nor deaf. "Well, it *is* getting close to lunch. . . ."

Shankey nodded in a friendly way and led off back to the inn, an unpretentious two-story structure called "Clem's Place," according to the sign. The bar was open, and the woman behind it informed them she could do them some cold meat, cheese, and bread, but if they wanted anything hot it would be another hour. They ordered accordingly and took their tray and huge flagons of foamy beer to a quiet table at the far end of the room. There they could put their backs to the wall and each keep an eye on the front entry. Their training made such caution second nature.

After a healthy guzzle of beer, Shankey gave a shuddering sigh of relief in reaction. "Damn, I needed that. Dry work out there."

"Dry work," agreed Debreban, belching. "What might that be?"

"I'm buying this round, so you go first."

"Fair enough. Lord Cadmus told me to follow you and find out what you were doing."

"That's all?"

"Sadly, yes. I wish he'd get a more interesting hobby than mooning after your lady all the time. I'm pretty sure it's to do with Lady Filima."

"He knows I'm on one of her errands? How's that?"

Debreban, who was slicing cheese with his fighting knife, waved it carelessly. "Probably something to do with magic. He has Talent, you know. Dabbles like some of the rest," he added, meaning the clan aristocracy in general. He lowered the knife and stuffed cheese in his mouth.

"Yeah, I've noticed that. They have way too much time on their hands." Shankey helped himself to bread and butter, laying the latter on generously. Being more respectful of his battle equipment, he used the flat, dull knife provided by the inn, sparing his own cherished blade for less mundane purposes. "But, what the hell, so long as we have a job."

"That's for damn-sure. Now . . . what's your side of it?"

Shankey took on a resigned expression. "Lady Filima wants me to find a man wearing a cat mask."

"Excuse me?"

"That's what I thought. Couldn't say it, though. Not to her face. Pisses her off when people question her orders. Have no idea why she wants him; I just do what I'm told. Makes life a lot simpler."

"A cat mask?" Debreban shook his head. "Is there a circus in town?"

"She said so, but I've not seen or heard sign of one. Been feeling like a fool asking around after him, too. Seems more like a job for one of my errand runners, but she wanted me to see to it personally, so it must be important in some way I don't know yet."

"He could be a thief," Debreban suggested. "Uses it as a disguise. But why wear a cat mask when a hood and muffler would do just as well?"

"Thought of that, too. It's nuts. Between you and me, I don't think she knows who he is either or she'd have given me a name. Must be doing that magic stuff the same as your master. Why couldn't she have gone in for embroidery or horse racing like some of the other clans in the city?"

"They're a strange bunch, aren't they?"

"That they are, my friend." Shankey hoisted his beer, relishing the moment. He enjoyed talking shop with another professional even if the fellow wasn't nearly as experienced at the work. "At least the pay is good."

"When you get paid." Debreban was justifiably morose about the topic. It was well-known Lord Cadmus Burkus was forgetful when it came to the timely remuneration of his retainers. "Sorry, didn't mean to air clan laundry."

"That's all right. If you weren't sworn to his service, I'd invite you to come work for Lady Filima." Shankey thought Debreban would do well once he got some proper training.

"You would? That's decent of you. The whole house is hoping it might happen anyway."

"What? That Lord Cadmus finally marries her?"

Debreban nodded. "We're hoping, but most don't think she'll accept him."

Shankey gave an expressive shrug. "Not unless Hell freezes over." In truth, he had no idea what the weather conditions in Hell might be and tended to conduct his life in such a way as to never find out firsthand.

"I wish it would," Debreban stated softly, but with a great deal of feeling under the words.

"Oh, yeah?" said Shankey, in a drawing-out tone.

"Don't get me wrong, Lord Cadmus is a great master. He's got no political ambitions, so there's not a lot of work, just drills and stuff like that to keep us all polished."

"Much better doing that than real fighting," Shankey agreed. He drained away his beer, signed for another round, and dug into a slice of cold ham.

"But he needs a keeper. Someone to see to the practical side of running the household, you know?" Debreban finished his first flagon and welcomed the next.

"Someone to see that he doesn't overspend himself?"

"Exactly!" Debreban said. "Lady Filima would be perfect for him. She used to have to earn her way like the rest of us, so she knows the value of a penny. There's no waste in your house, is there? Everyone gets paid on time? The whole town knows she's smart that way."

Shankey felt a warm glow of pride that his lady's reputation was taking on a new facet. In the early days of her marriage to Lord Botello the oochie-coochie dancer past had been rather hard to live down. "True, all true."

"Then there you are," said Debreban conclusively.

Shankey nodded several times in agreement and made a mental note to return to this inn for more drink. Whatever they did with the beer here was inspired. It usually took more than just two to make him feel this relaxed. Debreban was also looking happily mellow—in between his thoughtful frowns. It was good for a man to be so concerned about the welfare of his master, too bad that master was Cadmus Burkus.

Both men ate. And drank. On his fourth flagon, Debreban said:

"If they got married *she'd* be able to keep my lord Cadmus in line. Of course, there's also the risk that he could beggar her. You know how some women get when they fall in love. She could go silly and give him all her money."

"Won't happen. *Won't* happen. Her falling in love. With him. She's met him already. No offense."

Debreban grunted, apparently used to popular opinion concerning his liege-lord. "Wish we could *make* it happen. It's time my lord settled down, got himself a proper heir. He's the last of his line, y'know. If he dropped dead today the whole household would be . . . be . . . something." With his flagon empty, his memory lapse was excusable. "Shouldn't be allowed."

"Seems to me," said Shankey slowly, for he'd also found the bottom to his fourth beer, "seems to me, that all the advantage is on *your* side. What would my lady get out of such a match?"

"Well, he's a handsome fellow, has pretty manners, and makes a good joke. Very dedicated to the gentlemanly arts. He'd never mistreat her. That's a fact. You know . . . you know . . . *all* his old girl friends still like him?"

"Really?"

Debreban nodded solemnly.

"How does he manage that?"

A shrug. "Something to do with being a gentleman. Got himself trained up right. He'd give her good entertainment and some fine-looking children. If they got her brains and his looks—not that she doesn't have a face a man could die for . . . but then that could be all reversed. The kids could end up with *his* brains." He frowned again.

"That's getting too far ahead. What benefit could my lady get from such a match *now*?"

"Not a damn thing that I can see—wait, she'd have a fine lover."

"I don't want to know how you know that," said Shankey.

Debreban laughed himself into hiccups. "Ever'one knows he got some special *training* in *that* area."

Maybe that was why his old girlfriends still liked him. "Oh, yeah?"

"From what I understand, my lord is *very* exceptional when it comes to putting a female into a good mood. Nothing keeps a woman home and happy more than a man who knows how to please her. If once your lady ever sampled his goods I'd bet she'd not be wasting time on magic and sending you off on errands looking for fools in cat masks."

Shankey hiccupped a few times, too, but managed to pull himself together. "You've got summin' there. But how d'we make it happen? The very sight of him . . . well . . . it seems to annoy her to no end."

"I'm sure we can work out something to cure that," said Debreban, also making an effort to overcome his beer. He cut loose with an extended belch when he made himself sit up straight. "I am also, also, *also* sure that we won't work anything out while we're in this state."

"I am not drunk, my friend. *This* is just a little buzz."

"Didn't mean to imply that you were. I was referring to this huge meal we just had." Indeed, their shared tray was bare of food, including crumbs. "I'm too full to think. But later today, after we've walked this off, we can *start* thinking up something. A 'master' plan." He giggled. "As in a plan for my master—get it?"

But Shankey had his head sideways on the table, his eyes thickly glazed over. He managed to drool hearty agreement, though, to the idea of thinking up an idea.

A Few Streets Away from Clem's Place

The screaming had nothing to do with Terrin, for a change. Not at first. It did seem to have to do with a big guy dragging a little guy around by the neck. They emerged, yelling and cursing, from some tavern, and it looked to be a full-blown brawl. I didn't know who started what, but my sympathies automatically went to the smaller fellow. Big guys who beat up on not so big people piss me off. I wasn't planning to get involved, but they both careened into me, knocking me hard over. Only by some fast footwork and an instinctive shift in balance did I manage to land square on my feet.

"Hey, asshole, you might hurt yourself," I called out to the big one, annoyed. He'd done all the klutz-work. "He's way out of your league, you know."

"Huh?" Still holding onto the other guy's neck, he loomed toward me. Oh, boy, was *he* ugly, though it might have been the rage distorting his features. His eyes were pretty rabid. Must have been the booze. At two yards I was getting high off his breath. "Whazzat to you?"

"I mean you'll strain something if you keep dragging him around like that."

"Shaddup, freak!"

Bet he worked all day thinking up that riposte. He dropped the man and took a swing at me. He was big and fast, but I ducked, dancing clear, drawing him away from his original target.

Luggo rushed at me, roaring, but I dodged, and he plowed into a slower-moving bunch of people. None of them took the sudden assault too well and began beating on him in response. They seemed to be having a great time. He straightened and brushed them off, launching toward me to try for another round.

"Myhr! What the hell are you doing?" Terrin came out of one of the shops to glare at me, probably pissed that I wasn't there to pay his bill.

"Just a little exercise." I avoided another fist. It also cut close. Too close. I couldn't let this guy connect or he'd snuff me. "But I'm getting bored now."

"You started it, you finish it."

"It's not my fight. He was after *him*." I pointed at the little guy, who was still on the ground. He looked confused and unhappy.

"Oh, okay." Somewhere deep inside Terrin had a rusty sense of honor. His black candle still in hand, he stepped into the street and addressed the man trying to kill me. "Hey, you big-ass jerk. Pick on someone your own size!"

Terrin's just an inch or so over five feet. Nearly everyone he got in a fight with was taller. I'd yet to see him lose.

Mr. Drunken Lug turned on him. "Shuddup, shorty."

Remarks on his height never bothered Terrin. "Both my feet are on the ground, that's all that matters," he'd usually say.

But in this case his feet ceased to be on the ground. Launching a lightning-fast crescent kick, he caught Luggo's chin solidly with the heel of his purple high-top sneaker. Our mutual non-friend dropped heavily to the cobbles and stopped moving.

"Ouchie," said Terrin, rubbing his butt. Apparently he was still sore from last night's dragging down the stairs.

"He'll kill me when he wakes up," said the victim-guy.

"Not if you leave," I said. "After a knockout like that he won't remember anything that happened today."

"He'll *find* me!" he wailed.

I looked at Terrin. "He did seem the type."

He grumbled and grumped. "Why's it always me?"

"Because you're the best, of course." He liked being talked into things. Flattery helped.

He growled, but gave in to his fate. He went over to the unconscious man and held a hand out over his head. I saw a very faint shimmer, like heated air. "Okay, he's fixed."

"Fixed in what way?" Never liked that word, "fixed."

"Every time he tries to hit someone, he'll get an instant migraine."

"He won't be able to defend himself, you know."

"I know. But he's about due for some karmic payback."

"You hear that?" I asked the victim. "You're safe now. He can still yell at you, though."

"What'd you do?" he wanted to know.

"Community service," said Terrin. He snagged my shirt sleeve. There was sweat on his white face, making all his freckles stand out. He *did* need some rest. "Come on, I need you to buy me some herbs."

I went with him. The street theater scene over, the crowd went on with business as usual. I hoped they'd bring some of it to Clem's. Before I could make an announcement to that effect, Terrin hauled me into an herbalist, and bang went what was left of my tips.

"You sure you need this stuff?" I asked, paying out. As ever, it was a painful experience. "I know you have a stash in your pack."

"That's my own personal recreational weed; *this* has to do with my magic. It's always better to use local organics for spell work. The energy connection to the ley lines is stronger than if I bring in something alien."

"Oh." Tech stuff again. Boring. "I gotta get back to Clem's. It'll be time for the lunch crowd soon."

"Great, take this with you." He foisted his candle and bag of herbs onto me.

"Where will you be?"

He shrugged. "Walking around. I need to feel out the lines, see where the power points are . . ."

"Get laid." I wondered how he spelled the "ley" in ley lines.

"That, too. I saw a place where—"

"Thanks, spare me the details." Terrin could spot a sex business through solid walls, and in all our travels I'd never once seen him pay for services rendered. Girls just seemed to *want* to give it to him. He never used magic, either. Some guys are born lucky. I didn't begrudge him, though. If he didn't get laid fairly often he tended to implode. I hated that.

"An' there was something about the big drunk, too," he added.

"What kind of something?"

"When I did the whammy number on him, it took a lot more energy than it should."

"Maybe he was just resistant 'cause of the booze."

"I don't think so. There must be some heavy-duty vibes going on here, only I'm not feeling them, and I should."

"And that's a bad thing?"

"It could be. I've never run up against anything like it before, so I don't know what it means. A deserted astral plane, that fog river, and me being this kind of tired from doing a simple restraining whammy."

"Maybe it's jet-lag."

He snorted, more to himself than toward me. "I'll see ya later. I gotta go get some energy."

Sex tended to charge him up again. It did the same for me, but in a different way, since I wasn't into the magical side of stuff. Terrin said he fed on all levels, whatever that meant. I never asked for an explanation, filing it in my Too Much Information cabinet. He went off in one direction and I another, heading back to the inn.

Greta gave me a wave hello, reminding me it was time to get started. The place was a little sparse for lunch customers yet, just two soldier-type guys in a corner. One was passed out on the table, and the other seemed fast asleep with his eyes wide open. He wore a really awful purple-and-green uniform that clashed badly with his blond hair.

I stopped upstairs long enough to drop off Terrin's stuff and get ready for the lunch show. Over my white pirate-style shirt I pulled on a dapper vest to dress things up. Then I stood just outside the front door and did my warm-up act.

Like I said, my face is my fortune. It was enough to

gather a street crowd just to stare at me, but the key is to make them see past my face to the talent beneath. Having been blessed with a decent singing voice, this wasn't a tough job, and I rounded it all out with the jokes, muggings, and double-takes whenever a pretty girl came in view. They ate it up. I duly invited everyone for second helpings over their noontime meal.

I brought in enough takers to draw a smile from Clem, who was helping behind the bar while Greta and their various kids dished out the food. My stomach growled expectantly, but it would just have to wait until the show was over. I never ate beforehand; it's too embarrassing to interrupt a perfectly good song with a badly timed burp.

This did happen, though. I was about to launch into "The Lion Sleeps Tonight"—my signature piece, it never fails to please a crowd—when the guy in the purple and green cut loose with a monumental belch. I'm talking the kind that shakes the rafters and it happened just as I opened my mouth. Well, there's no following that sort of thing until the audience settles down. They were laughing too hard. In an attempt to win them back I announced a belching contest. It seemed the perfect thing for this group.

"What's the prize?" someone demanded.

"Prize? You expect a *prize*?" I didn't have to pretend shock.

"Aye, 's only right. You 'ave a contest, y' should 'ave a prize!"

Damn. I was faced with a situation I'd not thought all the way through. Thankfully, Clem saved me from having to volunteer my tips.

"The prize is a free flagon of beer," he called out.

I shot him a grateful thumbs-up for the rescue. He grinned back and proceeded to sell beer to a dozen eager contestants. He'd more than make back the money for the freebie.

Playing emcee to the full, I got things going. The contest grew louder by the minute, and smellier. I figured out quick which end of the room was upwind from the belchers and stood there for the duration. By the time it had devolved down to the last two, the soldier guys in the corner seemed to have woken up fully and were giving me what I'd always thought of as "the hairy eyeball." I wondered if there was some kind of permit required for what I was doing. Clem hadn't mentioned anything about it.

"Okay, last and final round," I bellowed. "Rick the Roaring Bear against Werdel the Wondergut!"

Rick and Werdel drained off their flagons of fuel and after a moment to let the fizz build in their expanding bellies, each had a turn cutting loose. The rafters not only shook, but a quantity of dust sifted down. They both sounded the same to me, but I'd left the judging to the audience. The cheers were loudest for Werdel. He accepted his free flagon with good grace, took a swig, then generously passed the rest of it to Rick.

"Gotta see a man about a dog," he announced, looking all tense as he sprinted for the back door.

I offered a few choice lines wishing him additional success, then finished out the act by passing a hat and singing "Show Me the Way to Go Home," after first reminding the audience that the song was for me, not them. I'd put in a good hour and a half and needed a break.

Clem was well pleased. "That's triple the business I usually get for beer this time of day. We'll do the same tomorrow if my stocks hold out."

"Glad to have been of service." Maybe I should have felt guilty contributing to the area's population of alcoholics, but didn't. I had a nice chunk of change left over after Clem took his cut. Not enough to buy gems, but maybe I'd at least go check on their prices. The sooner

I left the sooner the locals could get back to normal drinking habits, right?

Just as I slipped the coins into my pocket, the purple-and-green-cloaked soldier guy came up. His blue eyes were somewhat red-rimmed and dull. "My friend here wants a word with you."

His friend wasn't here, but still at their table. "Is something wrong?" I'd traveled enough to develop a certain respect for people in uniforms. It's great when they're your chums. Not so great otherwise.

"He jus' wan's a word with you."

There'd be no information forthcoming from this one. Maybe he wanted me for their version of a USO show. Feeling safe enough, I went along to the table. The guy there was stocky and balding; what remained of his dark hair was combed straight back. He wore what I'd come to recognize as civilian clothes, but he was definitely some kind of military. With practice, you can just tell.

"Captain Shankey of House Darmo," he said about himself, like I would know the name. I thought I did, too.

"Hi, I'm Myhr."

"Hah?"

"Myhr—rhymes with 'purr.' A nice play on the cat angle, don't you think?" I flared my lip whiskers in a way I hoped would be taken as a friendly expression.

He squinted. "That's not a mask, is it?"

"Just my own wonderful face." I spoke slow so he'd catch everything. His breath was very beery. "Was there something I can help you with?"

"You're not from around here, are you?"

"Just got in yesterday. Is there a problem?"

Shankey straightened a bit. "My Lady Filima Botello Darmo requires that you come to her house."

From my chat in the apothecary shop I belatedly recognized the name of one of the city's main clans. I couldn't recall if they were Fortune 500 rich, though. "Oh, yeah? Did she say why?"

"She doesn't have to say why."

Uh-oh. Types like that make me nervous. "Look, I never met her or anything, so how is it she even knows me? I appreciate the invitation and all, but—"

"I'll put it this way," he said, lurching to his feet to come around the table, looking more sober by the second. He and his friend had me bracketed. "You're coming with me. If my lady wants to see you, then she *will* see you. Understand?"

Before making a run for it I weighed a lot of factors, like both of them having knives, swords, authority, and stuff like that. Bolting seemed more trouble than it was worth. Maybe this Filima dame had seen me doing PR work and just wanted a closer look. I hoped she'd be more reasonable than this guy. He seemed a friendly sort except when his dark eyes went hard. They were like chips of onyx now.

"I understand, but—"

They each grabbed one of my arms.

"Oh, Mr. Myhr!" called Greta from behind the bar as I was dragged past, backwards. "What's this about?"

"These guys want me to see Lady Fillerup Bordello, I think. Tell Terrin what happened or I might be a little late getting back." If I ever *got* back.

"I don't hold with arrests in my place," Clem pronounced solemnly.

"Nyuhh," said Captain Shankey, lifting me, I presume, to spare my shoe leather.

"Yuhhh," added his blond buddy in the bad clothes, also lifting.

My feet were inches clear of the ground. They hauled ass toward the front door.

"Say," I chirped optimistically, legs swinging, "will there be any money for me in this gig?"

CHAPTER FOUR

One Long Walk Later, at Darmo House

I *love* how the other half lives. You just can't beat it. Lady Filima's mansion definitely put her on the side that has the really good stuff in life. It was bigger than any other building I'd seen in Rumpock and cleaner, too, made of smooth, whitewashed stone, looking like an art-deco wedding cake. Once past the wrought iron gates, we had a quick stroll up a paved, garden-flanked drive to a set of huge doors with gold-leaf trim. It impressed the hell out of me—in an intimidating kind of way. People with this kind of money and power could be dangerous.

Shankey and his friend cut over to a smaller side door on the left. I didn't rate the main entrance, but at least the goon squad had stopped carrying me. A dozen feet from Clem's they'd stopped the come-along routine, allowed me to face forward, then we'd walked more or less normally if you call being arm-braced by two humor-less guys normal. Neither of them answered my questions or loosened their grip. Cozy.

67

Shankey gave a yell and some kid within opened things up. We trooped into a dim hall. The kid gaped at me as he shut the door. Shankey told him to take off, then turned to his partner.

"Debreban, it was great for you to help like this, but you should keep out of sight. I don't want to have to explain you. Her nibs can get touchy seeing those colors."

"Then I'll lose them," said the blond fellow. He let go of my arm long enough to shrug clear of his garish cloak and throw it on a table.

"She might recognize you anyway."

"Doubt it. She's never noticed me before. Come on, Shank, I gotta see this through to the delivery. My lord will skin me if I don't have something to report."

"But maybe my lady won't want him knowing what's going on."

"She'll get her way then, 'cause neither of *us* knows what's going on."

"Count me in, too," I said. They glared, apparently having forgotten my presence. "Listen, guys, let's just go see this lady and get it over with. My guess is she won't be looking at either of you once I'm in the room. You can hang back and play fly on the wall, then *everyone* will know what's going on."

Shankey opened his mouth as though to object, then clammed up. "Okay, why not?"

I relaxed a little, reassured by his show of common sense. "Cool. Now where do I freshen up?"

"Freshen up?"

"If I'm going to meet a lady I want to look my best. You got a place where I can brush off the dust?"

Debreban shifted on his feet. "Sounds like a good idea. I'm feeling a little pressure, myself. All that beer . . ."

"Now that you mention it . . ." began Shankey. He finished by leading the way to an indoor facility that was down a flight of stairs in a stuffy basement chamber. The flat, low-browed windows, shoulder-height here, ground level outside, were for ventilation only. No way for me to squeeze through any of them. Along one wall was a long bench, with dividers between the holes: a three-seater with no waiting.

"This wasn't what I had in mind," I stated. There wasn't a mirror in sight where I could check the lay of my mane. I was still in performing clothes, so hopefully their flashiness would make up for shortages in my grooming.

Shankey and Debreban were too busy imitating Niagara Falls—American *and* Canadian sides—to pay attention to me. I waited them out. Afterward, they looked a lot less tense. We went upstairs again.

"Now what?" I asked Shankey.

"Now you shut up and speak when spoken to. Show respect."

Well, he didn't make any friends with me for that answer. He sent someone ahead, then we all marched upstairs to the more refined areas of the joint.

The house looked like a movie set for a Cecil B. DeMille epic, but on a *really* big budget. I gaped a lot, admired paintings and sculptures, and fiercely wondered what the hell I was doing here.

Our hike ended before a set of elegantly tall double doors, painted royal blue. Their detailed trim sported enough gold leaf to give me and Terrin room and board at Clem's for the next year or so, no singing for my supper necessary.

The great doors silently swung wide just before we reached them. I looked for hidden wires, but spied only a couple of page boys in matching blue tunics. Like the kid below, they stared at me. I smiled back. Anything to brighten someone's day.

A mournful-faced man in black and silver emerged,

stopped, and made like one of the pages. I smiled at him, too, my lips together. The fangs tend to alarm neos.

The doors wafted shut again, blocking any glimpse of the next room.

"Good afternoon, Lord Perdle," said Shankey, with a slight bow.

Perdle recovered fairly fast. "Hello, Captain. Erm . . . who is this person, if I may ask?"

Shankey hesitated, then made a quick introduction, but I doubt if Perdle heard any of it. I gave a little bow as well, but could tell by his eyes he thought I was some kind of performing nutcase in a mask. It seemed best to preserve that illusion, so I kept my smile fixed in place.

"Friend of Lady Filima, what?" He spoke to Shankey, not me.

"I think so, your lordship."

"Is there a circus in town?"

"Not that I'm aware of, your lordship."

"Too bad. Might have added to the Mid-Summer Festival, what?" He frowned at me, then noticed Debreban. "Hello, Captain. What are you doing here?"

"Just visiting with my friend, your lordship." Debreban nodded at Shankey.

"Good to see everyone getting along. And how *is* Lord Cadmus?"

"He's very well, your lordship."

"Excellent, excellent. Well, carry on, then." He moved out of the way. Shankey and Debreban closed ranks next to me.

Once Perdle was out of earshot, Debreban snickered. "Did you *see* his face?"

"*That* was funny."

"Not to me it wasn't," I put in. Just to remind them I was there. Neither chose to respond. Maybe I could get a job here as wallpaper.

"Why is *he* here, though?" wondered Shankey.

"Who knows?"

"Overduke Anton. He'll have word about this little encounter ten minutes from now. Perdle repeats everything to him."

"Why should the overduke bother about me?" asked Debreban. "I told the truth. I *am* visiting."

"He'll figure Lord Cadmus sent you over, then think up ten good reasons why, even if they aren't true."

"The first one will be. Everyone knows my lord's interest in your lady. I wish she'd accept his suit and they'd both settle down."

"Don't worry, we'll hatch out some kind of plan. Come on, let's get this over with." Shankey tapped three times on one of the doors, two quick, one slow, and they opened. The pages were still there, now able to have a clear view of the Myhr and Two Stooges show.

The big room beyond had a blue theme all through it, but not in such a way as to bore you. Tall windows allowed in plenty of light and air. The floor was a large-scale mosaic in a hundred shades of polished blue stone; the ceiling was always summer with a painted sky full of fluffy clouds. Very oddly, smack in the center of the room, was a circular pavilion-style tent made of black velvet. The top was suspended from a ceiling rafter like some kind of fabric chandelier. Maybe it was a bed chamber of some sort.

Then I noticed *her* and the whole room just melted away.

I didn't know they made them like that any more, sort of an Elizabeth Taylor crossed with Josephine Baker type. There was no way to see her all at once; she was a series of quick, intense perceptions that hit me all over. I wanted to root myself to the floor and stay for a few years to absorb every nuance of this feminine phenomenon.

Eyes, the kind that grab you, beat you up, yet you keep coming back for more. They were a pale crystal blue that made the blues of the room look like so much sludge. To call them living gems leaned toward insult.

Her skin was like honey on cinnamon. I wanted to taste it, to find out whether that smooth-looking texture was as sweet and spicy as it appeared.

And her figure . . . it was seven or eight miles beyond *wow*. I could have written symphonies just on her breathing alone.

Yes, I drooled. On the inside. Outside, I just stood and gaped a lot. My brain had disconnected, the speech centers shut down, but other parts of me were very much up, alive, active, and real happy. If I didn't start thinking baseball scores soon she'd be able to tell whether or not I'd been circumcised.

"Captain Shankey?" she said.

Ohh, I could float to Tahiti on that voice.

"My lady," he responded briskly, bowing.

How could the guy act like nothing extraordinary was in front of him?

"My lady"—he straightened—"here is the . . . the *person* you wished to see. Mr. Myhr."

She nodded. Man, she could give lessons to queens on how to get it right. Regal clothes, too; her long, dark blue gown seemed painted on, hugging her every move.

Rowhr-rowhr. And then some.

Shankey looked at me. "This is the Lady Filima Botello Darmo of House Darmo."

I had just enough brains still working to know what was expected and swept into a low bow. "An honor, lady." The gesture earned me a small smile. Woo hoo.

"Thank you," she said. "You may remove your mask if you will."

Shankey cleared his throat and shot me a narrow-eyed warning. "My lady, he's not wearing a mask. That's his *face*."

She stared for a full minute. It seemed that long. No

one else moved the whole time, either. "You're kidding." Her dulcet tones jarred with abruptly informal speech.

"Uh . . . no, my lady."

Then she stepped close enough so I could feel her breath and inhale it for my own. She'd been eating fruit. Strawberries. Sweet ones. Mmmm.

"You're *not* kidding." She reached up and yanked on my nose, jolting me from my Strawberry Fields Forever fog.

"Ow!" I said, backing away. "That's attached, if you don't mind."

"You're. Not. Kidding!" She drew back as well. "What *are* you?"

I flared my lip whiskers, annoyed. "I'm a who, not a what, and the name has been mentioned. Myhr. Rhymes with *purr*."

"Show respect," Shankey muttered through his teeth.

"Where are you from?" Filima went on, oblivious to him.

"Dallas." There was no recognition of the name from any of them, so I could assume no equivalent city was in this world. "Dallas, Texas? As in deep-in-the-heart-of?"

"Texas? Where's that?" she demanded.

"It's a long way from here, a whole other country if you can believe the tourist hype."

"Are all those from Texas like you?"

"I don't know. I haven't met everyone who lives there yet." Her eyes blazed, sapphires catching the sun. Amazing. But I couldn't let them distract me. "It's my turn. Why did you have me dragged over here?"

"What?"

"Where I come from it's not considered neighborly to go around kidnapping people. I've got nothing against these guys, they're only doing a job, but I'd like an explanation of why you wanted to see me. How do you even know me? We've never met." I would have remembered. So would she.

She did a wonderful thing with her lips, tucking them in, then pursing them out again. I wanted to do wonderful things with them, too, but the way her eyes went all glower-like the possibility of that seemed remote. "No, we haven't, but I had . . . knowledge of you all the same."

"Oh, really?"

"And I know that *you* are connected to the Hell-river." She spoke like a TV lawyer about to crack the star prosecution witness during the cross-examination. Raymond Burr would have been proud. Shankey and Debreban, in the midst of their fly-on-the-wall opportunity, shifted on their feet as though startled. Apparently a large clue had been thrown out on the nice blue floor.

But it only got a blank reaction from me. "I am?"

"You will tell me everything about it," she said, with much certainty.

Maybe she was talking about that black mist. "I'd love to, but I don't know anything. Really. I'm just a tourist passing through. What gave you the idea that—"

Some invisible sign must have passed from her to Shankey. He cuffed the back of my head. "Answer," he snarled.

I paused to turn and shoot him a withering look. "I *am*. You guys got something against the truth? I don't know squat except what I saw last night, and that scared the hell out of me."

Filima smiled, all sexy triumph. "*You* were able to *see* it."

"Yeah, and I wish I hadn't. You guys have a serious pollution problem here."

"Very, very few others are aware it exists; certainly none of the ordinary folk of Rumpock."

I shrugged. "Well, sometimes a tourist notices things a resident misses. What is it, anyway?"

"That's what you're going to tell me."

I almost went "hah-whazzat?" then sealed up quick.

She didn't seem the type to take ignorance for an answer; she was way too nerved. I recognized her kind of tension. Some guy in a casino I'd been in had bet everything he owned on the turn of a roulette wheel. Filima had that same intense look in her eyes that he had while following the little white ball around the wheel. I'd left before the ball came to rest on either his salvation or destruction. No such freedom for me here. But before I could come up with an appropriately clever response that might get me on the other side of her front door, my stomach growled. It didn't just growl, it put on an extended chorus with curtain calls.

Shankey frowned, Debreban tried not to smile, and Filima blinked.

"Sorry," I said. "Haven't had lunch yet."

She blinked again, seeming to take me in on a different level. It was subtle, but I sensed an easing in her luscious body. The blaze in her eyes cooled. "How remiss of me not to offer you refreshment. Captain Shankey, would you be so good as to ring the bell? Three long and two short."

Shankey must have twigged that she was going to try for a softer kind of campaign to get information. He nodded with sudden cordiality and went to drag on an embroidered bell pull. I was just able to pick out a distant ringing from the far depths of the house. Middle C. Before too long a tubby geezer in formal-looking clothes ushered in a small parade of servant-types in identical blue smocks, all carrying trays. The smells of perfectly cooked food plucked the air like music. The gastronome gang set up a table for two with gold plates and utensils. Within a minute Filima and I were seated opposite each other, and I was invited to pick what I liked from the mobile buffet.

Talk about a change in gears.

I'm pretty adaptable, though, and common sense told

me to eat up while I could. I pointed to dishes that I had no name for, but which appealed to my instincts. In the worlds I'd been to it's better not to inquire too closely about the strange food, just trust that if the natives survive on it then you will, too. Besides, it usually *does* taste like chicken, even the chicken, which I was sucking down like it would go out of style. Filima had a goo-ood cook.

And a crafty wine steward. My glass was filled to the brim. I drank deep to quench my thirst, secure that my weird body chemistry would keep me out of trouble. Terrin and I had made a few pub crawls in our time, usually running out of money before we ran out of sobriety. Even Clem's potent beer had only given me a pleasant buzz and then mostly because I'd been tired.

"Tasty," I said, grateful.

Filima barely touched her stuff, mostly sipping what looked to be ice water from her goblet. She watched me scarf away, trying to smile pleasantly, but could have saved herself the effort. My back hairs were up—in a very literal sense—and she'd have to do more than just feed me to get what she wanted. I had enough human DNA to resist that bribe. Of course, it also helped that I was clueless. The black mist, or Hell-river as they called it, was Terrin's area of expertise. *He* should be the one here, not me.

So . . . I ate enough for two.

"You live here long?" I asked.

"Why do you ask?" she countered.

I hate when people read ulterior motives into banal conversation. "Because when you answer it'll cover up the noise when I belch."

Her mouth tucked in again and her eyes flickered. She didn't seem offended. Amused. Good.

"You gonna answer?"

She lifted her chin. "I've been here for three years, since my wedding day."

Damn. She was married. "What's your husband's line of work?"

"He doesn't work. He died just two weeks ago."

Damn. She was widowed. "I'm sorry. My condolences."

"Thank you. May I ask what your line of work is?"

"I'm an entertainer."

Another one of those subtle-change things took place. She straightened a little and her eyes got brighter, if that was possible. "Really? What do you do?"

"I sing and tell jokes."

She came down a notch. "A patterman, eh?"

I shrugged, filing the name away for future use. "It's a good life. I travel a lot, meet fun people." At this I glanced at Shankey and Debreban, who were doing their best to be invisible with the rest of the servants.

"I used to do that," she said. "I don't miss the travel, but the applause was great."

"You used to sing?"

"And dance. I was the best oochie-coochie girl in the five provinces." No little pride in her tone.

I gulped as my imagination put Filima's superb figure into an oochie-coochie outfit. I'd never seen such a costume, but my internal picture made me think of a Vegas showgirl wrapped in the final silky wisp from the Dance of the Seven Veils, with more beads and feathers than fabric. "I bet you were. Wish our paths had crossed earlier so I could have caught your act."

"You're sweet, but I've hung up my dancing shoes. I'm all out of practice."

"Aw, you're just waiting for someone to talk you into them again."

"Maybe so, but with all this—" She shrugged as though to take in the enormous house. "I have to keep within the dignity of my station."

"That's too bad. Everyone needs to get out, cut loose, and boogie through the night."

"Oh, we have parties. It's not the same, but better than nothing."

"Yeah, I've been hearing about some summer fest that's coming up. Could you tell me about it?"

"It's a big celebration, singing and dancing in the streets, games and contests of skill, horse racing."

"Sounds like a blast. Need any entertainers?"

She smiled. "Perhaps."

"Paid entertainers?"

"Perhaps. I've just been placed in charge of planning it out."

"Coo-ool. Maybe you could find a spot for me. I'm really great at Master of Ceremony work."

"A place might be made available." She'd stopped being sincere, turning to coy. I don't like coy unless it's sincere.

"What do I have to do to get it?"

"Tell me about the Hell-river."

I put down my fork. My plate was empty anyway. Someone whisked it away and a wine server topped off my goblet. Another server slipped some kind of elaborate dessert in front of me that smelled of brandy. I sensed a conspiracy. "I'd really love to help you, but I don't know anything about it. What I saw was huge, black, and spooky as hell. Last night it tried to ooze into my room at Clem's inn and I stampeded downstairs yelling the house awake. But when Clem and his wife looked outside they didn't see any mist. That was freaking weird."

"Yes, many folk are not magically sensitive, so they don't see most of what's around them. You're different from them, obviously."

"I guess so."

"Please." She leaned forward, so casual that she was intense. "Please tell me about yourself, then."

Wow. A beautiful woman who feeds me and wants me

to talk about myself. What are the odds? And was she any good at belly-rubs?

"Well," I began, then out of nowhere started singing to the tune of a hillbilly sitcom song.

> *Lemme tell you a story 'bout a cat named Myhr*
> *A poor patterman with really soft fur;*
> *He travels around with a dude named Terrin*
> *And their poverty thing really is wearin'.*
> *(Cashless they are, ain't it a shame?*
>   *Donate, please!)*

I did NOT know where *that* had come from. Maybe the wine was working on me after all.

> *Well, Myhr sings and jokes and Terrin gets laid*
> *They have lots of fun but rarely get paid;*
> *They're aheadin' home when the stars are right*
> *In the meanwhile, remember their plight*
> *(Pockets empty, thumbing rides. Donate, please!)*

Filima, with her sagging jaw, had obviously expected something along the lines of where I'd been born—which I didn't know, having been too young at the time—and other dull stuff like that.

But why should I tell my whole life story to strangers? This wasn't a bank loan application.

Elsewhere, at Overduke Anton's Palace

"She was a bit surprised at first, of course, but after expressing to her your complete confidence that she was indeed the very best choice, Lady Filima at last accepted the honor of putting together the festival."

Anton lifted a long hand an inch from the arm of his chair, halting the flow of Perdle's droning voice. The man tended to turn even the simplest of reports into epic drama. "That's good. See to it she has whatever she needs to organize things."

"Yes, my lord. There is quite a lot in the palace archives she will no doubt find extremely useful."

"People, too. She'll want an outside staff that knows what it's doing. Find those who have worked on the festival before and make sure they're sent 'round to her."

"Excellent suggestion, my lord."

A pretty damn obvious one, thought Anton.

"Lord Cadmus must still be presenting his suit to her, I think."

Anton shifted, restless. His throne was very comfortable, but he'd been in it far too long and wanted to stretch his long legs, maybe look in on Velma to see what she was doing and if she'd like some company for it. But Perdle had made a leading comment that wanted a response. "Why do you think that?"

"Captain Debreban of his guard was at Darmo House. I couldn't tell if he had a message in hand. Said he was visiting his friend Captain Shankey. He didn't appear too comfortable, but I suspect I sometimes intimidate a few of the lower echelons. You know how it is, my lord."

Perdle couldn't intimidate so much as a rabbit, but it would have been impolite to say so. "Yes, I know," Anton said agreeably. "The burdens of rank and all that." He should have a word with Cadmus about Filima. The idiot would have better luck with her by backing off for a month or so, allowing her a decent interval for mourning. Anyway, she'd be busy with the planning work.

"I think perhaps her ladyship might have had an inkling of your festival proposal before I ever arrived to deliver it, though." Perdle shuffled his papers, tucking them under one arm, ready to bow himself away.

How could Filima have an inkling? Anton hadn't thought of giving her the job until that morning. Unless she'd been scrying on him. Not likely. The palace's shielding spells had been in place for decades and still worked just fine. Besides, everyone knew Filima got awful headaches whenever she tried magic. "How so?" he asked casually.

Perdle sounded pleased. "Because she already had some sort of circus performer on the premises, though there's no circus in town. A rather odd-looking fellow."

Anton gave a mental shrug. "Probably an old crony from her oochie-coochie days."

"He was most amusing, yet didn't say a word. I suppose he couldn't with that mask on. It was quite a charming bit of work. Very realistic rendition of a cat's face it was. Thought it was a sort of man-cat creature at first. Took me back a step when I clapped eyes on—"

"A cat's face?" Anton's heart sped up, but he was careful to keep his voice normal.

"Yes, my lord. If he is one of her entertainer friends we must have him perform here while he's still in town. The mask alone is well worth seeing, though what he does besides I could not venture to guess. An acrobat or an actor, perhaps?"

Anton managed not to twitch. Crystal sharp, the nightmare vision returned to his mind's eye. Some *thing* with a cat's face and a human body pushing him into the Hell-river. With that idiot Cadmus helping. Cadmus was no worry, but this other creature . . . Anton took his visions seriously, because too many of the bad ones tended to come true in a very literal sense. He had hoped this new one would only prove to be symbolic. In vain. Dammit.

"What news have you on the Hell-river?" he asked.

Perdle gave an apologetic cough. "Forgive me, my lord. I'd quite forgot about that report. Very puzzling business it is, too. It didn't behave in its usual manner last night."

There was *nothing* usual about the damned thing. Anton wished Perdle would realize that. "Go on."

"One of the Talents on watch noticed a section of it

flowing up the side of an inn near the bell tower. Someone had a window open on an upper floor there and was looking out. That might have attracted the river's notice. The tenant closed the shutter and the river hovered outside for a goodly while, then subsided. It's happened before. No one was hurt. But very strangely the river vanished away from the streets shortly after, hours ahead of its usual time at dawn."

"Who was in the room?"

"I don't know, my lord, but can find out."

"Do so."

"At once."

"Yes, my lord."

"And write out some sort of informal invitation to send to Lord Cadmus. Ask if he's free to come 'round for dinner tonight. I think Velma would enjoy the diversion." Unless required by the demands of his office, Anton preferred just the two of them alone at dinner. It had been especially true since the coming of the fog. With his curfew in place guests had to stay overnight and he disliked imposing on people. Perhaps *they* were flattered by the invitation, but there was the risk it might go to their heads. Bloody politics. Ah, well, this was as good a time as any to give Cadmus that talking-to about Filima. Velma would put in a few words herself. Perhaps some of it might sink in.

"At once, my lord."

"And Perds?"

"Yes, my lord?"

"Have someone keep an eye on Filima's house. When that fellow in the cat mask comes out, ask him over. I'd like a look at him."

"Oh, *yes*, your lordship." Perdle seemed pleased. "I'm sure you'll find the workmanship most amusing."

Gooseflesh crept along Anton's arms. He was anything but amused.

In the Streets Near Clem's Place

Terrin poked his nose into yet another herbalist shop, but sensed nothing of magical note. At least it wasn't full of wannabe wizards, tree huggers, and kids in black trying to scare their Bible Belter parents with pentacles and over-dyed hair. Dallas had been full of those, but so long as their checks and credit cards cleared he never minded them coming into his shop. Besides, he'd put plenty of wards up to keep out the real riff-raff, seen and unseen.

No shortage of Talents back home, but this world was a freak show for having none at all. His nape hair had been on end from the first moment. The exact cause of his unease still eluded him, but he had a pissy feeling he was on the right track for it.

In search of others of his kind he'd asked around Rumpock, carefully phrasing his questions so only insiders would understand. Sometimes he'd get a deep enough conversation going to openly ask about magic. People here were fairly comfortable about it; they'd heard of Talents, but no one knew where to point him. Some gestured vaguely toward the east side of town, saying that some of the titled types "did that sort of thing," but they couldn't recall who. It was like trying to track down an urban legend; everyone had a story, but no real source to name.

The empty astral plane bugged him, too. Deeply. It was just too damn fricking weird, like those movies where New York City's deserted because someone had dropped the bomb. He wanted to find a local wizard to tell him what was going on. If that was normal for this world, then okay-fine, but if not, then he wanted out. A-s-a-p. Sooner, if possible.

But none were to be found. Usually he couldn't help

but sniff out another Talent. In fact, they tended to trip over each other. But here, nothing.

He did find a few mysteriously closed shops that gave him the creeps. He'd pass by their sealed doors and shuttered windows and feel a strange tugging, but it vanished when he drew near. Touching the buildings to pick up leftover vibes didn't work. All he felt was brick or plaster; any latent emotional signature of the previous tenants just wasn't there. That was *very* wrong, particularly for the older structures. Nearly everything was capable of absorbing that kind of energy and holding it for a time, like a scent lingering on still air. In this burg it was like a great wind had swept through and swept away all the magic.

And oh, lordy, was he *tired*. The two nimble girls he'd spent some athletic afternoon hours with had cheered him a lot, but not powered him up as much as he'd expected. They'd all parted company on buoyant terms, and though he felt a little better for the psychic feeding and physical exercise, he should have been bursting with energy, not dragging around like a sloth on downers.

It seemed to get worse by the minute. Better get back to the inn for a nap, then pow-wow with Myhr about speeding up their departure from this dump.

Maybe I'm going through techno withdrawal.

Terrin *did* miss the warehouse raves down in Deep Ellum. Nothing like the deafening blast of electronic music thrumming through his body with crowds of kids mashed together, jumping and weaving to the hyper-beat like one gigantic animal, throwing off more energy than even he could pull into himself. He wanted a big dose of that right now, just to crawl back up to feeling low-end normal again.

Terrin hadn't been this bad since his gall bladder had done a meltdown a few years back. The docs had had to suck it out with medical vacuum hoses because it had liquefied. Too bad. He'd wanted it in a jar as a souvenir. The painkillers had been fun, though. He could use a few right now for a little flying. Nothing specific hurt, but being knocked out for a day or so might draw his strength back. Taking that street bruiser on hadn't helped; not the physical part, but the magic. Gawd, he was drained. . . .

Free association of memory made something click in his head.

Mirror. He wanted a mirror.

On this tech level the only place that might have one would be a shop selling women's clothing. Not a Walmart or Rodeo Drive chain store in sight.

He found a likely prospect, walking through the open door like he owned the place, sketching a wave at the startled proprietress. Was she staring because this was a chicks-only place or was there another reason? A framed mirror stood on her front table where she could keep an eye on it. Not large, and kind of warped, but valuable enough. Vanity and thieves were universal, he'd found in his travels.

The shop was nearly too dark for him to properly see himself. He angled the glass to reflect outside light onto his face and got a *good* look.

Oh. Shit.

CHAPTER FIVE

Back at Darmo House

Man, was I full. All that food. I'd lost count of my seconds, thirds, and fourths and had to loosen my top pants button. Good thing I wouldn't be singing for some hours yet. No way could I take a deep breath now. If Filima offered me a wafer-thin after-dinner mint, things would get Monty Python messy.

Our conversation throughout the meal had gone rather well, considering that when it came to the Hell-river we had wildly opposite views. She was positive I could help her, and I was positive I couldn't, not unless she came up with a lot more background that I could give to Terrin. And money. Despite the lyrics of my improv song, she'd missed their message and hadn't once mentioned money.

That black velvet pavilion had begun to nag at me, too. I asked her about it, but she just shrugged and said it was a "retiring place." What the hell did that mean? Was it an upper-class toilet?

Heh. No way.

Just because I'm not interested in magic doesn't mean I can't sense it. That curtain-shrouded question mark was definitely a hot-spot. Not a big one, but enough to make my muzzle whiskers twitch. It was the first whiff of real magic I'd detected since we got here. I'd have to tell Terrin. He'd be all over it like a cheap suit.

"Lemme make sure I got this straight," I was saying to Filima. "One night a couple weeks back this Hell-river just appeared?"

"Yes."

"And no one can say what it is or where it comes from?"

"You know that to be true."

"Pretend I don't know anything." Which was way too right. "Something happened to cause its appearance here. Rivers don't change course without a reason, even the metaphysical kind."

"Yes, we're all aware of that. Those of us who *can* see it have discussed nothing else."

"The 'those' being a few people in high society. Why is that? What makes them different from the rest of the townspeople?"

"We're high-born and wealthy, I suppose."

That couldn't be it. She was wealthy, but in my experience damn-few high-born ladies go into oochie-coochie dancing for a living. I didn't mention that, of course. "Do you all practice magic?"

"Not everyone. Just those with Talent, and not many of them."

"None of the townspeople have any Talent?"

"Of course some of them *did*, but they're not around anymore."

"Hah?"

"When the river appeared they left."

"Where'd they go?"

She looked unhappy. "No one knows."

Uh-huh. "Someone must. They had relatives and friends, maybe a nice little job where they'd be missed."

"They didn't leave in that sense. They just weren't around any more."

"Like they vanished—poof?"

"Exactly."

Not good. Maybe the river had sucked them in. The way it crept up the outside wall of the inn like a misty version of the Blob still gave me the heebies, though I realized now it probably hadn't sensed me at all, but had been sniffing for Terrin. That guy was a magical power station, broadcasting twenty-four/seven to anyone or anything geared to pick up his kind of signals. "That's pretty serious," I said. "Didn't you try to find them?"

"Once we worked out what had happened, Overduke Anton had investigators running all over town looking for them. No one knows where they are. It's as though they'd all been forgotten by all their friends."

"If they'd been forgotten, then how did you know they were missing?"

"Those of us with Talent who remained remembered them."

Oh.

"But it took us *days* to work that much out." She snorted disgust, whether for her slowness or that of her friends was hard to judge.

"And nobody's upset about it? Like this overduke?"

"Of course he's upset, we all are, but he can't draw a lot of attention to it or there might be a panic."

"If there was going to be a panic, it'd have happened by now. Maybe you *should* have a panic, a real big one. It might stir up an answer." I could use a few of those. "The Hell-river appears, a few practitioners in the upper classes can see it, but the rest of the town folk don't, and all the magic-types down there vanish, only no one else notices or misses them. A conspiracy or mass hypnosis?"

She shrugged.

"Aside from the river coming, what else happened a couple weeks ago?"

Behind me I heard Shankey shift on his feet. I turned to glance at him. He seemed like a guy with something on the tip of his tongue and it wasn't an after-dinner mint.

"Yeah, Captain?" I said encouragingly.

Filima's turn to shift. She added in some throat-clearing, too.

I turned back to her. She had the same look as Shankey. "Yeah, lady?"

"I don't see *how* it could be connected . . ." she began. Her trailing off gave me to think otherwise.

"How what could be connected?"

"Well, it was about the time my husband died that the river appeared."

I sensed major pay dirt here. "Did he, by any chance, go in for magic?"

"Actually, yes. He did. Yes."

"And no one's put together that there *might* be a connection between the two?"

She lifted her chin, frowning a lot. She was still gorgeous. "I have. But I don't know what it could be. You do."

Gawd, she was still playing that tune. I'd have to do some creative jamming to get past her chorus. I gave a deprecating shrug. "Maybe so. If I do, I'm going to need your help."

"What sort of help?"

"The truth, the whole truth, and nothing but. Accept no substitutes."

The frown turned into a scowl. An adorable one.

I gave a bigger shrug. "It's not really a lot to ask. Wouldn't you want the same?"

A quick thinker was this babe. She stopped making faces and nodded.

"Okay, then it's cards on the table time, Lady Filima. First: How did you know to find me?"

She shook her head, plump lips sealed shut. A quick thinker but with a really bad stubborn streak.

I kept a patient I-don't-care kind of tone. "If you want my help, you need to tell me everything. It's in the rules."

"What rules?"

"Myhr's Rules for Magical Investigation 101. You talk or I walk."

Shankey shifted again, maybe getting ready to contest my challenge, but neither of us needed to worry about who was faster at the fifty-yard door dash. Filima made a capitulating sigh. She sounded like she meant it.

"Very well, I'll show you."

It took some effort for me to lever myself and my meal out of our comfy chair and follow her to the "retiring place." Man, what a lunch. I hoped there was a bed in the pavilion so I could take a nap. Filima drew back a fold of black velvet just enough to allow us to slip inside, then let it fall into place again.

Drat. No bed, just a simple stool and small table, lighted by a single candle on a sturdy floor stand. It was very dark and stuffy with the smell of old incense. Not a very fragrant brand, either. Flat on the table was a scrying mirror similar to the ones Terrin and I sold at his Dallas shop: round, about a foot across with a highly polished black surface. Terrin worked the things all the time; I prefer a big-screen TV with a remote and cable.

"You know what this is?" she asked.

"Sure, I've seen 'em before. *That's* how you found me?"

She nodded, solemn.

"Cool that you can use one of those; not many people have the knack."

"It's difficult, but not impossible."

"Were you looking for me in particular?"

"I asked the mirror to show something that would help against the Hell-river."

"And it picked me? For certain?"

"I clearly saw you coming from a building near the bell tower and sent Captain Shankey to find and bring you here."

Oh, lucky, lucky me. I should be so blessed when it comes to picking lottery numbers.

"You *are* the right one to help us, Mr. Myhr. The magic never lies. I know that for a fact."

Boy, did *she* have a lot to learn. Like the river, her mirror had probably sensed Terrin and geographically focused where she could find him. A literal interpretation to her request. I'd just walked onto the stage at the wrong moment. It happens to the best of us, only this time it brought me more than guffaws from a bemused audience. A quick exit would be the wise course, but I hadn't heard Shankey or his pal Debreban move from their posts. No way could I get past either of them without a fuss. Besides, I was still too full of lunch for feats of derring-do. Hanging around here didn't appeal since I wasn't eager to get involved with this Hell-river stuff. Not without pay. She'd still not mentioned money yet. Wizards don't work for free, especially Terrin.

On the other hand, Filima *had* fed me, so that made up a little for the kidnapping. I could also understand why she was hanging on my every word. Under all the gorgeous trimmings and posh airs, she was scared. Really, really scared. "Just what is your stake in this?" I asked.

"Stake?"

"Why's it so important that I help you? What do you get out of it?"

She blinked. "I don't get anything. I just want the Hell-river sent back to wherever it came from."

"That's pretty civic-minded, but aside from making all the town magicians vanish and scaring the pants off tourists like me, what is the river doing right now that's especially threatening?"

That one netted me another scowl. It was still adorable, but I'd touched a nerve. "It's come to a place where it shouldn't be! That's more than enough threat for anyone. You can't leave things so seriously out of balance without consequences."

I had the feeling she and Terrin would get along just fine. He was really big about cause-and-effect stuff in magic.

"If we don't find a way to put the river back I'm positive something truly dreadful will happen," she continued, voice rising.

Talk about a stress case, she needed calming. "If this river has been running for a couple of weeks and no harm done except for some missing persons"—Terrin might be able to sniff them out; he could find other Talents almost as fast as a sex business—"then maybe things won't be as bad as—"

"Don't you *see*?"

"Not very well, no." It was pretty dim in here, even for my eyes.

"Every night the river gets a little bit bigger."

She could have mentioned that sooner. "That's a threat?"

"I've no reason to think otherwise. It grows in strength, but the change is so gradual I don't think even the overduke is aware of the potentials."

"Such as . . . ?"

"Compare it to a normal river. Ever see one in flood? I have, and the devastation is the most horrible thing you can imagine. I think that when it gets large enough the remaining people with Talent will also vanish. There will be no one left to remember them, or try to get them back. Please, Mr. Myhr, please help us."

I'm a sucker for a pleading dame, but usually the

circumstances are a lot more romantic. "I'm not sure I *can* help. . . ."

"I'll pay you anything."

Hello. My favorite magic word: money. Or gems. Filima probably had a dusty old diamond tiara lying around somewhere that Terrin could use. Something like that would power us a lot farther toward home than the quartz crystals stuck in his fishing hat. "No promises, but *maybe* we can work out a deal."

She jumped for it like we'd already signed contracts. This babe *was* scared. "You've a plan?"

"Not yet. I'll need to study the river some more—without your captain breathing down my neck."

"Shankey won't bother you, I swear."

Filima had gotten agreeable way too fast. There had to be a hitch, but I'd find it later, after I was clear of the house. "Sounds great. I'll just go back to my place and settle in for a good bout of research." And do some serious data dumping on Terrin. With this info he might be able to figure out what to do. The prospect of getting some real diamonds for his travel-whammy might even make him hurry.

"But you *must* stay here as my guest," she said, dropping the shoe I'd expected.

"I must?"

"Yes, of course. My house is infinitely more comfortable than anything you'd find in town. I also have supplies of every kind of herb and incense, magical equipment, books, whatever you'll need."

Hmm. A cushy place to nap, regular meals, servants, and—compared to the facilities at Clem's Place—decent plumbing. This just turned into a no-brainer. Add to it the sight of the glorious Filima wafting through the halls and I was ready to apply for a long-term lease.

"It sounds pretty good, but I'll have to consult with my partner."

"Your partner? Why didn't you mention him?"

"Already did—when I was singing. His name's Terrin."

"I thought that was a nonsense song."

"Nope, all true. I have to go back, find him, and do my late afternoon show at Clem's Place. He'll expect me to draw in the early supper crowd for a couple hours."

"No need. I'll see to it he's compensated for your being elsewhere."

"But I've got an obligation. He's been advertising me all day, and the lunch crowd might be back for more. You know how it is, the show must go on, at least for one more time so I don't look bad."

Filima grinned. Much more adorable than her scowl. "You like the applause, don't you?"

"Almost as much as chocolate."

"What's that?"

"An old Aztec love spell."

Somewhere close I heard a choking noise that sounded like Shankey lurking nearby. Having swivelly ears on top of one's head is a heck of an advantage at times. If he was any good at his job he'd have been listening in on this little conversation in Filima's retiring place. I chose to ignore him, and Filima hadn't noticed.

"Love spells?" She snorted. "Those things never work."

"I've seen them work very well indeed. It's getting them to stop once they're up and running that's the big problem." I was more or less quoting Terrin. We stocked harmless love charms at the shop. I say harmless since Terrin always neutralized what he sold to infatuated girls and horny guys. It was an honor thing with him. That kind of emotional coercion and manipulation rankled the hell out of him. If something did happen between the caster and the castee it would have happened anyway, was meant to happen. Love is its own magic, after all, but none of the lovelorn customers were ready to believe that. Everybody wants an edge.

Filima looked a little wobbly all of a sudden, putting a hand to her forehead.

"Anything wrong?" I asked.

"I get like this in here. Scrying gives me headaches."

"You're not scrying, though."

"The incense, then. I'm sure I'm allergic to it."

The leftover stink of whatever she used was pretty strong. "You need to switch brands."

"But that's the kind you have to use for scrying."

"Who told you that? Never mind, there's others that work just as well you might not be allergic to. Nag Champa is a good all-purpose one, and it smells the same burning or not. . . ."

She'd stopped listening to my sales pitch, which was a leftover habit from when I helped out at Terrin's shop, and stared down at the surface of the dark mirror. "Something's coming through. That's never happened before, not unless I'm initiating it."

Now I stared at the mirror. Its polished surface did seem to be shifting, reminding me too much of that black fog of the Hell-river only this time in red. "Maybe we should leave."

"No, I must see. Perhaps your presence has set off some magic."

I had solid doubts about that, but was curious. She sat on the stool, and I kibitzed over her shoulder. It was hard to concentrate with the scent of flowers coming off her hair. From my vantage point I not only saw the mirror, but had a wonderful grandstand view down the front of her low-cut dress.

Oh, baby!

What a perfect spot: I could stare at those beauties all I wanted—so long as I didn't drop any drool on them.

"There!" she exclaimed, leaning forward.

Damn, she'd blocked my view.

"Do you see it?"

Reluctantly, I transferred my attention. The blood-red fog roiled and boiled, and though I first thought it my imagination, there seemed to be a form emerging from the mess. The image was distracting enough to take my mind off appreciation of Filima's hypnotic figure.

A man's face shivered in and out, like looking through moving layers of smoked glass. He was no one I knew, just the usual collection of eyes, brows, nose and mouth . . . but somehow he was very, very *wrong*.

Sulfur? Why was there a whiff of that in the air? Or was it just rotten eggs? It came and went, replaced by the stink of something putrid and festering, which also whipped away, stirred by the wind—a hot wind that should not have been in this small, completely enclosed area.

The candle went out, but light remained, coming from the mirror. It originated *from* it, absolutely was not a reflection.

All my back hairs were up, and yes, my spine began to arch outward. Instinct from my cat DNA boomed a red alert at full force; it wanted me *away* from there. My human side fought it, trying to see more. The conflict caused me to hiss, actually hiss.

The face in the mirror came closer, the mouth open and working in a scream or a curse. It seemed to touch the surface and begin to raise itself up, a three-dimensional thing trying to squeeze its way through.

The light—now turned pale green like from a rotting corpse—flowed from the mirror, bathing Filima. Black specks tumbled in the glimmer. They spun around her head, then swirled down to the emerging face. Its mouth yawned wide to receive them.

Filima's eyes rolled up in her head, and she slumped forward with a soft moan.

Elsewhere in Rumpock

Terrin hoped to gawd he was on the right street this time. Every twisty-turny way in this hellhole looked alike to him now, and they all seemed to be uphill, even the downhill ones.

He staggered along like a drunk, keeping his legs under him only by an act of concentrated will. The air was way too thin to breathe; his lungs worked overtime and then some. Sweat ran freely down his face, but he shivered with cold. People hastily got out of his path. Maybe they thought he had plague or something. Good and fine. No one offered to help. That was fine, too. It would have delayed him, and he couldn't afford a delay. He had to get to shelter—magical shelter.

The bell tower, yes, there it was, useful landmark. But what direction was it from Clem's inn . . . from . . . somewhere . . . um . . . someplace. . . .

The thought slipped from his head. Dammit.

Where was he? *Tower. Move.*

He plunged toward it, running a few steps, slowing to gulp air, running a few more. What if he couldn't make it to the inn? Had to consider that possibility. Just getting under any old roof wasn't the problem, he had to be in a shielded area. Those weren't too common. The ones he'd sensed were weak, nothing compared to the safe zone he'd set up . . . um . . . where?

The inn, Clem's Place.

More steps. Blinking and wheezing, his strength drained out like water from a tub, a steady, swirling stream that would take him with it in the end.

No way. No fucking way!

Anger helped him focus. He looked up and charged forward again, certain he'd spotted a familiar door ahead.

No, not that one, the next one over.

Yeah, red letters spelling out the serving hours for drink and food, the smell of both drifted from the wide-open front door.

Terrin dove through headfirst, landing hard on the bare flags of the floor.

Air. Lots of air here. He lay like a dying fish for a few moments, gradually becoming aware of Clem and Greta staring down at him.

"Usually they stagger and fall over after they *leave* here," Clem remarked.

"Are you all right, Mr. Terrin?" asked Greta. "You look sick."

He recovered enough to show his teeth. It wasn't the same as a smile. "Tired. Just tired. Need to rest."

"But you look feverish," she insisted.

"I don't hold with people being feverish in my place," Clem added. "Bad for business."

"Got too much sun is all," said Terrin, making an effort to stand. He dragged himself onto a bench, and squinted outside. The street shimmered violently in his vision. It wouldn't stop. Dizzy-making. What the hell was going on out there? "Is Myhr around?"

"He got taken off awhile back," said Clem, with a nod toward the door. He didn't seem to notice the shimmer at all. "Couple of fellers carted him right out just like that. He told us to tell you."

Huh, what? "What fellers? What happened? Was he kidnapped?"

"Looked more like a pretty firm invite. Could be an arrest, but they wasn't city watch. One of them was in Burkus House colors, and I think the other might have belonged to Darmo House. Mr. Myhr yelled something that sounded like Lady Filima's name as he was going out. She's important in these parts."

"Arrested? You think he was arrested?"

"Maybe, but the clan houses don't have the authority

for that, only the overduke's people are allowed to make city arrests. I'm not too happy about all this fuss; Mr. Myhr's supposed to do a late afternoon show—"

"Who took him away?"

He got a more detailed report from Greta, who cheerfully provided some background on the house names involved. "Those two men came in, had a huge lunch, and drank like tomorrow wouldn't come. Real chummy they were, then they had a little nap, but perked up when Mr. Myhr began the noon show. They seemed to know to look for him."

"And they took him away just like that? People can do that here?"

Clem shrugged. "It happens. Usually for a good reason."

"Good for who?"

Another shrug. "Well, if he don't come back, you'll have to pay a proper rent on the room. Nothing personal, just business."

Room rent was the least of Terrin's problems. He'd gotten his breath back, but still felt weak. And cold. And sweaty. And . . . itchy. Like his skin was on inside out.

"Are there any healers around here? *Magical* healers?" No time for circumlocution. He'd take the risk of getting burned at the stake. Wouldn't be the first time.

"Magic?" said Greta, surprised. "There may have been, once upon a time. We usually call in Doc Warty. She's not magic, though."

"I don't hold with that weird-fangled magic stuff," said Clem. "Too unpredictable. Scares off customers."

Terrin groaned, but wasn't surprised. If there was some kind of draining field floating around this berg, little wonder all the Talents were gone. But had they vanished, been sucked dry, or just moved out? And why couldn't anyone remember them?

And what the *hell* was out there that was so efficiently

sucking him dry of magical energy? He was safe in here
for the time being. The shields and wards he'd set last
night seemed to be holding up well enough, like a brick
house against a storm. Perhaps he could shrink them down
to cover a smaller area and recharge himself with the
leftovers. That would confine him to his room, though,
unless he could establish a moving shield he could take
with him. Those never lasted very long, though.

He had to find Myhr. Clem and Greta might be talked
into going on a search, but they'd have to know where
to look. Terrin excused himself and crawled upstairs.
Literally. The last few yards of steps he took on all fours
to conserve himself.

Myhr had left the black candle bought that morning
on a small table. Good man. Cat. Whatever. Terrin
fumbled for a Bic lighter in his backpack, pulling out a
few other useful items. Sitting cross-legged on the floor,
he lighted the candle, then held it in front of him, gaz-
ing at the flame, working up a good strong visualization.
Gawd, it was hard.

Usually he had no need of props. When he did use
things like candles it was only to keep the energy up and
running while he went off to do other stuff. Sort of like
setting the VCR to catch a show.

Not this time.

He focused on the flame, took it into himself, and
surrounded himself with its glowing image. He began to
warm up a little. Illusion only, but wasn't everything?

Myhr! Where the hell are you?!

CHAPTER SIX

Back at Darmo House

I caught Filima before she hit the mirror, before she could touch that *thing* trying to come through. She was in a dead faint.

The face glared at me, sucking in more black specks, pausing to mouth more stuff I couldn't hear. Well, screw him. I swatted at the table and sent it and the mirror crashing over. The sickly light abruptly winked out.

Scooping up Filima, I pushed past the velvet curtains.

"What happened?" Shankey demanded. He was right there, making no apology for eavesdropping, or rather pavilion-dropping.

But it was nonstop for me to the nearest couch, which was next to a nice, bright sun-filled window with lots of fresh air coming in. Perfect, we needed both. I put Filima down, then sat rather suddenly on the floor next to her. There hadn't been a lot of lifting effort involved since she didn't weigh much, but I felt like I'd run for miles.

Shankey patted her cheek. "Lady Filima?"

"Fainted," I gasped. "Don't. Know why."

"What did you *do*?" Debreban wanted to know.

"Nothing. Just. Rescued her. Is all."

Shankey snarled, yanked on the bell pull, and yelled orders. Definitely a man of action. For the next few minutes the place was full of freaked-out servants shouting, waving their arms, and running around. Very intense. Finally, a matron-type woman came in, sensibly told everyone to calm down, and passed an open vial under Filima's nose. It must have been the same stinky stuff Greta had used on Terrin last night. I sniffed ammonia again; Filima popped wide awake.

"Argh! Agh! Foo!" she said, waving it away.

Now they were asking her if she was all right, and she had no immediate answer to give, probably trying to figure it out herself. No one asked about *me*, of course. It must be that aura of competence I give off that makes people think I'm a hundred percent all the time. I shut my eyes and rested.

"Myhr?"

Her hand on my shoulder. A light caress. Nice. The kind that makes me purr.

Then an impatient thump. "Myhr!"

"Hah? What?" I jolted out of my fog.

"You all right?" Filima was up, blinking, concerned. Scared, too, judging by the ashy tint of her cinnamon skin.

"I think so. What was that all about? And please don't tell me I should know, 'cause I don't."

"That makes two of us. I've never seen anything like it before. Had no idea the mirror could do that."

"Who was he?"

"He?"

"The face in the mirror. Who was that guy?"

"I saw no face, only a horrible cloud thing coming at me."

"My lady . . ." began Shankey, who wasn't happy, "what went on in there?"

"I'm not sure, Captain. Something was trying to contact us. In my scrying mirror. A psychic-message, perhaps."

"More like a psychic-mugging," I put in. "The image was coming *through*, going all three-dimensional. I'm no expert, but I got the impression it was using you to do it."

"Me?" Filima went a shade more ashy.

Shankey and Debreban exchanged looks. The worried kind.

I could relate. "I think it was taking strength from you. That's probably what made you faint."

"But how? My mirror has only ever shown me ordinary visions of people and places I know. Nothing like that's happened before. Where did it come from?"

Hell, maybe. The sulfur and rotting-meat stenches, blackness, clouds, the ongoing Hell-river situation, *lots* of spooky stuff that could connect together way too well. I decided against sharing; things were stirred up enough for now.

A scowl from Shankey, directed at Filima. "My lady, for your own safety, may I respectfully suggest you leave that magic stuff the hell alone?"

A shocked look from Filima at his language. She started to reply, then zipped up. "Sounds like a very good idea, Captain." She addressed the rest of the crowd of servants. "Show's over, gang, beat it."

She was in quite a state. Her formal mode of speech had slipped badly, along with some of those dulcet tones. I couldn't blame her, still feeling pretty shaken myself.

"Oh, my head." She lay back on the couch, rubbing her temples. "Someone get me some mint tea."

The matron lady muttered an acknowledgement and left, herding a bunch of other servants ahead of her, until the room was mostly clear. Shankey and Debreban remained, the latter eyeing the pavilion as though he expected something to jump out of it at him. He had a hand on his sword hilt, for all the good it might do him. In my experience not a lot of metaphysical phenomena are affected by solid weapons, though cold iron would be a help. I wondered if his sword had any in it. A metallurgist I'm not.

Filima groaned again. Lady in distress. And a nice distraction from my tail-chasing speculations. I pulled myself together and stood, going around to the end of the couch so I was behind Filima. "Sit up," I ordered.

She did so, no questions. Made for a nice change.

"Now close your eyes and relax."

"What are you doing?" Shankey asked as I was about to lay hands on his lady.

"I know a couple of pressure points that should help her head. It's okay, I know what I'm doing." Terrin had taught me a thing or three, but I think I already had an inborn instinct about therapeutic massage. It made me very popular with women, I can tell you.

I tried a pressing light thumb on her lower neck, taking it slow and gentle, working my way around the nerve clusters. (Don't try this at home, people, this is for trained, professional stunt-Myhrs only.) Almost instantly Filima gave out with a delicious moan. Oh, to have different circumstances, the things I could *do* for this babe.

Shankey kept up with the suspicious bodyguard thing for awhile, then eased back as he saw her obvious enjoyment.

"Ohhh, that's wonnnderful. . . ." She sighed, going all limp as I massaged her shoulders and back. She'd been granite-hard when I'd started; it's very gratifying to get an immediate and positive result from one's efforts. It's much more gratifying to follow through on them, but this wasn't the time or place—though if she named a time, I'd pick a place. Rowhr-rowhr!

Man, was *this* fun. Took my mind right off that terror in the tent. A little too much off. I gave her one last squeeze and prod—in a very gentlemanly way—and stopped for *my* own best good. No baseball scores came to mind just then, but looking at the black velvet curtains helped calm me down a bit. I'd stand up later.

"Thank you!" she cried. "I feel fantastic!

Always good to hear *that* from a woman.

"I think my headache's gone. It's a miracle."

"More of a Myhr-acle," I chirped. "And you're welcome. Now how about shutting down the shop for real like the captain wants?"

She swung her legs to the floor, turning to see me. "What do you mean?"

I motioned at the pavilion. "Take down the curtains, put the furniture in the attic, dump the mirror in the river, and go on a nice, long, magic-free vacation."

"I can't do that!"

"Sure you can. I bet the captain here will be the first volunteer for the dismantling crew."

Shankey nodded enthusiastically.

Filima's voice went up a notch. "But I need the mirror so I know what's going on!"

"It pointed me out, didn't it? You want my help, don't you? Trust me on this, you *don't* want to use that thing again. Even if you don't sink it, I want your word of honor as the best oochie-coochie dancer in five provinces that you won't go in there again for any reason."

A protesting noise from her throat.

"Promise?"

She made a growl this time, but it sounded like the agreeing kind. "Very well."

"Maybe after we get this Hell-river business smoothed out you can play Presto the Magician, but until then leave that kind of play to the experts."

"Experts? Does that mean your partner is also a wizard?"

During lunch she'd gotten the idea I was a Talent in the magic sense. It seemed best not to correct her. "Last time I checked. He's probably wondering where I am. Clem, too. The sooner I'm out of here, the sooner Terrin and I can return and look into things."

A maid came in with a drinks tray. Mint tea for two. I helped myself. Yum. Filima gulped half her goblet, probably not tasting it. She must have used the brief time for thinking instead. When she put her tea back on the tray, she was sitting up straight, like for a piano recital, and had recovered her posh tones.

"Captain Shankey, you're to escort Mr. Myhr wherever he wants, then guide him back here before sunset. He is to be my honored guest."

His chain of command reestablished, he came to attention. "Yes, my lady."

Well, this was cool. Come in as a prisoner and go out as a celeb. Nothing like a little rescue derring-do to put a fella in good with the boss-lady. I just hoped Terrin could figure things out for her or it could become a prisoner gig again. For us both.

"You'll be back soon?" she asked.

I love when a woman says that to me. "Soon as I can."

She smiled. Mmm, you could have used it for rocket fuel to the moon and back. Then her smile faltered. She looked narrowly past my shoulder at Debreban. "Excuse me, but don't I know you from somewhere? You're not on the house staff, are you?"

Debreban started to open his mouth.

I saved him from putting his foot into it. "He's sort of with me, lady. Was acting as native guide in the city. Don't think I'll need him anymore if Captain Shankey takes over. Come on, guys, daylight's burning."

We all hastily bowed good-bye to Filima, then Shankey and Debreban walked me through the doors.

"Thanks," Debreban muttered out of the corner of his mouth.

"You're welcome," I muttered back. I didn't know why he was so hinkie about her knowing him, but good old trustworthy instinct said I should do him a favor. I'd collect an explanation later.

With my change of status in place we would use the front door, but now it was my turn to take a detour to the basement facilities. That wine at lunch may not have given me a buzz, but it was liquid, and I had plenty of it on board, plus the tea. The guys were polite and didn't stare while I did my business—some people want to know just how far down the fur goes—and looked out the basement windows instead.

"Wonder why *they're* here?" said Debreban in an idle tone.

"Who?" asked Shankey.

"That lot just outside your lady's gate are all in Overduke Anton's colors. They're not doing much, just standing around."

Shankey grunted. "Pretty odd."

"Think it's to do with Lord Perdle seeing me here?"

"We could go ask them."

"I don't want to. Not just now. Maybe I should get back to my lord's house first, find out what's going on."

"It's probably nothing to do with you."

"I'd better make sure, though."

"Debreban, you and I may have a fine opinion of you, but to the clan lords you're just a face in the crowd."

"Until you get noticed. Like Lady Filima almost did. I don't want to be noticed by Lord Anton."

"What have you got against him?"

I zipped up and found a washbasin and towel, moving quietly so as not to interrupt.

Debreban shrugged, apparently not possessing an easy answer. "His eyes. Ever see them? They look right through a man. They say he can turn a person to stone when the mood's on him. He works magic, too. Bigger stuff than scrying. Lord Cadmus says he has visions. Bad ones."

"So I've heard, but there's never been anything harmful come of it. My lady's only ever said good of him. She's best friends with that new lady he's been seeing. The talk I've heard is he's a decent enough fellow. That troop out there probably has a message to deliver to the house."

"Then they should ring the bell and hand it over, not stand around like a raiding party waiting to be called."

Shankey frowned. "You've got a point there, my friend. Let's go up and see what they want."

"It's your house."

"That it is. You hang back and watch my lady's guest, and I'll go talk with them. They'll expect me to come out, anyway."

All finished, I was peering over their shoulders with interest. When they turned to find themselves nose-to-muzzle with me we all gave a little jump of surprise.

"Urgh," said Debreban. Edgy type for a guard. He should switch to CPA work.

"What's the deal?" I asked. Outside, beyond the gated opening to the grounds of Darmo House, stood a few big guys in black-and-silver cloaks.

"Nothing you need trouble yourself about, Mr. Myhr," said Shankey. "If you don't mind a little delay, I'll go see what they want."

"It's all one to me, fellas."

We went upstairs. Debreban and I cooled our heels in a big hall.

"So who do you work for again?" I asked.

"Lord Cadmus Burkus."

I refrained from saying *bless you*.

Elsewhere in Rumpock, at Burkus House

Cadmus lay collapsed on his scrying mirror, biting back the knife-sharp agony that threatened to split his head in two. The shock lasted only a moment, but he remained still for much longer, panting like a dog, wishing he'd not gotten himself into this mess. If only Botello hadn't offered him so damn much money when they'd started working together. Money and advanced magical training—it seemed like a good idea at the time. Cadmus had known there would be a few strings to the arrangement; he'd just not suspected they'd be so bloody painful.

From within the mirror came Botello Darmo's grating voice. "Get up, you idiot! Let me see you!"

Tiredly, Cadmus pushed himself off the mirror. Dizziness threatened to twist his belly inside out. He barely heard the tirade of cursing aimed at him. The fact that the curses did indeed originate straight from Hell held little intimidation for him. He always had trouble focusing on larger issues when his guts were woozy.

"If you'd held your concentration I'd have made it through!" Botello carped. "She was right in front of me, her magic *flowing* into me. You stopped it! I'll make you pay, Cadmus, don't think I'll forget this!"

Cadmus ran a hand over his sweating face. He was secretly elated that Botello's experiment had collapsed, but couldn't show one hint of that to the grumbling bastard. "It wasn't my fault; there was someone else in the room with her. Didn't you see the chap with the circus mask?"

"That was some damned cat, nothing more!"

"A cat the size of a man? With a man's body? Your mirror may distort things, but not by that much. Filima's hooked up with one of her old touring chums, you mark me."

"I'll rip you to shreds, you mean!"

"Botello, rant all you like, but I did warn you it was too soon to attempt a manifestation. You've not stored up nearly enough power yet—"

That set him off again.

Cadmus waited him out. The more Botello gave in to his temper, the more magic he squandered. Perhaps if he wasted enough he'd be unable to use the mirror. Pleasant thought, that: with Botello trapped forever in Hell Cadmus could devote all his time to forgetting this whole unpleasant episode and pay court to the lovely Filima. Perhaps in some way could even atone for today's ill-turn for her. He'd really not wanted to help Botello, had done quite a lot of arguing to dissuade him—

"Do you hear me, Cadmus?"

"Yes, I hear you. So will everyone else in the house if you keep shouting."

"You didn't answer."

"Sorry, old man, would you repeat the question?"

"The magical source by the bell tower. The wizard. I want that person tracked down before sunset. I've told you to do that, why isn't it done?"

"Yes, I remember, but the captain of my house guard is the only one I can trust for such a task and he's not back from . . ."

Botello exploded again. The word *idiot* dominated the outburst. "You didn't hear a damned word I said! I told you to see to it *personally*!"

"You did not. I distinctly recall you wanted me to make sure the person was swayed to our side. You never said anything about *my* going to look into it. In fact, I got the impression you preferred me close by the mirror in case you needed to talk. Certainly if I'd known you wanted me out and about I'd have done so ages ago—"

Another crash of pain. This time Cadmus cried aloud. He lay still for a much longer period. Various fragments of thoughts came drifting to him, the largest being that he wasn't getting paid nearly enough for this abuse. He was a clan lord, dammit, one of the oldest houses in the province with heaps of honors amassed by his ancestors. Why should *he* have to put up with being treated like some inferior servant's dogsbody?

Grimly, he choked on the fact that he had no choice in the matter anymore. Botello owned him. Not completely, but nearly so because of his assistance in his experiments. Gawds, if anyone found out, he'd be ruined.

Cadmus had thought it a lark, just a harmless bit of fiddle faddle and an excuse to visit Darmo House and feast his eyes on Filima during dinner. By the time he understood that all the castings performed in the cellar were for a more sinister purpose than improving scrying skills, it was too late. He should have known better, he really should. There were plenty of cautionary tales about that sort of thing, but Cadmus had never been much for reading, and the money had been right there on the table, enough to keep his tottering household going for months.

Too late now.

"Wake up, Cadmus, I know you're not that hurt."

He groaned, pushing himself away again. "What? What do you want?"

"The wizard. I felt him, I still feel him. He's like a great bonfire of power."

"You're sure it's a man?"

"Yes, I am now. He's so powerful his energy is coming through even during the day. That's why I tried manifesting this soon. There was enough to bring me through, but the flow was cut. He must have gone to ground in a shielded area. I had to take from Filima. The stupid bitch has power, but not nearly what's needed for the job."

Cadmus shut his eyes a moment to hide any reaction he might give about the name-calling. Botello's attitude toward his widow had gone very sour in the last two weeks. Being in Hell might account for his constant bad mood, but he was quite over the top whenever she came into the conversation. "Then you shouldn't have to bother her in the future."

"I'll do whatever I please with her!"

"Yes, of course. I'm sure she'll be delighted to see you again once you've solved this bodily displacement thing. I was wondering . . . why were you trying to come through *her* mirror? Wouldn't it make more sense to come through mine? It *is* larger, you know, less of a squeeze for you."

"The doorway size doesn't matter, it's the power. The aetheric structures I set up at Darmo House are still in place and tuned to me. I should have manifested in my work-chamber, but the mirror there is broken. Hers is the closest in proximity to it. It was my bad luck she happened to see me coming through, but good luck so she could provide a boost. If *you'd* just held out a moment longer . . ."

Cadmus had held as long as he could. He'd made an honest effort. It rankled that his hard work went unappreciated. "Her mirror might be broken now. That cat fellow did some mischief, I warrant."

"Then find out who he is. I never heard her talk of any clowns in cat masks in that traveling troupe she danced with. Maybe he's an old lover sniffing after her money. *My* money. Find him and tell me what's going on over there, but get to that wizard *immediately*!" Botello's distorted image in the mirror went black as he cut their link.

Blinking, Cadmus woke up a lot more. Damnation, if anyone was entitled to Filima's money it was himself. He'd put significant labor into his pursuit of her; time to start forging ahead in earnest. Gawd knows he was more Filima's type than some scruffy entertainer hiding under a cat's mummery. Maybe the fellow was covered in warts or had a horrible skin condition. If he didn't now, he soon would. Cadmus had a spell for that lying around somewhere in the house. . . .

Of course Botello was something of a snag in the marriage stratagem. Cadmus had been reasonably sure Botello would stay bodily displaced, since in the history of known magic—not to mention ordinary life and death history—no one had ever escaped Hell before. Displaced or truly dead, he should have been there for keeps, but he'd somehow set up a route out that might work for him, providing he had enough power. Even the Hell-river was insufficient to the task, but this new wizard might upset the applecart in a bad way.

Perhaps . . . if he were taken out of the picture. Botello would be none too pleased losing a power source to feed from, but to hell with him. Literally.

Cadmus did not relish violence, but, as a necessary means to an end, was confident he could inflict it. The means was easy enough: most magical Talents were highly allergic to cold iron—especially in the form of a blade-thrust to the heart. Hmm. Yes. There were possibilities in that. Cadmus rose from his chair and escaped his scrying chamber, fresh purpose lending him new energy and nerve. Now where the devil had the butler hidden all the dueling weapons?

Elsewhere in Rumpock, at Overduke Anton's Palace

Anton writhed in a death-struggle with the bedclothes. His body ran with sweat, eyes rolled up in their sockets, limbs thrashing. He fought to wake himself from the dream, the nightmare, groaning like a dying man.

Someone had hold of his shoulders, shaking him hard. "Come on, honey, come out of it!"

Velma. Sweet, sensible Velma. He managed to open

his eyelids enough to glimpse her concerned face, which was very close to his.

"That's it, stay right here with me," she said. "You're safe."

His body relaxed as he gratefully exchanged illusion for reality. "Oh, gawds."

"You said it, honey." She lay next to him, arms cuddling him tight.

He liked that, reaching for her, holding her desperately hard.

"Oof! Easy, now, I'm breakable at this angle." She shifted to a more comfortable position with his head on her bare shoulder, settling in to stroke his brows and hair.

He breathed deeply of her flower perfume, trying to will away the lingering shreds of his latest dream.

"Must have been a bad one," Velma commented after awhile. "I've never seen you like that before. Scary. I've got an uncle who has those kinds of fits, but only after he's been in a tavern for a week."

Anton grunted. "The price of my Talent. They've been getting worse. It's that damned river."

"I know. What was this one about?"

He shook his head. He didn't like to share the really bad ones with her. She didn't need the burden.

"Oh, come on, honey. If you aren't gonna see a doctor about them you need to talk to somebody. Might as well be me."

After a time he sighed, picking one of the lesser visions to relate. "I saw something trying to break through from another world. There was a black room and a table with a hole in it, but instead of a floor showing under the table it was a doorway, a tunnel. A creature was coming through."

"What kind of creature?"

"A Hell-being. Huge. There was smoke and clouds obscuring things, but I saw its eyes, heard its voice, a horrible squalling shriek, like all the souls that ever died crying in torment at once. It was reaching toward me. All I could do was watch. Couldn't run or fight."

"No wonder you got into such a state, and in the middle of the day, too."

That troubled Anton, as well. Usually his nastier dreams took place at night when the veils between the worlds were thin. He'd hoped to catch up on his sleep with a nice afternoon nap—after a little healthy leisure fun with Velma. She'd enthusiastically helped tire him out, but not enough to dispel the visions.

"I think . . ." he said, "I think it's going to get worse. Soon."

"Can you do anything about it?"

"I don't know. Probably have to call a meeting of the remaining Talents in the city. Gawd, I hate meetings. They expect me to hand them all the answers, then they debate about them for hours."

"You need to do that delegation of power stuff."

"Tried that. Appoint one of them to do something and he appoints a committee, then they swill wine over an endless series of meals before coming up with exactly nothing in their 'study.' I should have it so easy."

"You'll have to get tough with them. Declare an emergency, a call to arms. Rumpock hasn't had a decent crisis in decades, so they take the peace for granted. You've traveled, seen what it's like in other provinces. You know what's needed to pull them all together."

He made a rumbling sound, turning it into a grim chuckle. "Yes. They won't like it much, doing some real work."

"You won't like it much, you mean." She twiddled his earlobe.

"Hmm?"

"You've got a nice comfy throne without a lot of work or hard decisions to make. Makes a guy lazy."

Had it been anyone else but Velma making that accusation he might have gotten a little cross. "I suppose you're right."

"Of course I am, but you can prove me wrong. Call the Talents in for a meeting and kick their butts into doing something. You can exaggerate the vision stuff, stir them up."

"I won't have to exaggerate."

"I was afraid you'd say that, honey."

He reluctantly dragged himself from her side and got dressed, but came back to kiss her forehead. "You're lovely," he told her, then left for his audience chamber. Carrying her smile in his memory was much better than that damned vision.

Perdle was at his worktable at the far end of the chamber. He looked up as Anton stalked across the long hall.

"Good afternoon, my lord."

Anton changed course, guided by Perdle's voice. He just made out a blurry figure next to one of the windows. "Hello, Perds. What's the news on that cat-masked fellow?"

"None, my lord. The welcoming honor guard I sent out for him hasn't returned yet."

"Honor guard? Why send that many for a casual invitation?"

"Keeps the troops on their toes, sir. Makes them feel useful having something to do. The drills get boring for the poor chaps. Besides, does the city good to see their overduke's colors marching on the streets. Reassures them that authority is in place and on the job."

The palace colors were black and silver, flashy, but hardly vibrant; Anton thought Perdle's expectations were a touch inflated, but knew his heart was in the right place. "Very well. Let's hope they don't scare him off. What about Lord Cadmus? Has he replied to his dinner invitation?"

"Not yet, sir. The page bearing it was dispatched about three hours ago; he's not yet returned with a reply. Lord Cadmus might have shut himself into his Black Room to delve into this Hell-river problem. He goes all incommunicado when he's playing with his magic, you know."

Anton pursed his lips to keep from making a crude observation about what sort of activities Cadmus might pursue when alone. Perdle could be quite oblivious at times. "Send another page to find out what's going on. I'd like to talk to Cadmus tonight. Now I've an errand for the rest of the house guard to run."

"At once, my lord." Perdle shuffled his work papers together and made to leave.

"Hang about, let me tell it first."

"Ah, yes, just so, my lord." He put the papers down, striking an attentive pose.

Anton outlined his desire to have a meeting first thing the next day with the remaining magical Talents in the city. "All of them," he clarified. "Whatever their level of skill and experience, I want them here. You won't need to notify Cadmus, I'll tell him over dinner."

"There's quite a number of those people on night-duty, sir. From watching the Hell-river, you know."

"That's why the meeting will be one hour after dawn. They can go home and sleep later."

"Dawn, my lord? You plan to get up *that* early?" Perdle seemed quite stunned.

"Yes, Perdle. I'm sure I can manage. Just have my tea ready as usual. I don't know how long the meeting will last, so notify the cooks they might have extra mouths for breakfast. You need to be there, too, and a few scribes to take notes."

"Sir, may I ask the prompting of such a gatherage? To summon them all on such short notice might be construed as an emergency.

You've gotten that right, old friend. "I had another vision."

"Oh. My sympathies, sir. Something of a serious nature, then?"

"They're all serious these days. See to it, Perds, there's a good fellow."

Anton left the audience chamber, his boot heels echoing hollow on the marble floor. He wanted air and made for one of the palace towers. The climb was a chore, but worth the effort. He pushed up the trapdoor to be greeted by a gust of clean, head-clearing wind.

Wanting solitude, he slammed the trap down again to discourage interruptions, and spent the next few minutes just breathing. He wondered how much longer that would go on. In addition to the Hell creature trying to break through, Anton had once again seen himself drowning in that damned river. This time its black fog was solid, viscous as jam. It had clogged his nose and mouth, blinded him, yet, strangely, he was still able to see Cadmus and that cat thing pushing him down deep. Anton had struggled and cursed and fought desperately, but they—

He shook his head to dislodge the image. It was a deadly warning of some sort, whether literal or symbolic remained to be seen. The dreams weren't always specific. He'd long ago accepted that frustrating aspect of his Talent, but still, it was no easier to bear. Few friends in his inner circle could appreciate the burdens of precognition. Those who did not would congratulate him on his gift and express a desire to have it themselves. No doubt they thought it would help them at gambling. The better-informed regarded him with respect mixed with sympathy. Anton would rather chuck his gift in the Rumpock River with the rest of the rubbish and have a normal life, but one couldn't change what the gawds ordained. He might as well have wished to be taller or shorter. He was stuck, might as well make the best of it, as always.

Going to the waist-high wall of the tower, he stared out over his city, what he could see of it. His eyes could pick out the general shapes of structures, blobs of color, light and dark, the smaller moving blobs that were people navigating the streets. He thought some of them paused to wave up at him. Just in case, he waved back.

"Long live Overduke Anton!" someone called in the distance, sounding quite cheerful.

He waved again. It was nice to be popular, but was their affection well-bestowed? If he and the other Talents couldn't find a solution to the Hell-river problem, send it back to its source, they were all . . . well . . . doomed.

All too clear on his inner eye was the worst vision yet: the whole of Rumpock in flames with Hell-creatures everywhere greedily feasting on his hapless people.

CHAPTER SEVEN

Back at Darmo House

Debreban spun off nervous energy like a generator. After all the standing and playing fly on the wall in Filima's blue room he probably wanted to end our wait for Shankey and get going. I could tell by the way he buffed the floor with his boots. Watching people pace makes me dizzy. I blinked out of the hypnotic pattern. "If this Lord Cadmus is your boss, what are you doing over here?"

"Helping out Captain Shankey." He paused to look at a painting, a portrait of a Darmo ancestor, perhaps. Couldn't say much for the artist's skill or the subject's taste in clothes. Maybe that's why it was hanging in a drafty hall.

"You do that a lot? Helping Shankey?"

"First time, actually."

"Why now? Is it me?"

"Not that I know of. My lord Cadmus wanted me to . . . well, that's house business, nothing to do with you."

He started up and down the hall again, but his rhythm was interrupted by the arrival of one of Filima's young pages, who came in carrying a purple-and-green cloak. Without a word he gave it over to Debreban, who thanked him and put it on. In full daylight the colors made my eyes hurt; in the shady indoors they weren't so bad.

"I gotta ask . . ." I began when the page was gone.

"Ask what?" He carefully adjusted the hang of the cloak. It looked a little threadbare around the hem.

"Is Lady Filima allergic to purple and green? I was wondering why you wanted to be incognito."

He frowned. "It's more like she's allergic to Lord Cadmus. Just the sight of these colors can put her in a bad mood, so it seemed best not to distract her with them."

"Oh, yeah?"

"Well, it's no secret that he admires her a great deal. If she'd give him even half a chance she might see what a fine man he is, but she's not interested in him."

"No accounting for a woman's taste, but if a lady says no, it's the smart thing to listen."

"More's the pity. They'd make a good match. A great match. Shankey and I were talking about it today." An idea visibly appeared on his face. "Mr. Myhr, with you being a wizard and all . . ."

Uh-oh.

" . . . perhaps you can help us out in this matter—after you're done helping Lady Filima, I mean."

"Help you out in what?"

"With the things you know you must have a really good love spell or potion or charm or something."

I shook my head. "Listen, if I knew of one that worked I wouldn't have to sing for my supper at Clem's inn. I'd have that money-machine patented in one minute, on the street in two, and retire a zillionaire about an hour later. Everyone wants love. But you can't get it that way. Sorry."

The poor guy looked pretty disappointed. "Don't you have anything that might get my lord and Lady Filima together? He already likes her a lot; it would only have to work on her."

"Nope. If they're supposed to fall in love it'll happen if and when it happens. Trying to bend the will of one person to match the desires of another is unethical. That goes on often enough without using magic. It never turns out well."

"Even if it would be for that person's own best good?"

"Lemme ask you this: when you were growing up, how many times did you hear 'I'm only doing this for your own good'?"

He shuddered. "Too many."

"How would you feel if you heard it now?"

"I see your point, but this is different. It *really* would be doing them both a favor."

Jeez, I'd get a dozen a day exactly like him in the magic shop, twice as many on weekends, ten times more girls than guys. They all seemed to have a killer crush on some geek, deciding that he was their soul mate, and they wanted him right then and there. They didn't want to hear their symptoms were hormones, not destiny. A few I was able to persuade to sense, but most didn't want to listen. They all thought they were the exception to the rule. I'd sell the really stubborn ones neutralized love charms to wear and off they'd go, happy.

Then there were the new Talents, most without a real teacher to guide them. They had the magic, which was what drew them to the shop, but some were getting into it because it was cool, it would freak their parents, or they'd watched *The Craft* one too many times and wanted the power trip.

They'd read—make that skim—one book about magic and decide they were ready to alter the whole Multiverse according to their desires. I was grateful about the

Multiverse being mostly tolerant toward such neos until they learned better, but had seen a few mess themselves up by not thinking things through. You've heard the stories, someone wishing for a ton of wealth, and they get it via an insurance company paying off a claim on their broken leg or trashed car. Or a gal throwing a love spell on some guy and ending up with an obsessed stalker or an emotional leech. Or both.

You *do* have to be careful about what you wish for; it's true, true, true, true, true, true, true, true.

"Nope," I said again to Debreban. "Let nature take its course. Trust me on this, it's a lot safer." I went to look at the brass inscription of the portrait painting. Good grief. It was the late husband himself, Botello Darmo. What was he doing out in the house boonies this soon after his demise? Maybe Filima didn't want any reminders of him peering down from the walls at her. That or she just had good taste in art. This depiction of his kisser was on the gloomy side. There was also something familiar about him in a creep-out sort of way. . . .

Shankey came back just then. "I don't believe this," he announced. "Overduke Anton sent that whole lot over here to invite him"—he jerked a thumb at me—"to the palace."

"I always wanted to play the Palace," I said brightly. They gave me a blank look. Okay, for a joke that creaky I could forgive them for not getting it. "Is there a problem?"

Debreban made a kind of mournful growling sound. "Lord Perdle must have told him. I knew he would. But why would he want to see him?"

"You're talking about Anton wanting to see me or Perdle?" I knew what he meant, but they'd slipped back to referring to me in the third person and needed to be jogged out of it.

"He means Lord Anton wants to see *you*," Shankey answered.

"So this is a bad thing? Why would he want to see me?"

"Look in a mirror," he grumbled.

"I do, as often as possible, and the view gets better with every passing day."

"I better tell my lady about this. She might prefer you to avoid the invitation for now."

"She's got something against my making new friends?"

"It's not that, but if you go making side trips to Lord Anton's palace you won't be able to do what you need to do and get back here in time for the sunset curfew."

Yeah, and maybe Filima wanted to keep me for herself. Pleasant thought, if that was all there was to it. I came up with my own reservations, as well. This Lord Anton was also into magic; he could have been scrying around, asking the same questions she'd asked and getting my face in his mirror. I'd have to do the same song and dance with him, explaining myself and including a side trip to my life story. Once a day was more than enough, and anyway, I was still full from lunch.

"Okay, you won me over," I said. "You didn't tell them I was still here, did you?"

"No, but they're certain you're inside."

"Is this going to cause Filima any trouble?"

"I don't think so. They all seemed friendly enough, just another errand for their lord."

"If this is all so friendly, then why send so many men after little ol' me?"

"Good point. They wouldn't say. Maybe it's an honor guard."

Yeah, sure. "Well, they can't 'invite' me over until I come out, but I do need to get back to the inn. Is there a back door out of this pile?"

"They'll have it covered. I would."

"What about the secret passage?"

Shankey's eyes widened. "How'd you know about that?"

"I read a lot." Places like this *always* came equipped. I looked at Debreban. "You got a secret passage in your clan house, too?"

He went stone-faced. "I'm not at liberty to say."

"Thought so. Let's use it to get me out and back again. Filima can take me around to visit this Anton dude later when it's more convenient for everyone."

"That's duke. Over*duke* Anton," corrected Shankey. "And I can't take just anyone through the secret passage."

"Or it won't be a secret anymore, yeah, yeah, I've heard that one, but it's only the three of us. Unless these murky catacombs are guarded by hordes of rats and alligators flushed down the drain in centuries past—"

"There's no such things there!"

"Then let's get moving. If you're worried about security, just remember that Debreban's your good friend, and I'm a passing tourist. With any luck I'll be gone before too long, never to return."

"Maybe I should blindfold you . . ."

Debreban came in on my side. "Aw, Shank, let's just go. I don't want them seeing my leaving here, either."

Shankey grumbled and rumbled, but gave in, and led off back into the house. "Why are you so against Lord Anton?"

"I'm not, but he might ask Lady Filima why the captain of the guard for House Burkus was here, and she'll ask you, and it'll get back to my lord in some way, and he might not be pleased that you and I got to talking."

"He wants to keep things simple," I translated.

"Should have said so in the first place." Shankey shook his head.

We returned to the door leading to the basement facilities, but struck off in a different direction once downstairs. No windows, just a lot of dark, but a couple

of lanterns stood ready on a table, along with candles and
a tinderbox. Shankey struck some sparks, made a flame,
and lighted things up. Debreban got a lantern, I didn't,
but that was fine with me. Shankey raised his own lantern high and forged ahead through dusty storage areas,
threading past old furniture, trunks, and what looked to
be party decorations. Compared to the stuffy interior of
the pavilion it was positively cheerful.

But the creeps began to sneak up on me, nonetheless.
They began when we left the flotsam and jetsam of
the household and entered a real tunnel. About five or
six feet wide, seven feet high with an arched ceiling
carved, apparently, out of solid rock, its rough, dust-coated
floor slanted down at a gentle slope. Everything was dead
quiet except for the noise we made walking along. I
couldn't see the end of it; the lantern light didn't reach
that far. Facing the overduke's honor guard seemed the
lesser of two evils right now.

The air was dank at first, then got drier.

"We walking away from the river?" I asked.

"River?" Shankey said, alarmed.

"The Rumpock, not that Hell-river."

"Oh. Yeah, we're moving away from it. Makes sense
not to dig a tunnel through a river, you know."

Or even a river I didn't know. "Where does this one
come out?"

"The Darmo stables across the grounds."

"Must be some big grounds."

"They are, but the stables have to be a distance from
the house what with the smell and the horseflies."

I could agree with that. If I didn't keep myself squeaky
clean all the time flies tended to buzz me mercilessly.
They love the fur. And you thought having a piece of
spinach stuck in your teeth was a social embarrassment.

"The tunnel's about eight hundred feet long," Shankey
added. "Seems longer."

"Yeah," Debreban agreed. "Who built it and why?"

"About two centuries ago one of the Darmo House heads decided walking across to the stables in winter was a pain in the ass, so he started digging. Legend has it he began with a teaspoon, but I don't believe that because those kind of spoons hadn't been invented back then. Cook told me so. She collects them."

"She collects teaspoons?"

"Yeah. Has them all over her room in little display cases."

"Really?"

"Yeah, nice ones with glass covers. They're on the walls like paintings."

Debreban didn't seem the type to have much interest in the history of household utensils but it was something to get our minds off our surroundings. The farther we went down the tunnel the more the darkness piled up behind. Maybe this worked for moles, digging forward with the dirt closing in their wake, but not for me. I wanted out. I wanted air. I wanted more light than just two tiny little flames that could vanish at any given importune instant.

"Shankey . . . ?" said Debreban.

"Yeah?"

"Just how is it you know what the cook's room looks like?"

"Debreban?"

"Yeah?"

"Shut the hell up."

Debreban snickered. I felt a half-hearted grin come and go on my face. We needed more jokes. Okay, I needed more jokes. Cracking them was usually my job; it was first nature to me, but I just couldn't work into the mood. All the hilarious stuff I'd ever heard or invented wasn't the least bit hilarious down here. The only thing that kept popping into my head was some line Lon

Chaney, Sr., once said about a clown not being funny in the moonlight. That clown would be a laugh-riot for me now, though; moonlight would mean we were in open air and free of this pit.

I'd been in dark, tight places before; this one shouldn't have bothered me so much, but there was something nervous-making about the atmosphere. When my whiskers started quivering on their own I recognized the feeling.

"Shankey? Did Lady Filima's husband do a lot of magic work?"

"I guess so. He kept quiet about it. Didn't want to scare people, I guess. Some don't like it much; I don't care one way or another so long as it doesn't hurt anyone."

"Just where did he set up shop? He had to have a workplace."

"In his private chambers. He had a room set aside for it. Nothing much to it, just a table, lots of books and papers, that kind of junk."

"Think he might have had more than one retreat?"

Shankey paused. "Why would you ask that?"

"Because *all* my back fur is up and to do that for a guy like me takes a humongous amount of magical energy."

"You can *feel* that stuff?"

"Like an itch you can't scratch. I think we're close to some source. Is this the only secret tunnel for the whole joint?"

"There might be one or two others," he reluctantly admitted. "But we don't have time for them."

"Um, we may not have a choice." My ears perked forward. "You hear that?"

They didn't, at first. The sound was too deep for human ears to pick up. It was like a subwoofer on a really good quadraphonic system; you don't hear it so much as feel it thrumming through your body. They suddenly flinched and drew their swords.

"What is it?" Shankey asked. "Sounds like a dragon breathing."

"You got dragons here?" It was an honest fear. I'd been on worlds that had them. They're not always fun.

"Figure of speech," he explained. "It's getting closer, isn't it?"

"Yup, I think it is, yup, yup."

"Let's go back to the house," Debreban suggested. "If we run like hell—"

"Sounds like a plan," I said, starting to back away.

Shankey hesitated. "If something's down here I have a duty to find out if it's a threat to my house."

"How about figuring it out with lots of well-armed reinforcements for company? If that noise has a magical source we're going to be out of our league, anyway."

"If it's magical, then *you* can handle it." Somehow Shankey had gotten behind me. He had to shout to be heard above the welling sound. "You're a wizard, aren't you?"

"Oh, hell," I said, my ears going flat.

The low sound intensified to an extended growling roar. The blast of it in the confining walls of the tunnel was too much. I put my hands over my head and dropped, doing a half-remembered duck-and-cover routine. Shankey and Debreban did the same, the three of us cowering against the walls as the sound grew in power, swelling like thunder.

"Iron!" I bellowed at them.

They looked up, scared, perplexed, way out of their league for sure. That or they couldn't hear me.

"Have. You. Got. *Iron?*"

Shankey missed it, but Debreban must have caught enough to understand. He gave me his lantern. I started to push it back, then realized it was metal. Iron or not, cold iron or not, it would have to do. I grabbed the ring handle, stood, and threw it down the tunnel like a grenade.

It had about the same effect. The hideous roar ceased so abruptly that you could hear the softer clang of the lantern rolling to a stop on the stone floor.

We were left with one pitiful little light. And eardrums. Functioning eardrums were good.

"What *was* that?" Shankey whispered in awe.

"A burglar alarm, I think."

"Will it come back?"

I shrugged, brushing off my knees. I wanted a good all-over combing-out to get my back hairs down, but knew it wouldn't hold. There was still something nasty hanging around. This time I could *smell* it. Nag Champa incense it was not.

"Hoo," said Debreban, his face screwing up in reaction. "What's that?"

"Lots of things," I said. "You don't want to know about them, either." I wished I didn't. My nose was into overtime picking out graveyard stench, rotting fish, rotting flesh, *eau de* Dumpster in hundred-degree weather, sewer stink, month-old armpit sweat. All the bad smells I'd ever experienced in my whole life seemed to be down here having a convention.

"Ugh." Shankey found a handkerchief, but had trouble pressing it to his face while juggling with his sword and lantern. I took the latter from him and held it out. The tiny flame still burned a normal yellow color, meaning that despite the stink there was plenty of oxygen for us.

"This is another kind of burglar alarm," I told them. "Revolting, but not life-threatening."

I hoped.

We hesitantly moved ahead, retrieving the lantern I'd thrown. It was a tough piece of workmanship, just a dent or three and the glass broken. Some of the oil had

leaked out, but enough remained to re-light it, which
we did.

"Faugh!" said Shankey. "Let's go. I can't take much
more of this."

"It's an illusion," I said. "Ignore it and it'll fade."

"You sure?"

"No. But I think its presence means there might be
a magic hideaway nearby. The noise and smell are supposed to discourage visitors. When was the last time
anyone was down here?"

"A couple of years, maybe. It's not a popular place."

"Try a couple of weeks." I pointed down. The coat of
dust on the floor showed signs of recent traffic. There
was a thin path worn in it, and even the marks of something heavy having been dragged along.

"Huh." Shankey's attention shifted from the stink.
"Wonder where that leads?"

"No one uses this to get to the stables anymore?"

"No need. When we want a horse or carriage we just
send a page running across to have them brought to the
house. The lord who made the tunnel should have thought
that up instead of going to all this work."

"Maybe he was part-gopher."

Shankey stared at my cat's face and slowly nodded.

I went back to studying the tracks, then following them.
They stopped in mid-tunnel on the right-hand side. "Who's
wants to bet there's secret door here?"

No takers. They were both closely checking the wall.

"I'll bet it can only be opened by a spell," said Shankey,
cautiously prodding with his sword tip. "I heard stories
about these things. You have to have a certain magic word
or you get turned into a frog."

Debreban hastily backed away. "We should let the
expert deal with it."

I knew what he was thinking: with me already being
part-cat a little frog in the mix wouldn't be noticed. To

hell with that. "You're right. We'll talk to my partner; he's great at opening up all kinds of things." Besides, my whiskers were twitching so much they tickled. "We can bring him back this way. He loves scary places."

"Let's hurry, then." Shankey pushed himself from the wall. It responded with a grinding noise.

Uh-oh.

He stopped in mid-motion and poked at a long, vertical crack that had appeared. "This could be what we want."

I could argue against that assumption. A lot. Outside.

But he pushed again. The crack widened to a dark opening. The pivoting door was narrow, but sufficient for a man to use. There was a change in the air quality, shifting to a stifling chemical taint, like you find in the insecticide aisle at a store. Shankey held his lantern ahead. The flame remained reassuringly yellow.

"Look at the stuff in here!" he said.

We couldn't do that until he went in, which he did. I reluctantly followed. Debreban was content to hang back over the threshold.

"Watch where you step," Shankey cautioned.

Glass and crockery shards were all over the floor, crunching underfoot. The chemical stink seemed to come from them, or what had been in them, which was also on the floor, dried pools of multicolored whatever. The chamber was round, completely enclosed, and a good twenty feet across.

Shankey found some candles on a tall metal stand and lighted them, revealing more detail.

A few tables, lots of paper, lots of books, not a lot of fresh air. The walls and low ceiling were black, from soot or paint, I couldn't tell. Either one would be depressing. Was depressing. The latent magical power in the room pulsed at me like radiation. Oh, yeah, Terrin would *love* this.

"Looks like your lord was into some heavy shit here," I said. My voice fell flat between the thick walls. They were fuzzy, as though coated with sound-dampening material. I didn't check too closely in case it turned out to be some kind of disgusting super-mold.

"Uhn," agreed Shankey. "What's this?" He pointed to a scattering of polished stone fragments in the exact center of the place.

"Might have been a scrying mirror. Someone must have dropped it."

"Or smashed it." He indicated a wooden hammer with a metal head attached that lay nearby. It looked like an overgrown croquet mallet and was pretty battered.

I picked it up. Cold iron again. Solid. I felt better with it in hand and held it close. My muzzle whiskers calmed down a little.

"This is interesting." Shankey pointed to an oddity in a room full of weirdness.

At our feet was a vaguely man-shaped outline in the broken glass. I made out the trunk and out-flung arms as if someone had been lying on the floor while someone else smashed things around the body. I'd seen an identical setting in a Sherlock Holmes movie. From there I followed a dragging path in the debris that went straight to the door.

"Just how did your lord die?" I asked.

"His heart failed him. Best healers in the city said so. The overduke held an inquiry to make sure."

"Where did he die?"

"In his bedchamber. Happened while he slept. Lady Filima said he was gone and cold when she woke up that morning. She was in quite a state. You don't think that it was him who made those marks?"

I shrugged. "Who else knows about the secret tunnel?"

"A few in the household, myself, Lady Filima."

"Who else knows about this room?"

"Hell, *I* didn't know about it 'til we got here! I thought I knew every inch of the house and grounds. That's my job."

"It could have once been an old grain storage bin," suggested Debreban.

"Why hide it with a concealed door?" I asked.

"Famine. Times past weren't always so good in Rumpock. If food was short you'd want to keep your hoard safe but easy to get to. Or it could have been a weapons cache, or a place for the household to hide out during a siege."

"Then the lord of the house stumbles across it and turns it into a private den for spell work?"

"Why not? Especially if whatever he was up to had to be kept secret."

"You think he was up to something?"

Debreban nodded. "Nothing wholesome, either. A couple of my mum's relatives used to do small magic, healings and such. They told stories about the people who went in for the dark side of it. Secrecy was a necessity. They had to work in hidden, out-of-the-way places to keep from being detected by others who might stop them."

It made sense. If Filima's late hubby was up to no good, he'd want a shielded spot close to home to play. This sure filled the bill. Terrin would probably confirm everything once we got him here. While he did that I would have a private chat with Filima. Maybe Botello Darmo didn't mention his getaway to the head of his house guard, but sure as anything his wife would know. He might not have mentioned it to her, either, but she *would* know. Women are like that, so I do my best never to lie to them. It never pays.

"I think this is enough for now," I said. "Let's split."

The slang translated just fine. Debreban backed clear of the door. Shankey and I went through and pushed it into place. The balance was perfect; it swiveled easily.

"You can't see the seam at all," Shankey marveled,

holding his lantern close. "I'd better mark it so we can find it again. He pushed on the door, wedged a handkerchief into the crack, and let it close again. The square of white cloth hung at shoulder height.

"Did you hear that?" I asked.

"Not again," Debreban groaned. "Hear what?"

"A voice. Someone calling my name. Quiet a second." They obligingly went silent, listening.

"There it is again," I said, turning my head back up the tunnel. But that wasn't right. I looked down the tunnel, still hearing someone calling to me, but unable to fix a direction. As there were only two to choose from it was confusing.

"I don't hear anything," they said in unison.

"My ears are better, but . . . something's off here."

Myhr! Where the hell are you?!

I jumped. The volume was at conversation level, loud and clear, as though the speaker stood right next to me. Shankey and Debreban were still deaf to it and giving me funny looks.

Myhr! Come back to the inn. Now!

Terrin's voice? What the hell was he doing in my head? I asked him. Out loud. And I thought my escorts had given me funny looks before.

SOS, mayday, mayday, mayday. Get your ass back here! Myhr!

Okay, he could send, not receive, and something was seriously wrong. He'd never done this before.

"Come on, guys," I said, starting briskly down the tunnel, my fear of the dark shoved aside. "I got a situation. Wizard stuff. Let's move."

Outside Clem's Place

First the failed love spell, then Botello's needling and psychic assault, Debreban not reporting back, more orders and assaults from the imperious Botello, and finally the surprise invitation to dinner at the overduke's palace. Lord Cadmus hadn't had such a full day in ages.

At least the dinner and a comfortable sleepover in the palace would be a pleasant experience. Anton had a famous cook, and with Velma playing hostess Cadmus would have someone decorative to feast his eyes upon and practice complimenting.

Then there was the plumbing. Like Filima's house the ducal palace had the very latest in water pipes, with bathtubs that didn't require an army of servants to heat and carry water. Thus far only the rich could afford this, so Cadmus had yet to install any at his place. To repay his host for the luxury of such a bath, Cadmus would be cheerfully entertaining for the dinner conversation. Talk would probably be about that dreary Hell-river and how to get rid of it, but he was certain he could subtly shift things over to the topic of Filima. She and Velma were old friends from their show business travels. Old friends always knew useful things about each other. Cadmus welcomed this opportunity to press Velma for courtship advice, so he'd sent the overduke's patiently waiting pages back with an enthusiastic acceptance of the invitation.

Then he had to leave on Botello's errand. Drat the man. *I have better things to do, like deciding what to wear tonight.* That crucial decision would have to wait, though, until Cadmus found this wizard or mage or whoever it was Botello was in such a furious twist over.

During his tedious trudge through the city Cadmus concluded there was entirely too much red paint used on signs in Rumpock. He'd been all around the bell tower district, on the lookout for red letters, his other senses wide open to pick up the smallest whiff of magic. Too much lettering and no magic at all: Botello would throw another fit. Well and good if he wasted his power, but Cadmus wondered about surviving another outburst. Each one had gotten progressively stronger and more painful. Botello would be in an even nastier mood when the time came to deliver the awful news that the Talent had inconveniently died in a street brawl. *I'll deal with Botello somehow or other,* Cadmus decided.

And hopefully live another day.

He paused outside a structure that seemed to be half-tavern, half-inn, seeing then forgetting the name on the sign, just noting the ubiquitous red paint. He went inside. The place had a solid business going and the food smells were good. Tempting, but he didn't dare stop for a late lunch, though something cold to drink would not be unwelcome.

"Yes, your lordship," said a tall man behind the bar, apparently drawing conclusions from the new customer's fine clothes. "How may I serve you?"

"Have you cold cider?"

"Hard or soft?"

"Soft." Cadmus wanted a clear head. He could get drunk later tonight on excellent palace wine while the Hell-river flowed. Damned thing. Literally. It had certainly put a dent in the social season. If informal evenings out were ever allowed again he could go back to winning Filima over, and this time succeed. Since his love spell hadn't worked, he'd revert to personal charm. He had *lots* of that.

The barman gave him a hefty crockery mug; its chilled contents proved quite a restorative for all that hard walking. Cadmus had nothing against physical exertion, provided it showed his manly form off to good advantage. Simply *walking* around was so mundane, though he did cut a dashing figure, even in his less than best clothes. He'd dressed in dark colors, not those of his house, as he was desirous of anonymity and anticipated the need to hide bloodstains.

Anchored to his hip was an elderly small-sword with

a black blade. The newer ones were of a more flexible alloy that made them less prone to breakage and able to hold a sharp edge for longer, but they wouldn't have suited his purpose. This antique had cold iron in it, and that's all that mattered to him. One of his ancestors must have had it made up special just for the job of killing magicians, though gawd knows why. Kill one and the others all knew about it, worse than stirring up a nest of hornets. That had changed, though, since there were no more with Talent left in the city. Botello had seen to it.

Cadmus drained his mug, dropped a coin on the counter, and turned to leave. He froze, staring through the open door to the street beyond. It was all wavery, like the air above a fire. What in hell was *that*?

None of the wavering people walking past seemed aware of the phenomenon. This was *very* interesting.

He caught the barman's eye and pointed toward the door. "Do you see anything odd out there?"

The tall, thin man squinted. "Can't say as I do unless you want to count old Marloe across the way being awake this early in the afternoon. He usually don't stir 'til supper hour."

"But you see nothing odd about the air?"

"Can't see air, your lordship," the man stated.

A sensible answer, unless one possessed a touch of Talent. "Very true. Then tell me, have you any interesting guests staying here? Anyone new? Perhaps from well out of town?"

"There's Mr. Myhr, very unusual-looking fellow, but friendly. Packs a good crowd in for lunch and supper with his show."

"Show? What, he does tricks?"

"Sings, mostly, tells stories, lots of jokes, and you should see how he gets the room laughing when he spots a pretty gal."

"But no magic tricks or illusions?" Cadmus had heard of some few Talents who went in for doing gaudy demonstrations of their craft, but there was no profit in it. Too exhausting and costly. The only ones who made a living at it were the fortune tellers, and it was rare you could find ones who had a true gift for it. The rest were frauds. Overduke Anton had regular checks made on those practicing in Rumpock to make certain they were real and not cheating the public. Of course, they were all gone, too, thanks to Botello.

"No magic, your lordship. I don't hold with magic in my place. Unpredictable stuff, scares off the customers. Mr. Myhr's friend was asking after that stuff; had to tell him the same. You can talk to him about it."

Oh, to hell with his friend. Probably some hanger-on. Cadmus wanted the real wizard. "Where is this Mr. Myhr?"

"Don't know. He got picked up and carried off by two fellers. One of 'em might be with Darmo House, Lady Filima's name was mentioned, the other was in a purple-and-green cloak, so I reckon he was with Burkus House." Cadmus hid his utter surprise with a deep frown. "You're sure about those colors?"

"Hard to miss or forget. Anyway, these two fellers seemed to be looking for Mr. Myhr and carried him right out the door. I hope they bring him back soon, else I'll be stuck for a show for my early supper crowd. Popular he is, with his songs, stories, and 'specially that cat face he's got."

"Cat face?"

"I didn't believe it myself when I clapped eyes on him, but it ain't no mask, that's his real face. Looks just like a cat, ears, mane, eyes, and all. It don't half mystify everyone."

"Cat?" Cadmus worked hard to get his head around it. Perhaps if the wizard wanted an impressive disguise or to advertise his skills, he'd cast a glamour on himself. But why bother?

"Cat, your lordship." The barman spoke slowly. "Cat."

He *had* to be the creature that had disrupted Botello's manifestation attempt. Which meant he was very probably the wizard Cadmus needed to kill. Odd, though, that Botello didn't sense its magic and draw it off. Too busy with Filima, most likely. "When did you say he'd return?"

"I didn't. I said these two fellers took him away. Maybe he's singing at Darmo House, though how them up on the hill heard about him so quick is past me."

Filima and her scrying session this morning, that was how. Like all the other remaining Talents she was trying to understand the mystery of the Hell-river and discover a way to get rid of it. Cadmus didn't think she was aware of Botello's connection to its appearance, not for certain, not in a way that could be proved. Botello hadn't said anything on what she might know. Whenever Filima was mentioned all he usually did was seethe. Maybe there was something to the murder rumor, but how could *she* have killed him without leaving a mark? Not magically, she just wasn't powerful enough. Well, no matter, work that one out later.

Perhaps she'd stumbled upon something important about this Myhr fellow. If he was a wizard, the impossibly powerful one that Botello wanted so badly, there was a chance he could do something about the problem.

Hmm. If the wizard turned out to be up to the task, it might be better to not kill him. Let Filima charm him into helping. Or pay him. Not too much. If he found a way to send the Hell-river back and closed off the planar opening, then Botello would stay in Hell, leaving Cadmus free to console his grieving widow. If only she would grieve a little more openly. He was quite good at lending a shoulder to cry on, and what better way for him to get a set of well-muscled, comforting arms around her—

Another *hmm*. If that wizard had a halfway decent love spell . . .

All right, so be it.

Cadmus was set to leave when the sight of the wavering street again halted his first step. He thought he knew what caused the effect and why he'd not detected any magic while outside. A shielding spell or guardian wards around the inn would do that. Either would have to be terrifically strong to hold up against the Hell-river and Botello's daylight leeching. Also very advanced, so as to be unnoticeable to those within it.

Now that he was conscious of the possibility, Cadmus shut his eyes and reached out beyond himself. Yes, by concentrating he could feel the presence of a magical wall. Myhr must have set it up and let it run, definite indication of a powerful talent. Even Botello couldn't do it on that advanced a level. Not before his displacement. It might be a different story at present, but worry about it later.

Right, nothing for it but to go to Darmo House and inquire after the long-strayed Debreban. He'd been gone all day, and instead of following Filima's man as ordered he'd somehow teamed up with him. So they *were* gossiping, about gawd knows what. Everyone did in Rumpock. It was the town's second most popular pastime.

While there Cadmus could make inquiries about this Myhr fellow. Filima should have no reason to keep him to herself, not if she was sincere about getting rid of the Hell-river, which she was. Why else expose herself to those miserable headaches with all her scrying?

But he couldn't go up to Darmo House on foot and ring the bell like a common peddler. And he couldn't let Filima see him in these unsuitable rags. No, a trip home to change and have his horse saddled was in order. Her prince of hearts would arrive in style on a prancing, arch-necked charger. With flowers. But not

a too-large bouquet, something small and friendly,
tasteful . . . cheap . . .

He plunged into the whirl of the street. Now that he'd
attuned himself to the magic, he felt the difference
between the shielded indoors and the unprotected outside. Cadmus detected a very slight internal tug, easily
mistaken for indigestion or the like; no wonder he'd
overlooked it before.

He strode away from the inn, but missed a step, having
caught a flash of green and purple in the corner of his
eye. He halted in mid-stride, which resulted in a minor
collision between himself and some house woman walking behind. She snorted disapproval and moved around
him.

Cadmus searched the crowds narrowly, seeking another
glimpse. Had that been the missing Debreban? If so, he
was in for a good tongue-lashing. The nerve of him,
running off all day to swill drink and gossip when he was
supposed to report back about Filima's captain as ordered.
Had he done as he was told, Cadmus was certain he'd
have learned about this Myhr-the-cat-faced-mage a lot
sooner; then Botello wouldn't have been so painfully
unpleasant.

On the other hand, Cadmus now had an uncontrived
excuse to drop in on Filima, so it hadn't turned out too
badly. He must be off quickly though, or he wouldn't have
much time to spend with her before leaving for the palace.
Had to get there before the sunset curfew.

One last futile look, then he hurried away, grumbling.

CHAPTER EIGHT

Outside Clem's Place

"Gawd, that was close," breathed Debreban. "He nearly saw me."

"He nearly saw all of us," corrected Shankey.

"You guys wanna get off me?" I asked, somewhat muffled and breathless. "Friendship is great, but I think we're moving way too fast here."

Debreban was on me, Shankey was on Debreban, and the three of us were face-down behind a cart full of radishes. Shankey removed his sturdy weight, and with a few *oofs* and *ughs* we got ourselves upright again. Lots of people stared, particularly the radish seller, but no one was curious enough to inquire why three adults were playing hide-and-seek in the street.

Debreban had spotted his master coming out of Clem's Place and acted reflexively, tripping me flat. He dropped on top before I knew what was happening, then Shankey joined us.

"Why'd you do that?" I wanted to know. "It doesn't

matter if this Cadmus dude sees me or not. We've never met."

"No, but he might have been curious enough to come over to talk to you like everyone else since we left the stables."

True. Once back in the town proper I'd collected another quasi-parade of kids who must have heard about me from their friends and wanted a first-hand encounter with the cat-guy. Any other time and I'd have been glad to oblige, but I was in a hurry to get back to Terrin.

"He's in a bad mood," Debreban fretted about his master. "Didn't he look like he was in a bad mood? Bad."

"I didn't see him," I said, futilely brushing at the dirt and other stains I'd collected here and back in the tunnel. "This is my favorite shirt."

"My lady will see that it's cleaned," Shankey promised. "Let's keep moving. Don't you still hear your friend?"

I'd told them about Terrin's walkie-talkie-in-my-brain summoning. They'd been skeptical, but had seen enough magic to give me the benefit of the doubt and cooperate. Shankey had saddled three of the Darmo horses to speed our return to the inn. We'd just been tying them to a hitching post when Debreban spotted his boss and hit the dirt. Or in this case, the Myhr. "Thanks for the reminder."

We pressed forward before more kids could gang up on us. My chief distraction from them was Terrin's voice in my head keeping up a constant stream of talk with a single theme of me getting to him. The annoying, but worry-making, call was like a radio station playing my least favorite commercials with no volume control or on/off switch. I tried mentally replying to let him know I had the message, but it was one-way traffic.

About two minutes ago the internal noise stopped. I didn't know whether to celebrate or panic.

Clem was cleaning a mug behind the bar as we rushed

in. He called something after me about the show, but I charged past and up the narrow stairs, pushing the door open.

Terrin sat cross-legged on the floor with his back to me, his usual meditative posture. With Shankey and Debreban crowding each other in the doorway, I cautiously moved around to see his face.

His eyes were open, with only the whites showing. In his hands was that black candle, alight; some of its wax had melted and flowed over his fingers. His breathing was shallow and fast, which was wrong for meditation.

"Terrin? Hey, what's the emergency?"

His eyelids shivered, then he took a deeper breath, and shivered all over.

"You sick or something? What do you want me to do?"

He blinked out of it, his eyes wandering a few seconds before focusing on me. "It's about time you got here. Where were you, Timbuktu?"

Gracious as always. "Pretty much, and I've risked life and limb to get here—"

"Yeah, sure, okie-dokie, lissen up, we got a problem. I told you something was wrong with this world. I finally figured out there's a magic drain here."

"Yeah, it's to do with that black fog."

"Not during the day it ain't! I've been feeling tired from the first and it kicked in big time a little bit ago. It's in the fat part of the curve and sucking me dry. I made it back here where I have shields, but they aren't gonna last. We gotta find a way to get off this world before I'm husked out, or we stay here for good. You will, anyway. Much more of this and I'm hosed."

"How hosed?"

He suddenly turned to glare at my guests. "Who are those guys?"

"It's okay, they're cool—"

"You think everyone's cool. Who are they?"

I made a quick introduction. "Shankey's boss lady has invited us to come stay with her and help out on this Hell-river problem."

"Hell-schmell, I gotta leave this planet! We have to find gems and leave now while I still have the strength to do the travel spell."

"I'm on your side for that, but—"

"It's dead serious, Myhr. We'll have to lift some and pay out the karmic debt later. I can't wait for the quartzes to recharge. They won't recharge anyway since all the latent magic is gone."

"Lady Filima has gems. Doesn't she, Shankey?"

"Oh, lots," said Shankey enthusiastically. "Lots of jewels."

That was the right magic word to use with Terrin. "Great. Get two and bring 'em here. I want out of this dump before sunset."

Man, he was totally freaked. I'd rarely seen him like this before. "It's more complicated than you know."

"I don't care. We're outta here a-s-a-p or I'm dead!"

Okay, that was hosed and a half. "What about your shields and the protective wards?"

"They're too weak to hold for long."

"Ahh," began Shankey in a helpful tone, "Darmo House is magically shielded. From what I know of 'em they've been in place for centuries, added onto over time. They may be why Lady Filima didn't vanish with the other Talents. She's the same as ever."

"Huh? What?" Terrin demanded.

"We need to get you caught up on all the stuff I've learned today," I said. "I got inside information you need."

"Just gimme the headlines."

I did so, with Shankey and Debreban nodding vigorous confirmation as I outlined the city's problem with the Hell-river, the disappearance of all the town Talents and described Botello Darmo's hidden workshop. "If we can get you to Darmo House you'll have better protection than in this place."

"You sure about that?"

"No, but sooner or later your wards and stuff will give way, right? You'll have a better chance surviving there than here. Besides, you need to *see* what we've found."

"When I get there. *If* I get there."

"We've horses outside."

"Not fast enough; it means leaving my shelter. I won't last five minutes. There's something ugly out there sucking magic off like a frat house empties a keg."

"Can you make a movable shield?" asked Debreban. "I've heard talk of such things."

Terrin gave him a cockeyed look. "I like you, blondie, you think like me."

Debreban offered a weak smile, perhaps unsure whether or not to take that as a compliment. Terrin was still in his wrinkled Hawaiian shirt, holed jeans, and purple high-tops. By no stretch of imagination on any world we'd ever been to did he look like a wizard.

"Okay, gang, I gotta work," he said. "You guys beat it and have the horses ready. Soon as I'm downstairs we go and don't stop. How far away is this place?"

"About a mile," I said. "But with the street traffic it might take us a bit to get there."

"So long as I don't have to walk I should be able to make it."

I grabbed up our backpacks, stuffing them with scattered odds and ends from the room. "See you when you show. I gotta talk with Clem before we split."

Zipping the packs shut, I herded Shankey and Debreban down to the common room.

"Lady Filima said she could reimburse the landlord here for me leaving before my run was over," I said to Shankey.

"Yeah, I remember."

"Can you help square things with him so he's not sore with me?"

"No problem."

Shankey and I told Clem about our need to whisk away a sick Terrin while Debreban went for the horses. Before venturing forth, he folded his distinctively colored cloak under one arm and looked both ways on the street. When he came back we'd settled everything with the easy-going Clem, who accepted Shankey's offer of Darmo money in place of my show. I let him do the bargaining since he was more familiar with the currency values.

"I'll return when I can, if I can," I promised Clem.

He continued polishing a mug. "Fine by me. I don't hold with people being sick in my place. Business'll be better for a bit, though. Crowd here has some new songs to sing and that belching contest is going to be a regular tavern event now. You done me a favor."

It was good to know that I'd left behind a fresh cultural tradition they could enjoy for years to come. Beatles and belching. Who would have thought it?

"Shankey?" Debreban called us over to one side, fidgeting with his bundled cloak. "I should get back to Burkus House. Lord Cadmus has been waiting all day. Maybe he even came looking for me here."

"He was *here*?" I asked. I thought he'd only been passing in the street.

"Saw him coming out."

"Of all the gin joints in all the towns in all this world, why did he come into mine?"

He shrugged. "He'll probably tell me once I'm back. I was supposed to be following Shankey; gawd knows what I'm going to report about today. I went well outside the bounds of my orders. That sort of thing annoys him."

"Well, if he dismisses you," said Shankey, "come over to Darmo House and I'll see that you get into my guards. It's regular pay, you know."

"Shank, you are a true friend and anyone who says otherwise will have to deal with me."

I'd have gone all misty-eyed, but Terrin was coming downstairs. He looked almost normal.

"Horses," he said, tossing me the black candle as he zoomed past. I hastily put it away. We were on the clock, now, and I didn't know for how long.

Elsewhere, NOT in Rumpock, in Hell

"You're *not* getting results," the demon said to Botello Darmo. It wasn't the one who looked like Great Aunt Matilda. Instead, it bore an equally disturbing resemblance to Uncle Fraddlip, who was still alive in a mental hospice somewhere.

"These things take time," said Botello.

"That runs differently here. You should have results by now."

"I am limited by how time is reckoned on Otherside." *Keep your manner nice and even, Botello. Don't let it see you sweat.*

Sweat was a major by-product in certain segments of Hell. Botello presently stood in the center of one of them. He felt heat, but not at the same intensity as some of the souls being roasted only yards away. The demon who had summoned him for a conference had temporarily removed their voice boxes, so the only sounds they could produce were of the breathy variety. It was like being in a room full of leaky bellows. Botello made a point of not looking at their faces. They all bore an uncanny likeness to his own and he knew damned well the demon had done that to make a point.

"Nonetheless, we want a show of results now."

"I will have some shortly. It is nearly sunset on Otherside. The river will vanish. I believe I understand what needs to be done to restore its flow here."

"Sunset or dawn, it's all the same," the demon stated.

Very true in a place where there was no sleep and the light—if it was light—remained the same throughout, except in those places where they had none. Lots of those.

"I understand that, but I am limited to Otherside reckoning," Botello said patiently. "I *will* make progress tonight, though."

"What sort of progress?"

"It's an experiment. I won't know until after it's done. What happens then will give me a direction, *then* I will be better able to provide results."

"You didn't answer the question."

"I did as best I could within the language. What is up here"—he pointed to his head—"is not easy to express. Much of it is very abstract, intuition-oriented."

The demon frowned. It had a permanent frown, but this one was deeper than usual. "You will make progress, you will achieve results," it said. Unmistakable orders. "If not . . ." It waved a very long talon at all the soundlessly screaming Botello Darmos around them. "But worse. Far, far worse."

The original Botello nodded, feeling pale and hoping it wouldn't show in the low light.

The demon quietly vanished, taking the audience chamber and the wheezing floor show with it, leaving Botello alone by the dim banks of the Hell-river.

He did not sag in relief. His guardian demon was presently out of sight, but probably looking on. It wasn't smart, but good at its job, like reporting Botello's "excessive use" of scrying with an Otherside human under the guise of getting information. A few extra, quite necessary contacts and everyone goes into a spasm. Typical. Just typical. They wanted things fixed, but begrudged every step he took toward achieving that goal. Perhaps they suspected—no, make that they must be certain—he had something else planned. Which he did, but how could they know about it? He'd been extremely careful. They must be watching him more closely than he suspected.

Making his boots, socks, and lower pant legs vanish, Botello sat on the edge of the bank, thrusting his feet into the black stream to feed. It took longer than usual; the magical energy was thinning. Or his appetite was growing. What he'd fed on earlier from that wizard had been wonderful, even if most of it had been squandered in the attempt to materialize. He wanted more of *that* energy.

If only Cadmus hadn't given out. And that business with the cat interrupting. Botello had thought there was something odd about it, but dismissed its apparent great size to a distortion produced by the mirror. Could it have indeed been man-sized and man-shaped as Cadmus insisted? Where would Filima have found such a creature and what was its purpose? Or was it one of her old traveling show mummers done up in a mask?

He would ask her later himself. When the time came. He would ask her about a lot of things.

The one mistake Botello could accept as his own fault had been trying to materialize by recreating his old body. Obviously it was far too difficult and costly in terms of magical power. The conversion of ephemeral energy into something solid was always a tricky calculation, especially when emotions were involved. Though magic worked better with the inclusion of strong emotional energies, those were the most difficult to control. One could get too easily diverted.

Using Filima's mirror might also have been a touch misjudged, too. If only the bitch hadn't been present. The mere sight of her had infuriated him. Though it added to his strength, the anger disrupted his concentration just the tiniest bit. Add that to Cadmus's weakening and of course the whole structure collapsed, closely followed by one of the overlords of Hell appearing to ply a number of unanswerable questions. Why couldn't they mind their own bloody business and let him get on with things?

Botello had covered the small disaster well from this side. Even his personal demon had noticed nothing. So how had the overlord found out?

Scrying, perhaps, or something like it. They had tremendous powers, but strange limitations he was still trying to identify.

But later. Botello stood, willed his clothing back into place, then conjured up a scrying mirror. That idiot Cadmus was taking too bloody long.

Elsewhere in Hell

The overlord demon dismissed the image of the silently screaming Darmos and waved in the image of the real one, who was sitting on the riverbank again, laving his feet in the river's black stream. That creature was always hungry. Much more feeding and he'd become a real problem.

He didn't belong here like the rest of the souls, not in the usual sense. He'd not come in the proper way through the gates. The Outer Guardians hadn't found out about him yet, but there would be Hell to pay—in the absolute, most literal sense—if they did. It was part of the Great Balance that all souls had to enter Hell through the gates. How Darmo managed to get around the judgmental process had been the main perplexity occupying the overlords for what seemed like ages now. They were all impatient for an answer and even more impatient to get rid of Darmo.

As he wasn't doing anything but sitting, the demon waved his image off and focused on a different plane, shifting time backwards to see if more dreams had come in.

No, nothing new. The little spheres of dream and

thought floated about undisturbed, meaning the human in the Otherside city gifted with the visions was probably awake. Why they spent so much of their pathetically small ration of time conscious was a mystery. Why be up and about when they should be asleep and dreaming? It was much more rewarding than playing their incomprehensible social games.

Few of them ever put their dreams to use, either, and this fellow was no exception. He accepted his gift, but was unwilling to understand and exploit it. Was even afraid of it at times. His dreams were Outer Guardian warnings, of course, vague and full of portents as usual, though lately they'd all been clear enough. The dreamer didn't seem to know what to do about them.

Little matter. The overlord demon found the visions of the future a ripe feast, a wonderful view of better things to come. It reached forth, again relishing the one of that frail city in flames, with demon hordes feasting on the remaining souls. Here were no rancid leavings thrust through the gates, but fresh, sweet innocence and complacency, still alive, and all ripped to glorious, bloody shreds. The Guardians would hate that, try to stop it, but after such a feasting the demonic overlords would be strong enough to fight them off this time.

"What are you doing?" asked another demon. It was much larger, uglier, and more powerful, appearing out of nowhere, of course.

The overlord shut down its viewing. "Nothing."

"So you're all done with your work?"

It dared not reply to that one. Work was never finished here and they all knew it. In reply, it waved the images of the screaming Darmos back into being again, this time with their voice boxes restored. The awful chorus drowned out all possibility of further conversation.

The other demon nodded and vanished, one of its more annoying traits. You never knew where or when it would show up. The overlord demon wished it could do that, too, travel anywhere, commanding beings as strong as itself.

After Darmo sorted things out, perhaps that would be possible. But he had to be watched. He was up to something else. And it was connected with the Hell-river. He had told the truth, but not all of it.

The demon brought back the image of Darmo, who had conjured a scrying mirror. Again? Was he aware of just how much power it cost to use those things?

Back in Rumpock, at Burkus House

Cadmus decided against wearing his usual clan colors for his visit to Filima. Better that she see him as himself, not a household, though the peacock mix of purple and green looked remarkably well with his coloring. He'd heard every joke there was about the combination and had learned to reply with wit and good humor, backed by his absolute certainty that of all people, *he* could carry them off.

Instead, he chose to wear a somber red so dark as to nearly be black. He'd been told it was a rather rare dye to achieve, and it was almost hypnotically eye-catching. He did a turn or two before his dressing room mirror and struck a pose; casual, yet manly. Yes, this would suit just fine. Sober enough to be appropriate for visiting a recent widow, yet festive enough for dinner at the overduke's palace. A light-colored under-shirting would set it off nicely, showing just the smallest bands of cream at the throat and wrists. Now, how did the whole ensemble look with his clan honors?

He draped the thick gold chain around his shoulders, centering the medallion on his breast. No, that didn't work at all. Far too pretentious. Save that thing for public appearances when one was expected to make a bit of show for the cheering throngs. He hurriedly stripped it off and replaced it with a thinner, more subtle piece that had a small, teardrop-shaped black pearl attached. *Much* better.

Cadmus thanked the gawds for the wisdom to have invested in so much gentleman's training, else he'd be putting his foot into things all over the place, like Lord Wattle, always overdressed and ill-prepared for the rigors of Rumpock's social whirl, poor fellow. He was stinking rich, so few minded his ways; some even liked him, too. Filima once mentioned she found the man's clumsy quirks a touch endearing, like a sad-faced clown.

No accounting for a woman's taste in men, though on second thought Cadmus considered he might have dismissed Wattle too swiftly. The fellow was never without female companionship, after all. His money had seemed the best reason for that, but equally wealthy women often sought him out.

Perhaps if I tripped and looked sheepish once in a while, Filima would warm up to me. Cadmus disliked the idea of appearing the least bit maladroit, not after all his sword-fighting and dancing masters had drilled a near-perfect sense of balance into him. But the *appearance* of vulnerability . . . there might be something to it. He'd seen a play once about a handsome man who couldn't get a lady's attention until he was injured, then she nursed him to health, falling in love at the same time. But the idea of allowing himself to be skewered in a duel held little appeal for Cadmus.

"I could fall down her stairs and pretend to twist my ankle," he said to the image in his dressing room mirror. The image looked thoughtful and interested. "Then I could be very grateful to her as she helped me. Perhaps I could even fake a touch of fever, confessing my love to her in my delirium so she'd know my sincerity."

Oh, my. That was ever so *much* better than a love spell. Why hadn't he thought of it before?

Because he'd only been at this courting business for two weeks. To charm, to seduce, those he was very good at, but to truly get a woman to fall in love with him . . . oh, the complexities, but he was positive he could work through them all. The man in the mirror looked back with bright, beaming confidence. What woman could resist all that?

This staged accident would take a bit of planning. He couldn't fit it in tonight; his dinner with Anton precluded that, but later this week . . . yes, while he was at Darmo House he'd wrangle an invitation from her or could make a light-hearted promise to call on her later in the week— as a concerned friend, of course.

The only snag Cadmus foresaw was the need to avoid actually *falling* down any stairs. He should be discovered already at the bottom, artistically sprawled and groaning with bravely suppressed agony. He knew a small illusion spell that caused a show of redness and swelling good enough to fool a healer. The hard part would be achieving enough privacy to get away with the ruse. Her servants were always about. He couldn't just lie down, they'd see that and the spell-casting. Damn, he might have to fall after all. At least he'd be realistically bruised, but what a price to pay.

His thoughtful reflection in the mirror began to warp and churn, as though in disagreement. What in the world . . . ?

Botello Darmo's distorted form suddenly appeared, nearly filling the frame.

Cadmus jumped back, startled.

"Stay where you are, you idiot!" Botello ordered. His voice was as uneven as his swimming image.

"How is it you're here?" Cadmus demanded. His heart thumped violently at this new and unpleasant show of magical power. It should have been impossible. What was Botello up to in Hell that allowed him such an awful freedom? "This isn't my Black Room, and I'm not scrying."

"I know that! You should be there now telling me why you've not found that magician yet."

"I found him, but he's at your house. Lady—"

"*My* house?"

"Lady Filima seems to have found him first. I'm told he runs about wearing a cat mask, or it might be his real face—"

"*What!?*" Botello roared.

Cadmus flinched. "I was just going over there to track him down."

"Shutup, shutup, shutup!"

The image spun about, highly agitated. Cadmus had never seen this wide a view of Botello; until now only his face had been visible. How odd that he still wore his working clothes, the ones he used to put on when engaging in spells, which included his long robe. It seemed more likely that he should have been in a nightshirt, since that's how he'd been dressed when his body was found. Legends ran that one spent some portion of the afterlife wearing the memory of one's last outfit. Because of that, Cadmus made a point of always being well turned out; even his night clothes were beautifully tailored.

Botello settled down. He almost looked sane. "Listen closely to me, Cadmus."

Cadmus gave him his guarded attention, hoping this wouldn't involve another jolt of pain. It wouldn't do to turn up on Filima's doorstep all shaking and pale, though that might be better than throwing himself down her grand staircase.

"Listen to me," Botello whispered. "Come closer. I can't let anyone else hear this."

"I'm alone."

"Anyone on *this* side! Press your ear against the mirror. Hurry!"

Damn Botello for doing this *now*. Cadmus wouldn't
have any time at all with Filima. A brief, dropping-in visit
was exactly right for the desired effect, but a flying stop
was just plain insulting. Besides, a man in a hurry gave
the impression of disorganization, not busyness.

"Couldn't this wait until tomorrow? I'm to dine at the
overduke's palace tonight and I've got to get there before
curfew."

"The overduke? Perfect. What I have to say involves
him. Something you need to know."

Gossip? Gossip from Hell? Cadmus wanted no part of
it, but the enticing lure of truly interesting information
tugged at him. Anyway, the sooner he got this over with,
the sooner he could depart. "Oh, very well." He pressed
his ear to the chill surface of the mirror.

Then he shrieked.

Just Outside Burkus House About Ten Minutes Later

Debreban ducked guiltily through the wrought iron
gates, then remembered to stand up straight, squaring
himself. Just because Lord Cadmus might be angry didn't
mean the rest of the meager household would embrace
his example. Though most of them looked on Cadmus
with the kind of indulgent affection usually reserved for
wayward, but charmingly cute, infants, none took their
emotional cues from him. They were a sensible lot, and
gawd knows, where the eccentric Burkus clan was concerned, one needed to remain sensible.

Toward that end, Debreban paused to put his cloak
back on again, so as to present a competent facade when
he made his report. Drat, there was a seam parting up
near the shoulder. He'd have to get one of the house girls
to mend it for him; his own sewing skills were too limited. It was too much to expect Lord Cadmus to notice
and replace the cloak with a proper new one, not until

more money came in, but dammit, the head of the guard for Burkus House should not be seen running about in thready rags.

At least it was clean. Mostly clean. Trudging through that tunnel and then the streets had certainly caked on the dust. Well, that could be brushed off. . . .

From up the carriage drive came the sound of hooves going at a smart pace. The only horse left in the stable capable of that much energy was his lordship's showy war charger. As there'd been no war here for ages many thought the animal should be traded in for something more practical, like a flock of egg-producing, edible chickens.

Debreban broke off toothsome thoughts of roasting fowls as the big white horse nervously cantered up, Lord Cadmus astride it. One couldn't fault him for his looks; he cut a dashing figure in the saddle, but why was he wearing the cloak with the house colors with *that* outfit? The purple and green clashed horribly with the deep garnet red. Had he suddenly been struck color-blind?

"My lord," said Debreban, executing a bow as horse and rider approached. "About that errand you sent me on . . ." He had thought up a reasonable excuse for his lateness; not a good one, but reasonable.

"Out of my way," Cadmus ordered, rather shortly.

Debreban stepped back, though he was nowhere near the horse's path. The great animal still skittered, head plunging up and down, its iron shoes striking sparks on the carriageway cobbles. Cadmus pulled the reins sharply, which upset the horse even more, making him buck.

"Bloody bastard, don't you dare!" Cadmus snapped, hauling the reins tighter.

Debreban judged that things could get out of hand if he didn't interfere. He jumped in quick, seizing the bridle. The horse started to rear back, dragging him along, but weight and muscle saved him. He spoke the horse's name

in a calming voice, hand on its nose, and that eased the
crisis. His mum had always maintained he had a way with
animals and should have stayed on the farm.

"Let him go, you lout! You think I can't handle him?"

Sheer surprise made Debreban let go. He'd seen his
lord annoyed, but never to the point of name-calling. It
wasn't the gentlemanly thing, even to servitors. Cadmus
looked incensed beyond the measure of the situation.
There was something seriously wrong here, you could see
it in his red-rimmed eyes.

"My lord, I—"

"Are you deaf? Out of my way, you clot!"

Debreban got out of the way, and the horse went back
to its frantic dancing. Whitestone was usually very well-
mannered; what had gotten into him? Cadmus dug in his
heels and otherwise did things he shouldn't that only
added to the problem. The horse finally leaped forward,
heading toward the gate. Poor Whitestone was already
patched in sweat. The only time Debreban had seen its
like before was with an animal panicked by a nearby fire.
What could have this one so spooked?

"Brainless bloody idiot," Cadmus snarled over his
shoulder as he charged away.

Debreban stared open-mouthed after his master. Now
that was just *mean*.

CHAPTER NINE

Outside Darmo House

Whatever Terrin had done about shielding himself worked, but he got very white during the trip. Even his freckles went pale. Shankey and I rode on either side of him in case he fell off. Terrin didn't say a word the whole time, very unusual for him, but his horse-riding skills were intact. He'd worked on a ranch as a kid, which came in handy with all these low-tech worlds between us and home. I was pretty good myself, and since I couldn't remember taking riding lessons, maybe it was an instinct thing.

Once clear of the more crowded streets we made good time to Filima's, opting to go to the front gate of the main house rather than use the stable tunnel. Shankey was unsure if the house protections extended that far. Of course we were seen by all those overduke guys in the black-and-silver cloaks who were still hanging around. They could hardly miss us, especially me.

"Hey! Shankey! How'd you get out?" one of them called.

"Wouldn't you like to know?" Shankey called back.

"Come on, we been waiting here all day for that guy. The overduke wants to see him. If we don't show up, Lord Perdle will throw a fit."

Shankey muttered something about Lord Perdle throwing like a girl, even fits. Then, louder, "Sorry, we got an emergency. I'll tell Lady Filima."

We pushed past. None made to stop or follow us, though I got the usual curious looks. Maybe there was some kind of protocol rule at work; I didn't care so long as we kept moving.

Terrin's balance lasted until we reined up at the front door, then he began to sway.

"Ulps," said Shankey. He threw a leg over his horse's neck and slipped off to grab Terrin before he fell. I did the same and between us we kept him from hitting anything hard. He seemed strangely heavy as we hauled him up the steps and inside.

There was a long, padded bench in the entry hall, and that's where we eased him down. His eyes were shut, and he'd gone all limp.

"Oh, jeez," I said, not sure what to do. I tried his pulse, which was fast and strong, maybe too strong. A couple of veins in his forehead were throbbing big time.

Shankey bawled orders to the pages who had opened and shut the doors, and in a minute the hall teemed with more servants. It wasn't as crazy as when Filima fainted, but still a good crowd. They had cold cloths to put on Terrin's face, and a cute girl chafed his wrists. There was talk of fetching a local healer. What I wanted was a fully loaded Star Trek-style sickbay with a smug and smiling hologram doctor asking me to please state the nature of the magical emergency.

Instead, I got that matron-looking lady again. With a phlegmatic expression, she passed the ammonia-smelling vial under Terrin's nose.

"Argh! Agh! Foo!" he said, waving her off as he struggled awake. She nimbly avoided his thrashing arms and left, smiling grim triumph. I wondered if that was her only job.

"You okay?" I asked Terrin.

"Urgh!" he replied, dragging a cold compress from his forehead. He shook the wet cloth open and blew his nose in it. "Day-um, what *is* that stinky stuff? And why are you always shoving it in my face? What'd I ever do to you?"

"The day isn't long enough to answer. How are you?"

He paused wiping his nose to take stock. "I ain't dead, so that's something. You guys were right about the protections here. I don't feel anything sucking at me."

The kneeling servant girl who had chafed his wrists snickered. He threw her a big, showy grin.

"Later," I told him. All he ever needed with most women was to smile at them, but he probably wasn't in shape for anything strenuous. "You think you'll be safe here, then?"

"For the time being."

"What about tonight? That's when the river appears. Will you be safe?"

"If it's not come inside this house yet, then I should be fine. Stop fussing."

"I'm *not* fussing."

"You are so. I know fussing when I see it, and that's what you're doing, so stop it."

I looked at Shankey. "You got anything to eat? He gets like this when he's hungry."

"I do not!"

"What's going on?" This from Filima who had just swept in. She was the sort of woman who could do that sort of thing, sweep into a room and make it look good, both the sweeping and the room.

"Day-um," said Terrin, looking her up and down. "What a babe."

That got both her eyebrows up. "Is this . . . ?"

I nodded. "Lady Filima Botello Darmo, this is Terrin the Whiz. Wizard, I mean. Wizard."

He scowled at me, knowing exactly what I meant.

"You are welcome to my house," she said politely. "Are you all right?"

Terrin continued to loll on the padded bench, taking in the view. Filima was well worth the time. "I could do with a drink. Got any Captain Morgan Private Stock? Cold?"

How that translated, I couldn't guess, but Filima was spared from answering when Terrin tried to stand. He was sitting up with his feet on the floor, but that was his limit. "Houston, we have a problem," he said.

"Just stay there," I told him. "Don't rush things."

"I couldn't rush if you put a rocket up my ass." He lay back down again.

"Can we get you anything?"

"I could have done with a couple of gems a little bit ago. Too late now."

"What do you mean by that?"

"No travel spell power."

Uh-oh. "How do you feel?"

"Terrible."

Filima moved in close and held her hand out over him, fingers spread. A warping of the air, like a heat shimmer fluttered between them and Terrin's body. "You *are* weak."

"Magically weak?" I asked.

"On the nose, fur-face," said Terrin. He shut his eyes. "Feels like a migraine, but all over."

"What do you want us to do? How do we help?"

"A travel spell off this ren-fair reject world would be handy."

I looked at Filima. "You know anything about travel spells? The kind that bounces you from one world to another?" Her blank reaction was not unexpected, but, hey, I had to ask. "Okay. Option one is officially tossed. Let's try option two. How about getting my partner out of the hall? You got any magically shielded rooms, something like a vault where he can be safe?" I gave her the short version of Terrin's power drain crisis.

"There's my scrying area," she said. "But he probably shouldn't be there, not after what happened with the mirror."

Shankey put himself forward. "My lady, what about the late master's chamber in the tunnel?"

"Chamber?" She had the innocent tone nailed, but her eyes flickered. "What chamber?"

"Cut the act," I said. "We found where your hubby used to play hardball magic."

She cut the act, swapping the innocent tone for rising alarm. "You were in Botello's Black Room? How did you even find it?"

"He left the burglar alarms on." I looked at Shankey. "I told you she'd know about it. Wives always know what their husbands are up to." Which was probably why, among ten thousand other reasons, I'd never gotten married.

"You—?" But she bit it off, going as white as Terrin.

"Was our being there a problem?" Boy, did she look like she had a tale to tell, but I didn't think she'd spill it here. Maybe Terrin could work on her. I'd be along to chaperon, of course. Couldn't let him have all the fun.

"N-no. Not at all, as long as you weren't hurt by anything."

"What d'ya mean?"

She recovered some lost poise. "Many who use their Talent tend to be secretive. They try to protect their works. It's like a cook with a favorite recipe, a practical necessity. Black Rooms can be dangerous unless you know what you're doing. Touch the wrong thing and . . ."

"Boom? Okay, no sweat. Nothing jumped out at us.

Shankey, that's a brilliant suggestion, but the place smells pretty bad, and it's a long way to carry him."

"But wouldn't it be extra well shielded?" He appealed to Filima, really liking the idea.

"I don't know," she said with such absolute sincerity that I knew better than to trust it. "Botello had talent, but might not have been skilled enough to manage such precautions. Mr. Terrin will be more comfortable in one of the guest rooms, I think."

That said, she got four sturdy guys to lift Terrin, bench and all, and carry him upstairs like it was the last act for *Hamlet*. A short hike from her blue room was a fancy suite that would have done any five-star hotel proud. It even had indoor plumbing. I'd have been jealous, but one of her people led me to the next room over. It also had a bath. I could have a *bath*. In a gigantic tubby-tub. Oh joy, oh, rapture, oh, gawd, there was room for two, maybe three in that thing. I wondered what plans Filima had for the evening.

I broke off drooling at the prospect, dumped my pack, then returned to Terrin's room. They'd shifted him from the bench to a big red-velvet bed. The cute girl was trying to get his purple high-tops unlaced while Filima and Shankey had their heads together.

"Go tell them not tonight, Captain," she said, looking at me.

"Hah?" I asked, my ears perking forward.

"The overduke's invitation," she explained. "His men have been waiting for you for some time."

"Oh." I was too distracted to put on a show, anyway. "Maybe later."

"He also sent a message for all those with Talent left in the city to come to the palace early tomorrow morning. I got my summons just before you arrived. He's going to want a solution to this Hell-river problem; you'll have to be there to help."

Drat. Confession time, but I didn't think she'd toss us out just yet. "I can provide the entertainment. Terrin's the real wizard. The *only* wizard."

Her brows drew together. A frown. It was still adorable. "But I thought you—"

"I'm a patterman, remember?" Or cat, as the case happened to be.

"You've no skill in magic at *all*?"

"In a word, no."

"You misled me?" Her voice went up.

Shankey rounded on me to frown on behalf of his lady. In contrast, he didn't look at all adorable.

"You gave me to understand you could help!" she continued, voice still on the rise.

"And you'll get my best shot, just not in the magic department. Terrin's the wizard," I said, pointing at him. He waggled his fingers at her to show he was still alive. "A real good one."

"And in rather poor condition," she observed. "How can he help us put the Hell-river back? He can't even stand up."

"He'll get better, he always does." I *hoped* he'd get better. The grin he had for the servant girl working on his sneakers didn't have the usual evil spark that he could put into things. He *was* in bad shape.

"Why did you—? *How* could you—?" Filima was going kind of purple. Stress can do that to a person.

"Look, I got dragged away against my will, hauled up here to get the third degree with you making all kinds of assumptions about who I am and what I can do. You practically insisted that I be a wizard. It seemed like good healthy survival sense to just go with the flow. What would you have done in my place?"

That brought her up short, but she wasn't going to turn apologetic just yet. She made a growling sound, shifting mental gears. "Captain Shankey, will you go see to the overduke's men? Tell them something suitably polite, then make sure the house is locked before sunset."

He gave a kind of salute, then went off, but seemed to be grinding his teeth. Whether it was from my misdirecting the boss lady or because his fly-on-the-wall routine was ended, I couldn't tell.

Filima shooed people away to various errands and eventually had me and Terrin all to herself. I could have done without Terrin just then, but she didn't have amusement activities in mind.

"Master Wizard," she said, going all formal.

Terrin's grin got wider. "Wassup?"

She started to speak, then paused. This seemed to be the first time she got a real good look at him. The mindbending color combinations of his clothes were enough to shut anyone up, but his Hawaiian shirt was off, revealing the T-shirt beneath. Its silk-screened front showed a cartoon of demon lesbian babes with fluorescent orange skin cavorting in a cartoon hell. They had long forked tongues and tails, both appendages being used toward pleasurable pursuits on one another. It was one of his favorites.

Filima just sort of gulped and put on a brave face. She started to speak again, but couldn't quite get into the swing of it. Instead, she cleared her throat and muttered something about hurrying the food along. Then she got out, shutting the door firmly behind her. Couldn't blame her; she had a lot to think about.

Terrin fell into one of his snickery fits, but with less energy than usual. Since he was under the weather I wasn't as stern as I might otherwise have been. "She's got gems," I reminded him.

"I know that." Terrin lay back on the velvet pillows with a long sigh. "A dump like this has to have plenty floating around. When I'm feeling better we can check the sofas for loose diamonds."

"And I got her to agree to pay for any magic work done to get rid of that black foggy thing no one wants around."

"You're sure she'll pay in gems?"

"If you don't scare her off with your taste in clothing. That gorgeous dream that just stampeded out of here at warp eight is a bona fide *lady*." So what if she'd been an oochie-coochie dancer once upon a time and had probably seen a lot of life. Still a lady. A smart guy can tell.

"Okay. I'll change."

I could assume he meant his shirt, not his manners, but knew he'd behave himself. The prospect of getting paid in jewels would inspire him to new heights of decorum. Well, *his* version of it.

"Myhr, gimme the dope again about this problem, with details. When she recovers her sensibilities and comes back I'll need to know what I'm doing."

It was a familiar drill, brief him so he could give the illusion of knowing all and seeing all like the Great and Powerful Oz, impressive to less sophisticated types. Filima would be more difficult to astonish, especially since she dabbled in magic herself. Terrin's problem, not mine.

I recounted what I learned wandering around town, the lunch conversation with Filima, her fainting fit with the mirror, the nasty noise, smells, and signs of recent traffic in the escape tunnel, and the magical energy permeating the late Botello Darmo's Black Room.

"It's strong?" he wanted to know. "How strong?"

"Got all my back fur on end, which is quite a feat. Felt like I was walking under a power line."

"Good, I might be able to use that to recharge."

"Just how bad off are you?"

He shook his head. "Tell me more about her husband."

"You'll have to ask her, I'm scraped out. She won't wanna talk about him, either."

"Now, I wonder why that is?"

"Maybe she's still dealing with the grief thing. Apparently his death was pretty sudden, must have been a shock."

He grunted, visibly thinking, then glared at me. "Hey! What's the idea of *carrying* her out of danger?"

"Hah?"

"When that mirror thing tried to come through and she fainted."

"And I say again, 'hah?'"

"Me you dragged downstairs butt last. My ass still hurts. *Her* you *carried* out."

I shrugged. "It's a guy thing."

Filima's mobile buffet corps came in just then, sparing me from listening to more about my shortcomings in the hero department. I was still digesting that big lunch, so Terrin had most of the feast to himself. He was disinclined to leave the bed; I couldn't tell if it had to do with his weakness or if he just enjoyed being waited on so thoroughly. I helped myself to a plate of odds and ends and lots of cold mint tea. There was booze available, but I was more interested in losing my thirst than gaining a buzz. Terrin had half a glass of something that might have been related to rum and paced himself, making it last through his meal. Very out of character. I'd seen him drain whole bottles of the stuff in one chug.

He wasn't all that hungry, either. Whenever magic was involved he tended to gorge to keep up with its physical demands. So as not to be accused of fussing again— I *never* fuss, I just show concern and make helpful suggestions—I didn't ask why his appetite was down, but signed to the servers to keep the plates coming. He nibbled lightly, flirting with the girls. A trickle of his usual ruddy color returned, but he wasn't back to his version of healthy yet. I couldn't specifically identify what was nagging me about him, only that my back fur was saluting

and on the march again. This world was giving it one heck
of a workout.

I asked after Filima, but her people couldn't say if she
planned to return anytime soon. Terrin seemed to be all
right for the moment, so I went to my room to decom-
press. My clothes and the body that held them up were
grubby from running through secret escape tunnels and
being squashed down behind radish carts. My favorite shirt
was starting to look like one of Terrin's Salvation Army
discards. I hoped Shankey had been serious about someone doing my laundry.

The bathtub was beyond wonderful, once I figured out
how to work the plumbing controls. Hot and cold running water equals paradise. It seemed like pretty sophisticated stuff for this world, about level with the late
nineteenth century where I'd come from, which still put
it ages ahead of Clem's Place. Luxuries like this were rare,
so I went all out and filled it up, planning to soak myself into an advanced state of pruney-ness.

I was up to my neck in steaming hot water, even dozing
a little when the door to my suite opened. A ceiling-high
tapestry that ran all around the tub to protect bathers
from drafts and peeping toms also prevented me from
glowering at the intruder. With my yellow eyes I had
glower down to a fine art. It was probably one of the
servants with towels or something. I'm not overly modest, but everyone has a limit, and when I'm in the tub
I want to be alone. Unless it was Filima. *She* would get
my best welcoming smile.

What a fantasy: Filima in her oochie-coochie outfit
wafting in to gently draw aside the tapestry to smile down
at me. Then she'd do a spin or three around the tub,
shedding bits of silk until there was nothing left to shed,
ending her dance by diving in with me. We had room for
all kinds of possibilities in this thing.

She sure had a heavy walk, though. How could her

little dancing slippers make such a clumping? Unless she was in some kind of military storm trooper get-up. Hmm, jackboots and black leather . . . ohhh, baby . . .

The tapestry wasn't gently drawn so much as yanked back.

By Captain Shankey.

We both gave yelps of horrified surprise.

"Hey! A little privacy!" I snapped.

"Ee-yuh! Get a towel for gawd's sake!" He retreated, letting the tapestry fall into place. Then he started laughing.

"What's so damn funny?" The water was opaque with soap. What the hell had he seen?

"Y-you look like a drowned cat!"

"No shit." If that was his idea of hilarity he needed to get out more. "Why are you here?"

"Came looking for you."

"Can't it wait? I'm kinda involved."

"Yeah, I noticed that."

I checked the water again. It wasn't as opaque as I thought. "What do you want?"

"To know why you told my lady you weren't a wizard."

"Because it's the truth."

"But you made that noise go away in the tunnel."

"Anyone can throw a lantern." I felt like throwing one now.

"You knew how to find the secret chamber."

"I'm sensitive to magic, doesn't mean I can do it."

"And you know about love spells."

"Learned that by osmosis."

"Huh?"

"Hanging around with Terrin. Back where we came from he had a nice little magical supply shop. I helped out and picked up a few of the basics. You want any magic done you gotta go to him. Just don't expect much. He's wrecked."

Shankey made a disappointed sound. "You can't do a choglat asdek love spell?"

What the hell was a—oh. "Ahhh . . . no. Don't have the ingredients or the skill." I started to launch into the reason why love spells are a bad idea with or without chocolate or Aztecs, then gave up as a waste of effort. I wanted some peace and quiet and maybe a nap on that huge guest bed. If I was lucky I would dream about Filima. Minus mood-destroying interruptions.

"Can your wizard friend do a love spell?" he asked.

"Maybe, when he's in shape, which he ain't. What's with the obsessing on romance? I thought you had a thing going with the cook."

"Not for me! *I* don't need help there!" He was insulted. "It's for my lady."

"Debreban mentioned he wanted to put his boss together with your boss."

"We need a plan. We planned to make a plan, and with you turning up like you did it struck me that the gawds really want those two together."

How he arrived at that conclusion was not my concern. "The main hitch being I don't do magic and the ones who can are low on power or have vanished. I think you should wait until this Hell-river mess is cleared up and *then* make a start on leisure-time activities."

A heavy, heartfelt sigh. It made the tapestry flutter. "Oh, okay. That might be awhile, though."

"Where'd Filima get to?" I asked, wanting a change of topic.

"My lady went to her suite. She dresses for dinner about this time, even when we don't have company."

"But you do have company. Me and Terrin."

"Oh. Yeah." He wasn't too committed to the idea.

"Or are we not company? Are we guests or hired hands?"

"Both, I think. Hard to tell with her these days. She's

been a bit . . . eccentric ever since his lordship died, then
everyone's gone crazy with this Hell-river thing. Everyone with Talent, that is."

"You ever see it? The Hell-river?"

He snorted. "No. Glad I can't; I got enough to worry
about."

"How many people know about it?"

"Hard to say. The Talents know and probably their
families and so on, but the ordinary folk in the city don't
pay much attention to the rumors. Some don't like the
curfew, of course, but most would be in bed by dark
anyway."

"How can a curfew be enforced if everyone's in bed?"

"The overduke has his guard out on patrols, and some
volunteers with Talent are on the watch through the night
in protected areas to keep an eye on the river. They're
scared, though. Don't need to see a Hell-river to notice
that. When I first heard of it I thought it was a strange
joke, but some of my friends in the other house guards
tell me otherwise. They say it's real, and if that many
people say it's real, then it must be. I just want it to go
away so things get back to normal."

No argument there, even if I didn't know what normal was in this world. Probably the same as it was now,
but with a lot more wizards and minus the Hell-river.
Terrin and I would have to find out what the connection
was between it and Filima's dead husband. I didn't believe
in coincidence, especially where magic was concerned.
Botello dies and the Hell-river changes its course. Could
one man, all on his own in a basement workshop, swing
so much power? It seemed a pretty steep order. Even
Terrin didn't have that kind of magical clout. Or if he did,
he'd not mentioned it.

"Did Filima love her husband very much?"

"What do you mean by that?" Shankey sounded like
I'd touched a sore spot.

"Nothing bad, she just seemed to have adjusted pretty fast to his loss, and with you and Debreban trying to get her married off so soon after the funeral . . ."

"Oh. That's all Lord Cadmus's doings. He's the one who's anxious to snag her. He's got money problems and wants to put himself forward first before some other fellow pushes in. From what Debreban tells me Lord Cadmus really does like her, it just turns out to be a good thing for him that she's wealthy, too. She might learn to like him back if she gave him half a chance."

I grunted, not wanting to get involved in the local soap opera. "What was Lord Botello Darmo like?"

A long silence.

"Did I say something wrong?"

"Him being dead and all I suppose it's safe to say he wasn't that easy a man. Stern he was, short temper. He had a soft spot for my lady, though, seemed to treat her well. She could make him laugh, but in the last year he got more and more interested in magic. His last months he was always working on it. Didn't leave much room for her."

What an idiot. If I had a babe like Filima to myself I sure wouldn't be wasting time on magic. "How did they meet?"

"He went to a circus and saw her dancing. That was enough to decide him. His lordship was the sort to go after whatever he wanted and get it, and Lady Filima was no exception."

"Did she want him back?"

"It seemed so. She's very smart, studied up on how to be a proper lady so she'd do him proud. They got along as well as any and better than most. They had fights like any couple, drifted apart like any couple. I'd say it was his magic studies that displaced her in his heart. She has a bit of the Talent and tried to share the interest with him, but not being as single-minded she got left behind.

Someone had to see to the running of the house, so she picked up the slack. The last few months they hardly saw each other, so her maid told the cook."

Who certainly told Shankey during their pillow-talk. "Months? Was he lurking in his Black Room all that time?"

"Probably. He'd be around at evening meals and for the parties. I thought he was shut away in his study, but after seeing that chamber below—"

"And nobody noticed him running up and back from the basement?"

"Well, if his lordship didn't want to be seen he could manage easy enough. The house is big and there's more than one way to get downstairs. Hardly anyone ever goes there. If he was up to something private, nobody would know about it."

Except Filima. Damn. It looked like I'd have to forgo a nap for a talk with her. With her going all ghosty every time her dead spouse was mentioned she *had* to be hiding something. If it was just me and Terrin in the room with her she might share. Shankey would have to be out of the loop, which was too bad, as he struck me as being a good guy to have in your corner, but sometimes you can confide to a stranger things you'd never dump on family or friends. Or house guards.

I boosted to my feet. Water sheeted from my body. Shankey had been right about the wet cat thing. "Hey," I said. "Hand me a towel, would ya?"

He pushed one through an opening in the tapestry.

"Thanks." I made a start on drying off. "Got any more?"

"Yeah. How many you need?"

I looked down. "All of them."

Terrin finally got rid of the flock of servants and lay out flat on the velvet bed, wiggling his bare toes. This was the life, what was left of it, anyway. The magical drain had slowed considerably, but he still felt its tug in the background. He had breathing space, but sooner or later the protections around this museum would give out and the last of him would be sucked away, probably into that black fog.

From Myhr's description of last night's event the stuff was attracted to magic. Was it intelligent or a mindless thing, like an amoeba in search of food? Or was it under intelligent direction? And if so, who was directing it and why? And how had it come to this world? The hot money was on Botello Darmo being at the bottom of things what with the timing of his death. Terrin didn't believe in coincidence, especially where magic was concerned.

Chances were the guy had been up to an oddball conjuring and released something way out of his league. No wonder his heart had given out. He'd probably opened up the wrong doorway and whammo-blammo, he's on a slab. Oh, well, and too bad, one less fool in the gene pool, but what a load of chaos for the remaining swimmers.

Where had Myhr gotten to? Terrin wanted to see the secret chamber. And talk to her nibs. Filima the babe had hotfooted out way too quick after a squint at the T-shirt. If she'd once been some kind of wiggle-waggle dancer she should be used to the rougher side of life, so something else about it had spooked her.

Terrin groaned as he levered himself up and after a minute decided he'd be able to get to his backpack across the room. It had taken some severe and sharp tones to convince the butler or valets or whatever they were not to unpack it for him. He had protections on the thing, and woe to anyone who dared to poke around in his stuff.

He padded slowly across a thick carpet to the pack, got it open, and rooted around. First, a fresh shirt. *Not* that Myhr's warning about respecting the lady of the house had anything to do with it; Terrin just wanted to put on something clean. The new T-shirt was just as loud with a card-playing maniacal clown gibbering from its cotton front. Each card in the deck was a joker. Yeah, that one would be suitably enigmatic for the masses.

Pulling it on, he went to the window for a check on the darkening sky.

Nearly sunset.

From this height and angle he had a good view of the city and the tall towers of what looked like a fancy church or palace not too far distant. Filima sure had ritzy neighbors. Trees obscured a lot of the goings on, but he glimpsed people hurrying along, trying to make it indoors before the curfew began. Some overdressed maniac on a big white charger caught his attention, simply for going too fast in a street crowded with pedestrians. He was having trouble keeping the horse in check. It moved forward quick enough, but was torn between bolting and bucking. The rider kept jerking the bit around, stressing the animal even more. Twit. They should have a driving test for would-be horse people.

Then Terrin saw a kind of dark shimmering around the duet. The horse settled down and proceeded forward at a sensible trot. It soon vanished between the low buildings.

"You son of a bitch," Terrin murmured at the rider. "What are *you* doing tossing control magic around like confetti when I'm up here starving?"

He wanted to have that jerk dragged in feetfirst so he could tap into his magical energy and then ask a few pointed questions. Like why the dude was apparently immune to being drained. And where could Terrin get a nice, loud purple-and-green cloak like *that* one.

Too late, the man was gone. Another time then. Very shortly, if Myhr's briefing had all the facts right, the black fog would be rolling in, hopefully bypassing this house. Terrin was not one to place too much trust in another wizard's protection spells. He'd have to find Myhr and get to that basement chamber, and see what sort of energy was lying around. There was likely to be one unholy mess down there waiting for a clean-up crew. Unpleasant, but to put it off might be fatal.

So far Terrin had camouflaged things with grins and flirting, but cutting him up inside was one hell of a sharp edge of fear and desperation. He hated that feeling. The prospect of dropping dead at any given second nearly always interfered with his fun.

He usually tried to avoid trouble—unless he was its instigator—but if it got in his way then he preferred to be in the middle of the problem, kicking its sorry ass. No way would he let some piss-ant magical drain keep him from getting home again; he liked his techno raves too much.

In the Street Leading to the Palace

Finally, he'd gotten this *bloody* beast under control. Leave it to that idiot Cadmus to buy himself more horse than anyone else could handle. For show, all for show, not a serious bone in his body, though it felt fit enough. It was good to have a body again, a real one. Botello worried that he'd not have full use of it, but Cadmus was either too cowed or catatonic to put up a fight. His feelings were there: abject terror mixed with outrage and fury. They gibbered in the background, nothing Botello couldn't ignore.

He found he was also privy to some of Cadmus's memories. From there Botello got the gratifying confirmation that Cadmus hadn't slept with Filima yet. Ha! She didn't want anything to do with him. Wise of her to still be faithful to her dead spouse. One less thing to deal with when next he saw her. He had quite enough to sort out with the treacherous bitch.

He kicked the horse to a trot, scattering the people on foot who were unwise enough to be in his path. The sun was nearly gone; he had to get to the palace and quick.

He passed some of the overduke's volunteers on the way to their posts. They'd spend the night keeping an eye on the Hell-river cowering behind their protective shields. Fat lot of good they were. Blind watchmen, unable to see what was *really* swimming in the fog. Some of them waved at him in a friendly manner, one Talent to another. Talent. Humph. Squandering their skills on parlor entertainments, healings, or trying to influence people. Love spells, even. Bloody amateurs.

The palace gate was a great cast iron thing that gave him a shiver even from a distance. He forced himself to smile at the gate guard. Smiles came easily to the likes of Cadmus. This one hurt. The guard nodded respectfully and passed him in, shutting the gate behind. As Botello crossed into the overduke's influence, he felt the smallest of tugs, indication of the layers of protective spells that had been woven into the fabric of the property over the years. They would keep out something as Otherside as the Hell-river, but not for long. Not after he'd finished with things.

At the palace entry someone hastened out to take his horse. He dismounted a little stiffly. The body was fit, but he'd never liked riding. Once off the horse the beast went into another panicked fit of stamping and snorting, nearly carrying away the stable lad. Other men rushed forward to help.

Botello indifferently left their hubbub behind, taking the steps up to the main door, which was already opening for him. One footman relieved him of his gaudy cape and another led the way to a receiving room. The overduke was already there with his latest fancy, Velma, enjoying a bit of sherry to judge by the shape of the stemmed glasses.

"Hallo, Cadmus," he said, nodding vaguely in his direction. "Good of you to come on such short notice."

"I was delighted to receive your invitation, my lord." He gave a formal bow, flashed a charming smile at Velma, and graciously accepted an offer of sherry from her.

Anton's piercing blue eyes raked him, but Botello continued to smile ingenuously back, well aware of the overduke's extreme nearsightedness. He was not liable to notice any changes in Cadmus, visible or otherwise. Anton had a good store of Talent, ironically for visions, but often forbore from using it. Had he truly focused on Cadmus he might have experienced a moment of doubt, then dismissed it as imagination.

There were dozens like him still left in the city, possessing Talent, yet never fully exploring or exploiting its limits.

So foolish of them.

But so ripe for the coming feast.

CHAPTER TEN

Darmo House, just outside Filima's Blue Room

"Shouldn't she be finished dressing by *now*?" I asked. After all, *I* was ready.

Shankey shrugged. "That's ladies' stuff; I don't know how long it takes them to change."

"Forever." Usually when there was a movie I was anxious to see so we'd miss the trailers or worse, opening credits. I knocked on Filima's blue and gold-trimmed door again. Perhaps the first time I'd been too soft. Now I gave it several brisk wake-it-up, shake-it-up raps.

I really did have to use all the towels to dry off from the bath, but it had been worth it. My fur was all fluffed and shining, I had on fresh clothes, and some invisible servant had even polished my boots. Ready for most anything, I was impatient to get started on . . . on whatever came next. Sneaking suspicion told me that step one required I get Terrin and Filima together and let him take the lead. Having looked in on him I knew he was in a different shirt and able to at least walk.

In fact, he was ambling slowly down the hall toward us. Not his normal no-time-to-waste strut, but better than being flat on his back. He still didn't look right.

"Wassup?" he said.

"Trying to see if Filima's receiving." I knocked again.

He moved past and tried the door knob. Yeah, it worked.

"I'd have done that next," I said.

"No you wouldn't," said Shankey. "That's my job."

"Then you go first."

He obligingly went first. "Lady Filima?"

The painted clouds on the high ceiling were muted this late in the day. Shadows filled the corners of the huge room, frowning at us. Incense hung heavy in the air, a really nasty, head-numbing brand that made my whiskers twitch. The place was no longer cheerful, but gloomy and cold.

And she'd not taken down that black pavilion thing.

"Oh, shit." Suddenly flushed with foreboding, I made a beeline for it, pulling the curtain aside. Filima was slumped on the candlelit table within, her head on another scrying mirror. I picked her up and took her to the couch.

"See," Terrin grumbled. "*Her* you carry. *Me* you drag like a sack of potatoes."

Shankey sheered off to haul on the bell rope a few times. He grumbled as well, displaying a surprising store of gutter language, all of it terrifically appropriate for the situation. I felt like repeating some myself as I tried to bring her around.

"Terrin, can you do anything?" I called over my shoulder.

"She'll be all right," he said, his attention on the black curtains. He must have spotted the aura of magic permeating them. He went inside.

A lot he knew. I lightly slapped her cheeks and wrists,

the extent of my first aid for fainting. Feet up, that was another trick to try. I grabbed her ankles and did that elevation thing like you see in the emergency manuals. Maybe overdoing it.

"Hey," said Shankey, coming over quick. "What the hell are you—"

"I'm copping a peek up her skirt. Here, you take 'em." I put her feet into his startled hands and went to a table that held a carafe of water and other drinkables, returning with the water and something that smelled like brandy. I flicked one in her face and got her to take a sip of the other. She didn't like it, but tough love and all that. "Come on, wake up, ya dizzy dame."

The matron lady entered. With her bottle of stinky stuff.

"Argh! Agh! Foo!" went Filima, waving and sneezing.

The matron lady left. With a satisfied expression. She herded out the other servants who had charged in. You'd think they'd be used to this kind of riot by now.

Filima's eyelids fluttered and peeled back. She stared at Shankey. "Captain? What are—?"

Shankey hastily dropped her feet and pointed at me. "He told me to do it. I didn't look!"

"Yo," I said, drawing their combined attention. "End of emergency. It's the rake-over-the-coals hour. Filima, what the hell were you *thinking*? After what happened the last time—"

She waved some more to shut me up. "I know, but I had to have a look. Oh, my head."

"You're lucky another one of those creepy-crawlies didn't come through your mirror again."

"If that's what was really there."

"It was there, all right."

"Regardless, whatever happened earlier began on its own. I've never had any trouble before. Anyway, nothing hurt me."

"Yeah, sure, except for passing out cold again."

"That was my headache. Could you rub my neck . . . ?"

I grumped and growled, one of my more effective vocalizations with all the cat inside me, but obliged, standing behind her to work on a few nerve clusters.

"Ohhh, that's so much better."

And I thought *I* could purr. But I couldn't let her moans of pleasure distract me. Not too damn much. "*Why* were you messing around with the magic again?"

"I had to see what else was going on in the city."

"Again, why?"

"It's what I do this time of day. If I study the initial manifestation of the Hell-river enough, it might provide a clue to getting rid of it."

"Excuse me? You've got a wizard right here. You can't talk shop with him?"

"I had to see to this first," she insisted.

Terrin's muffled voice came from behind the black folds. "Never mind that, Myhr, she's throwing out more fog than the river. Ask her why she freaked when she saw my shirt."

"What's he doing in there?" She shifted from under my massage and started for the pavilion. I caught her and made her stay put. Shankey might have objected to his boss being manhandled—or rather cathandled—but he'd pulled the velvet out of the way for a look inside himself.

"Terrin's checking things out," I answered. "You got magic all around that thing. He's going to go over it. What about his shirt?"

"Shirt?"

"The one with the orange demon babes that you saw him in. Soon as you flashed on it, you split. I thought it was just a sign of your good taste, but . . ."

Filima squinched her face up, then shook her head, her shoulders slumping under my hands. "I'm so damn tired."

"Uh-uh, no continued-next-week crap. Talk, lady."

She remained slumped. And quiet. But after a moment or three, she gave out with a deep sigh and a shudder. "All right. What he wore was a vision."

"Hah?"

"A vision of Hell."

A short bark of laughter came from Terrin across the room. Whatever he was doing in the pavilion had Shankey riveted.

"A vision of Hell? Little more info, please."

"I saw it once in my mirror." Another wave, vaguely at Terrin and presumably his previous shirt.

"There's a lot of weird shit going on around here," Terrin put in.

Like I hadn't noticed. I turned to Filima. "And that's what set you off?"

"I had to find out if he was a Darkside creature, so I tried scrying to find out about him. Nothing came through, just blackness, like a horrible gaping, hungry maw. . . ."

"Look, I know Terrin's hard to get used to, but he's hardly—"

He poked his head out, peering past Shankey. "It's like a football game, Myhr. She thought she was sitting all safe in the home bleachers, then she sees my shirt and thinks I'm a spy for the other team."

"The other team? There's *teams*?"

"Yeah. And the other guys are pretty tough."

"The Hell-river?"

"I dunno yet. But Filima does."

"No I don't!"

He threw a sour, cranky look. "Oh, hush," he told her. Surprisingly, she did.

He retreated inside and I heard a low humming, not the kind of sound that comes from a human throat. Filima noticed it, too, and froze. My ears twitched and flattened, ditto for my lip whiskers. Magic stuff, fairly heavy-duty. It went on for about a minute, rising in force, then falling to nothing.

Shankey backed his way out of the pavilion, his mouth open. "You should have *seen* what he did," he said. "He went all glowy and there were these black specks whirling around like snow and they went right *into* him! That was magic, wasn't it?"

"Terrin?" I called. "What's going on?"

He emerged, his ruddy color nearly restored. "Just recharging my batteries. There was energy in there, not a lot, but it might get me through this mess. Jeez, it's dark. Somebody put on a light."

Shankey reached into the pavilion and came out with a table candle, using it to light others in the room. He looked excited. "Wasn't that magic? Someone tell me if that was magic. Was that magic?"

"You got it," I said agreeably. Filima by candlelight was absolutely devastating. I got the massage thing going in earnest. A cat can dream, can't he? Her mind wasn't on me, though—she wasn't moaning like before—instead she stared out the windows, her shoulders bunching up under my hands.

She pointed. "Oh, gawds, here it is again."

We all looked. The streets and ways of the city below had movement, not of people, but of a black, slowly undulating mass. It seemed solid and wispy all at once, growing out of nothing all over, all at the same time. In a very short while the city was choked with it to a depth of about head height.

"What's that?" I asked, pointing higher.

On the roof of one of the taller buildings were several small bobbing lights. As my eyes got used to the darkness I saw they were lanterns in the hands of people shifting nervously about.

"They're the overduke's volunteers," Filima answered.

"Those few remaining Talents are in shielded sanctuaries keeping watch on the river. They've not asked me to help yet because of the mourning period for Botello's death or else I'd be with them, too."

"You need to be here," said Terrin. "It's time for show-and-tell, and you're up first."

But none of us could tear away from the window, not even Terrin. His head was cocked and slightly tilted back, upper lip curled just enough to show his teeth, eyes half shut. He seemed about to have a sneezing fit. That told me he was using his inner sight on the river. With it he could see things invisible to most others. I had some of that ability as well, but since it's a normal part of me I don't have to concentrate to make it work.

Shankey, however, was frustrated. "I don't see a damn thing," he complained.

"That's the idea," said Terrin in a distant voice. "Trust me, it's out there."

Out there and then some. The black fog butted right up against the front gates of the grounds. It should have been able to ooze through the wrought iron, but didn't, apparently held in check by the house's shields.

"Do the magical protections extend as far as the stables?" I asked.

Filima nodded absently, still staring. She had a lost, frightened look that made me want to gather her in close and go all cave-cat on her.

Not the time or place. Dammit. "Gang . . . I think we should have a tour of the dungeon."

Elsewhere, at the Overduke's Palace

Botello liked the palace dining room; it had the only true grandeur in the whole wretched city. The ceilings were overwhelmingly high, and like the walls, heavy with ornate decorations and gold leaf. The vast table and its many chairs were on the same scale. This level of luxury should have engulfed the three people seated at one lonely end, but those three were extraordinary enough in themselves to suit their surroundings.

Overduke Anton, tall and spare in black discreetly trimmed in silver, could fill a room all on his own. He had the presence needed for his office, a rare kind of stillness that commanded attention. By his remaining in one place the world had to necessarily move around him; however, he possessed enough charm so as not to be annoying about it.

Seated to his left was Lord Cadmus Burkus, considered to be the most handsome man in the province. His looks, combined with a certain flippant wit and a mastery of the physical skills of hunting, swordplay, and horsemanship, made him an essential guest at all the fashionable parties.

Then there was Velma, a quite devastatingly beautiful young woman, come from the humble origins of a traveling circus. A dancer, of course. She'd met Anton at one of the Darmo House parties, invited there by her old friend, Lady Filima.

Botello suppressed a growl of displeasure at the thought of his treacherous wife. He also brutally suppressed a violent surge of resentment and fear emanating from the mind-imprisoned Cadmus. So, the fop *did* have real feelings for the bitch. Serve him right if he ever got her.

"Does the strawberry sauce not agree with you, Lord Cadmus?" asked Velma, noticing his expression.

"It's delicious," he countered. "I'm just a touch distracted by this Hell-river puzzle."

"I've not heard it defined as a puzzle before," said Anton. "Have you learned something new about it?"

Until now the topic of the river had not been broached. On purpose, Botello thought, so as not to spoil the dinner, but that suited him. How good it was to eat real food again, even when in another's body. It had cost him some effort of will not to bolt everything down like a starving farmhand. He was bodily sated, but on the astral level still ravenous. That would soon be remedied.

"Sadly not, my lord," he replied. "I've been busy with study, but it remains an enigma to me."

"What about your portal theory?"

Portal? What had that idiot Cadmus revealed? "I'm still investigating that area. Nothing of significance has presented itself."

Anton sipped his dessert wine, making a brief face. "Well, I hope you can be more forthcoming with details in the morning. I've invited all the other Talents over for a general meeting, very early. This Hell-river nonsense has gone on quite long enough; we're going to put an end to it. The curfew isn't popular, and if it's still on by the time the Mid-Summer Festival is upon us, it'll spoil everything. Can't expect people to be done with their drinking and debauchery by sunset."

"No, of course not." Gawds, he only saw the river as an inconvenience to some ridiculous celebration? It couldn't be; the overduke was a much more subtle man than that. Botello committed an otherwise unthinkable breach of etiquette—he was beyond such trivialities now, anyway—and used his inner sight for a look at Anton's aura. What an interesting pattern . . . and the colors . . .

Ah. So that's how it was; the man was terrified. He hid it well, having had decades of practice with the public life he led, but there it was for those with the Sight. What visions of the future had he seen to put him into such a state?

Velma was in a similar state of strain, but on a much lesser level. Her concern would be for Anton, not the future of Rumpock. She had rather sharper eyes than her lover, though.

"Anything wrong, Lord Cadmus?" Her delicate brows were up, questioning.

Filima would use that exact same expression when she was about to catch him out in some lie—that is, misdirection. Botello had to smother a strong urge to throw a psychic shock at Velma. Not the time or place and he couldn't afford to waste magic.

He smiled instead. "At the risk of giving Lord Anton cause for jealousy, I must confess your beauty quite enthralled me for a moment. I hope not to give offense, though." He bowed to her from his chair. There. Exactly the sort of pretty speech a twit like Cadmus would make. It had the right effect, too. Velma beamed and Anton nodded once to indicate that respectful admiration for his girlfriend was acceptable.

Velma's good cheer didn't last long, and her face sobered soon after. Did she know anything or was she back to worrying about Anton? That had to be it. She couldn't know Cadmus well enough to detect anything wrong, and Anton was too wound into his Hell-river worry to notice. Botello dabbed the corners of his mouth with his napkin. Velma, playing hostess rather well, nodded at this silent signal that their guest was prepared to quit the table and suggested they remove to one of the parlors. They rose, Botello with difficulty, for he was *very* full. Anton offered Velma his arm, she accepted, and they ambled from the dining room. Servants with candles in hand guided their way along a vast hall.

Social rituals . . . Botello had had a bellyful of them before his displacement. Good manners were quite useless in Hell—unless one was one of the demons, of course. Then one commanded respect, based on the fact that any demon with power could make existence extremely unpleasant for those with less power. And if he didn't do something to help himself soon, Botello would be back there and at their mercy—ah, there was the catch, they had none—in a very short while.

"Perhaps," said the overduke, "even something of insignificance could prove useful in our quest."

"Pardon?" said Botello.

"Your portal theory. You've found nothing significant, but much may hang upon a small detail. This business is too important to overlook anything. Perhaps a fresh pair of eyes is needed."

"Indeed, my lord. I didn't want to trouble you over trifles, though." Botello tried to call to mind all he'd ever related to Cadmus about portal-travel. Pity he couldn't be questioned, but the mind-prison he was locked into only allowed for the most basic communication of feelings. Anything more complicated and he might manage an escape. No problem for Botello, though; the way to prevent being caught out in a lie was to just be vague and let the other person take the lead. It had worked often enough on Filima. Almost often enough.

"After that wonderful meal I'm in a mood for trifles," Anton countered. Beneath his fear a tiny flame of hope warmed his aura. Hope was an excellent tool for manipulation.

Botello nodded. "Very well. I could try recreating one of my experiments. With your help, we might be able to make some sort of progress. That would require the use of your Black Room."

"It is at your disposal."

My, but isn't he being generous? Most Talents held their special chambers aloof from visitors. It could disrupt all their stored magic. *Generous or desperate.*

Velma paused before the door to one of the informal parlors. "This sounds like it might take a bit of doing."

Anton also paused, with a questioning look at Cadmus.

Botello gave a rueful smile. "It is the nature of the art. I hope you'll forgive me for stealing him away."

"Anything to get rid of that Hell-river," she said. "I'll say goodnight now, then."

Botello brushed his lips on the back of her outstretched hand, then Anton affectionately pecked her cheek. She wafted into the parlor; they took another direction toward Anton's private apartments. Neither man said anything. Ahead of them silent servants padded along, lighting candles and opening doors. The last door at the end of the hall remained shut. The two guards flanking it came to attention at their approach.

Anton had a key on a neck chain and used it to deal with the lock. Botello took a candle from one of the servants, holding it high. The door, a black slab of oak with touches of silver, swung wide. A breath of chill air flowing from the room within made the flame shiver. Having seen Hell, Botello found nothing to intimidate him here. He walked in behind Anton and solidly shut the door, sliding the inside bolt into place. They would have total privacy, now. Lovely. Botello looked eagerly around, this being his first time here.

The overduke's own magical chamber was larger than he'd expected. Instead of a pavilion of black velvet to help focus the power, the walls themselves were covered in that plush fabric. The ceiling, too. In the center was a table with a scrying mirror on it, and a simple chair. Botello lighted more candles on tall stands, but they helped little against the darkness.

"You anticipated something more elaborate?" asked Anton. He pulled a cord that caused a thick sheet of velvet to close over the doorway, cocooning them utterly. The layers of plush fabric muffled all sound. That was good. The men outside would hear nothing.

Botello ignored a stab of worry that Anton had picked up on his thoughts. The man had prophetic dreams, but was not clairvoyant. "I suppose so."

"I don't need more than this. I wish there was no need

of any of it, but one must accept one's path." He flicked a handkerchief over the mirror, whisking away a thin hint of dust. He stared long at the blank, polished face of the device, then puffed out a brief sigh. "The visions have gotten worse, you know."

Gawds, the great man was actually unbending a bit. That was a decidedly confiding tone, as one friend to another. Excellent. All the better to catch him off-guard. Sympathy was in order. "I'm sorry to hear that. I take it they're distressing?"

"They're damned hard on my sleep. Haven't had a good night's rest since Botello died."

He gulped to hide his smirk. "Yes, it was terrible what happened to him."

"We should all have so easy a passing. Go to sleep with a beautiful woman, wake up in . . . well, wherever it is the gawds store souls until it's time for them to come back again."

"He will be missed." Botello took care not to grind his teeth. What had Filima told them? Dead in his bed? The lying bitch.

Anton took a deep breath, clearing his throat. "Past and done. Let's see to the present and try to save the future. What have you in mind for this experiment? Do you require anything special?"

"Only your cooperation, my lord. If you will seat yourself before the mirror . . . and I shall stand opposite."

"What do you want me to do?"

"Shut your eyes, and compose yourself as you would for a scrying session."

"I was hoping to avoid that," said Anton in a wry tone. He sat and followed instructions. "I never see anything I like."

Botello took his place and held still for some minutes, stretching forth with his astral senses to determine the level of magic in the chamber. Quite a lot of it was stored up—years of it. His heart hammered frantically with anticipation, but he couldn't feast just yet.

Between them the black scrying mirror went dull, the black turning to gray. Clouds formed within its bounds. Anton must have felt something. He opened his eyes. There was a roiling image within the mirror, formless, but taking on color, going from gray to blood-red.

"*That's* never happened before—" he began, startled.

Botello slapped his right hand upon Anton's forehead. Anton gave a brief gasp, then froze, his blue eyes wide, his mouth sagging in shock. Visible now, his aura writhed like burning silk in a high wind. Botello reached toward the mirror with his left hand. Instead of stopping on what should have been hard surface, he slipped right through into the churning red clouds.

Something within them suddenly seized Botello's hand in a death-grip. Yes, they would be eager to know what he was doing, eager to tug him back. As whatever it was began to pull him in, he forced a wrenching shift in the magical flow. Anton's aura went flooding from his body. Botello heard his cry of anguish as the man's consciousness passed through him, down his arm, and into the clawing grasp of those on the Other Side. Then Botello cried out himself as he fled from Cadmus's body, diving blindly into Anton's empty vessel.

He crashed heavily to the stone floor. Disoriented, fighting nausea, he desperately tried to locate Cadmus. There. Over there, swaying, looking dazed. Fully conscious again Cadmus Burkus stared down, stupefied, at the mirror and at his arm, which was lost in the soft surface up to his elbow.

Yelling panic, Cadmus wrested himself free, twisting and falling. While he tried to sort himself out, Botello used the time to stagger to his feet. He could barely see the images in the mirror, only a blurred impression of blood and fire and . . . yes, he could hear Anton's screams now. Not in his own voice, but that of the astral body Botello had left behind in Hell. Anton would have a fine time dealing with the politics *there*. . . .

Botello flipped the mirror over, shutting off the noise. He gathered himself, peering around the dim room. Damn, he'd known the overduke had bad eyes, but the man was all but blind. It would have to do for now.

"My lord?" Cadmus now lay flat on his back, obviously exhausted and very shaken.

"I'm right here." Botello stood over him like a mountain. Smiling.

"Are you all right?"

"Yes, but what exactly happened?"

"It was Botello Darmo, I can't explain how he did it, but—gawds, my gut's full to bursting." Cadmus groaned and turned on his side.

Yes, well, Botello had indulged quite heavily at the dining table. Time to indulge some more now that he was in a body and in complete control of it. He was so very, very starved.

"Let me help you, my boy." Reaching down, he took Cadmus's hand. The man was a fool, but he *did* have magical energy, a goodly amount, and taking it fresh was far better than the stored stuff of the room.

Cadmus passed out long before Botello finished draining him.

CHAPTER ELEVEN

Just outside Botello Darmo's Black Room

Shankey held his lantern high. The handkerchief he'd left behind seemed to be sprouting right out of the stone of the wall. "Still there," he said, somewhat unnecessarily. He must have been nervous.

I understood the feeling. We were all twitching a little, except Terrin, of course. Botello's burglar alarms were still in place, first hitting us with the dragon-with-a-sore-head noise routine, then assaulting us with bad smells. Knowing they were harmless didn't help. Filima had a tight grip on my arm—which I didn't mind—and Shankey kept muttering—which I did. Terrin ignored all of us, forging ahead. All he did was to raise his arm once, and both noise and stink had ceased.

"Tasty," he said. There was a decided bounce in his step again. He must have been sucking down magical energy like ice tea on a hot day.

The distractions gone, Shankey trotted ahead to the site of the secret door. He tried to pull the handkerchief out, but it stuck fast until he pushed. The stone slab door swiveled easily. Must have been a hell of a good engineering job to make that happen.

Terrin had his own lantern and plunged inside. I gestured for Filima to proceed me, but she balked.

"Nothing in there but broken junk," I told her.

She gave me a funny look, as though she might burst into laughter or sock me one and couldn't quite make up her mind. "I'd rather wait out here."

"So would I, but his nibs will want you inside. Come on. He won't let anything happen to you."

She made a little sound to indicate faint confidence in that promise, then gathered her skirts up and stepped in. Shankey hesitated, like he wanted to bolt someplace very much elsewhere, then duty overcame desire and he followed his lady. Muttering.

"Day-um," said Terrin. "Don't you have maid service down here?" He kicked at pottery shards with his purple high-tops.

"No," she said, looking around, visibly shivering. "Botello never told me about this room."

"I just bet he didn't. If I had a hidey-hole like this I sure wouldn't share. But you found out about it, anyway." He shot her one of his patented, don't-you-tell-me-no-friggin'-lies looks.

She totally missed it, busy being wall-eyed about the surroundings. "Yes, I found out. I followed him one night."

"Through all *that*?" asked Shankey, pointing toward the tunnel and its defunct alarms.

"He dispelled the protections whenever he came down," she explained.

"Meaning you followed him more than once?" I asked.

"Yes. He'd tell me he'd be going for a midnight walk on the grounds or be reading late in his study or something like that. He expected me to be stupid enough to believe him."

Lot of disgust there. Couldn't blame her. On the other hand, Botello had been stupid enough to leave a raving gorgeous gal like Filima all on her lonesome. What a dickhead.

"Instead," she continued, "he would come down here."

"Can't see the attraction myself," I said. "But didn't he have a magic room upstairs?"

"Yes, but not like this one. I'd have sensed something of what he was up to."

"And that would be . . . ?"

"Nothing good."

From the heebies I was getting by being here again, that went without saying, but I wanted her to be more specific.

"Was this his scrying mirror?" asked Terrin, pointing to the floor and a scatter of especially lethal-looking shards of polished stone.

She nodded.

"Where's the table it sat on?"

"There was none. He had it on a stand, like a dressing room mirror. It was quite large."

"How large?"

She held her hand up just above her own height. "Wide, too. Like a doorway."

"Huh," he grunted. "Check this out." He bumped stone with his toe.

I dropped to my haunches for a good close look, seeing a few dozen small replicas of myself peering back from the pieces. In a normal mirror it should have been just parts of me in the reflections, but scrying mirrors are different. I thought it had to do with polarization and the material, but had never followed up on the idea. "What about it?"

"There's not that much here. I've broken mirrors before and they make a nasty mess. A big one."

"Maybe the rest is under the other debris."

"Not in this spot."

I noticed that there wasn't much broken pottery stuff near where the mirror must have stood. Then there was the body-shaped clear area right next to it. That Sherlock Holmes movie I'd once seen came back to mind. Too bad *he* wasn't here to help out. I'd have preferred to have him do the talking for the next few minutes, not me, but he wouldn't know how to push the issue to get Filima to talk.

"Uh, Captain Shankey . . . you got some armor on, don't you?"

He gave a start at being addressed, but recovered. He must have the heebies, too. Bad. "No, the house guard only wears armor on formal occasions."

"Well, that's a leather vest, isn't it? That should protect you."

"From what?" Now he looked as uneasy as his jumpy pal Debreban.

"The floor. I want you to lie down right here." I pointed to the body-shaped bare spot.

"Why not you?"

" 'Cause I don't have the vest."

"I'll loan it to you."

Terrin scowled. "Just do it!"

Shankey very gingerly did so. Muttering. Couldn't blame him. He made a good job of it, though, spreading his arms out to fit the space. "Like this?"

Filima's turn to make a noise, a soft choking. No fainting, but she didn't look well. It was hard to judge her color by the lantern light, but I could guess she'd gone all ashy again and then some.

"Was that how you found him?" I asked her.

Shankey gaped at us both, then shot quickly to his feet. "Found who?"

"Lord Botello," I told him. "If he died here, that would explain the floor's condition and those drag marks in the tunnel dust."

"My lady, is it true?" He turned a little ashy himself.

"I want to leave," she said, starting for the door.

Terrin got in front of her, not in a threatening way—he had his hands in his jeans' pockets—but his attitude stopped her cold. "Uh-uh. Time to spill. What happened the night Botello died?"

"I can't talk about that here!"

"Sure you can. This is the best place."

"It's horrible. I hate it!"

"That's just you; I like things just fine."

"Terrin . . ." I began.

He glared at me.

"You're freaking her out. If she's too freaked out . . ."

"Awright, awright!" He waved his arms. There was nothing magical in the gesture, just him venting impatience. "Lady, you are in a heap of trouble and so's the rest of this sorry planet. You wanna save the world, you gotta tell us what happened, and I mean *everything*."

"Oh, gawds," she moaned.

Darmo House, Two Weeks Ago

Filima had spent a fortune on the silken wisps of pale fabric that floated about her otherwise nude body like smoke, but had Botello noticed?

No. Damn him.

He'd simply walked out of their bedroom with barely a grunt of acknowledgment for what should have been a spectacular erotic surprise. She had yelled after him how much the outfit had cost, hoping to spark some kind of reaction, if only a fight. He seemed not to have heard and continued down the hall to his private study.

She executed a perfect dancing turn in front of her dressing room mirror, then spoiled the finish by scowling. Her face would freeze like that unless Botello likewise turned himself around. Thinking of the diverse effects of both honey and vinegar on flies she composed herself, attempting a more cheerful expression and didn't quite achieve it. Her face was somber and sad, like those of other women in unhappy marriages.

Dammit. How she hated being one of their number.

And damn Botello for losing interest in her. Maybe she should go ahead and let Lord Cadmus follow up on his puppy love crush on her. At least then she'd get some appreciation for her efforts. If only Botello would—

Oh, forget it. You're not getting any tonight.

What was he up to? What could possibly be more entertaining to him than an eager, hot, half-naked woman? Magic? She dabbled in magic to please him, but it always gave her a headache. What was the attraction?

He wouldn't be in his study, that was for certain. Was he going to take another walk around the grounds? Read another book he had to finish? What an insult to her to think she'd fall for those old excuses one more time. He'd be down in that not-so-secret chamber of his again. Not with another woman, either. Filima had eliminated that possibility early on. She'd know how to deal with a flesh-and-blood rival. His obsession with magic was something else again.

Her image in the mirror was back to scowling again. It didn't look good, but that was how she felt, dammit.

All right. Enough was too much. To hell with whatever he was working on; she was his wife and it was past time he realized he had to show at least a minimum of consideration to her. Gawds, he was more polite to the servants. If he couldn't scrape up a little respect then they had no business being married. She'd go back to the dancing stage and life on the road rather than deal with this kind of frustration day after day.

Edge-of-a-cliff time, she realized. Or, less dangerously, a crossroads. She'd come to one without being too consciously aware of having traveled. The last time had been when he'd proposed. Yes or no. Either answer promised to lead down profoundly different paths for her life. Right up to the last instant she'd not known what her reply would be. She'd finally smiled, blurted out *yes*, then they'd embraced and celebrated. What had prompted that answer? Oh, yeah, she'd been in love with him. She could be in love with him again, deeply, sincerely, if only he'd wake up to what wasn't happening between them.

Well, she'd wake him up tonight, one way or another.

Filima changed out of her fragile seduction costume and into a more practical dress. Not one of her newer ones; the basement and the tunnel were a filthy mess, so there was no sense in wrecking anything nice. No need for anything alluring, either. If he hadn't noticed her new sleeping gown, he certainly wouldn't be swayed by anything else in her wardrobe. She slipped on sturdy shoes, too, being disinclined to collecting stubbed toes while wandering around in the dark down there.

Thankfully, the hallway was clear. Good. She had no fondness for every servant in the house knowing her private business. Gawds, the whole town would hear of this brawl before breakfast if she wasn't careful. She knew rumors were afoot; Velma had told her as much during their occasional lunches together.

"You need to dump him and get back on the road," her best friend from the old days cheerfully advised. "You don't need to put up with that kind of crap. There's a hundred other guys out there better than him. Maybe not as rich, but better."

"I didn't marry him for money," said Filima. "Not too much, anyway. He was nice at first, really cared for me."

"They all do, honey. Once they get that ring on your finger it changes them. You're fun to start with, then sooner or later, if they get stupid about it, you become part of the furniture."

"But they're not all like Botello."

"Doesn't matter to you so long as Botello is like Botello," Velma pointed out. She was very pragmatic about such issues. "Like me and Anton. He's a good egg, but the moment he drops to one knee and proposes I'm out of there."

"But you could be the overduchess of Rumpock."

"I'm a person, not a title. No thanks. I like being his girlfriend, but 'wife' is a job with too many strings attached."

The trouble was, Filima *liked* being Lady Filima Botello Darmo. And she liked Botello. Had loved him. Could love him again. When he wasn't being such an ass. He'd been an ass for a very long while now.

Time to sort things out one way or another.

Filima eased into the hall, walking sedately so as not to draw attention from some sleepless lackey. It was past midnight and unlikely anyone would be up so late. Two back staircases later and she was in the basement fumbling to light a lantern with the candle she'd brought. She dripped wax all over, but got a good flame going. Not that it was much help down here. Why couldn't Botello have his pastime in a better section of the house? When this was done, she'd get all the servants organized into a cleaning army and make a serious assault on this jumble. Gawds, there was junk here going back for generations . . . but if she decided to leave then it wouldn't be her problem, so why waste effort planning something that might not happen?

Because I don't want it to be over. If he'd just wake up . . . I'm the best thing that ever happened to him. How could he forget THAT?

She found the door leading to the secret tunnel and hauled it open. It had been no great surprise to her to learn of its existence; every old house was supposed to have a hidden tunnel. But the adventure stories she'd heard as a child involving romantic trysts or escaping royalty had made them much more exciting or even scary. This stuffy foolishness was just another route to the stables, and a grubby one at that.

The secret chamber was something else again. The first time she'd followed Botello down here, she'd lost him, thinking he'd gone on to the stables to meet up with some woman. Only on the third trip had she noticed the marks in the floor dust, the hairline crack in the wall, and discovered his workroom. She'd felt both relief and annoyance that it was only a second Black Room for him and not a love nest. She'd opened the door just enough to see he was in the midst of some spell, then left in disgust. Well, not this time. There would be no casually dropped questions over dinner about his magical projects, allowing him an opportunity to open up and share—make that confess. He never answered anyway, poring over a book instead. Had she tied some pages to her body he might have looked up once in a while.

Putting the lantern down, she pushed gently on the swiveling door, peering ahead. He had only a few candles lighted and the air was filled with—whew!—that really horrible incense that smelled like burning manure and old socks. She'd forbade him to ever use it in the house. Even the stuff that gave her headaches was preferable. Fine for her this time, though; it put her in the proper mood for a confrontation she knew she would win whatever the outcome.

He had his back to her, facing the largest scrying mirror she'd ever seen. Why did he need anything *that* big? When did he get it? And how had he wrestled it down here? It had to weigh more than a horse. She stared around at the strange contents of the chamber and began to understand just how much effort he'd put into things. Quite a lot.

And what was that awful feeling of foreboding creeping up her spine? She only felt that at funerals when she forgot to shield her magical senses and could pick up echoes of sorrow and anguish left behind in the grave-yard by mourners for the dead. Filima lowered her personal wards just a little and the sad stuff gave way to something deeper, darker, positively threatening. The magical energy here was thick as the stink of death at a butcher's shop, anything but wholesome. What *had* he gotten himself into? She squared herself for the reckoning.

"Botello," she said, firmly, in a clear voice. "We need to talk. . . ."

He whipped around as though struck by lightning. What a look on his face, first a flash of abject shock, a guilty start, then he turned positively murderous. "What are *you* doing here!?"

"I'm your wife, remember? And I'm asking the same thing. What is all *this* about?"

"None of your damn business! Get out!"

"Don't you curse at me like that!"

He only cursed more and louder and the grand denouement she'd envisioned devolved into yet another dreary salvo-trading domestic clash, no different from a thousand others that probably took place every night in Rumpock. Gawds, she'd even played such scenes on the stage when filling in for ailing leading ladies. The make-believe dialogue had been much more clever then.

"You've no business here, so get out!" he shouted.

She stood her ground. "Not just yet. I'm here because this was the only way I could get through to you. We've been drifting apart for ages now and I want to know—"

"It can wait until morning. I've no time for this." He moved toward her.

"You'll just have to *make* time. Our marriage is more important than some magic experiment."

"Yes, yes, of course, but I can't talk *now*. Forces are at work that I can't stop; you couldn't have picked a worse moment to interrupt."

"What *are* you doing?" What sort of spell existed that couldn't be shelved if necessary? Unless he was into . . . the out-of-the-ordinary equipment, the smells, the unhealthy fuzzy growths on the walls, the feelings of dread, suddenly added up to disaster in her mind. "Oh, my gawds, Botello! You're not doing *sorcery* are you?"

"No, of course not!" He looked scandalized.

But he'd hesitated just an instant too long before replying. He never could hide his guilt from her. "Don't lie to me, I read enough in those books of yours to know the difference between normal magics and Darkside sorceries."

"That's just in the books, written by ignorant people too afraid to do any real research. There is no Darkside, only neutral magical energy—gawds, woman, just get out of here and we'll talk it over in the morning." He took her arm, hustling her toward the door.

She balked. "Not until I hear exactly what you think you're doing." She knew her man. He was clever about many things and utterly stupid about others. She'd blundered right into one of his more spectacular stupid patches.

"It's a very crucial experiment, and I can't waste time telling you about it. You'll hear everything in the morning. If I'm not in the right spot by the time the moon reaches its height—"

"Moon? How can you see the moon in this pit?"

He didn't answer, but shoved her at the door, rather too hard. She tripped on something and fell. Instead of a contrite apology for his roughness, he only cursed again and dragged her up. "Dammit, get out of here!"

In all their time together he'd never been violent. She shook him off. "All right, but this is the end!" She marched away, fighting an unexpected surge of tears. "You hear me?"

No reply. She decided not to look back. Nothing she

saw would make her feel better. She stumbled through the swiveling door and swung it shut again. It ground softly into place with no satisfying slam of finality. She was glad she'd left the lantern in the tunnel, else total darkness would have been her lot. Botello hadn't offered her so much as a candle stub, the thoughtless bastard.

Damn the man! Filima found a handkerchief and spent several minutes sobbing hard and blowing her nose until the fit passed and she was ready to think again. Leaving him would be no problem; she could stay with Velma at the ducal palace until the overduke dissolved the marriage. Thank the gawds he was an easy-going man about matrimonial disputes. And fair. Filima would be able to retain all her clothes and jewelry. No starving in the gutter until she was on her feet again. The parting would be simple enough, she had only to pack and go; no one would blame her. Botello's secret magical vice was enough to disgust anyone.

Sorcery—hardly so minor a thing as a vice. Dark magic was *not* the done thing among the Talents of the city. It ranked with the lowest of all common crimes, like murder and rape. She would have to tell someone what was going on. As a Talent herself, albeit a minor one, it was her duty to notify others of the possible danger. People who fooled around with such magics always came to a bad end, or seriously imperiled things for others. That was the whole point of Darkside spells, to purposely cause injury. It went against everything the Talents believed in.

But could she have been wrong? Botello was not an evil man, just full of himself. Always thinking he was right. He could have convinced himself that just one little experiment in sorcery would be harmless.

Filima was well aware of her own faults, the foremost being her willingness to give anyone she liked the benefit of a doubt. She was well tangled up in doubt now. Perhaps she had misinterpreted things. Before she threw away three years of marriage and turned Botello in for succumbing to a fit of bad judgment she had to be absolutely certain. After all, if he'd been up to something *really* awful he'd never have let her leave, knowing she'd go for help to stop him.

All right, she'd give him *one* more chance. Instinct told her it was likely to be one too many, but if he blew it, then to hell with him.

She once more gently pushed the door open.

The smell—make that smells—were even more disgusting. How could he stand it? They seemed to emanate from the rows of glass and crockery on shelving that lined the chamber. Some had small candles underneath, heating the liquids inside to steam. The fumes visibly rose to mingle with the fuzzy black fungus growing out of the walls. He was doing more than just raising weird mushrooms, though.

Botello had resumed his place in front of the scrying mirror. He wore a heavy robe of some kind, an absurd, oversized garment with a huge hood and sleeves that fell down past his hands. Why ever for? Other Talents she knew had no need of such props, but then they were not doing Darkside experiments. Apparently certain rituals required protective clothing. You didn't require protection when dealing with normal magic.

Too involved with the mirror, he did not hear her stealthy return. She stood quietly behind him, his taller, robe-shrouded body blocking her reflection from his view.

He was chanting. Something about the words, their pronunciation, the language itself made her flesh itch all over, as though she was crawling with tiny bugs. She resisted the urge to look at herself, focusing on Botello. It was dim in here, but she could just barely make out his aura.

Oh, hell. That couldn't be good. Black on black on top of more black. What had he *done* to himself? How could she have missed it before? He must have shielded that from her whenever he left this place, else she would have sensed the change ages ago. No wonder he'd been so distant.

He directed the chant at the mirror—which no longer reflected the dark room. How odd to see scrying working so well and so easily. It was always a painful struggle for her. But the image coming into view was not like the simple little visions of the future that she usually sought. Instead of a small, blurred view of something symbolic, this something was very large and specific and mobile. The placement of features made it a face, but not like anything she'd ever seen before, and gut instinct told her it was right out of Hell. The real Hell. The my-gawds-you're-not-kidding-it-really-exists Hell.

All right, she'd seen enough, more than enough, to withdraw from her benefit-of-a-doubt fantasy. She would run as fast as she could down the tunnel to the stable then saddle a horse to take her straight to the overduke's palace. This was too important to delegate to any servant. Whatever Botello was up to had to be stopped before anyone got hurt.

The thing in the mirror seemed to be speaking to Botello, using a muted whisper that felt like cold slime in her ears. Botello nodded eagerly, his arms stretched forward in a greeting gesture. A snow of black flyspecks flowed from the demon's—it had to be a demon—side of reality and swirled around the room. Some of them landed on her like cinders from a fire. They didn't sting or burn, yet she made haste to brush them off, calling to mind a protective prayer from childhood. Even as she quickly mumbled out the words, the black stuff drifted away from her as if repulsed.

No Darkside magic, my ass, she thought at the end of the prayer. She repeated it, louder than before. Neither Botello nor the demon heard. Perhaps the protective warding within its words made her inaudible to them. What about invisible? As she began the prayer a third time, a comforting counterpoint to Botello's previous chanting, she looked about for a weapon. No clear plan came to her, she only knew she had to stop whatever was taking place. For reasons best known to themselves, the gawds had put her here. Filima had never been particularly spiritual before, but now she felt absolutely certain she was the unlikely instrument of divine intervention. She would have felt more confident with a legion of ducal guards and Talents behind her, though.

What could she do? It had to be simple and fast. That unholy duet was building up to something. She could hardly see Botello for the flyspecks. They'd clustered themselves so thickly around him he seemed engulfed in a black fog. The stuff washed out from him in a slow whirlpool motion, beginning to fill the room. She was yet clear of it, but not for long.

Should she upset all the crockery? The stuff boiling away in them seemed connected to the spell. If their smelly contents were that important then the least disruption might stop things. She didn't want to get too close, though. A weapon . . . over there on a table with a number of tools, a big mallet with a long, sturdy handle and a metal face on the striking surface. Cold iron. Perfect. It was heavy, but balanced, and keeping up with dancing practice made her strong for her size.

Filima smashed the nearest container with a good solid whack. It made a fearful mess, exploding all over, splashing her dress. Thankfully the liquid wasn't boiling or acidic, but what a stink.

She heard a bellow from her soon to be ex-husband, but had no time for him, busy smashing two more jars, wielding the mallet like a broadsword. She shouted her prayer like a war cry, her blood up, the frenzy of destruction seizing her.

Smash! Wallop! Gawds, this feels great!

Months of pent-up frustrations lent her unexpected strength and speed. She'd nearly cleared a whole shelf when Botello grabbed her from behind.

"You stupid bitch!" he screamed.

She laughed at the name-calling. Once upon a time it had been important to her; she was above that pettiness now, fighting the good fight. Or she would if he let go of her waist. He lifted her up and away from doing more damage, bringing her around to face the demon in the mirror. It was the only thing she could see clearly in the whirling black fog, filling all her sight.

My, what an awful grimace the creature had for her, and it reached with a knobbly claw—actually coming *out* of the mirror—to take her from Botello. No, he was *giving* her into its grasp. *What a bastard!* Snarling, she raised the mallet high and brought it down on the demon's outstretched appendage. The cold metal head struck a blinding spray of sparks off its flesh, and a lot of things happened at once.

The close air of the chamber suddenly thundered with a howl of pure agony. Botello unceremoniously dropped her, falling away. The black fog turned thick as syrup, closing over her head. Instinctively holding her breath, she lashed out with the mallet, and was gratified when it punched a hole in the smothering reek. She gasped out her war cry prayer again, snatches of words she couldn't hear for the roaring around her. The room shook from it.

Filima staggered toward another shelf, but the quaking was already making short work of the objects there. Things jumped and smashed themselves all on their own.

Botello . . . where was he? Under all that black muck. It was creeping up over her knees. She waded over to where she thought he might be and felt around for him. Ouch, nothing there but broken shards and more muck.

Maybe if she disrupted the flow from the mirror it would clear away. Too bad she didn't know any powerful disruption spells. All she had was her childhood prayer and the mallet.

Not enough. The demon's face writhed about within the confines of the mirror, then pushed through, raging at her, all fangs and hot, stinking breath. Damned abomination, daring to come into *her* world and throw its weight around? Not bloody likely.

She thumped it a hard one on the nose. A burst of white fire. Another howl of pain and fury. More breakage. Where had that ass Botello crept off to? Just like him to run away and leave her in the lurch. She shouted his name, but again, could not hear her own voice.

Something stirred under the fog. One flailing hand broke its surface. So, he was hiding down there, probably smothering. She made a grab for him, connected, and pulled hard. He should drown in the stuff, but that would be too good a fate. He was going to face Overduke Anton if she had to drag him to the palace herself.

Botello floundered upright, blinked around in horror, and staggered to his feet. Shaking free of her, he faced the mirror and its demon, raised his arms and began that sickening chant once more.

Or tried to.

The demon suddenly withdrew itself, leaving behind a glowing red afterimage of its last grimace. Filima thought it had retreated, then realized it had only taken itself out of the way. It was her only warning. The next thing to fill the mirror was a vast rolling wave of that black fog, crashing through like a river in full flood. She braced herself against it, hoping her prayer and weapon would hold out.

Not this time. The force of the wave sent her tumbling. She rolled into a ball and tucked her chin down, hanging onto the mallet because she had to hold onto something solid in the chaos. She was thrown about like a leaf in a windstorm, all her senses crushed and overwhelmed by its shrieking force. It seemed to last for hours, with her holding her breath the whole time.

Finally she had to take in air or explode. She gasped once, loudly, and was surprised to hear herself. Her ears rang like Rumpock's famous bell tower at noon, but she could make out sounds beyond the deep drone that rumbled through her body.

Like Botello's pain-filled whine. She crushed a twinge of compassion for him; the idiot had brought this on himself, after all. Served him right if he was bruised black as that damned fog . . . which was no longer in the room.

She blinked, astonished she could see anything. With all that sound and fury the candles should have blown out, but they remained perversely lighted, their flames tall and still, as if in defiance to what had ripped through here. Filima had read and heard of metaphysical storms, maybe she'd just experienced one.

A shadow of movement made her look up. Just in time. The last shreds of the black fog were oozing through the otherwise unyielding walls of the chamber, leaving behind a layer of shriveled fungus.

"Oh, no . . ." whispered Botello. "Oh, nooooo. . . ."

She looked where he was looking: at the mirror. No demon. In its place was a blood-red swirling with a black hole in the middle, like bathwater spinning down a drain. A sound like rising wind came from it.

Not again.

She'd had her fill of otherworldly weather. Time to shut the damn door and be done.

Using the mallet to push herself up, she stalked toward the mirror. Botello was just beginning to stand as well and was in her path. Filima started to push him aside when the red vortex emerged from the mirror like a waterspout. She ducked and rolled as it lashed at her. The hot breeze of it tugged her body, but ultimately passed her over.

Botello made a dash for the door. His movement seemed to attract the thing, which whipped at him fast as lightning. It caught at his feet, crept up to his waist, and pulled him toward the mirror. He screamed and fought, kicking and hitting with his fists to no effect. He frantically called to her.

Filima uncoiled and struck out with the mallet, aiming for the fattest part of the flow. The streaming thing was like a snake made of air. She could halt its spin, but only for an instant before it recoiled and reformed, still carrying Botello.

She struck again. No effect. It slowed, but did not stop. Now Botello was caught fast in its swift swirl. She got one blurred glimpse of his face, mouth hanging wide, eyes gone to pits, then he was sucked straight into the mirror. Gone. The polished stone surface abruptly shot through with a thousand cracks. Bits of the center flaked off and followed Botello. More broke away, tumbling into the vortex until little was left but a few inches of the outside rim.

Then it buckled completely, the edge blowing outward before collapsing to the floor. The remaining glass and crockery vessels in the room also collapsed, spewing their contents everywhere. Filima covered her eyes, but none of the stuff touched her. The force had gone out of everything.

The next sound she became aware of was a soft drip-drip-drip of fluid. She ventured a peek, gaze drawn to an overturned pot, dribbling out the last of its diabolic soup into a pool in a low spot of the floor.

She waited before moving, unsure whether the storm was done or not. When nothing more happened for the next few minutes, she cautiously stood, mallet raised over her shoulder, ready for further assault. None came.

Gawds, what a mess. And poor Botello. She could feel sorry for him now. What had happened to him? Had the Darkside forces he thought he could control turned on him? That's what they usually did to sorcerers in the scarier stories.

She made a slow survey of the damage, then caught herself, stopping and staring. Botello lay prosaically sprawled on the floor just a pace or two from where the mirror had been. Had the vortex somehow silently returned him? She went over to kneel by him, slapping his cheek with the back of her hand to get him to wake. His head lolled. His eyes remained shut. He was terribly, terribly still all over.

Oh, no. Oh, damn. Oh, everything.

Her ear against his chest, she detected no sign of breath or heartbeat. In fact, he'd gone quite cold. She felt the same, inside. Empty, too.

For quite a long time she couldn't think. She only stared at him, at the wreckage around them, and not one thought or feeling came to her. It was as though she'd been hollowed out and had nothing to fill the space. Perhaps it was a good thing. Thoughts and feelings were dangerous, painful.

She sat and stared . . . until a really bad muscle cramp manifested in her left calf like a spear thrust. With a soft cry she straightened her leg and brutally massaged the excruciating knot until it passed off. Little by little she became aware of a hundred other aches and pains such as she'd not had since her days on stage in the circus.

Tears again. Not a lot. Just reaction. She swiped them away, glaring at Botello.

"It's all your fault," she snarled. "If you'd just been a little—oh, damn it all!" Filima made herself stop crying, which she managed within a few brief, forceful hiccups. This wasn't the time or place for self-indulgence, she had to *think*.

Right. Botello was dead, his Black Room an unholy—in every sense of the word—shambles, and she was smack in the middle of it all. Whatever his reason for dealing with Darkside matters, would anyone believe that she had nothing to do with them? Had known nothing about them? It was one thing to go self-righteously marching off to the palace to turn her live spouse in to the overduke, quite another to be . . . here.

Those members of Rumpock society who were not near and dear friends, lots of those, had taken it for granted that she'd married Botello for his money and an easy life. Yes, there was *some* truth to that. Botello's gradual, but unmistakable, estrangement to her was no secret, either. They might think she'd killed him to keep it all rather than lose the bulk of the estate to him in a divorce.

Then there was that handsome idiot, Cadmus. Suppose anyone thought she'd taken him as a lover? Everyone knew he needed money, too. Yet another reason to get rid of her spouse.

No, it was ridiculous. She would go to the overduke, tell him all, and let matters take their proper course. If she could survive a fight with a real demon, she could get through the gossip and finger-pointing from the town snobs. Certainly none of *them* could have handled themselves any better. She stifled a slightly hysterical giggle at the thought of the brittle and bitter Lady Sweggmit swinging a mallet in defense of her side of Reality. She wouldn't know which end to pick up. Or gads, she could break a nail in the process.

Filima cleared her throat. She had to focus.

She stood and brushed herself off, feeling stiff and sore, but otherwise unharmed. No cuts or scratches, which she regarded as miraculous. Maybe all that praying had shielded her from flying debris the way it had driven off the black fog. She hoped the stuff had harmlessly dissipated.

Then a truly bad feeling overcame her. The foreboding she had when first walking in was nothing to this awful sinking of her heart. She tried to shove it away, but it wouldn't budge. Something had happened. She just knew. On an intensely deep level, she *knew*.

Several minutes and one staircase and secret door later she quietly emerged into the relatively fresh air of the Darmo stables. They were on the large side; she didn't have to worry about waking the lads who worked here. Their quarters were on the far end of the building. The horses didn't matter either. A few poked their heads out, curious, but none made a fuss. Strange. They should have been all twitchy what with the earthquake. Unless its row had been confined solely to the chamber. Bloody metaphysics. More trouble than they were worth.

Making her way past the stalls, she unlatched a door to the outside. Real fresh air at last. How sweet it was, but she couldn't pause to breathe; she had to find out for sure.

Filima hurried along a graveled path toward the wall enclosing the estate grounds. She could just make out one of the gates in the waning moonlight. Beyond the gate was blackness.

Her heart caught in her throat and wedged there.

The gate, made of iron bars painted white, opened directly onto one of the roads leading down a gentle slope into Rumpock. That road was now completely hidden by thick, black fog, which was waist-high to her.

Oh, dear gawds, Botello, what have you done?

The whole town would see it. They'd panic. They would blame her once the story was out. Never mind the dead Botello, *she* would get the brunt of their fear and fury. Not even Overduke Anton could protect her then. They'd break into Darmo House, drag her and all the servants out, and after they'd finished tearing everyone to pieces hang those pieces from the bell tower.

Filima dropped back from the gate, fighting nausea. It wasn't just her skin at risk, but dozens of others. Even if she left town this minute, providing the fog allowed her passage, the whole of the Darmo household would suffer. She'd just inherited the lot of them, was responsible for the welfare and safety of dozens of her people. Maybe she'd not been high-born into such duty, but she fully understood the necessity that the show must go on.

But how? Pretend this disaster never happened?

Hmm. There was something useful there. Desperation was a wonderful clarifier. What if she pretended to be as ignorant as anyone else about that fog? That was one way out. How could she make Botello disappear, though?

Don't even try.

By the time she got back to the Black Room, she had it worked through. Of course, everything hinged on her getting him upstairs without being spotted by any of the servitors she was going to try to protect. She could trust all of them to keep a secret . . . for five minutes. Not nearly long enough.

Botello was as she'd left him, sprawled amid the fragments of pots, crocks, and scrying mirror. His heavy hooded robe had indeed protected him well. There wasn't a mark on him. Brushing off debris, she folded his arms tight over his chest, bent his legs up, grabbed a double handful of robe and dragged him out.

It wasn't as hard as she'd anticipated. Fear was a superb tonic, lending her even more strength than she'd shown against the demon. Facing it down was nothing compared to hauling Botello's corpse through the tunnel, up two flights of stairs, and into their bedroom. The last stage was almost effortless as the house floors were always in a state of high polish, making it easy to slide him along.

Once the last door was shut and locked she had to resist the urge to drop over in her tracks. Instead, she began the unpleasant task of stripping Botello to his skin.

She stopped once to flee to her bath chamber and throw up in the tub there. That took some time. It couldn't be helped. She ran water to wash away her weakness, then wet down a towel to wipe her face. The same towel served to wipe away all trace of the noisome liquids that had splashed them both. Within an hour Botello was clean, his usual night tunic pulled over him, and he was tucked into his side of the bed. Clean herself in her tunic, Filima bundled their clothes—robe, shoes, dress, underclothes, the lot—together and made one last foray down the back stairs to the basement. In a brick-encased side chamber she found the incinerator, an ingenious monstrosity for household debris that also kept a huge supply of fresh river water piping hot for bathing and other sundry purposes.

She threw the bundle into the firebox, pushing it in deep with a long-handled poker. When everything was fully aflame, she hurried back to her room.

Now she could drop in her tracks.

But not quite.

She had to drop in her tracks in the bed, lying next to Botello. They may have grown apart in the marriage, but they still slept together.

Had slept together. That was over.

Except for this one last time.

There he lay, cold and still and so very, very, awfully and utterly dead, and if she thought about it she'd get sick again or start screaming. Yet she had to lie next to him.

Filima was known to be a late sleeper. While dawn crept up and the morning wore on, while the house woke and went about its normal chores, she would have to lie there for hours on end until it was her usual time to wake.

I can't do that.

So what if she'd been an instrument of the gawds down in the Black Room? Up here she was just herself: scared, sick, tired to the bone, and wishing the whole night had never happened.

But she made herself do it. The bedclothes had to look right.

She took care not to touch him as she eased between the sheets. It was impossible to lie still. Tremors coursed through her body, making her shake as though from fever. The release of tears she had to put off. Once begun, she wouldn't be able to stop and it would seem odd if her face was found to be puffed and red.

Unexpectedly, she dozed off. Only a few minutes worth, but enough to disorient her. For several seconds all was well, then memory tilted her back into turmoil again. She didn't want to sleep. What if she tossed and turned right over onto him? Ugh.

She got out of bed and paced and sat and paced and looked out the window and brushed her hair and paced and sat and looked out the window and blew her nose and paced and wished the damn sun would come up and sat and paced. Had that fog blotted out the whole sky?

When the agonizingly slow process of dawn did finally begin, she peered anxiously down at the slice of town she could see. The black river undulated through the streets, still at waist height so far as she could tell.

And . . . people were walking in it. She could just make out the distant figures of early risers beginning their day. They went about their business without haste, without a sign that anything was amiss. What was wrong with them? They should have been ringing alarm bells and running around shouting their neighbors awake and sending messengers to the overduke's palace demanding answers and action.

Unless they couldn't *see* it. If that stuff was strictly magical in nature then most people would remain ignorant of its existence. Perhaps only those like her born with a measure of Talent would be aware. No town-wide panic

to worry about, but she'd still have to deal with some kind
of blame. Best to wait things out and see what happened.

Someone knocked softly at the door.

She stared at it, her heart thumping hard. Who
was—?

Oh. Botello's valet. The man was under orders to come
the same time every morning no matter how late an hour
his master had gotten to bed. Standing orders from the
lord of the house. Filima usually slept through it all.

In about three seconds the valet would come in to
shake Botello awake. She had to *not* be out of bed.

In two seconds she'd dashed from the window and dove
under the covers. Her eyes clamped shut, and she
assumed a relaxed sleep posture just as the door opened.
She heard the man's careful tiptoeing across the room and
the rustle as he touched Botello and murmured to him
it was time to wake.

Far a very insane moment, Filima fancied she heard
Botello's usual low grunt in reply and the shift and creak
of the bed as he got out. That was ever her signal to turn
over and snuggle deeper into her pillows. It didn't happen, of course, but the thought alone almost made it real,
almost made her scream.

The valet called again to his master, whispering. Silence
and a long pause. Another rustle as sheets were drawn
back, and then the man's gasp of shock. A longer pause
as he made sure. Then he made sure again. A heavy,
groaning sigh. He retreated quickly and used the bell pull,
having the presence of mind to use the codes for the
butler and Filima's chief personal maid. Both would be
needed for the coming crisis. Filima heard the bells ringing distantly within the house.

Then the valet was on her side of the bed, gently
touching her shoulder. She twitched, a sleeper who did
not want to be disturbed. Mornings were not a good time
for her and they all knew it.

"My lady? Please, my lady, you need to get up." The man sounded very unhappy, pleading. She hated the crack in his voice, knew she would hate the look he would have. When she opened her eyes to squint at him his expression was such as to tell even a stranger that something very bad was at hand.

"Yes, what is it, Jules?" she mumbled thickly.

"My lady, please come with me." He got her dressing gown from a chair and held it before him, ready for her. His hands shook.

"What is it, a fire?" She pretended to struggle to consciousness. When did she suddenly become such a great actress?

"No, my lady, please. Your maid is on the way. But you must get out of bed."

"What is the matter?" She shot a little more alert, sitting up. "Botello? What's going on? Botello?" She turned to him. Had to touch him. She wasn't acting when she recoiled from the stiffening corpse.

No need now to hold back the screams.

CHAPTER TWELVE

Botello's Black Room, Back in the Present

None of us had anything to say for awhile. Filima was all talked out, hoarse and blowing her nose for the umpteenth time. Even Terrin kept quiet, which was a singular feat for him. Shankey and I exchanged looks, then looked at Filima, then all around the chamber, trying to imagine what it had been like during the big fight. And how it had been for Filima having to haul her dead husband up to their room. And for two solid weeks keeping up the show of the fiction she'd invented about him dying peacefully in his bed, all the time with that black fog rolling in every night as a grim reminder.

"Whooh," I muttered, full of fresh respect for her.

Shankey echoed me.

She continued, her voice subdued. "After that it seemed best to keep quiet and hope the mess would resolve itself. Each sunset I'd pray for the Hell-river not to appear, but it kept coming. So I've been scrying every day, asking for a solution, asking for a cure, asking to find a way to put it all back and retrieve the lost Talents. Then when I asked to be shown someone who could really help—*you* were there in the image."

Lucky me, I said to myself.

Shankey made an *ahem* sound. "My lady, if you would, I was wondering one thing . . . if Lord Botello was pulled into the mirror how was his body still here?"

"I don't know." Her head was down as she stood over that bare spot on the floor.

"That's easy," said Terrin. "What got dragged off was his astral form."

"Huh." Shankey did some frowning. "I heard those were invisible. Not tangible."

"Hardly ever on this side of Reality, but back then this place was so charged up with magic energy his astral self would have been more solid than Gibraltar."

"Who's that?"

"Sort of a 'rock' star," I explained.

Terrin snarled. Good. He did his best work while annoyed. "Hush up with yourself, I'm on a roll. Botello's astral bod and all the brain and soul and the spirit luggage that goes with it got sucked in. When the mirror shattered that chopped his connection, what was left on this side—his physical self—died."

"I didn't mean for that to happen," said Filima.

"Of course you didn't," I told her, moving in with a comforting arm around her shoulders. I was sincere, not just trying to cop a feel. "He brought it onto himself."

"But he might not have died if I hadn't interfered."

"True," said Terrin. "But you did and it was supposed to turn out that way." He was a great one for Fate and karma stuff. It was from him that I learned about there being no such thing as a coincidence. "The big question is what was he trying to do? I don't mess around with demons like that. They can be fun and all, but he was screwing around with them in a dumb-ass way. Don't you have any idea what he was up to?"

Filima shook her head. "I've been over it a hundred times, and told you all that I saw. I've gone through his papers and notes, but he used a personal code that would only make sense to him."

"You still got that stuff?"

"It's up in his other Black Room."

"I wanna see. And why for is it always a 'Black Room' for doing magic here? Why can't it be purple? Maybe something orange with green polka dots. I never saw such a sorry-ass cliché world. You people gotta lighten up with yourselves, no wonder you got a black river. That's depressing as hell. Po-loo-shun all *over* the damn place . . ." He led the way out, grumbling at shortcomings of all kinds.

Shankey stuck a thumb in his direction and asked me, "Is he all right?"

"Oh, yeah, couldn't be better. It's a sign he's in a really good mood. The more he complains, the better for us. In case you hadn't noticed, he sucked off the leftover magical energy in here."

"When? Was it like what he did upstairs?"

"Nah. Just a little finger waggling here and there, like licking the bowl to get the last of the cake frosting." Only in this case the bowl had been brimming. The magic energy that had given my whiskers the twitchy itches was all gone now. Still didn't make this place any friendlier.

"Damn, I would like to have seen—oh, beg pardon, my lady!" He snapped to abrupt attention.

Filima was one of those gals who could command whole regiments with the lifting of one eyebrow. She had both raised at us, evidently wanting to go after Terrin. She was all recovered from her great confession, thank you very much, and ready to do something else.

"Uh . . . yeah," I added, and escorted her toward the tunnel door.

The Ouerduke's Palace, a Hallway

Cadmus Burkus only gradually became aware that things were not right and not right in a bloody serious way. For one, he was only partly conscious, yet walking. Not the sort of activity that becomes a perfect gentleman even when he's drunk. One tended to stumble into furniture and walls and thus provide much amusing but detrimental gossip for acquaintances to chew over for weeks on end. No, if one was drinking it was best done under circumstances where walking wasn't required.

But he was not drunk. Exhausted and suffering the ill-effects of overeating at a rich table, but not drunk. Pity. He wanted a good drink, because instinct told him something more was going on and it was bad. Very bad indeed, as in a bloody, bloody *serious* way. So what made him still able to walk?

Ah, that was it. He was being helped along. The assistance spared him from collisions with furniture and walls, but he was rather puzzled as to why two people were engaged in such a triplet exercise with him. It seemed to be two . . . holding firmly to each of his arms. Males. Large fellows. In the overduke's black-and-silver colors.

What the devil was going on?

Cadmus tried to work that one out, and at the same time endeavored to fix his geographic location, determine the time of day—or night, as it was dark—and how he had come to be in such a state of affairs. It was quite a lot to do all in one go, and frankly he was not at his best. He was still diligently at it when a very beautiful young woman appeared in front of him, halting his escorts.

"Captain Rockbush, what are you doing?" she asked of one of the men.

Excellent. The very question Cadmus planned to voice himself, once he got the hang of talking again.

"Orders from Lord Anton, ma'am," was the prompt reply. "Lord Cadmus is to be confined for the time being in the—"

"Confined?"

"—in the dungeon, until—"

"The dungeon?"

"—until Lord Anton calls for him again."

"Why?" She was very shocked. Cadmus felt the same way. Hardly any of the overduke's friends were ever tossed into dungeons. The man was a somber sort, orderly, not given to arbitrary judgments. If you were jailed it was for a damn good reason.

Goodness, what could have happened to put the overduke off to such a degree? He always liked me.

"Don't know, ma'am. Just following his lordship's orders. Seemed very keen about it, he was."

"Has Lord Cadmus done anything wrong?"

Yes, have I done anything wrong?

"Wouldn't know, ma'am. We was just called to his lordship's Black Room and told what to do."

The Black Room . . . something really awful had happened there. . . .

"Lord Cadmus?"

She was addressing him now. Who was—oh, yes, Velma, that dancer friend of the divine Filima. Stunning girl, just not his type. Needed to have more money. Still, she was very easy on the eye. Might as well be gallant to her, maybe she'd turn out to be an eccentric heiress run away from her wealthy family to be in the circus. Cadmus managed to straighten, then swayed into a droopy bow. Not his finest effort, he critically chided himself, particularly when he couldn't haul back up again. It put her very finely shaped breasts within his immediate field of view, though, so he had nothing else to complain about.

"Cadmus? Are you drunk?"

He discovered he could speak. Good show. "F-f-far from it, my lady. Deuced tired, though. P'rhaps if you could direct me to a guest room. I'd be uncommonly grateful for a nice lie-down."

She bent to peer at him, then felt his forehead. "My gawds, you're cold as ice!"

Now that she'd mentioned it, he was a trifle chilled. Her hand was lovely and warm, though. He sighed and leaned into her touch, but overbalanced and the two chaps next to him made themselves useful by keeping him afoot.

"Take him in here, Captain," said Velma, pointing someplace.

"Sorry, ma'am, we're under orders."

"He's sick and in need of help. I'm sure Lord Anton won't mind a little detour."

The captain hesitated.

"Oh, do bring him, Captain, he's obviously in no condition to escape."

"No, ma'am, but that's not the point. When the overduke gives an order it's my duty to obey."

"I don't question that, I'm just saying do it ten minutes from now. Do bring Lord Cadmus in here and ring the house bell for the doctor."

More hesitation. Velma not having any actual authority was the problem. Now if she had rank or was more than Anton's girlfriend that would make a difference. On the other hand, Anton had a (usually) lenient manner about him, was known to be a kind man, and positively doted on the lady. She wasn't being unreasonable, and it did help that she was pretty. Cadmus hoped she would win. He wanted to get to know her better. She could help him with his conquest of Filima.

Filima . . . there was some sort of trouble connected

with her. Had to do with somebody or other she'd been
married to . . .

"In here," Velma ordered. "Please?" Stern but charming
about it.

Captain Rockbush yielded. Couldn't blame him. Few
men would be able to hold out for long against her eyes.
Cadmus found himself being half carried into one of the
many palace parlors. A nice one with lots of comfy chairs.
They let him lie out on a long settee. Mmm. Velvet covering. Very soft. Now if he could just shut his eyes for
a little he'd sleep off this not-hangover and sort the rest
out in the morning.

"Cadmus?"

Damn, she was slapping his face and shaking him
awake. What was it with women that they absolutely could
not stand to let a sleeping man sleep? "Yes? Ad yer
serv'ce, lady. What d'ye need?" He'd be polite if it killed
him.

There was some sort of trouble involving killing, too.
Was it that wizard he'd planned to skewer earlier today?
No, he'd changed his mind about him. Had gone back
to Burkus House to dress for dinner with the overduke.

"Wake up, man, and tell me what happened in Anton's
Black Room. You two were going to try an experiment."

"We were?" When did he go to the palace? He'd just
been up in his room choosing clothes for the evening,
anticipating an overnight stay. He was going to make a
quick call on Filima so she could see how splendid he
looked in his dress clothes on his charger, off to see
the overduke himself about high and mighty matters.
That would have to impress her. Cadmus had been
undecided about whether or not to wear his great chain
with—no, of course he'd rejected the heavy gold and
gone with the black pearl . . . um . . . and then something
had interrupted. . . .

"Yes, you two went up there not half an hour ago. Why

does Anton suddenly want you in the dungeon?" Velma's
urgent voice yanked him into the present.

"Oh, it's not Anton, but Botello who wants me there."
Good gawds, what was he on about?

Velma asked the very same question, then urged
Rockbush to ring for the doctor again and to hurry. "What
do you mean about Lord Botello? He's dead."

"Only bodily displaced," Cadmus corrected. He winced,
vaguely recalling an evil memory of getting psychically
shocked by a not-so-dead man whose present residence
was Hell. Pity the bastard couldn't stay there. Hadn't
stayed there. Leaping about like a locust he was. And as
hungry. "He's being very difficult about it, too. Wish he'd
leave me alone."

"Who? Anton or Botello?"

"Both. Though it's mostly Botello. You haven't any cold
mint tea have you? Dinner was lovely, but left me rather
too full—"

"What are you talking about, Cadmus?"

"Mint tea. Good for the belly—I mean digestion. I do
beg your pardon. Didn't mean to go all vulgar. Do say
you'll forgive me."

"Delirious?" suggested Captain Rockbush somewhere
above him. "It's that or drunk and he don't smell drunk.
More like rotten eggs."

"You got that, too?" Velma again. "It's all over his
clothes."

Sweet of her to be so concerned about his scent,
especially since it wasn't very pleasant. Cadmus really must
send her some flowers or compose a modest poem to
show his gratitude. Nothing too elaborate, mustn't give
the overduke cause for jealousy or Filima the idea that
she had been displaced.

Displaced . . . now Filima's husband was quite another
matter on that topic. But Botello wasn't her husband now
that he was—for all practical purposes on this side of

Reality—dead. The mourners stuffed his body in the Darmo crypt, had a drink to his memory, and that should have been the end of the business, but the bastard just couldn't leave well enough alone. He should stay decently dead and let his dear widow move on with her life. If she was called his widow, what was Botello's designation of relation to her now? Was there a name for it besides "the deceased"? Might make for an interesting conversation some rainy evening. Just not with Filima.

"Cadmus!"

More shaking.

"Yes, m'lady, right here, at yer serv'ce."

"What's that rotten egg smell?"

Mmm? Was that a trick question? Or were they playing Riddle or Diddle? He always liked the game. Usually won.

"Doctor, thank goodness!"

Someone else had joined the party. Cadmus hoped to now be excused from the gaming circle so he could nap, but it was not to be. He found himself being poked, thumped, his heart listened to, his eyelids pried open, and his ears assaulted with questions. Shouted questions.

"Not so loud, if you please, I'm not deaf," he complained.

"Then wake yourself, Lord Cadmus," the man bellowed.

Damned if I will, so there! Cadmus purposely shut his eyes. The intrusion abated for a moment then he abruptly and nastily breathed in the most horrid, acidic, pungent, oh-my-gawds-get-that-away-from-me, stinging, nose-burning *stench*.

"Argh! Agh! Foo!" he cried, trying to wave it off. He sat bolt upright and stared around. The inventory of the room, besides the plush furniture, included Velma, two guards, and a bald young man with a squint who happened to be the doctor in residence for the ducal palace. The four of them stared back at Cadmus with varying expressions of concern, puzzlement, suspicion, and squinty satisfaction.

"Wonderful stuff," said the doctor, putting a cork stopper on a glass vial, the source of the smell. "My mother gave me the recipe. Good for all kinds of hystericals."

"I am not given to hysterics," Cadmus said, a trifle archly.

"No, but you weren't at all well. Bit of mental wandering, sir. Not the done thing in polite society."

"Oh, that's different, then." Cadmus instantly understood. This doctor fellow seemed a man after his own heart. Perhaps he'd had similar schooling in gentlemanly graces.

"You said some very interesting things, though. Would you mind explaining them to us?"

"I should be delighted, sir. And lady." He nodded at Velma. "If you would be so kind as to jog my memory, just the smallest nudge will do." He hoped. Something was stirring in Rumpock. Had to do with a dream or nightmare, only he'd been awake. Overduke Anton was— was . . .

Cadmus shot to his feet. *"Oh, my GAWDS!"*

Darmo House, Botello's Other Black Room

Terrin had fired up enough candles for a pope's birthday cake. When you're cut off from a culture with electricity all over the place, you miss the truly useful things like lightbulbs. We could have employed a bank of them here, the kind they put in baseball stadiums for night games. It would have made a good stab against the gloom of Botello Darmo's other sanctum. Though not underground, it was just as dark and seemed all the more disturbing for being behind an ordinary door.

Instead of using a free-standing pavilion, he'd shrouded a small interior room entirely with the trendy black velvet—layers and layers of it. So much that I wanted to own stock in the town's fabric concession and maybe go down in Rumpock history as the dude who invented their first vacuum cleaner. There was enough dust in here to dress an Okie set for a remake of *The Grapes of Wrath.*

"Whuuaa—aahhh—choooo!" was my first comment when we all crowded inside. Shankey thoughtfully loaned me a handkerchief. From the crumpling it was the one he'd jammed in the swiveling tunnel door. I used it anyway, so thoroughly that he told me to keep it.

While I wiped my nose and sneezed, Terrin and Filima got busy at a paper-blanketed formation that might have served as a work desk. It was so buried under books and other office-style clutter I couldn't tell. The dust got worse for their excavations, but I stuck it out until Filima, who already had a head start on nasal problems with her recent crying, called a sniffling retreat.

Terrin, apparently immune, stayed behind as the rest of us emerged into the hall. Filima and I then had a brief sneezing, nose-blowing contest, which I won, but only because my facial anatomy gave me a larger practice field.

"What a mess," she complained. "No wonder he forbade me to ever go in there. It wasn't because he had secrets, he just knew the first thing I'd do would be to call in the cleaning maids."

"He had secrets all right," I said. "Didn't you feel the magical energy?"

She nodded.

But Shankey shook his head like a guy trying hard to get a joke. "It gave me the creeps. Is that what magic feels like?"

"*His* kind." Meaning Botello, who had a very negative style.

My nose was clear now, and since Shankey was absolutely unaffected by the dust I got the idea that we'd run into another type of burglar alarm, one directed specifically at those sensitive to magic. Botello was looking to be a little more brainy than I'd estimated, or at least subtle. A non-practitioner would find nothing of interest or sense in the arcane books and papers. The ones who might would be so busy with allergy symptoms times twenty they'd be forced to leave. He'd probably worked a neutralizer into the spell so as to exclude himself. Terrin should have been forced out by now, but he was a special case, being a lot more powerful than Botello to the point of taking advantage of things.

"Dark magic," Shankey muttered.

"Don't worry. By the time Terrin's done the room will be sucked clean."

"But if it's a dark conjuring, won't that be bad for him?"

"Not Terrin. He's weird that way. Black, white, gray, green with orange polka dots, magic's all the same to him. He's trying to recover what's been drained out of him." Which could amount to a lot of whammy juice. He'd been seriously bad off earlier today. I hoped he'd get enough stored to allow us to split this world, but not so soon that we couldn't help Filima.

She brushed at dust clinging to her sleeves, but from her expression her mind was on something else. Breaking off in mid-swipe, she fixed Shankey with her gaze. Uh-oh.

"Captain, I have a very serious request to ask of you."

He did that coming-to-attention thing again. "My lady."

"A request, not an order."

Shankey went to an at-ease posture. "Ma'am?"

"It's to do with all that I spoke of downstairs in that awful room. I'm asking if you would not say anything about it to anyone until and unless I tell you otherwise. I could order you as your liege-lady, but I'd rather ask you as a friend."

The look that came over his face was a doozy. Right then and there if she'd asked him to jump off a cliff into a lion pit he'd have done it—as her friend. Heck, I might do it too, and I wasn't at all ready to commit to a relationship.

"My lady honors me," he said, pretty humble.

"Will you?"

"Yes, my lady. What was said in that room stays there. I understand the consequences."

"It's for Darmo House, not me."

"It's for all of us," he said, solemn.

If I hadn't known he was already involved with the house cook I'd have told them to get a room. Speaking of cooks . . . "Now that that's out of the way, how 'bout some food?" I suggested brightly.

They stared, but what the hey, I hadn't eaten since lunch, just some nibbles from Terrin's tray. Huge as it was, I'd finally used it up, especially in the last hour or so. Trudging through tunnels and listening to harrowing stories about fighting demons does that to me.

"But we don't have time to eat," said Filima.

"Where'd you get that?" I wanted to know. Tense lady, but she had good reason. She needed to relax; we all did. I opened the door to the room.

Terrin was seated before the pile of arcane stuff, focused on paperwork. There was noticeably less dust, and by half-closing my eyes I could make out a thin but steady stream of minute specks swirling into a spot between his shoulder blades. They swirled into it like water down a drain, going right through his Hawaiian shirt and the T-shirt he wore under it. He had a special tattoo on his back, which was linked to his magic, of course, like everything else about him. Some days it was hard to tell if he was dedicated, driven, or just filling in time between techno-raves and getting laid. Right now it was business as usual. "Dude . . . you gonna be awhile?"

He gave a grouchy grunt that could have meant anything.

"Ooo-kay. We'll be in the kitchen when you're done."

Grunt. Of the "don't bother me" variety.

"Boy, is he in a chatty mood," I said to them, pulling the door shut. "Thought he never would button it. Come on, I need a beer-and-pizza fix."

"What's pizza?" asked Shankey.

The Ouerduke's Palace, a Parlor

"Orders is orders ma'am," said Captain Rockbush stoically. "His lordship is the only one who can revoke 'em."

"But if what we heard is true, then it was *not* Lord Anton who gave those orders," Velma patiently argued.

"I was there, ma'am, I oughter know Lord Anton from Lord Botello, who was a sight shorter and dead these two weeks."

"But Lord Anton has been possessed by Botello!"

"Perhaps so, ma'am, but it's not my place to make that judgment. Besides, this here Lord Cadmus might be telling you a tale so as to make an escape. I will afford that it is very original. I've not heard better."

"But he positively reeks of sulfur—doesn't that tell you something?"

"Only that Lord Anton was at work in his Black Room. Maybe he had call for sulfur in his magics. Or rotten eggs. Not my place to make inquiries into his business, ma'am."

Cadmus, sitting on the edge of one of the comfy chairs, buried his head in his hands and groaned. "It's all right, Velma. This is the price of my trusting the wrong man. My gawds, a dead man at that. And they say the dead don't lie."

The other guard, posted at the door by Rockbush, stifled a snort of reaction. Whether it was amusement or derision was hard to say. Rockbush was rather more conscious of his training in palace deportment and shot him a glare. The doctor stood by a window, looking squintily thoughtful.

"Perhaps Lord Perdle might be of assistance," he suggested.

"Maybe," said Velma. "But he's not here in the palace. It would be very hard to convince him that anything was off with Anton, either. Perdle's a good minister, but doesn't have a lot of imagination."

"I'm really very, very sorry," Cadmus moaned. "I know it won't help, but there it is."

"I'm sure someone will forgive you," she said, not too consolingly. "But right now we need a way of putting Anton back where he belongs."

"No question about it. With Botello pretending to be overduke there's all manner of mischief he can get up to."

"I'm more concerned about getting Anton out of Hell," she snapped.

Cadmus winced. "Um, yes, sorry. That must be our first course of action."

"So what do we do?" she demanded.

He opened his mouth, but no brilliant solution came out. He tried thinking a bit, but came up empty there, as well. Had the few hours he'd spent in a mindlock destroyed his ability to reason? Impossible. Cadmus was fully aware and awake now and trying hard not to shiver as various possibilities about his own immediate future came unbidden to him. Those were gruesomely clear. Nearly all had him wasting away in a dungeon bound up in different kinds of torture devices; the rest had to do with quicker modes of death. It was one thing to hear about the stuff when at a party with a ghost story theme, quite another to face the prospect of learning about them firsthand. Botello would want this inconvenient witness quite thoroughly gone.

"Logically," said the doctor, "we must confront Lord Anton—that is to say Botello. If he is Botello. Are you sure?"

"Abundantly so, my dear fellow," Cadmus answered. "He will deny all, though."

"Certainly he would, whether or not what you told us is true. But the motivation behind the denial will be different for each man. If he is Lord Anton he will have one sort of reaction. If he is Lord Botello, another. But how to determine which is which? Perhaps the lady would be able to shed some light should she be a witness to—"

"Forget it," said Velma. "Let's just assume he's Botello and take it from there, 'cause if he's really Anton it's gonna be easier to get forgiveness than permission."

"Permission to do what?"

"I don't know! Cadmus has all the magic training, ask him."

Cadmus groaned again. "Magic training, but no magic. He scraped me clean."

"What?"

"It's all gone. I can feel it inside, that is, I can't feel it inside. This happened to me once before when I had a really bad cold, was flat on my back for weeks. Though I got well again physically I was still recovering astrally. Took me months to build up to full magical strength again."

"Indeed," said the doctor. "I've heard the same complaint from other Talents; physical ills and even pregnancy affects their working powers. What about now?"

"Now?"

"Recovering what you've lost."

"That's the dodgy bit; there's no magical energy to be had. Botello's drained it all away."

"All of it?"

"Yes! That's why there are no Talents left in Rumpock!"

"That's not just a rumor?"

"No! The Talents who were in town the night the Hellriver first rolled through were gone by morning. He never told me what happened to them, but I think they'd been absorbed into it."

"Absorbed. Uh-hum." The doctor sounded dubious, but lacking Talent himself it was understandable. "No one was reported as missing, though."

"Because of the river! It did something to nearly everyone's memory. Oh, bother. You believe it, don't you, Velma?"

"Anton believed it, and I believed him," she hedged. "But back to the main problem. How do we get Botello out of him and Anton back from Hell? Without magic?"

"We can't."

"We might come morning."

"What do you mean?"

"The dawn meeting of the remaining Talents? You and Anton talked about it at dinner."

"But *I* wasn't there. That was Botello in my body, remember?"

She nodded. "And neither of us noticed any difference in your manner, either. It could be real hard proving Anton's Botello."

Cadmus looked up, nonplused and annoyed. "You mean you didn't see anything odd about my behavior?"

"Sorry. It's not the sort of thing you normally have to look out for."

He bit back a very ungentlemanly word. Bloody Botello. Not only had he done a mindlock and impersonated him, but had been *good* at it. Cadmus hated the idea of being that easy to mimic.

"The meeting," reminded Velma. "Just after dawn the Talents are all going to come here. Anton wanted them to focus together and work out a way of getting rid of the Hell-river. They would either talk it all out or he told me something about pooling their power to help him get a really clear vision of a solution. Seemed like a good idea at the time, not so good now, unless they can put Anton back where he belongs."

"You'll have to warn them off or Botello will scrape

them out just like me, then gawd knows what he'll do next. He'll be the only one with magical power, mountains of it."

"There's not that much left," she pointed out. "And magic's not all that strong."

He gaped at her. People without Talent just didn't *know*. It was like explaining music to the tone-deaf. "Not on this side of Reality. It's more subtle here. But on Otherside . . . like in Hell . . . it's beyond imagining."

And evidently beyond Velma's immediate imagining. "Okay, fine, but Botello's on our side of Reality, so he'll be limited in what he can do."

"No he won't! I think he's going to have the same impact here as he did when he was in Hell."

"That's bad, right? So then we've really got to get Anton back. How?"

Cadmus was about to lose all sense of good manners and bellow out to her face that he didn't know, when a perfectly wonderful, absolutely *brilliant* thought blossomed in his mind.

But before Cadmus could voice it, Captain Rockbush clapped a heavy hand on his shoulder. "That's all for now, sir, your lordship's feeling better, and I've got my orders. Come along quietly, there's a good fellow."

CHAPTER THIRTEEN

In an Undetermined Otherside Location Not Quite in Hell

Overduke Anton was not a man given to hysteria. Life had taught him the wisdom of calm; it had been decades since his last outburst in childhood. He forgot all about self-control for a whole minute, though, as he tumbled helplessly in a terrifying, smoky abyss the color of blood. At any point in his long fall he expected to be dashed into something unforgivably solid that would silence his voice for good. Panic and shock required expression, so he vented them. Fully.

Then he had to draw breath, and a distant part of his mind informed him that he should have struck that unknown solidity by now. He risked opening his eyes a tiny crack—the blood-red clouds stinking of sulfur still unnerved him—to ascertain just what had happened to him . . . was happening.

Nothing pleasant.

He still seemed to be falling. It *felt* like falling, yet the clouds remained close, slow-churning about him, so they were either traveling at the same speed, or he was victim to delusion. Gathering his bewildered wits and forcing them to work, he concluded he was *floating* in some other place than his Black Room. As there were no cloudy red abysses anywhere near Rumpock, he eliminated one possibility after another—including visions, hallucinations, drugged kidnapping, and drunkenness. What remained he did not care for at all, as it meant that Cadmus had managed to shove him into an Otherside place, a not very nice one from the look and smell of things.

Look . . . by gawds, he could *see*! Never had his physical vision been so clear before. His circumstance was awful, of course, but the novelty of unblurred sight took away a bit of its edge. But where and how was he? He didn't feel right, not bodily.

His hands, he noted, were *not* his own. The fingers and nails were all wrong and the garment clothing him— he'd never worn this drab brown color that he could remember. The same went for the trousers, robe, and boots. He felt his face and hair. Oh, yes, those were wrong. What else? No . . . oh, *no* . . . not *that*. . . .

Fresh horror blooming, he grabbed his crotch, then sighed out gratitude. Everything was there, hopefully in working order. Hastily, he pulled up the hem of his tunic, opened his trousers, and checked their contents. Good gawds. That wasn't *his* wedding tackle. What in the name of everything had Cadmus *done* to him?

Before he could crumble into another bout of panic, there came a decided change in the sulfurous red air. The unforgiving hard surface he anticipated occurred, only he seemed to just *be* on it instead of smashing into it. That was good. So far as it went.

He stood upright just as the clouds began to thin and whisk away. Intuition made him do up his trousers again. He be damned if he got caught anywhere with his pants down.

Dignity restored, Anton looked about him with his sharp new eyesight . . . and promptly wished himself blind.

Emerging from the retreating clouds before him was a Hell-being. There was no mistaking it, as it looked exactly like the nightmare vision he'd had not so very long past. The eyes were the same; so was the voice, a squalling shriek like all the souls that ever died cried out their torment through its gaping mouth, as though trapped within. The demon was far uglier, larger, and smellier than the vision, and the earth—or whatever it was Anton now stood upon—shook as it walked.

It loomed over him like a great red mass of growling hate, then bared several rows of needle-sharp teeth, snuffling to get his scent, glowering down with fiery eyes.

Despite a profound instinctual urge to pelt away shrieking, Anton held his ground. In the vision he'd dreamed he could not run or fight. If he was where he thought he was, there would be no point attempting escape. No one ever got out of *this* place to tell the tale. "Hallo, there," he ventured.

The demon snuffled again, belched out fetid breath, and roared. A very unsettling sound. "You're not Darmo," it pronounced with dark certainty.

Anton didn't quite know how to respond to that. Darmo? As in Botello? What did *he* have to do with things?

"Not. Darmo," it thundered again, ominously.

"Er . . . no. Not as such." Anton didn't recognize the voice he used to respond. It wasn't the one he'd been born with, but someone else's. Almost familiar, but not. Was this how Botello sounded inside his own head? A tiny little inkling of the terrible truth began to trickle into Anton's consciousness.

Rumble. Growl. The demon stood tall as houses over him, burning slime dripping from its jaws. *"Then who the hell* ARE *you?"* it wanted to know.

Darmo House, the Kitchen

It was a good thing Filima had once led an ordinary sort of life, otherwise she wouldn't have been able to unbend enough to sit around a kitchen with Shankey and watch while I puttered and put things together for food. She had the demeanor of royalty required for her gig as the lady of the manor, but could drop it according to the situation. Anyone born to the life wouldn't have adjusted. She did a very nice slump with her elbows firmly on the table, looking all cute and adorable. I wanted to tell her that, but in her mood she might have slugged me.

Shankey turned out to be the snob of the moment, at first refusing to sit down until she specifically told him it was all right. He didn't mean anything against her; it was just his training. After I located and raided a stout keg we each had a beer and that helped things along. It wasn't as potent as Clem's, but worked well enough.

At this hour the staff was all in bed; we had the place to ourselves, and however huge the room, candles made our patch pretty cozy. Not a lot of light, but cozy. I had good night vision, but used my sense of smell more often than not to locate the needed ingredients for the feast I planned. Though Terrin had top cookery training, even he couldn't match my skill at made-from-scratch pizza.

As this wasn't the Earth I knew, there were differences in the food, but dough was dough and cheese was cheese nearly everywhere in the Multiverse. Tomato sauce was trickier, but I let my nose lead me until I found something like it in a cooler crock. They called it wolf apple smash, and warned that I'd need honey to take out the tartness.

I tasted the red sauce. Tomato/to-mah-to, a rose is a rose, and a cigar is a smelly leaf that costs way too much. *This* was what I wanted. "Just needs salt."

"Salt?" Filima was scandalized. "You'll ruin it."

"Trust me, this will work."

"What are we *doing* here? We should be helping Terrin!"

"Trust me, that *won't* work. When he's on a research binge just keep clear. You clean up the mess he leaves only after he's done."

"But I can help him with Botello's code."

"You've been studying it for two weeks, right? Not made a crack, right? Let the wizard-dude play. He's got the magic for it."

"So do I," she maintained.

And any little league player could throw a baseball, but not like Nolan Ryan. I kept the comparison to myself. One, she wouldn't get the reference, and two, if she did, she'd be mad at me for implying she didn't have the same level of expertise as Terrin. I was sure she knew that, but guilt and desperation to fix things had to be clouding her thinking. Now that she'd broken down and confessed all, she wanted action and to be a part of it.

"Just chill and go with the flow," I said, hoping to sound reassuring. "Terrin knows what he's doing."

He needed his space and isolation to concentrate. Sure, he could block out distractions, even hubba-hubba babes like Filima, unless she made a point to put herself in the middle of his work. As restless as she'd gotten that was a forgone conclusion. He'd turn *real* cranky then. Better to keep them apart until it was time.

Time for what, I didn't know, but I felt it. It was big and on its way.

Sooner or later.

Not now, but not never.

I'd have been bored (not to mention hungry) standing around waiting on *it*, though. Might as well have a snack.

My morning wanderings around Rumpock confirmed

that this world not only lacked pizza, but was woefully behind on the concept of delivery food, period. If it turned out we were stuck here permanently I planned to correct that lack and make lots of money. I could go into partnership with Clem since he was a friendly sort and had a good kitchen all set up. I could be "Myhr the Singing Pizza Cat, Your Order in Thirty Minutes or It's Free." Hmm. That might not be too cost-effective in a horse-and-wagon society. Have to come up with a different promotion ploy.

From the size of the measuring cups this place had a different system than Earth; good thing I never bothered to learn imperial or metric. I went by eyeball calculation and the feel of the dough. Shankey knew a thing or three about baking ovens—maybe from that cook girlfriend of his—and got a fire going for me. Man, back home I'd have had to pay extra for the taste that would come out of this kitchen and said as much to them. Though there were only two in my audience, I felt compelled to have a running patter going about pizza parlors back home as I mixed, rolled, and tossed. It kept Filima distracted. She actually smiled when I began spinning the dough overhead like a juggler.

I spread it out on a close cousin to a cookie sheet, poured on wolf apple smash spiked with salt, vinegar, and a touch of garlic, then loaded on toppings like sliced sausage, mushrooms, and cheese. Oh, for some pepperoni.

"It'll be great," I said in response to their horrified looks. Apparently no one had ever combined these items into a single dish before. I was the first ever to do so on this world and for many brave minutes felt a little like Neil Armstrong. My audience maintained the face-making shtick until I got another round of beer for the table.

"What's going to happen to me?" Filima asked.

I didn't think her question had anything to do with how

her digestion would react to the pizza. "In relation to . . . ?"

"When the town finds out what I've done. What Botello did."

"They won't," said Shankey.

"They could," she countered. "We all scry on each other unless we think to put up protections. I'm sure someone might know already."

"I doubt it," I said. "Botello had that spot shielded up the wahzoo or someone would have sensed it. The kind of power he was working down there would have been astrally noticed by someone long before you walked in on him. He had it locked tight."

Shankey agreed. "If anyone had found out, he would have stepped forward by now and spoken to the overduke."

"Unless it's that idiot Cadmus." Filima made a derisive *humph* sound. "He and Botello talked magic all the time, though I'm sure as often as not he came over to ogle me."

"You think Lord Cadmus knows anything that could help us?"

She shrugged, her eyes dull from the beer. "He's the honorable sort who would have stepped forward by now. He'd want to help out against the Hell-river. Even he's not that dim—except where I'm concerned. He'd keep quiet if he thought it would further his suit, I'm sure. I'm certain he scrys on me all the time. I put up protections, but he could find a way around them. Bloody puppy love."

"But"—Shankey shot a warning glance at me—"what if he's really in love with you?"

"I don't want to think about that. Poor Botello's not cold in his tomb yet."

Poor Botello???

Shankey was equally scandalized. "My lady, Lord Botello tried to feed you to a *demon!*"

"Which has *nothing* to do with me not wanting to get involved with another man until I'm damned good and ready!"

That would be about twenty years from now to judge by her tone. Standing behind Filima, I made a throat-cutting gesture at Shankey, who caught the message and nodded. He'd apparently dealt with enough women to understand when to shut up.

"Wooo, that's sure smelling good," I said, to change the subject. I peered into the depths of the baking oven. The crust was just starting to brown, the shredded cheese to melt. "Not long now."

Filima took a swig of beer. "Takes longer to put it together than to cook," she observed.

"And less time to eat it, which is why I made it triple-huge."

"We won't finish all that."

"No problem. Cold pizza's just as tasty. Ask any college kid who's pulled an all-nighter." If and when Terrin completed his code-breaking he'd want a sizable chunk of the feast too.

And speak of the devil, he sauntered in. There wasn't a speck of dust on him. He looked almost normal. "Wassup?"

"Sausage pizza," I said.

"Coolies." He sat at the table next to Filima. If she'd just look at *me* with that kind of anticipation.

"Well?" she demanded, eyebrows and voice rising.

He shrugged. "You want the bad news first? Or the *bad* news first?"

"That's supposed to be good news/bad news," I pointed out.

"Not this time. Got any beer left?"

"*Did* you find out what Botello was doing?" she asked, eyebrows and voice going higher.

"Yeah, and it ain't good from any angle."

"You broke the code?"

He curled his lip in disgust. "Code? You call *that* a code? More like shorthand notes. I didn't bother."

"But how did you—?"

"I just held the stuff for awhile and felt up the vibes he left behind. He might as well have put it in Times Square in lights. You guys are in deep kimchee."

"Terrin . . ." I handed him a flagon of beer. "You're scaring the lady."

"That's awright, she can take it. But one thing—that little tiff in the basement ain't nothing compared to what's coming."

The offhand way he said it pounded the point home. We stared at each other for a bad moment. They went pale and so did I—under the fur. It felt the way pale should feel, anyway. "Well, go on."

He slugged back the beer, all of it, and cut loose with a monumental belch. I swear the walls shook. "That's better." He leaned forward. "Okay, it's like this: Botello's studies got him into opening portals between planes. Myhr and I do that all the time when we travel, it's no big deal because I know what I'm doing."

I stifled a snort.

He heard. "*I* know what I'm doing," he repeated. "Your guy thought he knew, but didn't really. Most beginners are like that. All they see are the special effects, they don't get the wherefores of the underlying work behind them and only groove to the flash and dazzle. Lazy twits."

"The scrying mirror was a portal? Into Hell?"

"Give the cat a kewpie doll. Botello had enough personal power to open one and probably thought he could control whatever came through it. He was working in a fast and dirty way, not how you're supposed to. All those jars and liquids and junk were part of his conjuring. Amateur stuff. No real wizard who knows his noodles has to bother. It's a matter of power, will, intent, and some damned brutal training—years of it, which he didn't bother with—you get those four working smooth and you don't need silly things like props."

"Okay we get that, and that Botello was opening portals better left shut. Why?"

"Oh, *pul-ease*! For power, of course."

"Power." I felt a bit of a let-down. "That's it?"

"Pretty much. Of course, what he was after was a mash of Panavision, Technicolor, Cinemascope, Omnimax with Dolby Digital sound with subwoofers only elephants can hear kind of power."

I got what he was saying, even if Filima and Shankey were lost. "Serious shit kind of power."

"The most serious, shittiest kind, yes."

"Magic power?" asked Shankey, visibly floundering at what to him must have been a string of incomprehensible gabble-words. He was mostly right.

Terrin lifted his flagon for a refill. "Yuppers. Only kind worth having. There's just a few little problems: to *get* that high a degree you have to *give* something in return. The Multiverse is strict on checks and balances. Make it rain in one field, another one goes dry—those are the rules; you deal with them. Botello the do-it-yourselfer on a roll decided he was above that. He started small, like a guy who only snorts coke on the weekends, thought he was in control, and the demons he dealt with let him keep on thinking it. Then when he was thoroughly addicted to what they fed him, they kept upping the dose."

"And getting what in return?" I asked, topping off his flagon.

"Knowledge about this side of Reality. Anything they can use that might break down the barriers. They want to be here because Hell is hell. The more they find out about this side the more they want it, but hate it at the same time. The way other countries look at America. They want the mod-cons decadence—cheap fast food, blue jeans, and flush toilets—but since they can't get them, they gouge tourist wallets and blow up embassies. Copy for the evening news."

I looked at Filima. "You get that?"

She shook her head. "Botello found a way of bringing demons into this side of Reality? And they want to be here?"

"So far, they only managed it for short periods in his downstairs Black Room," said Terrin. "Crappy as that place was, it's *still* better than Hell. If that was all he showed them of this side they'd want it. Want it bad. Beer?"

I remembered the flagon in my hand and gave it over. "So if they got the idea that his room was just a small part of something better . . ."

"Then they'd want it *real* bad. They'd feed him up, offer him a sweetheart of a power deal, all he has to do is fix it so they can drop in for casual visits. That's what they'd tell him, anyhow, and he'd believe them because he'd want to believe. The way things are set up with the planes, demons aren't allowed to do crossings on their own. They have to be brought in under very specific conditions. The Powers That Be get *very* honked off with those who make the attempt themselves so *they* must have been paying attention to Botello's screwing around. That's how you ended up being the defender of all Reality, girl." He smirked at Filima.

"All Reality?" She seemed unconvinced.

"Pretty much. I wouldn't sweat it. Sooner or later everyone gets a turn and most don't even know it. Usually it's something subtle like holding a door for someone at the right place and time. Or not holding a door. That's going on all over so no one really notices. But— if something major is getting the balance out of whack more force is needed than a butterfly doing a wing-rumba in a rain forest. So this time they sent in a pissed-off, ignored wife swinging a cold-iron mallet like Hank Aaron on speed. Congratulate your fine self, girl. You saved the world. For a little while. I figure we got a couple of hours yet."

"Hours?" she squeaked. It was a cute squeak, but didn't suit her.

"Hours." I said evenly. "Then what happens?"

"Something bad."

"Define that, please."

He peered past me at the oven. "Hey, get that pizza out before it burns. I'm starvin'!"

The Overduke's Black Room in the Palace

Cadmus's contribution of magic energy helped Botello feel much better, but still not *quite* satisfied. He required a lot more power, not only to initiate what was to come, but to withstand the aftermath. Once he opened the Door Between the demons might not discern friend from food unless he had sufficient protections around himself.

In a few hours that wouldn't be a problem. The remaining Talents of Rumpock would come to the palace, singly, in pairs, in groups, all with the expectation of resolving the business with the Hell-river. There'd be a resolution, just not one they'd like.

Filima would be in their number. Should he scrape her out first or let her watch it happen to the others? Either way had its own appeal. Either would teach her not to interrupt his workings. "We need to talk. . . ." indeed. Bloody woman.

He began pacing around the room, wonderful new possibilities giving him a surfeit of nervous energy. Wonderful feeling.

Perhaps . . . he could send an escort to fetch her to the palace. The Hell-river would drain away her small store of powers as she passed through it, but it might be worth the sacrifice to have a private chat with her. He could ignore the curfew. He was the overduke after all; he could order anything he liked and people would jump to it. Lovely advantage, that.

Turning too sharply, he bashed into the overduke's table, nearly sending the reversed scrying mirror off its edge. Botello caught it only just in time, fumbling badly. If only he weren't so damned blind. It was like trying to see through overly thick, fogged glass. He'd have to find a way of correcting the fault, or see to it that his own body was manifested anew. There was no question of reinhabiting his old one. What shape it was in after two weeks of rotting away in the Darmo family tomb he didn't want to consider. While he was about it he could fix his manifestation at a much younger physical age, truly *fix* it. Imagine being perpetually twenty. He could be taller, too. And cure that lifelong nagging ingrown toenail trouble . . .

But later. First things first.

He checked his trousers. Well, Anton's trousers. Contents thereof.

Good *gawds*.

Apparently there were *some* compensations for being half blind.

Same Palace. The Dungeon

Cadmus decided that his situation—confinement in one of the overduke's dungeon cells—though bad, could be worse. The place was small, but thus far free of hungry rodents and obnoxious crawly bugs.

He'd had a good meal, even if he couldn't remember eating, so it would be hours yet before risking his digestion to the vagaries of prison food.

The delightful Velma had believed his story about Anton being possessed by Botello. She was a brainy, practical sort and would pool resources with that squinty gentleman doctor fellow. Between them they'd eventually come up with something helpful to their problems.

Captain Rockbush was out of the old school, meaning that prisoners were treated with a certain degree of respect no matter what their accused crime. He'd follow the letter of his orders and be polite . . . right up to the point where Cadmus ascended the scaffold.

Cadmus shied away from that one. It was one thing to run swinging into a duel to the death, quite another to coldly consider the idea of being executed. He was fairly certain Botello would have that uppermost in mind, only it wasn't likely to be a formal execution. He'd send some lackey down with a knife or garrote. Or see to it himself.

But Captain Rockbush wouldn't allow that on *his* watch. Being old school he would require no end of proper paperwork, even from Anton, which could take days. Botello couldn't hide behind the overduke's face for that long without someone noticing.

Sigh of relief. Cadmus was safe for the moment. Things could indeed be much worse.

So . . . now what? He frowned at the drab walls. He'd not been here long enough to justify scratching marks on them as had past incarcerates. Besides, he really didn't care to leave a written record that yet another member of the Burkus clan had ended up in jail. The family reputation was spotty enough. He'd really hoped to redeem it by marrying the divine Filima, fathering some lovely children, and raising them up smarter than he'd been raised. First and foremost: he'd keep them away from Burkus family history lest they take all those bad ends as a model instead of a lesson.

"Cadmus!"

The fierce whisper jarring him from his somewhat dented dreams had come from Velma. She'd changed from her fragile evening dress into a very flattering riding-type costume, all high boots and trousers. She might not have been born a duchess, but certainly possessed the good taste inherent to the class. With a better figure. No wonder Anton adored her. Cadmus got up from the plank bed upon which he'd been reclining and executed a superbly ironic bow to acknowledge his fallen circumstance. "Dear lady, how nice to see you again. So kind of you to brighten my lonely incarceration with the warmth of your presence."

"Oh, will you leave off the fancy talk, we're not at court now."

"One must keep up appearances, good for morale, y'see."

She came close to the bars of his cell. They were new bars and hadn't had time to rust yet. Not that this dungeon was damp. As dungeons go it was rather decent. "Were you serious that you knew a way of getting Anton back from Hell?"

Cadmus looked past her. Captain Rockbush stood a few paces away by a big slab of a door, his deadpan gaze well over their heads. It was an illusion of privacy only; Rockbush could hear everything, of course, giving no indication of what he thought of the proceedings. Cadmus supposed that so long as he and Velma didn't talk of escape there was no cause to worry.

"Yes, actually," he said, pleased she'd followed up on what he'd shouted over his shoulder when Rockbush and his man had dragged him off. "I had a positively brilliant thought on that."

"Then what is it?" she demanded.

"I suggest we try a séance."

Her face went a touch funny, and her tone went flat. "A séance. That's *it*?"

"As a way of contacting Anton; then he can tell us what to do."

"Unless he's too busy being tortured by demons to hear."

"There's that, but if he's not, then I think he is most likely to be in the best position to advise us on a suitable course of action. The advantage of a séance is that one does not require magic to obtain results. Of course, magic *is* a help. Otherwise there is a chance that whatever answers our call to the Otherside might not be Anton. I've heard some of the entities over there are very good at imitation and misdirection. Since they're not subject to the laws of time they love wasting ours, you know. Having a Talent on this side who can tell the difference between the overduke and an astral impostor would be handy."

"Yes, I see what you mean, but right now all the Talents are sitting around Rumpock roofs watching the Hell-river . . . except for Filima."

An awful thought occured to Cadmus. "What if she's helping Botello?"

"Filima? Don't be absurd, she has more sense."

He was suitably abashed. Of *course* his darling wouldn't dirty her hands with Botello's schemings. "Then we must bring her in."

"But the curfew's on. What do we say at the gate? 'Excuse me, mister guard, we have an emergency séance to conduct, let us through, please.'"

"Dear lady, we have the palace doctor with us. He has no need to explain himself. Just ask him to toddle over to Darmo House with a note for Filima explaining things. Or not explaining things. She might find them difficult to believe just written out cold. You can tell her everything when she gets here. And I would strongly recommend you both avoid contact with Botello. From past talks I got the impression he was none too pleased with his wife—er—widow, that is to say. If he saw *her* he might get the wind up."

"Don't worry, I know how to handle him."

"But it's not the him you know! Not Anton. He's Botello."

"He's a man. I know how they work."

Cadmus wasn't sure how to take that, feeling a vague need to defend his gender, but so long as she was lending a hand to the cause what did it matter? "Fine, now go write that note to Filima and bring her down here."

"Here? Why?"

"Out of consideration for Captain Rockbush. He won't let me out."

"Strange place to hold a séance," she muttered.

"Indeed, they are rather more associated with candlelit parlors, but one must make do. Now, *please* hurry along before Botello takes it into his head to chop *mine* off."

"You think he would do that?"

"At the earliest opportunity."

"Why didn't he kill you when he had you in the Black Room?"

"I wondered myself until I remembered some lore I once read about the energies of death. A lot gets released and transformed when one dies, and murdering me there would have disrupted whatever power construct he set up. He must need things left well enough alone for the moment. Probably waiting for dawn when the Talents come over."

Velma's gaze flicked at Rockbush. She leaned closer. "There's a little problem we have about sending the doctor to fetch Filima."

"Which is . . . ?"

"I already sent him out to warn the Talents not to come here after all."

"Oh. Then you thought of the emergency loophole, too." Cadmus had intended to recommend it at some point.

"Uh-huh."

"Well, that was very clever of you, but deuced bad timing. I don't suppose you could slip out of the palace and fetch her yourself?"

"If I have some help."

"I'd offer my services, but as you can see . . ." He gestured at his cell.

She straightened and turned. "I'll ask for the captain's assistance."

As she spoke in such a way as to indicate he was now a part of the conversation, Rockbush relaxed his "I'm not listening" posture. "Yes, lady?"

Velma told him she required an escort to take her to Darmo House.

He smiled and nodded. "I'll be pleased to see to it myself, lady. We can leave at first light."

She did not look overly surprised. "You must be aware that I need to leave now."

"Sorry, lady, but the overduke's curfew is on. Until he revokes it, or gives you a writ of exception, I have to follow my orders."

She gave a sigh. "Damn. I suppose you do. Even if the overduke is really someone else using his body?"

"Not my place to make those distinctions, lady. Now Lord Perdle might be able to help you if you're reluctant to speak with Lord Anton."

"What a marvelous suggestion, but Lord Perdle is not in the palace."

"It is a bit of a dilemma, lady." He was not unsympathetic in his manner, just tied by the restrictions of his office.

But Cadmus had enough. "Oh, bother! Let's have the séance here and now and take our chances. You know Anton well enough to tell the difference between him and an Otherside entity, don't you?"

"Yes," said Velma. "But since Botello is involved we really should have Filima in on things. She needs to know what her husband is up to. I'll just have to go myself."

"When you have a writ of passage, lady," the captain

reminded her. "My men won't let you out the gates without one."

"And if I should avoid the gates and sneak over the wall?" she challenged.

"Then they would have to arrest you. Sorry, lady, but they have their orders."

"Yes, one must have those, mustn't one? Damn and blast! Out of my way!" She stormed toward the door.

Rockbush made haste to remove himself from her path.

Cadmus called after her. "Velma! You can't risk arr—"

Velma, coming even with Rockbush made a very fast, strong uppercut motion with her near fist. She was quite a bit shorter, which put her into an ideal position to inflict the most awful damage to his groin area. Rockbush emitted a piteous sound—Cadmus winced in wholehearted sympathy—and doubled over. Without mercy, Velma struck again, this time with a flexible object she pulled from a pocket in her riding jacket. It made a nasty thumping noise upon connecting with the captain's head, and thereafter he ceased all movement.

"My gawds. You've killed him!" Cadmus observed to the abrupt silence that filled the chamber.

"Just put him to sleep for a while," she said. With some effort, she turned the body over and rifled his pockets.

"What did you hit him with?"

"A stocking full of coins. My mum taught me how to save my money and keep it safe all in one." She found a largish ring full of keys, pushed up, and came over to try them on the cell lock.

"Are you sure he's not dead?"

"Yes, I had plenty of oafs to practice on when I was in the circus. Some rubes just don't get that no means no. He'll have a headache but won't remember how he got it." She fitted a key in and gave it a twist. The lock tumblers fell into place, and she pulled the door open. "Quickly, put his cloak on."

"I won't fool anyone up close."

"So? We just don't let them get close."

"And if they do anyway?"

"Then run like hell."

CHAPTER FOURTEEN

Hours after his inexplicably ill-mannered master had ridden away to the palace, Debreban was still unsettled by the encounter. His evening meal did not sit well with him, either, his digestion being disturbed by all that he'd seen and heard that day. How a simple errand of following Captain Shankey around had turned into a major adventure involving catmen and secret tunnels and magic and grouchy wizards required much mulling over.

Debreban would have liked to talk it out with somebody, but the whole household was long gone to bed at this hour. Besides, he'd have had to provide an enormous lump of background explanation to his audience, which never worked too well in his experience. Better to speak with a person who had been there. That would be Shankey, of course, but he was at Darmo House, probably hearing all sorts of interesting tales from Myhr and the sickly young fellow he'd introduced as being a real

262

wizard. He'd not looked too terribly wizardlike, but it takes all sorts to make a world.

So Debreban tried to quell his restlessness with a bout of walking, hoping it would tire him out. He patrolled the grounds until the mosquitoes drove him indoors, then paced throughout the house. Fortunately it was a big square structure with an enclosed courtyard, enabling him to walk endlessly round and round without having to pay mind to his path. He kept to the upper floor, so the tramp of his boots wouldn't disturb the sleeping staff. Only Lord Cadmus slept upstairs, and he was gone for the night. Debreban could stalk the hallways to his heart's content, and did so for quite some time.

It didn't help as much as he'd hoped.

He partially convinced himself that the disturbing encounter with Lord Cadmus had been a misapprehension of some kind. Perhaps his lordship had received some upsetting news, causing him to be in a tremendous hurry to be elsewhere. That would explain his short temper. This did seem confirmed when one of the staff mentioned his lordship was off to dine at the palace. It did not explain the peculiar behavior of the horse. Though a fine-looking war charger, the animal had ever been as well-mannered as its master. Had he not known better, Debreban would have sworn a changeling demon steed had taken good old Whitestone's place. Strange how he kept trying to throw his rider. Lord Cadmus had barely been able to keep his seat, and he was the best horseman in the province.

Could he have been drunk? Not likely. Except at parties, his lordship was usually sparing in his consumption of spirits. Whether that was an economic stratagem or to do with the sodden demise of several dipsomaniac relatives was debatable. Either way, his lordship *never* drank while riding.

Yes, something was up. Probably to do with that Hell-river the Talents were in such a twist over. Debreban had never seen the phenomenon, but knew enough about magic to respect the concept. Magic was like air; you couldn't see the stuff, but it was very useful to have around, and when a storm was up you certainly could *feel* it.

That's how things had been in that awful tunnel. He hated closed-in dark places to begin with, and combined with the noise and stinks . . . well, it was a good thing that Myhr had been there to vanquish the bad stuff. Odd man . . . creature . . . whatever, but friendly. Why was it that Shankey had first thought him to be a man wearing a cat mask? Perhaps Lady Filima had seen a vision in her scrying mirror. Debreban did not approve of those. They were nothing less than an invasion of privacy. He'd been quite scandalized when he first learned of such devices. He was aware that Lord Cadmus had one in his Black Room, and made a point to avoid the spot.

Debreban happened to be walking past the door to that very chamber. He kept walking, and with some success quelled the creeping gooseflesh that was trying to take hold of his spine. His personal remedy for that was to mutter a childhood prayer and cross his fingers. There, he felt better now already. As usual, nothing leaped roaring from the Black Room at him and nothing ever would.

His confidence faded as he approached his master's private suite. The door was shut, as were all the others on this floor, but a strange wavery light now leaked from the threshold space. It had not been there moments ago when he'd last passed this way.

Debreban ran down a logical list of what might be causing the light, in short order dismissing the moon shining through an open window, a forgotten candle or lamp, or some impossible reflection from the Rumpock River. Nothing he was familiar with could possibly create that strange red glow.

The gooseflesh returned, rather forcefully.

Oh, damn.

He wished himself elsewhere, but it didn't work. Like it or not he was the captain of the guards for Burkus House, and it was his job to protect the place. Defending against magical threats was not specifically mentioned in his contract, though. Lord Cadmus should really deal with this. If only he was here.

Oh, damn again.

Hoping it would be something quite hilariously boring, Debreban drew his sword and cautiously opened the door. No reaction came bounding out, though the red glow got stronger, washing him with crimson color. He pushed the door wide with the tip of his sword and waited. All remained quiet . . . no . . . he heard a strange low hum coming from within. It wavered with the light and made the inside of his ears itch.

Bracing, he stepped in, looking around very quickly, wanting a few hundred candles to light the way and a host of Talents to back him up.

So far as he could tell by the lurid radiance, his master's rooms were in good order. A few clothes were strewn about the dressing area, but that was normal when there was a dinner engagement on, according to his lordship's long-suffering valet. Only the glow and the humming were out of place. Debreban eased forward to their source which turned out to be a huge dressing mirror.

A fine piece of art in a heavy, gold-leafed frame, it stood alone in one corner, and at first glanced seemed to be on fire. Its surface roiled with blood colored clouds, yet they remained confined inside, as though reflecting some other place than the dim room. He stared at it for some time, not coming to harm, but still nerved up.

The hum grew louder. Was it meant to be a burglar alarm like that dragon-breath sound in the Darmo tunnel? If so, then perhaps throwing an object made of cold iron into the works would stop it. His own sword wouldn't do, what would . . . a fire poker perhaps?

His gaze fell upon a long shape left casually propped against a chair: a sword and scabbard of antique style that he thought he recognized. Yes, it was one of the oddities of the Burkus House armory collection, supposedly a wizard-slayer because of the composition of its metal. Why was it off its stand and up here? His lordship must have had some use for it. No matter; Debreban accepted the opportune gift of fate and grabbed it up.

Weighty thing, but nicely balanced, with a slightly curving black blade that still held a killing edge. The pommel felt right and reassuring in his hand as he rounded on the mirror like a hero about to face down a long-sought-after adversary.

Of course it was all very well to strike a pose even if no one was around to appreciate it, but nothing happened. The clouds continued to churn, the hum steadied out. After some minutes of this they ceased to intimidate him. Perhaps he shouldn't even be here. His master might have cast some kind of spell to create this effect and would be annoyed to have it disrupted.

But Debreban's instinct went against that conclusion. No, there was something afoot that wanted looking into.

He extended his arm, very gently touching the surface of the mirror with the tip of the black sword.

Oh, my.

The clouds recoiled like a slug struck with salt. The hum rose to a high shriek and cut off into sudden silence.

I broke it!

Debreban fell back a step, holding the blade in a guard position, ready for whatever might rush forth. The clouds slowly recovered, only now there seemed to be some form to them, a roughly oval shape in their midst. Eventually he made out human features. Was this what scrying was like for the Talents?

The face—three times larger than normal—grew more solid, and though possessed of a red cast, its features seemed familiar. He couldn't quite place . . . yes, of course, it was Lord Botello Darmo. . . .

Who was dead.

Oh, damn. Again. A lot.

Darmo looked out from the mirror, his gaze sharp as a spike as it fell upon Debreban.

"Hallo there," he said politely. "To whom am I speaking?"

Debreban didn't have enough spit in his mouth to reply.

"Come now, man, answer. It's a simple question. Are those Burkus House colors?"

Debreban managed to nod.

The head, floating in red clouds, curled its lip. "Bloody hell." Darmo seemed to hear something and turned away to reply. "Sorry, just slipped out. I'm having trouble connecting with the Otherside. I think I've got hold of the wrong place." He flinched, as though in pain, then looked back to Debreban. "*Is* this Burkus House? Answer me!" Desperation crept into his voice.

"Yes, sir," Debreban whispered.

"Speak up!"

"Yes, sir!"

"Bloody—oh, never mind. Who are you?"

"Captain of the house guards." Remembering a cautionary tale with a particularly bad end featuring magical mirrors, Debreban knew better than to provide this being with his name.

"Where is Cadmus Burkus?"

"A-at the overduke's palace for dinner. Staying the night."

"No doubt. Is this the scrying mirror in his Black Room?"

"No, sir. This is his lordship's dressing room mirror."

"No wonder it's taking so much power to get through. Do you know who I am?"

Debreban did his best to overcome his trembling. "You look like the late Lord Botello Darmo, sir."

" 'Look like.' Wise reply. Oh, do buck yourself up, fellow, you're in no danger. Not yet, anyway. That's better. Right, now I want you to listen carefully, I can only say this once. . . ." His voice faded as clouds blew over his face.

"What?"

The face twisted with frustration. "Oh, bloody, *bloody* hell!"

Something on the Otherside happened, turning the red clouds pale green for a moment like a flare of lightning in a heavy storm; Darmo blenched in reaction, twisting in agony.

"For gawds' sake, *help* me!" he cried.

In the Streets Not far from the Palace

"That was very well, done, dear lady," said Cadmus, judging that they were far enough from the ducal gates to make speech safe.

"Thank you, but keep your voice down. There's Talents on watch and we don't want them reporting us," Velma said in a low, muttering tone.

He obligingly matched it. "Where did you learn such acrobatics?" Their recent flight from the palace involved slipping around the backstairs like ghosts to reach a side door, a hair-raising tree climb, some dicey walking along a swaying branch to get over a wall, and finally a jolting drop into darkness. It took Cadmus back to his school days and those occasions when he and the other boys found it expedient to break away from the restrictions of academics for a bit of illicit fun and frolic.

"The circus, where else? I didn't spend all my time dancing the oochie-coochie. I had a crush on a trapeze artist, then there was the tumbler, then the actor, then the . . ." She caught herself. "Never mind them. Which way to Darmo House? Everything looks so different in the dark."

Remembering that she was a relative newcomer to town, Cadmus pointed down a twisty, turny street. "This one. It's a bit of a walk, though."

"Then let's get going. Any sign of the black fog for you?"

Cadmus frowned into the night. It looked and felt perfectly normal. That had to be wrong. "Not a wisp, and I should see it. Botello did an excellent job removing my magical energy; I've no sense for the stuff now. What a bother. I shall have words with him about it at the first opportunity, I promise you. Strong words."

As it was very dark, she held onto his arm. That felt nice. Pity she wasn't Filima, but he would see her soon. All right, so he wouldn't be collapsed at her feet, a brave, injured warrior in need of tender succor, but bursting in on her with a spine-tingling tale of possession, unjust arrest, and narrow escapes from dungeons was just as good. He was certain Velma would put in a word or two on his behalf. She didn't out and out agree with him that his idea of a séance was utterly brilliant, but obviously thought it important enough to pursue. At any rate, it got him clear of the dungeon and the two of them away from Botello for the time being. Pity he had to leave his horse behind. He would have looked so much better galloping up to the Darmo gates with a fainting Velma in his protective arms.

Not that she'd have cooperated, but a heroic scene all the same.

"Someone's coming," she hissed.

He'd not been paying much attention and nearly stumbled as she dragged him into a small space between buildings. Holding his breath, he just barely made out the sound of someone's approach. Velma pressed against him—that felt *very* nice—and held her breath, too, going absolutely still.

The stranger wore boots, made no effort to be quiet, and seemed to be in a furious hurry. Cadmus saw by his faint silhouette it was a man, and one he recognized.

He stepped into his path. "Captain Debreban? What are *you* doing out?"

Debreban reacted as though he'd been hit with a hot lance in a tender spot. He jumped a full yard to the side, had his sword ready in hand, and gasped out a cry of shock all in one go. Agile fellow.

"L-lord Cadmus?" he wheezed.

"The same. Is there an emergency? Why are you here?"

"Can't tell you, my lord, important errand, can't delay, have to—"

"Errand? For whom? What are you doing with that sword?" Cadmus suddenly noticed it was the black-bladed wizard-killer he'd left propped by a chair in his rooms.

"Cadmus?" Velma emerged from the shadows. Debreban jumped again, just not as far. "Who is this man?"

"This is the captain of my guards, Debreban. Actually, I want to have a word with you. . . ." Cadmus turned back to his man, who seemed on the edge of bolting. What a strange look on his face, almost as though he'd seen a— "I say, Captain, has something happened?"

"Ah, no, my lord—"

Velma stepped forward. "Of course something's happened or you'd not be out past the curfew. Is there a problem at Burkus House?"

"No problem, lady. My lord, forgive me, but I must be going."

"Not until you explain yourself," said Cadmus.

Debreban peered hard at him. "And if I don't, my lord?"

The uncharacteristic challenge from a heretofore unshakably loyal man took Cadmus aback. "Well, I shall be very displeased with you, Captain. *Very* displeased. Now put your sword away and behave like a proper gentleman, you're upsetting Lady Velma."

Relaxing somewhat, Debreban abruptly grinned.

"Just 'Velma,' Cadmus, you know I'm not—"

"Velma?" said Debreban. "The overduke's uh—that is—"

"Girlfriend," said Velma patiently. "Is there a problem?"

"No! I've been sent to find you, to deliver a message from . . . er . . . someone." He finished up rather lamely.

"Who?"

"I can't say. I was told to speak to you and you alone." He stole a wall-eyed glance at Cadmus.

"Oh, very well," said Cadmus, taking the hint. "I'll stand over here and not listen, will that suit?"

"Yes, my lord."

Snorting, Cadmus stepped off a pace or two, put his hands over his ears, and hummed a favorite dance song. This was altogether a very aggravating situation. Shut out by his own guard captain. It smacked of intrigue or worse. Or . . . what if Debreban had a message from Filima? He'd been sent to follow her guard captain today, had made friends with him, too, according to that tavern keeper. What if she found out? Learned about his scrying? If it involved Cadmus she'd not want him to hear a single word. How bloody frustrating. Still, he was a gentleman, and ladies were entitled to their secrets. Besides, he could always catch up on things using his mirror. If he ever went near the damned thing again. Not likely after tonight. Hell, maybe he should just start sending her flowers like a normal suitor and damn the expense.

Velma tapped his arm to indicate the conference was over. He let his hands drop and tried not to look too curious.

"You'll never guess," she said. "He had a message for me from Anton."

Cadmus blinked. "You're right, I never would have guessed that. How?"

Debreban again displayed reluctance. "Lady . . ."

"It's all right, Captain," she assured him. "Lord Cadmus is no longer possessed by Botello Darmo. It's Overduke Anton he's using now. Anton doesn't know that Cadmus is free."

He shook his head and frowned, indicating a low opinion of the magical leapfrogging. "Very well . . ."

Debreban launched into a lightning-quick report of the recent goings on in Cadmus's dressing room mirror, which had to do with things they already knew: that Botello had traded places with Anton and was up to no good. Cadmus's questions bunched up so fast behind his teeth that he had trouble speaking in a coherent manner.

"So Lord Anton is all right?" he finally managed to blurt.

"Of course not," said Velma. "He's in Hell, trapped in Botello's astral body. That's very *not* all right."

"I meant he isn't being tortured or anything."

"He didn't specifically mention that, my lord," said Debreban. "I think he was being closely watched by . . . something. But he didn't look at all well and was in a great hurry to leave."

"No doubt. If it was truly Lord Anton and not some Otherside deception. Are you certain?"

Debreban had to admit to a shortage of certainty about many recent events.

"*I'm* positive it was Anton," said Velma. "He told the captain to remind me of a backrub I gave this morning as proof. Botello would know nothing about that."

"Backrub?"

"Yes. I happen to be very good at them. Now let's get going to your place."

"Not Darmo House?"

"Yours. So we can talk to Anton in your mirror."

"But Filima has a quite nice scrying mirror." He was not ready to give up his quest to see her.

"And a wizard," added Debreban.

That was unexpected. "A wizard?"

"Ah, yes, my lord. I learned about him during that—ah—errand you put me on this morning. He was ailing a bit, but I was told he's quite clever."

"Wizard?" Cadmus repeated, trying to remember the specifics of the day's errands . . . *Debreban* was supposed to follow the Darmo House guard. *Cadmus* had been told to go looking for wizards. Wizard. One with a cat's face on. So he'd taken shelter with Filima. Botello would be furious, but sod him.

"Yes, my lord. The wizard's friend is a friend of Captain Shankey of Darmo House, and the two of them were taking him there the last I saw. I was given to understand he needed to be in a protected area as his magic was being drained off."

By Botello who'd wanted to finish dining off the wizard. Greedy bugger. "Oh—ah—interesting. Then we should go meet the fellow and see if he can lend us a hand with this mess."

"I thought all the Talents were missing or on watch," said Velma.

"He's newly come to Rumpock, lady," Debreban explained. "Looked a bit washed out, though."

"But Filima will still have some magical energy left for us, I'm sure," Cadmus urged. "And a mirror. It'll be safer, too. Once Botello notices we're gone Burkus House will be the first place he looks."

"And Darmo House the second," Velma pointed out. "We'll sort it later, let's just get moving."

"Yes! Please *do* get moving!" a woman cried from a window directly above them. "People are trying to sleep, y'know!"

A chorus of annoyed agreement erupted from lots of other windows overlooking the street.

"Move along, ye bloody toffs!"

"Some of us have to work in the morning!"

"Have some consideration!"

"Call the Watch!"

"Plug yer flippin' pie hole!"

"You plug yers!"

Swallowing embarrassment, for a true gentleman never makes a nuisance of himself, especially in public, Cadmus seized both Velma and Debreban by their arms and hauled them away, double-time.

The Palace Dungeon

Captain Rockbush had a singularly unpleasant awakening. Not only did he have the most awful, horrible agony in his crotch and head, but the overduke himself was yelling at him for some reason. He had served in the palace man and boy for thirty years, and never in that time had the overduke raised his voice to anyone, much less cursed them out. Something was very seriously wrong. His lordship was positively screeching.

What happened, you dolt? Who helped him get away? Did he bribe you? Was that it? Where is he, you witless, brainless bastard! Where IS he?

One question after another hammered at him as he lay on the stone floor, each more insulting than the last. Rockbush would have attempted a reply, but was far too occupied dealing with nasty physical distractions. What had happened? The last thing clear in his mind was something to do with Lord Cadmus. Arresting him . . . then that fine-looking lady had come along and stopped things. Females just didn't understand the law. Took a bit to get her to come around, and then she *had* come around and . . . Rockbush groaned.

How had he ended down on the floor like this and in this condition? Obviously the overduke had no clue to offer, not with the fit he was throwing.

Eventually he finished screaming profanity and went away.

Rockbush remained very still and hoped his pain would likewise depart.

Darmo House, the Kitchen

Terrin had a gift for depression. When he was in the mood for inflicting despair and misery he waded in with both fists and maniacal glee; it was one of his great pleasures in life. He could bring down helium and not break a sweat.

"So," I said, "essentially the outcome is we die, you die, everybody dies? Consumed by flesh-eating demons who get off on death energy, terror, and destruction on a massive scale?"

"Pretty much," he said, picking a stray mushroom from his plate. He chewed on it, staring into space, exuding contentment.

This bummer news, I hardly need mention, totally eclipsed the historic and delicious debut of Pizza à la Myhr in Rumpock. Filima and Shankey ate a little, made some half-hearted yummy noises to be polite, and mostly stared in horror at Terrin, who scarfed nearly half the pie down as he talked of planetwide annihilation at the hands—or rather teeth—of starving hordes of demons who were likely to pour through onto this plane at any moment. I wanted to think he colored his narrative that dark on purpose just to have more pizza for himself, but the odds were against it.

"Botello can do that?" I had a hard time believing just one guy could wipe out a world that hadn't yet developed atomic weaponry.

"All he has to do is open the right astral door so the Hell-plane guys—demons to you—come rolling in to do their doomsday gig."

"Why would they want to?"

"Just because."

"But why?"

"It's what they *do*. If they were nice they wouldn't be in Hell!"

"Good point. And out of this Botello gets a bunch of magic power?"

"Which he can't handle."

"You know that for sure?"

"Pretty much. If his most advanced work has him still relying on props like that junk in the basement, no way could he be remotely ready on a mental or psychic level to handle the real-deal energies that will be slamming around out there. He'll get turned inside out fast, and that's only if he's lucky. If not, he'll get turned inside out slow. Let's open a pool on it. I'll bet fifty it'll be slow and they'll make it go on—oh—for a couple weeks, our time. Any takers?"

Shankey seemed to understand what he was getting at and scowled. Filima looked like she'd tuned out everything. As for me, I was used to the black attitude. And this after all his complaints about the color of the velvet curtains.

"You don't have fifty, in theirs or any other currency," I said.

Terrin shrugged. "When the end comes money ain't gonna help nobody, no how."

"What can we do to stop it?"

"Stop it? Who wants to stop it?"

"I do!"

He grumped. "Mr. Tree-Hugging Goodie-Goodie, of course *you* would. I'm tired of this incarnation. The Multiverse has been fucking around with me long enough, I'll be glad to kiss this life bye-bye."

"That's fine for you, but the rest of us aren't quite ready to leave yet."

"Hey, it'll be *fun* to start over. I've done it dozens of times. Nothing like getting burned at the stake or cut in two by cannon fire or—"

"Terrin . . ." The last thing we needed was a recital of his past lives and how they'd ended for him. Things were gruesome enough at the moment.

He laughed and sucked down more pizza.

"Anyway," I continued, "if the Powers That Be put Filima in the cellar with the mallet to delay things, I'm fairly sure it was to allow time for your arrival here so *you* could fix the problem. As you are so fond of saying, there's no such thing as coincidence."

"Prolly so. Just like them to screw me like that. I swear I might as well drop my pants, hand them a broomstick with a sandpaper condom, and bend over to make it that much easier." He looked up at the shadowy ceiling high above. "You *hear* me? I know what you're doing, and it ain't funny!"

"On the other hand, I seriously doubt this world is having an apocalypse just to inconvenience you."

"Of course it is. That's how things really work!"

I got a sudden flash of inspiration. "What about Heaven?"

"What about it?"

"Doesn't this world *have* one? They got a Hell, shouldn't there be a Heaven to balance things?"

"Yeah, they got one of those. I asked around. It's a nice one."

Filima and Shankey nodded agreement on that point, looking hopeful.

"So why don't we call for help from *that* side?" I asked. "Then we could have hordes of angels pouring in to stop the demons."

He rolled his eyes. "You ever see a real apocalypse?

They're ugly, lots of property damage, which includes people. You wouldn't like it, trust me. The idea here is to *not* let things get that far."

"Okay. Very sensible. Another question."

"Surprise me."

"All right. On one hand we got a bunch of starved demons wanting to vacation in this Reality. Why is it that there aren't a bunch of angels wanting to get in here, too, only instead of eating people they run around being nice to everybody?"

"Because they're in the Heaven-plane."

"So?"

"I'll put it this way: if you had the penthouse suite in Trump Towers rent free, guilt free, tax free forever with everything you always wanted right there and then when you wanted it, would you wanna visit a Third World trash dump to feel even happier?"

"I see your point."

"Exactly. What help we get in this Reality is the angel version of Peace Corps volunteers. They're dedicated types, and point the natives in the best direction, but it's the locals who have to do the work. If the trouble is truly over our heads, then *maybe* we'll get some kind of divine intervention, but don't expect it. The Powers That Be are a twisted gang with a warped sense of humor."

"Sure explains my life."

"And mine.

"Excuse me?" This from Shankey. "*Is* there a way to avert the disaster and save the world?"

Terrin slugged back more beer and belched. Yes, the walls did visibly shake. "Uh-huh," he said, then looked at me, smirking again. "But *you* won't like it."

That was a given. "Okay, what is it? Both barrels, don't spare the buckshot."

"You've no idea."

"We're all agreed on that point. What is it?"

"You go to the astral plane."

Hah? I blanked for a second. "But I don't have a ticket."

"Don't be a fuzzle. Think about it."

Digestion interfered with my cognitive processes. I was full of beer and pizza, having overindulged in the latter, figuring since it was my last meal, I might as well pig out. "I'm sorry, but I misheard. I thought you said I should go to the astral plane."

He tapped his finger on the tip of his nose. Grinning. Boy, did he have a lot of teeth. "Specifically, to Hell."

I was suddenly on overload with outrage and panicked butterflies. Neither combined too well with the beer and pizza. "What are you talking about? Did I hear right? What's going on? Answer the last one first."

"You go there so you can stop Botello."

At this Shankey leaned forward, all attention, and Filima sat up straight, coming alert. "Deal in what way?" he asked.

"Kill him," said Terrin. "What else?"

I choked, on the verge of blanking completely. "Kill a dead man?"

They all stared at me.

Well, *someone* had to say it. I waved them over to Terrin. "It's his idea! Talk to him!"

"You want to kill Botello?" asked Filima.

"Call it soul-death," said Terrin. "Just take him out of planar existence once and for all. Then he won't be able to reincarnate a generation or three down the line and start trouble all over again. I know his type, he doesn't give up."

"Isn't that kinda harsh?" I asked.

"Harsh? The guy is fucking around with ending this world, planning the deaths of untold millions, is in the process of ripping apart the very veils that keep the Multiverse running smooth and more or less sane, and you think one little soul-death to prevent it all is *harsh?*"

"I withdraw the question."

Terrin flapped one hand to indicate our surroundings. "You wanna save the world, snuff Botello."

"Great, fine, wonderful. But I heard you say *I* was going to the astral plane . . . with a side trip to Hell? No way, Jose. That kind of tripping is *your* department, as you are so fond of reminding me."

"Not this time around."

"Yes, this time around and for all times around! I'm not trained for visiting other planes. You've told me how dangerous it is."

"You'll be safe with me running the tour."

"That's not the issue. Why the hell are you even thinking of sending me?"

"I got my reasons."

"So share!"

He shot me an annoyed look. I flared my lip whiskers right back at him. "Excuse us," he said to Filima and Shankey. "Private conference."

He slipped off his chair and led the way out of the kitchen into a hall, then to another hall. Big place. He finally stopped at a window with a view to the outside. The house and grounds being on a hill, we could see down to some of the city—and the black fog flowing through its streets.

I crossed my arms. "Okay. Give. Why *me?* You're better equipped for that kind of thing, you float around the planes all the time."

"Yeah, but I don't bother with a physical presence there. To do what needs to be done requires a solid body on—"

"Wait, I thought an astral bod wasn't solid."

"Not on this side, and usually not over there. But for this job the rules have to be different."

This was way out of my league. "Which means you should go, you *know* all that stuff!"

"Yeah, but I'm needed here. Now shuttup and listen: when I'm playing tourist I don't establish a physical body on the planes. I can only do that when I have an anchor on this side to guide me back. There are no wizards left here powerful enough for the job, so you have to be the one to travel while *I* act as *your* anchor. If there was any other way I'd try, but we're on our own. We have to brilliantly improvise."

We he says. Uh-huh. Suuurrre.

He continued. "You'll need a planar equivalent of a physical body there so you can do the work. That's what takes so much energy. I'm going to channel it to you along the anchor line."

"What kind of energy?"

"We don't have time for Wizardry 101. Just trust me to get it right."

"Come on, there's plenty of people more magically inclined than me." I was in some ways magically un-inclined. Terrin said it had to do with my feline side. "What about Filima? Can't she anchor you?"

He shook his head. "It'd be asking her to hold a train in place with a string. And I can't send her; she's too emotionally involved to focus."

"Or Shankey? He's a soldier; he knows weapons. You wanna kill someone, that's his kind of job."

"Shankey doesn't have the magical moxie not to freak at the stuff he'd see."

"And I wouldn't?"

"You're used to special effects. Besides, those two don't trust me enough yet to forge a strong enough psychic link."

"Woo, I'm so surprised. Find someone who does."

He showed his teeth at me again, which wasn't the same as a grin. "I already have."

"Dammit, Terrin . . ." Like it or not, all the traveling we'd done together had established a bond between us. And, like it or not, I trusted him. So far as magic went I trusted him. Really. When it came to equally splitting a pizza that was another matter. "I'm not up to snuff when it comes to magic. My cat and human DNA mix—"

"Makes you ideal for the job."

Hah? Whazzat?

"Lissen," he said. "Cats are aware of magic, but it doesn't affect them in the same way as humans. You'll have a huge immunity to some of the stuff over there. And no one else here—including my otherwise flawless self—has your senses, reflexes, or strength."

He had a point. Though my body was mostly human, the cat in me gave me a hell of an edge, twenty-four/seven. I was so used to it I generally forgot it. "Flattering, if entirely true, but—hey!" Then the really big question popped into my buzzed brain. I'd been too busy making objections to think straight. Terrin's fault. Like any really good wizard he knew all about the art of misdirection.

"Does this require killing me?"

He did a double-take. His face screwed up. He was all over offended. Shocked, even. "Jeez-louise, NO!!"

That was a relief.

"What ever gave you such a fizzy-headed idea?"

"It's been my understanding," I said with much dignity, "that most people have to be dead to go to Hell,"

"Stick with me and I'll widen your horizons."

Well, they were broadening right now. With other possibilities. "Okay, it's time."

"For what?"

"To tell me the real problem. If this was just about Botello and astral travel we could have stayed in the kitchen."

He scowled.

"You forget that I've been hanging with you for way too long. I know how powerful you are and how you work. If bumping off Botello was all there was to the gig then you'd call him up in one of those mirrors, grab him by the family jewels, and drag him into this Reality for some terminal ass-kicking. Tell me I'm wrong."

Terrin glared at me a moment, then broke into another big grin. "You're learning, fur-face."

"So what's the real deal?"

"That is." He pointed at the Hell-river. "Rolling in each night, sucking off every last scrap of magic energy like some kind of psychic vacuum cleaner. It's gotten so its effect continues on a lesser level even during the day. That's what must have begun sapping me out the moment we arrived. I told you there was something wrong with this world. I'm safe behind these walls for just a little while. Soon it's gonna break through the household protections. That's gonna happen whether the demons invade or not."

I nodded. "Okay, I'm clear on that. And killing Botello will stop the river?"

"No, I don't think so."

Hah? Again. "Aw, shit. What's going on *there*?"

"It seems to be running its own program. Even with Botello soul-dead I'm probably still screwed, but snuffing him has to be done no matter what."

I rested my rump on the windowsill, my sense of reality shifting in a profound way. Terrin seemed to be going suddenly altruistic, was willing to save this world even if it didn't help him, but this wasn't the time to give him a big thumbs-up about it.

"There's no way to help you?" I asked.

He looked at me. His green eyes had turned silver gray, a sign he was truly serious. "With you on the Otherside, I *might* be able to figure a way to fix things and survive."

"How?"

"I won't know until you get there. Yes, I could yank Botello through to this side and whack him, but stopping the river is something more involved."

"You want me to go to Hell for you?"

" 'Fraid so, fur-face."

I thought it over as best I could given the short time and circumstances. From the first, without even knowing me or my past, he'd taken me in, fed me, given me a job at his magic shop and so on. So what if lately we'd been bouncing all over the Multiverse like a couple of bad checks; it had been lots of fun. He was asking a LOT, but I figured I owed him.

"Okay," I said. "Why not? But how will I get back?"

He gave me a funny look. "Back??"

I blanched under the fur.

He held his hands up. "Kidding!"

CHAPTER FIFTEEN

Up the Hill to Darmo House

"Are we there yet?" asked Velma. She sounded more irked than weary. "These boots were made for riding, not hiking."

"Not too much farther," Cadmus replied, sympathizing since he wore similar footgear. They worked much better on horseback than tramping over cobbled streets. Mostly cobbled streets. Their hasty jaunt toward Darmo House required detours into malodorous areas that made squelching sounds he did not care for at all. Normally he would have a lantern in hand to keep clear of them, but these were not normal times.

"You hear that?" she whispered.

Cadmus instantly froze in mid-step. He was taking to this sneaking around business rather well. They listened a moment. He picked up the commotion of several people trying to be quiet and not succeeding. "Next street over, I think," he murmured.

"Hoof it," she said. "Better to be a moving target."

He wholly concurred; they pressed forward with some speed.

Debreban had been the first to notice they were no longer the only people abroad after the curfew, spying in the distance marching men in black-and-silver cloaks. Concluding that Botello had discovered Cadmus's escape and sent forth the ducal guard to pursue and recapture, they were forced to take a more circuitous route to their goal. Debreban volunteered to lay a false trail and had cut away toward Burkus House, promising to catch up with them when he could.

Unfortunately, there were more than enough of the guard to cover the myriad byways of Rumpock. They were very efficient, too, and had obviously been informed of their quarry's potential destinations. When Cadmus and Velma reached the front gates of Darmo House, a group of men in black-and-silver livery were already there.

"If I had one of their helmets I might be able to bluff past them in this cloak," Cadmus mourned.

"Let's find another overhanging tree," Velma suggested. So they made a complete rounding of the estate, ducking onto narrow paths and behind hedges when necessary. No convenient foliage of a suitable height presented itself on their side of the tall boundary walls, though.

"That little gate has possibilities," Cadmus said, pointing. It served the stable yard and adjoining gardens. On informal visits to Botello, Cadmus had occasionally found it a useful entry.

"Except for those two left on watch."

True. A couple of exceptionally large specimens of ducal power paced alertly before the white-painted wrought iron gap in the wall. Cadmus, armed with Captain Rockbush's sword, had no doubt he could outfight them, but wasn't too terribly keen about killing the fellows. Not their fault they were following orders from the wrong overduke. A distraction was needed to remove them.

"I say," he said into Velma's ear. "I may have a cunning plan. . . ."

It was very gratifying when she readily agreed to his idea. They mapped out a quick strategy and separated, Cadmus placing himself just out of sight close by the gate, ready to dart forward when the time came.

Shortly afterward the two guards came even more alert, their attention drawn to a deeply shadowed patch of trees some yards away. On the still air, Cadmus heard what they were hearing, the wholly joyful, breathy giggling of a woman as she noisily made her way through the copse.

"This spot's good," she said in a loud whisper. Then came a rustle of branch and brush, then stifled laughter.

"That's it, nice an' comfy, ain't it, love?"

More thrashing. More giggles. Then deepening sighs.

"Gawds, you've done this before, haven't you?"

Cadmus had to remember to focus on the two guards. They nudged each other, grinning.

"Oh! Ahh!" went Velma. She sounded entirely convincing as she set up a strong rhythm that threatened to break branches. "Gawds, yes! Do me! Do me!"

The guards shifted restlessly, edging from their post, craning their necks in a futile effort to see the source of the excitement.

"Come on, big boy! Yeah! Yeah! That's good! Oh, gawd, ohhh, gawwwds . . . !" she caroled.

Velma's cries of pleasure gradually worked up to what promised to be a monumental peak.

Curiosity and lust finally overcame duty. The men bolted toward her. Cadmus bolted as well, reaching the gate. He tossed his sword through, then used the crosspieces like a ladder, going up and over, nimbly avoiding the spear-shaped points of the vertical bars. Once inside he felt along the wall for the long metal rod and catch mechanism that operated the interior lock. Releasing the catch, he gently swung the gate open, peering through the dark for Velma or the guards, whoever appeared first. He had the sword in hand again, just in case.

Happily, it was Velma. She emerged from the trees a short distance from where the men had gone in. Cadmus half-expected her to be in an advanced state of undress, but she was yet securely clad in her riding costume. She hurried across the way, dodged past him, and paused for breath as he quietly closed them in. He caught her hand, and they tiptoed fast over the grounds toward the house. No alarums erupted behind them.

"I say," he whispered. "That was brilliantly done!"

She huffed out a thank you. "Had to work from memory. I'm *much* better with a partner helping."

"Yrrgh!" He tripped, falling flat on his face. "Sorry. Foot caught on some ivy or something." They were on uncluttered open lawn. She did not point that out, for which he was profoundly grateful as he picked himself up. He was about to add a self-deprecating, but amusing remark concerning his odd lapse into clumsiness, but an authoritarian voice cut him off.

"Hold it right there! Move and you're dead!"

The Street Outside Cadmus House

Debreban was pleased with himself. Perhaps he wasn't all that good at following people, but he was exceptional at getting them to follow him.

He'd caught the attention of a whole pack of the overduke's guard, at least twenty, and was leading them a merry hide-and-seek chase through the immediate area around his master's estate. The fact that he did not plan to effect an entry there had not yet dawned on them. Many of their number were now posted at regular intervals outside the wall. As for the rest, all he had to do was make them *think* he was trying to get inside.

This made for a satisfying hue and cry, drawing more

and more guards into the area, which meant fewer men would be available to hunt Lord Cadmus and Miss Velma.

Creeping silently up the exterior stairs of a neighboring building, Debreban crouched in the shadows, holding his sword close to keep it from rattling. Black-and-silver capes fluttered about below like a swarm of agitated moths. They'd grown very noisy and, with windows open to take advantage of the cool night air, people were waking to the disturbance. Lights showed and doors creaked and, despite the curfew, annoyed and curious citizens clad in sleep clothes began to trickle into the streets. The guards now had to talk them all back inside again. It was too funny. Debreban couldn't wait to tell Shankey what he'd missed.

Then a door behind him opened. He nearly tumbled backwards into the sudden space. An old lady with a rolling pin in one hand stood over him. " 'Ere! 'O'er you?"

"City watch," Debreban promptly whispered. He grinned ingenuously up at her. "There's a thief loose we're trying to catch. Lock yourself in, quick!"

"Wotch? My eye! Yer that feller what marches aroun' fer 'is lordship over there. I seen yer ever day, don't I?"

"Madam—"

"Wotcher fink yer doin' sneakin' up my steps an' callin' me maderm? I ain't one ar' them fancy ladies wot 'is lordship ennertains, so be orf wif ya, 'fore I calls the real Wotch!" Her voice got inconveniently loud.

"Who's up there?" Someone from the street was taking an interest.

"An' 'onest woman tryin' ter ged 'er rest, that's 'oo! You lot be orf an' leave lawful folk in peace. An' take this 'un wif yer!" She poked Debreban in the ribs with her rolling pin.

"There he is!" the someone crowed.

Debreban wasted no time making a quick exit, which required that he clamber to the top of the stair's framing, which led to the roof. He'd planned to go there anyway, just not be seen while he was about it. Too late now, dammit, thanks to Mother Muddle-up. Usually he got along fine with old ladies; why did *this* one have to be immune to his nice blond hair and charming smile?

He left her well behind—she shouted after him using language not befitting her dignity—and shot across the slanted roof, dodging chimney stacks and trying not to slip. His leather boots, so practical for the street, worked against him on slippery tiles, but he had good balance to compensate.

"Get him!" cried several men from the street.

He heard pursuit, but judged he had an excellent chance of a clean escape since he knew where he wanted to go and they didn't. And all he had to do to vanish was pick a dense shadow and hold very still within it. None were at hand, though, so he kept moving, using the chimneys for cover as he worked his way across the roofs. In this section of Rumpock the buildings were crowded close upon one another, but they didn't go on forever. He'd have to descend sooner or later.

"He's over this way!"

This from an unexpected quarter, the bell tower. The people there weren't Watch or guards, but some of the Talents keeping watch on the Hell-river. Why weren't they doing that instead of bothering him?

"He's heading south!"

"West, now. He's turned west!"

Bloody tattles. Time to leave the heights. He had a better chance in the street. But where? He was following the edge of a building a good thirty feet up. Over there . . . a narrowing alley between this one and the next. If he got a good run of speed, he could jump it. He hoped.

But people were already on the roofs with him, egged on by the bell tower babblers. He ran flat out as best

he could over the uneven surface, then before he was
quite ready the gap was under him and he was flying
through space.

Too short!

He slammed hard on the perimeter wall of the next
roof, arms grappling desperately for purchase on its raised
lip, his legs dangling over an awful drop. Panic swelled
in his chest for an instant, then he realized he wasn't
falling just yet. His boots scraped bricks, found crevices,
and he pushed for all he was worth. Not enough to put
him over, but he gained a better hold. His scabbard
banged against his ankles, threatening to complicate things
until he kicked it clear. Panting and grunting, he hauled,
pushed, pulled, and heaved. Somewhat dazed, he rolled
onto a welcome horizontal surface.

That was close. He was still in one piece, not smashed
on the cobbles like a rotten apple.

"Here! That ain't Lord Cadmus!" This from a man on
the building he'd just leapt from. "Who are you?" he
demanded.

"Watch!" Debreban shouted back, using a flat city
accent. He kept down behind the lip to hide the distinc-
tive colors of his cloak. "Free Armsman Vylow. Who are
you?"

"Overduke's guard. Why are you running?"

"Thought you lot were some of them Hell-river
demons."

"Hell-river demons? What are those?"

"You mean you ain't *heard* of them yet? It's all they're
talking about, the Talents, that is. They seen 'em out in
the night. There was a man tore to bits by the east wall,
but they hushed it all up."

"Tore to bits?" This sparked some worried discussion
with several cronies who had caught up.

"It's true, I saw with my own eyes. Thought it was
butcher leavings. They told me to—"

"Arrh, he's lying his head off," put in a second man. "I ain't heard nothing about no demons."

"Well, of course not," Debreban said. "Them what's running things don't want it to get about. You ask any of the Talents on watch and they'll lie till they're blue, but I know what I saw."

"Then what are you doing up and about with demons all over an' a curfew on?"

"I reckon what business I had out was none of yours, 'cause it ain't polite for a man to talk about such things. I was on my way home when you lot started chasing me for no reason, and I'll be pleased to be on my way again if you'll allow it."

"We should take you in for wasting our time!"

A change in subject was in order. "Who are you after? Lord Cadmus you said?"

"That's right."

"Why didn't you say so? I passed him down by the river. Can't miss him in those dandy clothes."

"What part?"

"The docks. Seemed to want a boat but didn't know how to find an oarsman. Silly toffs don't know nothing."

"The docks. Hop it, boys!"

"What about *him*?" The first man pointed across the alley.

Debreban held his breath.

"Sod him. Shift yourselves!"

There was a general rout and Debreban was abandoned to his own devices. Perfect. He was thirty feet up and on the wrong end of town, but in no immediate danger. Half the guard would be on a north-bound chase to futility. All he had to do now was head for Darmo House and hope his lordship and the lady were having even better luck.

Debreban found a lower roof to drop to, then a lower one, until he felt confident of landing on the ground without breaking anything. This he managed; the jolt wasn't too bad. He straightened and dusted off, then set out once more, boldly striding forward like a man with a mission, which was somewhat true.

"Halt, there!"

Bloody hell. More of the overduke's minions. Hadn't they heard the news? A few carried dark lanterns and opened the metal shutters, bathing Debreban in watery yellow light.

"He's at the docks," he said to the figures closing on him. "Just got the report. Lord Cadmus is trying to hire a boat to escape by river."

"Then he will be caught. You are to halt, though." This came from a big man on horseback who seemed to be in charge. The backwash of the lanterns picked out the silver trim on his clothes, then the glint of his close-cropped pale hair. Debreban froze in his boots as the man's basilisk gaze fell on him.

"Overduke Anton?" he whispered. What was *he* doing out hunting with his men? But they weren't his men. If that face in the mirror was right, then this was Darmo Botello, wearing the overduke's body like a cloak. Debreban stared, trying to see any sign of the impostor beneath the shell.

"What an observant fellow you are. A bit more brainy than your master, though it wouldn't take much."

"M-my master?"

"Those are Burkus colors. You are going to tell me where Cadmus has taken himself."

"His lordship's at the docks."

"Where you would be were that so. He's gotten you to lead us away from him. Don't mistake me for the idiot he is. Where is he really headed? Darmo House? Does he think that bitch will be able to protect him from *me*?"

Debreban gulped. It was true. The man's manner of speaking, the way he pronounced "idiot," were identical

to the name-calling from their first encounter on the
carriage drive when he'd been in possession of Lord
Cadmus's body. Didn't any of these others know the
difference? Apparently not. Why should they? And it
wasn't something Debreban could just blurt out. Not only
would he be ignored as a lunatic, but Botello would shut
him away in a dungeon cell. Or kill him.

Stiffly, as if unused to riding, Botello dismounted from
the horse. It was a gentler animal than the sleek and restive Whitestone, and much less discerning; wouldn't know
the real overduke from a tree. Rather like the guards.
Debreban had never been comfortable about the
overduke, so much power in one man who knew magic
and had strange visions, but for all that he was known
as a friendly sort. This impostor was a definite threat. To
everyone.

Botello approached Debreban, squinting. The others
took a pace closer, but were waved back. Debreban
instinctively knew something more was up than a simple
interrogation. Botello smiled as though he fully expected
to get answers to his questions and would enjoy the
process.

*I won't talk, and he must know it. But what if he has
some magical means to force me?* Debreban felt in his
bones the absolute certainty of that suspicion. He possessed no Talent himself, but held a deep, wary respect
for those who did. Suddenly heavy on his hip, he felt the
weight of the cold iron sword. *But if I kill Botello, I'll
kill the overduke, and even if he's not really Lord Anton,
I'll be killed for raising a weapon against him.* Times were
peaceful, but treason was yet a capital crime.

The false overduke lifted his hand high toward
Debreban, fingers spread wide. That couldn't be good.
Debreban took his cue from the puzzled glances of the
men around them. Apparently this wasn't typical custody
procedure. He did not feel bound to discover what came

next. Quick as thought he drew his sword, holding it in a defense position.

"This is made of cold iron, wizard. Do you want to risk it?" he asked.

Botello flinched back, his eyes wide. "You dare?"

"I have to."

Bafflement turned to malignant fury. "You know the penalty for treason?" he hissed.

"I think we both do. *Sir.*" Mutual understanding flashed between them like lightning.

"Take him!" Botello ordered.

But before the men could act, Debreban swung the tip of his blade level with Botello's throat. "I'll split him! I mean it! Stand clear!"

They held their distance. Barely.

"Over there," he said, jerking his head to his right. "All of you face that wall and put your hands on it. Now!"

None of them wanted to cooperate. Debreban glared at Botello and applied enough pressure to dent his skin.

"Do what he says!" Botello snapped, then murmured, "I'll see you're gutted for this. You'll be days dying."

Debreban paid him no mind, urging the men to obey his instructions. When they were lined up with their hands in plain sight, he forced Botello backwards a few steps. "Your turn, the wall."

Botello seemed eager to remove himself from the range of the blade. While he was busy emulating the guards, Debreban seized the horse's dangling reins, jumped, and got a leg over its back. The quick move startled the animal, but Debreban clung tight. No time to find the stirrups; he dug in smartly with both heels, and they launched forward like the favorite at a racing meet.

Hands grabbed at him, but he beat them off, yelling his ride into a full-blown and dangerous gallop. He had to trust the horse knew how to run on cobblestones.

Behind him he heard a man's high shriek of rage. It was the overduke's voice, but such an unearthly sound could never before have passed his lips. Then a terrific flash of blue-white light bathed the alley. Debreban felt a scorching on his back and knew it meant death. He brought the flat of his sword down on the horse's rump, getting a burst of speed that nearly unseated him. The light grew stronger, the heat more intense; a loud roaring filled his ears like a rush of water at a cataract.

Heat, appalling heat. His cloak was on fire. He clawed at the knot under his chin. It tore loose, and the heavy fabric went flying off in his wake. Thank gawds for that, but he nearly lost the reins and his seat. He leaned low over the horse's neck, and kicked again.

Another gust of flaming white death swelled behind him, ironically lighting his way to the opening of the alley. It served a minor street, the opposite side blocked by a building. In scant yards he'd have to bring the horse sharp around without sending them spilling, but it was that or be roasted.

They burst from the alley, and he hauled on the reins, leaning into the turn. The horse's hooves skidded on the stones, but his legs kept moving. Probably panicked himself.

From the corner of his eye Debreban glimpsed a bright shimmering ball hurtling from the alley. He and the horse barely cleared from its path. The ball continued straight, slamming into the side of the building. Tongues of red shot out from it, taking hold of the old wood.

"Fire!" someone cried. Others chorused in.

"Fire!" he bellowed as well. It was the common enemy of the city. Everyone would converge on that spot to put it out, hindering pursuit. "Fire!" he called again and again. He continued long after leaving the immediate area. The more confusion, the better for his escape. Debreban felt fierce satisfaction knowing that Botello had brought the delay onto himself.

He would not be put off for long, though, and he already suspected Lord Cadmus would go to Darmo House.

Debreban had to get there, first and fast, to warn them.

"Fire!" he shouted to the night.

Darmo House

Amid the luxury confines of his suite, Terrin sat on the floor rooting around in his backpack, muttering crudities that would make a Marine blush. I paid no mind to him, being used to it and having other things to think about: such as nervously wondering what Hell would be like.

His reply, when I put the question to him, was less than satisfactory:

"About what you'd expect."

"But I don't have any expectations."

"Prolly better that way."

"What do you mean?"

Then he told me in no uncertain terms to chill out so he could work. Since my survival was likely dependent on whatever he was doing, I shut my mouth, paced aimlessly around his velvet-trimmed room, and chilled. And thought up other questions. And made myself not ask them. And chilled some more, which meant thinking up *more* questions. Hamsters stampeding to nowhere in their little wheels had nothing on me.

"Where's my frigging crystal ball?" Terrin snarled. "You can't go until I find it."

I perked my ears. "Oh, yeah?" I couldn't keep sudden cheeriness from my tone. "Why not?"

"I need it to watch you while you're there."

"Use Filima's scrying mirror."

"Can't. One of those Otherside critters might sleaze its way through."

"You can handle a demon."

"Yeah, but I don't need distractions that could break your astral thread. If that got snapped you'd be stuck."

"I'll help you look."

"Never mind. I remember where I left it." He looked disgusted.

"At the inn?"

"Naw, a circle of standing stones a couple worlds back. I was using it to scope out ley lines, see if they could lead me to an astral map home. Then some local deity showed up and it got ugly."

"You never told me that."

He shrugged. "Magic stuff bores you."

"What deity, what'd it look like?"

"Never got the name, but she was pretty pissed at me being on her turf, doubly pissed that I wasn't a virgin. We got into a slugging match."

"You hit a girl?" I didn't care for that.

"A deity who would have made Schwartzenegger look like Woody Allen with pneumonia. Metaphysically speaking, yeah. But she hit first. It all happened while I was in a trance, so there was nothing going on you'd have noticed. When I woke out of it my crystal ball was shattered. What a bitch."

"And you *forgot* all that?"

"Pretty much. Happens all the time. Go see if her ladyness has a spare. Real crystal. I don't want one of those glass rip-off jobs. I need a black candle, too."

"I still have that one in my pack."

"I'll get it. Meet you in the blue room that's got the tent."

Glad for something to do, I went downstairs, arriving in time for a patch of activity in the big reception foyer. The place was dark. The only lights burning in the house were still in the kitchen and a couple candles Terrin had taken with him. Not that I needed help seeing once my pupils were fully dilated.

Shankey walked in, just putting his sword in its scabbard. He fumbled at a table with a tinderbox, and I considered introducing the concept of strike matches to this world. They'd put up a statue to me for the idea alone.

He got a single flame going pretty fast though, which brought out the colors for me. He had company. With him was a *total* babe wearing something like a riding outfit and a guy resembling one of those overdone soap opera heroes: all shoulders, muscles, and chin. I paid more attention to the amazingly curvaceous babe where every part was a moving part, the whole of it beautifully synchronized. Wow. What a looker. She was sort of like Filima, but in vanilla instead of cinnamon. I *loved* the choice of flavors on this world.

The three of them, once the candle was burning, began talking at once. I skimmed bits and pieces off the top. Shankey had apparently found them lurking around outside; they were busy explaining the why behind their lurking and were pretty wound up about some major trouble that was on its way.

Filima walked in from another quarter and called out to the babe. "Velma! What's the matter?" She hurried toward them.

The soap opera guy said "Lady Filima" and executed a deep bow of greeting, but she just gave him a quick nod and passed him by. He seemed to want to say more, but zipped up.

Velma was bursting with six kinds of news, but rattling too fast for me to make much sense of it. Filima had the same problem.

"You're saying that Botello has taken over Anton?" she asked. "But Botello's dead."

"Just bodily displaced," said the guy helpfully. "He's been in Hell these past two weeks and when the chance came for him to possess someone he took it. Now he's out and about on this side of Reality."

"Botello's *here?*" She went green. Knowing what I now knew about how her marriage ended, I couldn't blame her reaction. "*Alive?*"

"He's using Anton's body. Everyone thinks he's Anton," Velma clarified.

Filima swayed. Not that she was anywhere close to keeling over, just a touch off balance. Soap-guy moved in, though, and swept her up in his arms.

"Cadmus, what are you doing?" she demanded. "Put me down."

He did so, but on a comfy settee. "I'm sorry. It's all my fault."

"What is?"

"He's sort of been helping Botello, honey," said Velma. "It's kinda complicated."

"*Helping* him?" Filima shrieked. She fought clear of his grasp. He fell away a few steps and hung his head low. If the word contrite hadn't already been invented he'd have inspired it just then.

"But he's trying to make up for it. Scream at him later; we gotta get Anton out of Hell and heard you have a wizard rooming on the premises."

"There he is!" said Cadmus, pointing at yours truly.

"Hah?" I said. "Not that again. Someone wanna bring them up to speed?"

"He's the one Botello wanted me to find," said Cadmus the soap king.

"You've talked to Botello?" Filima wanted to know.

"He kept coming through my scrying mirror. Always in a nasty humor. Told me to find a cat-faced man, that he was a wizard of great power."

I repeated the "hah?" and went the rest of the way

down to join them. "This guy in Hell knows me?" That did *not* sound good.

Velma went "Oh!" She stared a second, then I got the kind of melting look I love to see on women. She came closer and touched my face. I flared my lip whiskers invitingly. "Oh! He's real! Lord Perdle was going on to everyone that it was a mask."

"Just lil ol' me, lady." I wondered how she was at belly rubs. She looked like my sort of gal, beautiful, friendly, and extremely fond of cats.

"You're so soooffft. . . ." she cooed.

Well, parts of me were. She ran her hand up over my ears, making them twitch, which was great. Much more and I'd be purring like a fine-tuned Mercedes.

"Velma," said Filima. "This is Myhr, but he's not a wizard. His friend Terrin is, and he's upstairs."

"Does he look like you?" Velma wanted to know.

"Not a bit. I'm *much* more handsome."

"Then you're his familiar?"

My whiskers drooped a bit. *Not* the first time I'd heard that one. "We just hang together."

"He isn't a wizard?" said Cadmus. "But Botello told me—"

"He was wrong then, wasn't he?" Filima's voice was full of mood-destroying venom. "What else was Botello doing?"

Cadmus dropped his gaze. "He had me helping a bit with his magical experiments, but I swear I didn't know he'd be up to this sort of harm, the Hell-river, that is."

Velma reluctantly tore herself away from me. Darn. "Yeah, lissen to the guy. He's on our side for this."

"When you hear what we've been through . . ."

Then they were all talking again except for Shankey. I went over to stand next to him and watch. Things got pretty intense for awhile until they sorted themselves out. It boiled down to Cadmus and Velma wanting help to do a séance so the dispossessed Overduke Anton could himself tell them how to get him out of Hell. Sounded kind of nuts to me, but maybe it would save me a trip to the Otherside. To avoid that I'd gladly hold hands around a table and wait for someone to start cracking their toe joints.

"We've not much time," said Cadmus. "Botello has people out trying to find me. He could come through the gates at any minute. He won't be stopped by clan protocols."

Then we all gave a big jump when someone banged on the front doors.

Shankey drew his sword, went to a side window, and peeked through. He relaxed a bit and unlocked things. Debreban, breathless, sweating, and a bit singed, staggered in and spotted Cadmus.

"My lord, he's on his way here!" he announced.

No one asked who "he" was. "How long have we got?" Cadmus asked.

"I last saw him in the bell tower area. I took his horse and escaped, but he'll likely find another. He'll be here soon!"

"How did you get past the gate guards?" Shankey wanted to know as he re-locked the doors.

"I didn't." Debreban abruptly grinned. "Stood on the horse's back and hoisted over the wall. No one saw me."

"They'll spot that horse if they haven't already. Did it have the ducal colors on the saddle or tack?"

Debreban spread his hands. "I was too busy trying to get out of the way. Lord Botello threw flames at me. Twice!"

Cadmus stepped in. "What? Flames? How?"

"I don't know, my lord, but it had to be some kind of magic."

"Of course it was, but he shouldn't be able to do that. The spontaneous generation of fire, much less projecting it . . . the magical power required is unimaginable!"

"Unless you have a *big* chunk of it stored away." This conclusion came from Terrin.

We all looked toward the shadow-bathed stairs. Nearly invisible in the dark, he was seated partway down, hands clasped loose between his knees, and had apparently been listening in for some time.

"That's Terrin," I said to the newcomers. "*He's* the wizard." *And you're welcome to him, attitude and all.*

They gave him a good look. *Not* what they expected.

"What do you mean by that?" asked Cadmus. "Stored away magic?"

"If this is the same asshole who's been screwing things around—"

"It is, and I must ask you to moderate your language. There are ladies present."

Terrin looked down his nose at him. "Bite me."

Cadmus took a step forward, eyes blazing. He began to draw his sword.

Filima put a quick, firm hand on his arm. "We need him. What he says is nothing I've not heard before and thought myself. Let him talk."

He looked surprised that she'd spoken to him and strangely grateful. Not as though he was glad to avoid a fight with Terrin, more like hearing her voice made things all right for his whole life. Oh, yeah, he had it bad for her, terminally baaad. Cadmus reluctantly subsided with a nod, but there was still tension in his frame. He'd want to bust holes in walls. That or kiss her.

Terrin cleared his throat to get everyone's attention. "If it's Botello, and if he's on this side of Reality tossing magic around like that, then we have a change in plan to make."

I got hopeful. "So I don't have to go to Hell?"

"I didn't say that."

"What, then?"

"We just make sure he does what we want. Filima knows him best, she can help us figure out something."

"And just what is it we want?" she prompted.

"To delay him without getting everyone killed. If he's throwing fire around it might be a little tricky."

"He's after me," said Cadmus. "Except for Debreban, I'm the only other person he knows is aware of his possession of Lord Anton."

"And me," put in Velma.

"He can't know you've found out about him."

"Assume the worst, that he has. Go on."

"Well, if we make it look like I've not yet reached Darmo House he won't have any reason to come here. I'll leave and see to it he's led elsewhere."

Debreban shook his head. "My lord, protecting the Burkus clan is my duty. We need to hide you and the lady here while I lead him away. Lend me your clothes and sword and—"

"Blast you, you will not. *I'm* the one with a debt to pay—"

Filima got between them. "You're forgetting one thing: Botello is not an idiot. He'll search this place no matter how many fake trails you leave on the outside. He will come in regardless . . . because of me."

"I won't allow it," Cadmus stated, looking all manful.

"Yoo hoo?" said Terrin, waving. "He's a pissed-off jerk who can throw fire and who knows what else. Do you really want to get in the middle of a domestic disturbance with him? I don't think so. Filima, lemme ask you this: Botello's in Anton's bod, only you pretend you don't know it. He's gonna knock on your gate in the middle of the night. What would you normally do?"

"Let him in of course. He's the overduke, after all."

"That's right. Once in, what do you think he will do

when he sees you? Especially if he thinks he's got you off-guard?"

Her eyes narrowed, her lips thinning to a smile. "I understand."

Cadmus went red in the face. "Filima, I absolutely forbid you go anywhere near him!"

"I handled him before, I can do it again," she said. "You don't know what's at stake."

"Lady . . ." Debreban spoke up. "Begging pardon, but from what I saw he's not in his right mind. He won't react the way he used to."

"Then I'll just have to be careful. I know he's changed, and certainly for the worst, he's been in Hell for two weeks for gawd's sake."

I sincerely hoped she wouldn't say "poor Botello" again. "Couldn't we just hide behind the door, lure him in, then knock him out?"

Terrin showed teeth. "I was wondering when someone would come to the next part of my master plan."

My ass, I thought. He was just getting us do his thinking for him.

"That won't take care of the guards he'll have along."

"Debreban and I can see to them," said Shankey.

"But it's treason to raise a weapon to the ducal guard," said Filima.

"No weapons will be necessary, my lady. Not as long as we have kegs of beer handy and a store of sleepers in the apothecaria."

I took that to mean they stocked some kind of Mickey Finns in the house. "Aren't there rules against drinking on duty?"

He shot me a funny look. "Huh?"

"Never mind, after tonight there will be."

CHAPTER SIXTEEN

In Hell

Whatever titles and respect he'd enjoyed as overduke were entirely useless in the end, Anton decided. The only things that counted with this demonic lot—aside from demonstrating any aptitude for inflicting pain—were magical power and knowledge. Apparently little of either were to be had in this realm.

Anton found himself bereft of his store of magic. Botello must have stripped him during that awful moment when they'd traded places. Bloody thief. He'd not taken Anton's inherent knowledge, though, so not all was lost, just in a very, very bad place. Perhaps in time he could renew his energies. Only he didn't want to spend that time here.

The demons had shown in a most graphic way the consequences of lying to them, not on his own person, but upon some other hapless souls already in residence. Anton, after suppressing a strong urge to vomit, felt pity for them, but forced himself to be pragmatic. They were here because they'd brought it on themselves in some way. He was not of their number and reasonably certain the demons knew it. Though he was made uncomfortable, and thoroughly frightened, they'd not committed torture on him, just a few sharp nudges to keep him alert. Because of that tiny blessing, he was coming to the conclusion that they honestly didn't know what to do with him.

"Where is Botello?" they'd asked.

"He's gone Otherside," he'd replied. "He's taken my place, is using my body, having put me in this one."

"Get him back," they'd ordered.

His life experience in politics and diplomacy proved to be more handy than magic. Rather than unwisely admit he had not a single clue as to how to accomplish such a feat, he agreed to work something out.

Thus did they allow him some minor magical tools and freedom to work, but kept him under close watch. He got the impression that they had been more lax with Botello and weren't going to repeat the mistake.

Even with them looking over his shoulder, he did manage to make Otherside contact through a charged-up scrying mirror he willed into being, once they told him how to do it. Interesting feature about this place, the way thoughts could be made into form. Pity everyone here was so brutal, despairing or terrified, else they could turn the Hell plane into a quite nice place for them.

He'd hoped to find Botello with the mirror, but instead got that Burkus lackey. The poor man had looked right out of his depth. Anton did not have much confidence in him as a messenger. Suppose he was able to get to Velma, what then? She was a smart girl, but would she believe his story? Would she test things by speaking to Botello? Would he discover her out? And then what?

My gawd, if he hurts her, I'll have his skin on a wall.

The demons watched him; he watched the demons and fought an ongoing battle against giving in to shrieking panic. It's one thing to be condemned to Hell when the Powers decree you deserve the punishment, but quite another to be thrust in by the machinations of a fellow human.

I'm not even dead. There must be some provision for that in the Law of the Powers. He could not, offhand, recall any, having left the more esoteric matters of spiritual precepts to Lord Perdle, who quite enjoyed such canonistic convolutions. Making contact with him might prove more helpful. He could sort out the mess. If Anton—looking like Botello—appearing in Perd's shaving mirror didn't send the fellow into a spasm. It could take quite a lot of time, too, all the while with Botello up to gawd knows what. Probably finding a way to bring all these bloody demons into that side of Reality.

My vision coming true. No. Can't allow that. No, no, no, no, no.

The demons had altered their appearance since his initial encounter with that first creature. For some reason they now looked like warped versions of his courtiers. He decided it had more to do with his perception than the actuality. Whatever might really be beneath their facades he was in no hurry to find out.

Booooommmm.

Oh, yes, then there was that damned Gate. Literally. Far overhead an amorphous form screamed across the lowering sky like a shooting star, but minus the inherent beauty. He heard whisperings among his guards. *Another soul*, they said. *Another soul.* If there was any cause for joy in Hell, it was the arrival of fresh misery to feed upon. Anton never cared for that sort of company. Too much like some of his gossipy female relatives, only their echoing chant was more likely to be *Do you know who died today?* followed by a detailed report of the whole dreadful process.

Enough of that distraction. Enough of waiting. He had

to accept that things might not be going smoothly on the Otherside. With Botello there it was only to be expected. Anton would have to find a path out of Hell on his own.

Summoning up the courage to move, he made his way—with a demonic train in tow closely watching him— to the Gate. Perhaps his magical energy was gone, but he still had a mind well trained for problem-solving and the two-edged gift of his inner visions. That was one aspect of his Talent Botello could not touch. A player might be without his lute, but he could still create music if born with a genius for it.

Anton found a place where he could look at the Gate almost straight on, in the middle of a dry gully. The demons didn't seem to like him going down there.

"Is there a problem?" he asked.

"You are where the river flows," one of them replied.

The Hell-river? Well, fancy that. He wasn't too worried about being swept away in any black flood. His nightmare had been of himself drowning in the murk, not Botello. "Where is it now? On Otherside?"

The demon shrugged.

"Does the river vanish during the night and return at dawn?"

It stared as though not understanding the question. "The river comes and goes."

Not terribly endowed with brains, are you? "When is it due to return?"

It shrugged again.

Hmm. Interesting. They didn't have much concept of time. Not surprising in a place of eternity. His own time sense might well be confused. Hours in this place could be only minutes in his home Reality. Perhaps he should give that Burkus man longer to work. On the other hand, it would also give Botello longer to work.

Anton stood in the middle of the gully and walked toward the great black Gate. Formidable things. Opening inward. Beneath them a sizable crescent-shaped gap that would otherwise be filled up by the river. It was open and looked somewhat promising, but surely its hazy depths couldn't be an escape route. They'd have tried it by now. That is, if they'd *thought* to try it. In a Reality where thoughts could take on form the demons might be unaware of the possibility. Might not even see the same things he saw. Where there was nothing for him they might see acres of bear traps.

He couldn't quite make out what lay beyond that space; it was gray and blurred as fog. He hiked over. Demons on either bank of the riverbed kept pace.

He peered under the gap. Still a blur, but he thought he heard something within.

"Hallo? Is anyone there? *Hallo?*"

No reply, but the sound, a strange, soft whispering was definitely real.

Bending to duck through, he stepped toward it.

"You cannot go there," said one of the demons. Others nodded agreement.

"Why not?"

"Not allowed. You will stay on this side of the Gate."

"You want Botello back, don't you?"

"Yes."

"Then I have to go get him."

"He isn't there."

"How do you know that unless I look?"

The demons had no answer. He'd stumped them for the moment, so he proceeded before they got more forceful with their objections. He went slowly, well aware that souls don't just escape from Hell. It simply wasn't done. Nor should it be this easy.

He poked his head under the Gate. "Hallo. Anyone home?"

No reply or challenge. So far so good. He eased into the gray blur, straining to see. A light or a shape, anything solid. He raised one hand to touch the bottom edge of the Gate. That was solid. Thick, too; it took ages to reach an ending to it—unless he was walking lengthwise instead of across. No matter, he came to a place where he could stand upright and did so. He went dizzy for a moment, for there was no reference to up or down here, only the disorientating limbo.

The whispering was all around him, gibberish in a thousand times ten thousand voices. He called out again.

"My name is Anton. I was thrown into Hell by mistake. Is there anyone in charge to whom I may speak about this? Hallo?"

Now they were muttering, sounding none too pleased. He hoped this wasn't one of those members-only clubs, and feared he'd blundered in regardless.

"I'm not actually dead," he explained. "This isn't my body. I was dispossessed, you see, and I'd really like to clear the problem up and go back to where I belong."

The muttering abruptly ceased.

Trembling, he stared all around, finding *nothing* to focus on. It was almost as bad as Hell where things were far too visible. To offset another bout of dizziness he shut his eyes.

That's when things sprang into being for him. Oh, yes, his vision worked *perfectly* here.

Darmo House

I thought to stick with Terrin, but he and the girls took off pretty fast to Filima's room in search of crystal balls and other magical junk. Just like him to grab the babes for himself. I could have followed, but from the sound of things they'd be talking shop, even Velma, who had some catching up to do with her friend. It would be all magic talk, like hanging with a bunch of computer geeks. 'Puter chat I could relate to, but this world was a few

centuries short of developing microchips. Double ditto for
potato chips, even.

That left me and the other guys to take care of the
threat of the false overduke, if and when he decided to
show up.

Shankey stressed the importance of keeping lights away
from the windows. The house had to look asleep as
normal. He led us back to the kitchen and rooted around
in what looked like Dr. Jekyll's pantry, finding a bottle
covered with pasted-on cautionary labels. He squinted at
the curly lettering.

" 'Three drops per glass of water for a sound night's
rest,' " he read. He put it back on a high shelf. "Not strong
enough. What's this one? 'One drop per gallon of water
to soothe a panicked bull.' Yeah, that should do it. Okay,
I'll go check on the guys by the front gate. Back in a
minute."

He slipped out the kitchen door. I was curious to see
what he planned and followed quietly. Debreban and
Cadmus hung back to compare notes about escaping from
crazed, body-stealing, fire-throwing wizards.

Shankey opted for a casual approach, going up to
several men in black-and-silver garb who stood just outside
the Darmo House property, greeting them in a friendly
if surprised manner. My ears picked up enough of their
exchange to determine that he wouldn't need any help
fighting off invaders. Not for the moment. He pretended
to believe whatever story they gave him for why they were
hanging around his lady's driveway entry in the middle
of the night. His friendly offer of liquid refreshment was
readily accepted.

I was back in the kitchen setting beer flagons out on
the table when he returned. "How fast will that stuff
work?" I asked as he brought the bottle of knock-out juice
over.

He didn't know. "I saw it used once at a horse-racing

meet. One of the runners went into a fit, tried to kick its stall down along with a few stable lads. The animal apothecary managed to shove a drop of this into its mouth before getting bit. Not too long after the horse keeled over to sleep for a few hours. So did the apothecary, only he woke up a couple days later."

"Must be absorbed through the skin. You got an eye-dropper? We don't wanna risk touching this."

He found a thin glass tube like a delicate straw and used it to transfer a drop of the juice into each flagon. I filled six of them with beer. He put them on a tray and went outside again to play waiter, returning soon after with empties.

"They're in no pain," he announced, satisfied.

"Sure it won't kill them?"

"Not really, but if the apothecary survived, these guys should, too."

I hoped none of them suffered from bad hearts or sleeping sickness.

He and Debreban went to work hauling snoring bodies off to a gardener's hut. After the first trip they returned with twin wheelbarrows, and that made the job go faster. Shankey took over-tunics, weapons, helmets, and cloaks from two of the men, then he and Debreban put them on.

"Won't Botello recognize you?" After all, Shankey had worked for the guy for years, and Debreban was likely to be a fresh memory.

"Who looks at a guard?" Shankey pulled the helmet into position. It had some impressive and concealing metalwork around the eyes and over the cheeks. His impersonation plan might work. "Besides, it's really dark out, and if his lordship comes, he's going to be in a hurry." He and Debreban quick-marched out to the front gate.

"He'll come and soon," pronounced Cadmus, who was sitting at the table, looking morose. I offered him some leftover pizza, but he only shuddered, one hand straying to his stomach. "He'll know that I've talked to Filima and told her everything."

"He won't know for sure," I said. "If you keep out of sight, it keeps him guessing and buys Filima some time."

"You as well. He's assumed you're a wizard of great power. Wants to strip you of your magic. Why aren't you? With those looks you should be magical."

I shrugged. "Just not in the cards and I am delighted. Saves me a lot of headaches in the long run." Terrin was more than welcome to mess with the whammy tech; there were way too many details you had to remember to work it right without getting fried. Speaking of fried, what was Hell gonna be like? "You talked to this Botello dude a lot? After he was dead? Is that what I heard?"

Cadmus stared down at the table. "He'd speak to me through my scrying mirror. It was horrible the first time. I was trying to see—well, never mind—in place of what I wanted I got his face instead. Not ashamed to admit he frightened me silly. He was supposed to be dead, after all. Thought I'd somehow tripped and fallen into a bit of necromancy which is *not* the done thing around here. First he pleaded with me for help, later on he got more and more short, then demanding, then he was ordering me about like a skivvy. I expect the last two weeks of being in Hell did that to him."

No shit. I wondered if I needed to worry about losing my sanity and gaining an attitude. "Couldn't you have just not used the mirror?"

"The situation had turned too complicated by then. And I was really trying to help him escape. By the time I realized what a mistake it was I was too psychically linked to him to pull back. He was getting magically stronger, too. I couldn't block him." His shoulders bunched up.

"Did he ever explain how he got tossed into Hell?"

"Not really. Just said it was a mistake. Do *you* know?"

I didn't think Filima would mind if I gave Cadmus the headlines. He might need the information anyway, and if things went wrong tonight, then it wouldn't matter.

When I finished Cadmus was suitably impressed. "Poor Filima. What a burden she's been carrying, and I've been such a swine pestering her. I'll have to apologize right away." He began to scoot his chair back.

"Uh-uh." I waved him down. "It can wait. She and Terrin are cooking up some major mojo, so let them work. When you were talking to Botello did you see anything of Hell?

"Only his face and some red clouds. Sometimes they were pale green. Why do you want to know?"

"Just wanna be prepared." I suggested we wait in the front hall where we'd have a better chance of bushwhacking Botello in case Debreban and Shankey missed their window. Just as we entered the foyer, Velma was coming downstairs, candle in hand.

"Terrin said it's time," she told me, looking solemn. Apparently Terrin had briefed her.

My heart gave one terrific lurch. Oh, gawd, I was scared. Then my brain twitched and unexpectedly kicked out an idea. A wonderful idea. Why couldn't I have been this brilliant half an hour ago and saved myself some nail-chewing? "Great!" I said and bounded past her.

Terrin had set up shop in the fancy blue room, but not inside the velvet-draped pavilion. That was lying in a sloppy heap next to a pillar along with the table and shards from the scrying mirror I'd broken earlier. Four chairs were now in the center of the floor, arranged according to the compass points. My initial impression was that he'd had second thoughts about a séance.

Within their space was a big circle drawn in white chalk on the blue mosaic floor, about six feet across. He'd inscribed its perimeter with a lot of symbols and sigils using several different alphabets. It was enclosed in a

second, much larger circle where the chairs stood. Each
of them was in its own smaller circle like some kind of
cosmic basketball court. He'd lighted a ton of incense—
a nice-smelling brand—and the black candle, which would
absorb negativity. He had some serious shit going on here;
even from the doorway the magic radiating from the
circles set my whiskers to twitching a rumba.

"I may not have to go," I announced.

Terrin and Filima paused their conversation. He shot
me a look. "You better be sure, they don't have bathrooms
on that side."

"Get serious. I had this flash: why don't we first cap-
ture Botello and make him swap places with the
overduke? I bet you could get him to do that. We have
a séance to contact Anton and zap them both. But before
we do, we make Botello tell us how to get rid of the Hell-
river and stop things up so the demon hordes can't come
through."

He thought it over. For about a minute. A real long
minute to me. "Sounds cool," he finally said.

I sagged with relief.

" 'Cept I don't know how to do that."

"*What?* To hear you talk I thought you knew how to
do everything!"

"Magically that's almost true. If I knew everything we'd
be home right now and richer than Bill Gates on our own
tax-exempt islands."

"What exactly is it you can't do, then?"

"Getting Botello to body-swap with the overduke without the overduke being in the vicinity. I figure once those
two are in close proximity that problem will take care of
itself. To make it happen you have to go in and *find*
Botello's astral body. I'm not risking phoning him up on
a scrying mirror, 'cause we don't know who will answer
or try to break through. The other thing I can't do is force
Botello to talk—either in this Reality or on the Otherside.

He's gonna be plenty pissed wherever he is and in no mood to cooperate."

"So we keep him on this side and go medieval on him."

"Which would damage the overduke's body, and then *he'd* be pissed. If we had Pentothol we might be able to do something, but we don't. To get him to cooperate requires a lever or a bribe, and we ain't got squat. And there's no guarantee that Botello knows what we want him to know. For all his power he's an amateur, and they tend to cut corners when real work is inconvenient to their desires. I still need you over there to find Anton and help me work out how to deal with the river, but when it comes down to brass tacks, Anton is a side issue. The river is the big deal."

"So I go to Hell?"

"You go to Hell."

"Damn it."

"Ain't *that* the truth?"

Cadmus and Velma walked in. His gaze went right to Filima and took the rest of his body along. He guided her off into a corner for a quiet talk. Apologizing like crazy if I read his body language correctly. I could have listened in, but was too busy smiling at Velma. She came over to me, smiling back.

"I think it's a brave thing you're doing," she said. "Terrin told me how you're going to find Anton and bring him home."

The last I'd heard I was going to find Botello and kill him. Of course that was scrapped what with Botello being Anton. I switched gears quick, though. It's not often I have a major babe hanging on my every word. Very cheering, considering the circumstances.

"Well, it's a dirty job, but someone has to—"

"Can it," said Terrin. "We gotta get moving. You guys, front and center in the chairs. We're going to do a modified kind of séance."

"Really?" Cadmus perked up. "You liked my idea?"

"It has angles I can use, so listen. We're all going to sit, Myhr lies on the floor in the middle. I'm going to be his anchor for this side of Reality, you guys are gonna add your psychic energy to the pot. It means less work for me so I can focus on keeping him safe."

I was all for that.

"But Botello drained off my magical energy," said Cadmus.

"Good. Less static on the line. This is a mental thing, not a magic thing. Filima, you keep your power to yourself, don't try to help me."

She nodded, and everyone picked a chair, standing ready. They looked as nervous as I felt. He gave them each a small quartz crystal and told them how to hold it. I got a larger crystal and a sword.

Cadmus stared. "I say! That's my sword, the one made with—oh, ah, that is . . ."

"Cold iron," Terrin completed for him. "Yeah, I got it off of blondie-boy. Told me it was a family antique. What's your family doing running around making wizard killers?"

"Haven't the faintest," he said, looking uncomfortable. "The thing's very old. Forgot I had it."

"Yeah, sure, whatever. Myhr, there's two things you have to remember to make this work: hang onto the sword, hang onto the crystal."

"I get the drill. If I don't then horrible things happen to me, right?"

"Exactly—you lose these and we'd have to buy new ones 'cause they're borrowed."

"Then I won't be trapped in Hell and eaten by demons?"

"I never said that. And stop speculating on what you think might be there. It won't *ever* be what you think, besides I'll shield you from seeing the worst of it so—"

"Worst of what?"

"What do you *think*?"

Oh Gawd . . .

"Just tell yourself it's a movie with production design straight out of *Alien* and you should be able to keep from going into shock."

My back fur was up. In a big way. All over my spine like static electricity. "Terrin . . ."

He gave me one of *those* looks. No smart-ass grin, no patronizing, snarky frown, but something of the real person he kept well hidden inside. "It'll be fine. I promise."

Jeez, but I'm a sucker for sincerity. One of these days I'd have to get therapy before it killed me.

"Places everyone," he said to the others. They all sat except for Terrin. "We're going for a take. Myhr, lie down in the circle, your head to the south."

I did so. Terrin stood before the southern chair, looming over me. He had a small crystal ball in one hand, and a large quartz crystal in the other that he held out over me. He muttered some kind of chant, waving the quartz around in a power pattern. The chalk sigils surrounding me kindled and brightened, feeble at first, then glowing like embers from a fire. They began to pulse; it was pretty, until I realized their pulsing exactly matched the beating of my heart.

Oh, shit.

He stopped waving, stepped back, and dropped wearily onto his chair, pinching the bridge of his nose.

"What's wrong?"

"Nothing, just this gawd-damned magic-sucking world! It's trying to kill me. I ain't gonna give it the satisfaction."

Something about him had slipped. His aura was wrong. What in the world . . . I focused and realized he'd cast a glamour on himself. It seemed to melt from him, at least to my eyes. I didn't know if the others saw the reality.

He looked to be a hundred years older, hair turned bone white and so much color leeched from his skin that the veins underneath were visible. His weight was down, too; he'd gone gaunt, from cheekbones to hands, which were downright spidery.

We'd been here only one night, a day, and another night. At the rate he was deteriorating . . . I got a nasty, dark, cold feeling inside that he was dying and that it would be only a matter of hours.

"Yeah," he said, as though hearing my thoughts. Sometimes he picked them up if they were strong enough. "This is as serious as death." From the expression on his wasted face I knew he wasn't exaggerating.

He made an effort to straighten. I could see now that he was moving like an arthritic chicken. Despite the warm gold glow of the sigils he looked sickly. One-good-breeze-and-he-might-float-away kind of sickly.

Damn . . . and damn again. That wasn't fair. It sucked canal water.

"Yeah," he said. "It does. I can't do this alone, Myhr. I need your help."

Jeez—I knew what it had cost him to say *that*.

"What do I do?" I asked. I was nervous. Didn't like it. Couldn't help it.

"Close your eyes, breathe in through your nose, out through your mouth. The same for the rest of you. Clear your minds."

Easy enough, but I couldn't ask questions. Maybe he just wanted me to shut up so he could concentrate. I did the breathing for awhile until a dim flashing took place beyond my closed eyelids. That would be the sigils pulsing brighter. Their pace still matched my heartbeat—which was speeding up.

I gripped my crystal and the sword hard.

"Keep breathing," he said.

After a minute or three the flashing faded. The

room turned strangely cold. I thought I knew what that meant.

Okay, show me what you see.

My eyes popped open as much from surprise as anything else. I sat up. His voice was right *in* my head. "What the hell—?"

Yeah, pretty much, he cheerfully agreed.

In. My. Head. "You didn't say you'd be crawling around my skull! Get out!"

Cool it, Myhr, I already know what you do in the shower on Saturday nights, so chill. Your secrets are safe with me.

"ARRGH!"

Anguished screams cut no ice with him. He waited for me to settle down. *Look, we're stuck like this for the duration. Just do what I say and it'll be over that much faster. Okay?*

Like I had a choice in the matter. It was one thing to get a telepathic distress call from him, very much another to hold a conversation. "What else are you into?"

"Not a lot. I'm seeing through your eyes. It's coool. I gotta get me a set like yours when this is done."

I suppressed a groan. And shut my eyes for a second, just to annoy him.

Take stock. Are you all there?

Now that was a damn stupid question, until I remembered where and what I was: a projection of myself into the Otherside. I seemed to be in my own solid body, wearing familiar clothes, sword and crystal firmly in hand. One part of my brain accepted the reality, found comfort in it; another part was just as certain it was pure illusion. I didn't know why I knew that, must have been the cat DNA pulling some overtime. "It's copasetic so far as it goes. Now what?"

Look around.

I looked around. And listened. And smelled. And felt.

It was bad. Bad beyond bad.

No pretty blue room, but a strange, flat landscape with no specific light source. Earth, trees, grass, sky, clouds were an unrelieved cotton candy pink. My sensitive nose was jammed with the smell of burning sugar. The pink ground was sticky. I was being pelted by cobwebs of forming candy. The stuff fell on me like gossamer snow. Pink, of course. Sticky.

On the heavy air I heard the thin fruity voices of thousands of children singing. In Hell? That was wrong. Terrin had sent me to the wrong place. I was in kiddie heaven and any second some Otherside Shirley Temple in a fluffy dress would come tripping up to give me a chorus of "The Good Ship Lollipop."

The singing children abruptly launched into that particular song.

"Terrin? You messing with my brain? What's going on here?"

Your brain's already messed up. I'm doing what I can to shield you from what's really here.

"You promised me *Alien*. I'd rather have that than this!"

No you wouldn't. Shut up and walk. Hold your crystal out. See if it draws you anywhere or lights up.

"Okay, I'm walking. Gawd, it's like the floor of a dollar movie theater here."

He snickered. The son of a bitch had put me in circus hell and he was laughing about it. *You're doing fine. Bear left at that—er—ah—tree.*

"Tree?" It looked more like a giant gumball. "What is it? What are you seeing?"

Never mind, you don't wanna know. Oh, yeah—do me a favor and don't eat anything here.

Yeah, sure, like I was planning to scarf down this junk. *Not* that hungry. "How does that do you a favor?"

So I don't have to listen to you bellyache about it later.

He seemed to be following a theme here, so I decided not to ask him what was really raining on me.

I slogged forward, going fast. I guessed that this was costing him a lot in terms of effort, and speed would be a good thing, but I was without a clue to where I was going. The quartz didn't do any special effects for me. Once I glanced behind when I thought I saw movement. Nothing there unless you counted a faint silver thread winding away into the pink distance. One end was attached to my back somehow. Must have been how he was channeling to me. Man, this was *weird*.

"There's nothing here," I said. "Just miles and miles of monochromatic indigestion."

Okay. Dammit. I was hoping I wouldn't have to do this to you.

Before I could ask an obvious question I felt a rippling shift through my body, through the whole of everything around it. The pink landscape suddenly darkened to blood-red, the sticky rain stopped, and the children's singing changed to laughter like wind chimes, harsh and discordant. In another minute I would *really* hate this place.

You should see something. Look!

I looked, but even my eyes had their limits. Making a slow, in-place circle—without tangling my astral thread, it remained illogically straight—I held out the crystal. It flickered once, very faintly.

That's good! Go with it!

I moved in that direction, though the crystal remained dormant. "Not that I'm eager to see any of 'em, but shouldn't there be some demons here?"

Yeah, but I'm shielding you. They can't see you either, if that's a comfort.

It was. A big one.

I'll prolly have to remove it before too long. When you get closer to Anton. What shields you could hide him from view.

"Hey. I just thought of something. How will I know
Anton if and when I see him?"

Easy. He'll be the one not trying to eat you.

Oh, gawd . . .

CHAPTER SEVENTEEN

In a Street Near Darmo House

Botello's horse, commandeered from one of Anton's guard, wasn't as restive as that white monster belonging to Cadmus, nor as pliant as the one stolen by the Burkus House lackey, but somewhere in between. The animal was none too happy having him on its back, but not to the point of bucking, just balky and restive, ears flat, snorting and stamping all the way. Botello considered slapping a tranquility spell on it, but decided to save his power. Throwing fire had taken a bit out of him. Better to save himself for facing his dear, soon-to-be-departed wife.

Besides, Filima would have a quantity of useful magical energy with which he could restore himself. Not a lot, but fresh, better than the thin scraps flowing around him in the Hell-river. First he would drain her, then strangle her. Then he could go down to his Black Room and try to salvage his experiment.

Perhaps he should hold off the strangling, though. In dealing with the Otherside powers it was a good idea to bring an offering. So what if she wasn't a virgin? Her soul was innocent enough to make a meal for them. They relished innocence since there was none in Hell. The supply of souls they got was only the worst leavings sent there by the Powers. No wonder the demons were anxious to feast on living beings on this side. . . .

The horse stubbornly tried to turn back, forcing him to wheel it around. Bloody beast, he should offer it to them as well.

The move left him confused on his direction. Damn Anton's worthless eyes. Botello squinted, trying to fix on anything familiar in the dim blurs that made up his faulty vision. He spied a vague, flickering light. That would be the fire by the bell tower. It must be spreading. Bells were ringing all over Rumpock; people were emerging from their houses, muttering sleepy, uneasy questions. A few recognized him or rather who he seemed to be.

"Lord Anton! What is the matter?" asked one man holding a lantern.

"Nothing, which way is Darmo House?"

The man hesitated. Probably with his mouth hanging open.

"Answer me!" He pulled hard on the reins to keep the nervous horse in hand.

Several pointed. "Is there a fire? What are those bells about?"

He left them no reply, but dug in his heels and held onto the saddle pommel to keep from falling off. Damned animal must have caught a whiff of the smoke. Now it was only too glad to move along.

Botello thought he knew where he was now. Any street going in this direction would open onto the lane that ran around the whole of his property. Once inside he could find his way easily enough.

He made it to the lane and slowed his mount, peering anxiously for a break in the high wall. It was hard to tell if the amorphous blot ahead was a gate or a change in brick color. He decided it was a gate, flanked by two oddly shaped black columns. He had no such décor outside his wall. Had Filima changed things? Throwing his money around, was she? The columns came to attention as he approached, startling him.

"Lord Anton, sir!" said one of them, probably snapping a smart salute.

He quickly recovered. "Report."

"All is quiet, my lord."

"One of you hold this damned beast for me."

A guard, no longer a column, darted forward to take the horse's bridle. It calmed down for *him*. Botello dismounted and went toward the gate. Yes, this was the small one leading to the stables and gardens. Normally the overduke would go through the main entry, but Botello had no time for protocol. It would shortly become a useless concept, anyway. He felt inside the metal work for a hidden catch under the lock and swung it open.

"Do you wish escort, my lord?"

"No, I can manage."

Now . . . should he go through the secret tunnel by way of the stables or just take a side door into the house? He opted for the quickness of the latter. Filima would be surprised either way. First by the overduke's appearance in the house, then by his true identity when he revealed it to her. What a look she would have on her face; he'd have to be sure to stand close enough to see each nuance of her horrified realization.

Unless Cadmus or his man had gotten here ahead of him and alerted them all. There were other gates, other means inside.

But the house was dark, no sign of disturbance that he could see—which was very damned little with these eyes. No matter. He could deal with any trouble now, while in this skin. How satisfying it was to be in control of everything. And it would only get better and better.

The Main Gates of Darmo House

"Shankey?"

"Yeah, Debreban?"

"Does it look like the fire is spreading?" Debreban peered down the long hill to a distant, evil glow in the middle of Rumpock.

"Sure does."

"Lots of smoke."

"Sure is. Not your fault, though."

Debreban appreciated the sentiment. "Maybe we could yell and send people from here over to help fight it."

"I think they're already on their way. The bells and the Watch are doing their job of waking the city. We have to stay here and do ours until Lord Botello arrives."

Debreban grunted agreement, but it was hard to stand by and do nothing. He hated waiting. "Shankey . . . ?"

"I'm still here, Debreban," came the patient reply.

"What if Lord Botello *doesn't* come in by the front way?"

In Hell

The crystal flickered in my hand like a loose lightbulb. "Did you see that?"

Yeah, said Terrin. *Keep swinging until it steadies out.*

I waved it around, turning. "No dice. Maybe it needs fresh batteries."

There's too much psychic interference for it to fix on Anton.

"Where's it coming from?"

You don't wanna know. You guys really have to focus on him so I can cut through it.

By that I understood he was speaking to the others in his circle. Was he in their heads, too? Were they in mine? Yeeps.

Picture him clear in your mind like he was standing in front of you. Remember he looks like Botello, but Anton's inside the skin. Hold it steady.

The quartz glowed, but went out again. I moved forward. The closer I got to Anton the brighter it would get. Presumably. It had been hit or miss since my arrival, with me switching directions every few yards or so. The vivid red monotony of the landscape was getting to my overstressed brain in a big way, disorienting perception. The land, or whatever it was on this Side, seemed to slowly breathe. Hopefully it was only an illusion; I didn't need a bout of seasickness just now.

I began to hear another noise besides the bitter, chimelike laughter and Terrin's mental chat. Bits of low sound, almost a voice, but not quite, floated to me on the burned-sugar air, like a basso-fortissimo bear with a bad stomach. Sometimes it was close and loud, very cranky. My ears were twitching all over the place; my legs moved faster. Cat instinct was trying hard to cut in and take over; I couldn't stop if I wanted so I didn't. Strange thing, though, I wasn't tired or running out of breath. Astral bodies were tough, apparently. That or they had other kinds of weaknesses.

"I think I'm going in a circle, Terrin. That rock looks familiar."

Rock? Oh, yeah, rock. Yeah, that's a rock. Nothing else at all. Don't touch it, okay? You're right, we've been here before. I'm gonna have to crank up the volume. Brace yourself.

Pausing, I braced, knowing better than to ask him what for and rode out the next shifting, shimmering wave of change.

Things got darker and smellier, being too much like

the burglar alarm in Botello's tunnel. I'd need a week-long bath to get rid of the stink. If I ever got back.

Then I saw *them*.

Shadowy beings loomed out of the murk, *huge* hulking things with pointy teeth and glowing eyes and scales and attitudes. I was completely unprepared to deal with their immensity and ugliness. It wasn't just the surface fear of a bad surprise, this one went down to my toes and back again. All the cat in me, all the human in me froze, trapped in place by an abject primal panic so intense it hurt. My heart thumped a few times, crawled into my throat, flipped over, and stopped. I remained standing, but swayed.

"Are those demons?" I whispered, hardly able to hear myself.

Yuppers. Take it easy. I don't think they'll notice you unless you make a fuss. They're not too smart.

Neither are bulldozers, but they can still do damage. These things were about the same size.

"Terrin . . ."

Chill out, buddy. I mean it! Chill! I won't say it's okay, but you have to focus if you wanna leave. Try to get that damn crystal to work.

I felt like the proverbial cat in a room full of rocking chairs. Maybe I didn't have a tail, but a feeling of hideous vulnerability was all over me like a cheap suit.

The quartz began to glow very faintly when I swung it in a direction off to my left. It wasn't so much a swing as uncontrollable trembling.

Great! Follow it, Myhr!

Anything to get out of this place. It was ground zero for everything I hated most and a few I'd never thought about. The demons remained ghostly to me, and I could only hope I appeared the same to them. They seemed too busy with various activities to pay any attention. Those activities—I did *not* look closely—involved inflicting a wide variety of tortures on writhing forms and figures. Some of those looked human; others were too twisted out of shape to tell. What had once been hard laughter had become screams. The bear noises were from the demons. This was more like the *Alien* set Terrin had mentioned, only in comparison the alien was cute and cuddly. This was H.R. Giger on acid having a *really* bad trip.

I held tight to the sword and the crystal and let my feet do their stuff. The movement got my heart going again, but it was still jammed in my throat. I had to swallow a lot to be able to talk. "Terrin? The quartz is getting heavier. Not much glow, but it's putting on weight."

He made approving sounds. *You're getting closer. Hurry!*

Did that. The demons got louder and more solid-looking. One of them paused in its activity and looked right at me, glowing eyes going narrow with awareness. Oh, shit. I sprinted, hoping for concealment, and instead found a lot more like him beginning to perceive my presence.

"My cover's blown. Can you put me back in the candy hell?"

No.

No time to ask why not; I kept going. The crystal put on a few more pounds. Then I had to stop. Cutting through the otherwise flat landscape was a wide, deep gully, right across my path. It was steep-sided here, nothing I couldn't handle, but if I went down into it the demons would *really* notice me in its uncluttered emptiness.

On the other hand, maybe there was a good reason why it was so bare. If natives avoided a place it was usually because something nasty was already in residence. It had to be monumentally awful to scare off a bunch like this. I gingerly worked my way along the edge.

What are you doing?

I explained my reasons; Terrin subsided. For a moment.

Y'know? It looks like a dry riverbed.

"For the Hell-river?"

What are the odds?

In this place, considerably better than me winning a lottery jackpot. I followed the bank until a wall emerged out of the dark red murk. A really big wall, twice the size of the one they used to keep King Kong in his yard. The gully ran right under a massive-beyond-massive Gate. I couldn't see what lay past it.

"I think I have to go there. Will it be safe?"

How the hell should I know?

"I thought you'd been here before!"

Yeah, but not this spot. I party in better areas. You're in the slums.

Slums? Hell had slums? It made a creepy kind of sense.

"You. Come here." A deep, guttural, slow-motion, bearlike voice, *not* friendly, and much too close.

Oi vey, it was a demon. More teeth than Bruce the shark and his whole family of sequels. Solid. Hungry-looking. Looking right at me.

"Come here," it roared, making the air vibrate.

Yeah, right. I scampered into the gully and ran flat out toward the gap under the Gate.

This got *lots* of attention. Dozens of demons hulked over to line the banks, pointing, shouting up a major earthquake.

It's okay! They won't touch you so long as you have the sword!

"Do *they* know that?!?"

Terrin didn't reply right away; I ran faster. The gap yawned, but wasn't as tall as I'd thought. I'd have to duck to get under it. No problem.

"Noot alllooowed," said the demon, slow-motion pissed. It began to lumber down into the gully. Maybe it couldn't run, but being able to cover ground in sweeping five-yard strides it had enough speed to match my efforts. So this was how Jack felt when he was up the beanstalk loping through marathons.

After the one glimpse, there was no need to look back; I could hear the demon catching up. The ground rippled with each step it took. Red gravel shook from the sides of the gully like stony rain.

Boom. BOOM. *BOOM.*

Like it was home plate, I made a headfirst dive and slide under the Gate into the gray oblivion, slamming onto what felt like firm earth. Scrambling blindly forward, I sensed a low, confined space. The demon, yelling, was right on top of me. I rolled farther to escape its reach and lashed out with the sword. It connected, scraping against a giving surface. The next sound—which I assumed was the demon screaming—made nails on a chalkboard seem sweet as Mozart. Man, that cold iron stuff really did the job. When I pulled the blade back it had some green goo on it that smoked like burning rubber and smelled even worse.

The din and the monster retreated, but I wasn't going to wait to see if some of his friends might be brave enough to follow. I lurched to my feet . . . and abruptly cracked my skull against something hard. Light flashed behind my eyes, and my legs forgot how to take my weight. They slithered right out from under me. I pitched forward.

Hold on to the damn sword! Terrin yelled.

Sword? I had a sword?

Darmo House

Botello looked about his fine home with a mixture of smug contempt and frustration. The latter was the result of the overduke's rotten vision. Botello kept bumping into things in what should have been familiar territory. Had that bitch been moving the furniture around? His world was blurred beyond patience; he kept rubbing his eyes, trying to clear away the obscuring film.

What little he could see in the deep shadows was so dull, so utterly, pathetically, *mundane* compared to the wonders and horrors he'd recently observed. It was a symbol for the whole of this bloody boring Reality. How could he have thought to return when there were so many other places to manifest? He'd lived his life on a flat plain and almost too late discovered the addictive enchantment of mountains and valleys. Two weeks in Hell could indeed change a man's outlook on everything, especially when that man was the only one to ever escape the place. He'd fooled them all: demons, Outer Guardians, overlords, and Powers, and gotten away with it.

Just a little cleaning away of old business here and he could leave forever. A thousand times a thousand planes and more were out there waiting for him to find them. Of course to get to them he needed magical power, more than this world could provide, but that would come when he finished manipulating the river.

The truly laughable part was how Anton and Cadmus had helped him. Tucked away in their minds had been the keys Botello needed to open the Otherside Gate. Their researches in this Reality to solve their little Hell-river problem had plucked up arcane details he'd over-looked before in his own studies. Neither man had the whole, nor would they have known what to do with it. But when he'd passed through their minds the separate and well-scattered pieces jumped out as sweet, bright flashes of insight. It seemed so brilliantly simple to him now.

He cracked a shin on a low table. What was it doing here instead of in the side hall? Bloody woman. Prob-ably asleep in their room. Serve her right if he strangled her in what had been their bed, but no, he'd decided she would be more useful elsewhere. It would be just as unpleasant for her, and this time with no cold iron mallet in hand to spoil things. When had she gone so bloody *stupid* on him? No matter, he'd be shed of her very shortly.

He crept to the top of the grand stairs, blinking a lot, trying to get his eyes to adjust to the additional darkness of the upper hall. They refused to do so; he moved close to her door to see if any light showed through the keyhole. Nothing.

He eased it open and went in, fuming mightily when he found she wasn't in bed. Not even slept in it. Where had she taken herself at this hour? Certainly not out of the house or some drowsy servant would be up and wandering about waiting for her return, candles lighted to welcome her back. Was she with that idiot Cadmus? But he couldn't have arrived here yet or the whole place would be stirred up.

Perhaps she was huddled away in her so-called Black Room.

A poor imitation to his own chamber; she'd gone there often enough on sleepless nights, looking for clues to her tiny little future. She could have been helping him instead, working on something truly important. Had she been more open-minded about acquiring knowledge he'd have welcomed her in, but she was as terrified as the rest when it came to uncovering hidden truths. Bloody fools. Didn't they know that the best diamonds were always in the deepest, darkest, most dangerous mines?

He crept along the hall toward the blue doors with the gold trim.

Outside Darmo House

Shankey considered Debreban's question. The man had talent for guard work. It was an obvious detail that needed to be checked. "You got something there. I'll watch this gate, you make a quick rounding of the house. We may have to wait inside in order to nab him."

"Won't he be suspicious to find the front deserted?"

"He's gonna be that way no matter what. Give a yell if you see anything."

Debreban nodded and took off.

Just Inside the Great Gate

Oh, what a bummer. My head hurt so bad I couldn't hear myself, much less Terrin, who was wanting to know what was going on. I wondered if he'd felt the knock. It was my own fault, which made the pain worse. If I hadn't stood up so fast . . .

Growl, snarl, screech, and other similar noises expressing major annoyance began to rise and cluster behind me. I'd pissed off those demons in a big way. Had to put some distance between us. Maybe I'd lose them in the gray fog, unless I got lost myself.

"Terrin?"

Right here. He didn't sound so good.

"You okay?"

Never mind, check that crystal. You still got it, you got the sword?

"Yes and yes. Oh, my head."

I know. Don't do that again.

I was on his side for that. "The crystal's heavy as a bowling ball."

Go with it. See where you are.

"Can't. Foggy. Is this place safe?"

Just get moving. I'm losing it here.

So I got moving. Hard to judge how fast; I could have been on a cosmic treadmill going no place. The demon noises slowly faded. Maybe. All I was certain of was the quartz putting on more pounds. I could barely hold it in front of me. At least the pain in my head subsided as I walked.

The gray had no texture or smell to it, a bona fide limbo, with me the only real thing inside. Except I wasn't real, just a projection. I hoped my body back in the circle was doing okay. Probably better than Terrin. He'd sounded awful.

Faster, move faster. I used the sword like a cane, tapping ahead of my feet to make sure the ground was still there for them to land on.

Then . . . steps. Going down. In Hell, was that necessarily a good thing? But the quartz flickered once, so I went with it. If it got any heavier I'd need a truck to haul it around.

The fog began to unexpectedly break up, less limbo and more cloudlike, taking on a pale blue cast. There was a harsh, brassy quality to it, like a too-hot summer day, and it was getting warmer. The lower I went the more the clouds retreated. The steps ended. I was on a flat, spongy surface, visibility bounded within a slow-churning sphere of blue about ten feet in diameter.

"Am I still in Hell?"

Yes, Terrin said wearily.

"But where?"

He made no reply. I went with the quartz for a few yards, the limits of my vision traveling with me.

"Anyone here? Overduke Anton? Hello?"

"Well, hi there, big boy!"

I about jumped out of my skin, which is saying a lot after what I'd just been through. Whirling in a circle with the sword up, I tried to get a fix on the voice, which was bright, friendly in tone, and decidedly feminine. I didn't want to trust it, not in this place.

"I'm over here!" she called.

My ears swiveled, and I wheeled that way. A portion of the light blue clouds changed color, shifting to yellow, then red, then orange. The orange deepened and intensified. It took on form, a female shape, about my height.

She finally coalesced and solidified into what appeared to be a major, *major* babe, with a curvy rounded figure right out of a Mickey Spillane novel. She had glowing fluorescent orange skin, and royal blue hair, lipstick, and nails. I could get used to that. I was less sure of the blue horns and her blue forked tongue, which she was using to lick her delicate blue eyebrows. She wore six-inch blue high heels, a big smile, and nothing else.

Eeek. Yikes. I recognized her. She was one of those cartoon lesbian demon babes from Terrin's T-shirt, come to life.

"Ooo-ooo!" she said, looking at me like she just finished a month-long fast and I was made of chocolate. "You're cuu-uute!"

Darmo House, Outside the Blue Room

Botello felt the magical energy radiating from behind the closed door of the blue room like midday heat. It was the best he'd tasted since draining both Anton and Cadmus, but *much* stronger. What was going on?

Then he remembered the power of the wizard he'd sensed earlier. Filima must have brought him in, somehow. What were they up to in there?

Nothing good for me, he thought, softly opening the door.

A wall of sweet-smelling incense rolled out to greet him. He fought to suppress the urge to gag, waving futilely at the haze. Why wasn't she using the usual mixture he'd made up for her? The stuff that gave her headaches, that kept her scrying sessions short, kept her from learning too much. Someone was interfering.

Faint light came from a single black candle, fragile symbol of protection. A delicious wash of energy, both magic and psychic, was blended with the incense smoke. He took care not to feed from it just yet, lest he alarm anyone to his intrusion before he'd found out everything.

Treading lightly, Botello entered the room, hand on his belt knife. He'd have preferred a sword, but couldn't manage it and ride a horse. No matter. He drew no attention from the people within and was able to get quite close so even Anton's faulty eyes could see.

The black velvet pavilion was down. She *had* been busy.

Four, no, five of them, counting the one lying on the floor in the middle of a power circle. The others were seated at the compass points around . . . gawds, that was *not* a man. Not with those bizarre features. Cadmus had mentioned a man with a cat's face, and Botello had glimpsed something of it the first time he'd tried to manifest. He'd thought the veils between the planes had distorted the size of an ordinary cat and had dismissed it as such. Perhaps this creature was the wizard, but why put on so fantastical a form?

The others—Cadmus and Velma were in their number. How had *she* gotten caught up in this? At least it explained how Cadmus had escaped. They'd slipped past the ducal hunting parties and probably babbled everything to Filima . . . who was right over there, his dear, dear, *darling*, wife Filima, along with a short, red-haired stranger in odd clothes. They all seemed to be in some form of light trance. Each held a clear crystal, eyes closed, heads held high, their breathing deep and measured. He could see the psychic link flowing between their auras, thin, but strong enough for their purpose, whatever that might be. It swirled thickest above the cat-man on the floor who also held a quartz crystal and a sword.

So *that* was it. The wizard was on an astral outing. Looking for the lost Anton, no doubt.

Well, we can't allow that *to continue.*

Drawing his knife, Botello glided purposefully toward the wizard.

Darmo House, the Main Hall

Sword in hand, Debreban tread very lightly indeed, head cocked and ears straining for the least little sound. After finding a side door to the house left hanging open, his every instinct told him that Botello had slipped in. No time to call to Shankey for help; it might already be too late.

Debreban knew that the others were doing something magical and important to try to get the overduke back from Hell, but were they in the chamber in the tunnel or up in her ladyship's special blue room?

A strong smell of incense caught his attention. The chamber was too far away for anything like that to travel to the house. The special room, then.

He dashed up the stairs two and three at a time, moving soft and swift as a hunter. It was just possible, even in his sturdy boots. He had to worry about creaking floors, though. And anyone sneaking up on him. He edged along a wall to keep his back covered.

The door to the blue room was also wide open. Threads of incense smoke drifted out. He held his breath and peered inside.

Dark, except for one candle burning and a bit of light from the tall, narrow windows. He could make out four seated forms and a fifth figure lying on the floor. It was Myhr, apparently asleep. Looming over him was a tall, ominously familiar shape. Botello in the overduke's body. His back was to the door. None of the others seemed aware of him. None made a single move as he stooped over Myhr, a wicked, long knife in his hand raised to strike.

Debreban ran through his limited choices as he darted forward. He couldn't take Botello out by sword without killing the overduke, but he could crack him a good one from behind. With a lightning-quick shift, Debreban flipped his blade point-downward and slammed the hilt hard against Botello's skull.

Oh, yes, that made a very satisfying *whack*.

He'd been too gentle, though. Instead of falling, Botello staggered away with a pain-filled grunt. He tripped over Myhr's body and went sprawling. Debreban started after him, then froze as an uncanny wailing noise suddenly shot up from the chalk circle at his feet.

Magic. He did *not* trust the stuff, had little faith in those who claimed to be able to control it. One might as well try to control the weather; it was just too great a power, and now it seemed to be in protest of whatever they were doing here.

The wailing rose high, filling the room. The thick incense smoke was caught and swirled around by a hot, sulfurous wind that swept in from nowhere. It plucked at his clothes, made him retreat.

Lord Cadmus suddenly opened his eyes. He stared down at Botello, then at Debreban, lips parting for speech. His voice was lost in the otherworld uproar. Filima and Velma also woke up; only Terrin the wizard and Myhr remained as they were.

Botello pushed himself upright, turning. He squinted at Debreban, rage flooding his features.

Fearing another blast of fire more than the magic of the circle, Debreban charged forward. He leaped over Myhr, throwing himself bodily onto Botello, tackling him. For a few breathless moments they rolled wildly around the floor, cursing and punching. Debreban tried to get hold of the knife, at the same time bashing away with his hilt. Neither ploy worked, but it kept Botello from hurting anyone else.

The wind strengthened to gale force, howling around the circle like a confined beast. Debreban felt it seize hold of him like a giant, threatening to lift him up. It tugged at his legs, trying to pull him in. He kicked from its grasp. Still hanging on to Botello's knife hand, he tucked his head and tumbled forward. It was an awkward somersault; he landed on his side, but was clear of the wind.

Botello yelled agony for his sharply twisted arm, but still had fight in him. He brought his other hand up to take the knife, and lashed out. Debreban let go and rolled clear, blocking the thrust with the flat of his sword more by luck than skill. Botello made another swipe, but it fell short. He was being dragged into the circle by the wind.

Cadmus was on his feet now, unsteady, trying to brace against the storm force while making a grab for the knife himself. He managed to fall onto Botello, apparently landing hard, slowing him. He pinned Botello's arms and shouted. Debreban couldn't make out the words, but understood the intent. He reached into the flow and clubbed Botello's knife hand with the sword hilt. The knife fell free and went skittering over the floor. Debreban tried to grasp Botello's arms and drag him out, but the whirling force was too great; it would suck him in now.

Filima and Velma, their hair streaming, cried out as they were boosted right from their chairs. Cadmus quit Botello and stood to go to them, but was carried upward as well. They spun helplessly, three reluctant birds caught in a Hell-storm.

Debreban looked around, frantic for a rope to throw to them and spotted the discarded pile of black velvet draping. There had to be something in that mess he could use. He scrabbled over, digging quickly. No cording, but the velvet itself might work. There were yards of it in yard-wide strips. He pulled a long piece clear of the tangle and knotted an end around one of the room's support pillars. The length extended to the circle, but only just.

He wrapped the other end around his left arm. The windstorm had taken on a funnel shape, the widest part on the floor. In the brief time he'd looked away, it had swept Botello and Terrin up into its chaos. Myhr still lay oblivious on the floor. Debreban clutched hard on the velvet and leaned in.

It was like putting his arm in a vast fall of water. The wind was as solid as that, just as strong. He held on for his own dear life, but reached out, hoping to catch someone, anyone.

His hand closed around a limb, an arm, no time to see whose; he hauled for all he was worth to pull them both out of the maelstrom. He was weighed down for an awful yawning instant, then suddenly light. Velma came sailing clear. She landed hard, rolling into the remaining pile of velvet.

He couldn't tell if she was alive, too busy. He dipped into the current again, but this time it was so fast he was bounced back out like a stone skipping over a lake. He tried once more. Failed.

The small top of the funnel was lowering, and something had changed about its base. Instead of a blue mosaic floor there was a deep, dark opening with a red glow far down in its center. The sulfur stench overcame the sweet incense. Myhr seemed to float on top of it, serenely insensible to the abyss beneath him.

A blast of flame shot up around the edges of the circle, licking the high ceiling. Debreban fell back, covering his eyes. The heat beat him down; the roar deafened him.

And then . . . abrupt stillness.

The only movement he felt was his heart slamming against his ribs.

What . . . ?

He looked unbelieving on the aftermath.

Though the sulfur stink hung rotten on the air, there was no sign of fire or smoke. The floor was solidly where it had always been. The four chairs rested undisturbed within the circle. Velma lay just beyond—unmoving. The single black candle continued to burn steadily, untouched by the mad wind.

All the rest were all gone, though. All of them. Even the wizard. Only Myhr remained in place, and he was as still as death.

CHAPTER EIGHTEEN

In the Blue Limbo

I was almost nose-to-nose with an X-rated cartoon come to life. A hot—literally—demon babe who was way too cheerful for my peace of mind. I kept the sword raised between us.

She looked it up and down and flicked that long blue tongue over her full blue lips. On her they worked. "Well, honey, is that a sword in your hand or are you just happy to see me?"

"It's a sword," I said, trying to sound neutral, but my voice broke halfway through. I coughed to clear out the knot. "Who are you?"

She made a little yummy noise deep in her throat. Real deep. "Mmm. *I* am the stuff of dreams. The real *fun* ones, that is."

"Whose dreams?" I'd never had anything like *her* surface in my subconscious. More's the pity.

"Anybody's."

"Lemme put it this way: *what* are you?"

An amused pout. Damn, but it was cute. "Honey, what you have here is a Grade-A, ultra-terrific, low-down, get-down, let's-make-hay-in-the-howdee-do-me-now-baby-in-the-moonshine"—she took a breath—"succubus!"

Uh-oh. Not that I hadn't had a suspicion or three, but it was hard to think with her breathing all over like that. What an amazing set. Of lungs.

"I'm one of the red hot mamas who first taught men the necessity of washing their underwear." She sashayed—I'd never seen it done right before—in a slow circle. I got a heart-stopping view of everything, including her long blue tail. It had a little arrow-shaped point at the end, and she ran the tip up the inside of one of my legs.

Ohhh, man, that tickled. "I've—ah—ha-ha—heard of you. But don't you, like, have incubuses, too?" Or was that incubi?

She sniffed and whipped her tail back, lashing it restlessly around. "Losers, every one of them."

"Losers?"

"Only time *they* can get a date is when the woman's unconscious. You ever see one of those un-joy boys, you'll know why. Uhh-gaa-lee. But we succubae like a man up and ready and rarin' to go-go-go till the dawn-done-done-*does* us." She raised her hands high overhead and stretched.

Gawd have mercy. *Now* I was happy to see her. I coughed again, shifted in place, and casually held the sword a little lower. Okay, a *lot* lower.

She winked. "And honey, this is your lucky night. I haven't had any in *aaages!*"

"Any what?" I knew, but wanted confirmation. Hell is *not* a place where you wanna take chances on the wording.

She broke into a wide grin. Real white teeth. Lots of them, but I could get used to that. "Oh, my, sweetie-tweetie-piddie-pie, are you a *virgin*?"

Like when I had that lunch with Filima, it seemed best

not to commit myself to any specific direction until I had all the facts. "What if I was?"

"Ooohhh!" She screamed, throwing her head back.

Holy moley, if she made a noise like that just from anticipation, what else could she come up with if things got serious?

She slipped a very warm arm around my arm and snuggled close. "You are going with me, honey, as of now, now, now, and how."

Under any other circumstances and in any other place I'd have been more than happy to oblige. Terrin never had told me where he'd gotten that T-shirt, but I had my suspicions. "I'd like to, but I'm just passing through . . ."

"Aw, they all say that, but you can put your feet up for a little bit, can't you? Why else would you come here?"

"Actually, I'm looking for someone—"

"And you've found her! You just come along and I'll show you what *it* is allll about."

She looked like she could write encyclopedias about *it*, but that crystal was weighing way too much for me to shove aside. And no way was I gonna spend time with any cartoon-based lesbian demon babe while Terrin and who knows how many others were inside my head. Not that I had anything against a good healthy orgy, but those work better when everyone participates using their own body.

I tried to loose her grip. "It's real generous of you, but I just came here to get away from those big guys on the other side of the Gate, find someone, then get out."

"You came through the *Gate*?" She had night-black eyes, and they got real wide.

"More like dived under it. Those guys can't follow me, can they?"

"But you *can't* come here by that way. It's not allowed."

The pissed-off demon had said something similar. "Why not?"

"It just isn't. They have their side, we have ours. You go *in* by the Gate. You *never* go out. It's The Way Things Are." She stepped away from me, looking alarmed.

Hmm. Maybe Dante had a clue about different levels, but I couldn't recall if he had mentioned one-way streets. I wondered if he'd ever seen this world's Hell. Probably not or his *Inferno* would be a lot more popular with literature students; that, or he kept the high points about *this* section to himself.

"Okay," I said. "Probably better if I leave, so if you don't mind I'll take a rain check on you showing me the ropes and—"

Myhr! Terrin had been quiet for so long I figured he'd been laughing his ass off the whole time. His interruption was faint, though, his voice fading in and out like a bad radio. *Myhr . . . Botello's . . .*

"What? I can't hear you!"

Link . . . anchor . . . breaking the circle . . . back . . . pull you . . .

The succubus looked at me quizzically. "I never struck anyone deaf before. Blind, maybe, but not deaf. Are you all right?"

Opening . . . disrupt . . .

I checked behind me. That thin silver thread connecting my astral self with my body still extended long and strong so far as I could tell within my area, but it was whipping up and down like a phone line in a storm. That couldn't be good.

Let go . . . reel you in.

Let go of what? The sword? The crystal? Let go how? I felt a powerful tug on my back. What was he doing? It lifted me from my feet, pulling me, gliding, over the spongy blue ground as though I was weightless. The succubus ran after, easily catching up despite her heels.

"Honey, you can't go now, we haven't even started!"

"Can't help it. Don't worry, I'll call you. Terrin, what's going on? Terrin?"

No reply. Maybe he was focused on bringing me out.

I hit stairs with my butt, a very unpleasant shock. "Ow! Watch what you're doing! Terrin?"

The astral thread hauled me up a couple more painful steps. I did my best to stand, to speed things along, unsure whether I was helping or hindering. He hadn't exactly briefed me about how to make an exit.

Then sharp, hot agony flared in my back, and I suddenly pitched forward as though shot. A blast of heat and light exploded behind me. I caught myself at the last instant so the fall wasn't too bad, but that didn't register in my brain for all the other stuff crowding in. Wind, the hurricane-force kind, knocked me flat on my face and tore both sword and crystal from my grasp. They went spinning off, vanishing into pale blue depths like feathers in a storm.

Oh, shit.

It roared and rolled over me like a mile-long freight train. I ducked and covered and hoped not to get crushed.

Another hot flare, then . . . nothing. Total silence. Total nothing and then some, with more piled on top. Ominous nothing.

I cautiously pushed up. No pain. Twisted to look behind me. The cord was gone.

Maybe it was just slack. I got to my feet and turned all around. It was still gone. Once that fact sank in, I sat down again, feeling sick, shaken, and more scared than I'd ever been before in my short but very full life.

"Terrin?" I called. My voice was flat, no echoes. "You there? Terrin? Filima? Cadmus? Velma? Anyone??? Knock three times if you can hear me!"

No dice. Not one little whisper in my head.

The succubus came close, put a warm hand on my shoulder. "What's the matter, honey?"

Jeez, I felt like crying.

"Hey, you can talk to me." She did look sympathetic.

My hands twitched. "I—uh—I don't wanna jump to any conclusions, but I think . . . I think I'm dead."

She gave me a reassuring smile and squeeze. "Oh, honey, don't take on so! There's lots *worse* things!"

"I can't think of any."

"Well, let's get your mind off it for a while. You need a break."

Short attention span. We had that in common. I couldn't lose hope just yet, though. "But if my friends should try to contact me—"

"They'll get hold of you. That's the problem with this place, if anyone tries even a little bit to get in they can do it. Most don't bother. Keeps out the riff-raff."

"I thought Hell was full of riff-raff."

"*Some* parts. You'll like my place, though."

I thought I would, too. "Okay, but I gotta find that sword and the crystal I brought in with me."

"If they're still here. That was quite a big blast."

"Do you know what it was?"

She shrugged, not too concerned. "Probably another spat between the Inner Overlords and the Outer Guardians. They're always at it. Why can't beings just get *along*?"

That was a spat? I didn't want to know what a real war was like. "Outer Guardians? What are those?"

"No one you'll be seeing anytime soon. They see you, not the other way around. You come along and wait with me. Things have been so *slow* around here lately. For the longest time no one's been by, waking or sleeping. I shouldn't be out, but when I heard you I just couldn't resist taking a peek."

Well, I didn't have anything else to do. Something had gone badly wrong in the Blue Room, but Terrin would find a way to fix it. I hoped. If not, then there wasn't anything I *could* do, being dead. And in Hell. Though looking at the succubus, the situation wasn't as horrible as it might be. Keeping company with a horny—nice blue ones—babe was better than being on the menu of those big ugly guys on the other side of the Gate.

She urged me along, bumping a hip playfully against mine. We sort of halfheartedly looked for the things I'd lost, but the longer it took, the less important they seemed. I was dead. Didn't need stuff like that anymore.

We didn't go very far, that, or she was manipulating my perception. The brassy blue clouds retreated and changed color until we were in a kind of fluffy red chamber, all pillows and smooth curves. The place looked like one big bed. Even the floor was soft and squashy.

"This has possibilities," I said, my mood brightening considerably.

She was pleased. "Ooo, honey, I'm *so* glad you feel that way!"

"Ah, one thing: this isn't one of those bait-and-switch kind of things, is it? Me thinking one thing and getting another that's really bad for me?" I was still very much aware of my location.

"Sweetie-tweetie-piddie-pie . . . when I'm bad, it's better!"

"I just want to ask. Succubae have a reputation, you know. Not all the press has been favorable."

"And where did it come from? A bunch of pinch-faced prudes who couldn't get a date if they picked it off a tree. I'll let you know right off that their guilt trips bore me. You start talking a downer like them, and I'll just *have* to leave."

"Where would you go?"

"Who knows. Any lonely guy with a need for fun. It's What I Do."

That I could believe. "Here, there or where?"

"Any place, any position, big boy." Her whiplike tail

came up and tickled me under the chin. "Oooo! You're so soo-oooft!"

"Not all of me." Being dead was looking better and better every minute. Maybe this was it for eternity, hanging with this babe. I could deal with it. And her. Several times.

"Mmmm, you're not kidding," she murmured.

Somehow my pants were down around my boots. I didn't mind the warm draft. Neither did she. We ended up on the squashy floor. Woo boy, this was the life. Or death.

Then we rolled into something that gave a bit more than usual and voiced a protest.

"Hey! What's going on?"

One of the curvy, pillowy features of the place moved on its own, changing from red to fluorescent orange. It stretched itself out into another succubus. She was identical to the babe who had me pinned down.

"We got us a virgin!" she said to the newcomer.

"No! Really?" A huge grin blossomed on her face.

"Well . . ." I began, thinking it only gentlemanly to inform them of the misunderstanding. But they were *not* interested. My blessings had just doubled and gotten a lot noisier. I'd be busy here for hours on end, just *whose* end we had yet to work out. It could take years.

Then another orange succubus emerged from a soft wall, and another surfaced from the floor. "Heey!! We got companyyy!"

Oh, my goodness.

The rest of my clothes went away real quick after they lent a hand, or hands. Tails too. Those things got everywhere. I was at the bottom of a wonderfully, wiggly, squirming pile of happy, hot, eager flesh and feeling pretty damn good about it. No way to keep count of them all. I couldn't tell if the first one was still with me or not; we were all over each other.

"Save some for us!" more gleeful female voices chorused as they dove in.

I thanked gawd for my cat DNA. Lot of endurance in cats. These gals were having a Myhr-fest for sure. I never saw—or felt—so many tails, tongues, and hands at once, all of them on me. Delirious things were happening everywhere on my body. Complete and total turn-on. It was great.

As I looked to see how things were going for one of them, I recalled Terrin's warning that I might get eaten by demons. He never said it would be *this* kind of a chowdown.

Ohhh, mama!

In Another Part of Hell

Cadmus regretted not losing consciousness during that long and truly horrid drop. It recalled to him his occasional nightmares about falling, only those were tolerable since he always woke up before hitting the ground. Not so lucky this time. He struck hard enough to knock his breath out, but apparently not from as great a height as he thought, since he still lived.

He was *fairly* certain he was alive, anyway. He had to fight to get air back into his lungs, was frightened and angry at the same time, and by *gawd* once he was back on his feet he was going to *kill* Botello no matter whose body he was using.

Filima . . . where was she? Over there, just a few yards. He crawled toward her. She also seemed out of breath, confused. She opened her eyes, stared about and called his name when she saw him. *"Cadmus!"*

Oh, wonder of wonders, she was *glad* to see him. She looked almighty anxious, too. Understandable, if they were where he thought they—

It hadn't been a greeting, but a warning.

Hard, strong hands clamped around his skull from behind. At the same time something else pressed heavy on the middle of his back, pushing him down. He could neither turn, nor get enough leverage to break away. His head was pulled up, there was a painful twist, and he heard and felt his neck snap.

It was *that* quick.

He collapsed in the dust, boneless.

Now that's just bloody unfair, he thought.

Filima screamed his name in anguish. He could just see her standing, then launching herself toward him . . . no at someone behind him. He heard scuffling noises and Overduke Anton laughing and cursing at once.

"You bloody bitch! You won't—ah!" The last was full of pain.

She must have landed a good one on him. Served him right.

Cadmus tried to move, but was having a hard time of it. He could blink and that was the limit. Very odd. If his neck had been broken he should be dead. But if he was in Hell, he was likely dead already. It was all too much to take in, and Filima needed his help.

She and Botello danced into view. In Anton's body Botello towered over her. His hands were on her throat, but she raised her arms inside his reach and bodily turned, breaking his grip. Then she drove a sharp elbow into his belly. He doubled over, but too quickly recovered. Using a will he'd never called on before, Cadmus tried to grab at Botello's feet, anything to slow him, to give her a chance to escape.

But he *couldn't* move.

Botello caught her, pulled her toward him. She got her hands up to his face, then there was a flash. He roared out with real pain, let her go, and staggered away.

She's used magic on him. Good show!

Filima grabbed up a rock and threw it. Botello yelled

when it bounced off his head. She found another and another, and was extraordinarily accurate in her targeting. Cowering, he fell back out of view. She kept throwing. Tears streaked her face, which had gone dark from exertion and emotion, her hair was tangled every which way, her gown torn and coated with red dust. If Cadmus hadn't already been smitten with her he'd have fallen in love in that moment. *Gawds, she's magnificent!*

Then she stopped and stood, panting, a rock still in hand, but apparently Botello had taken himself from range. She looked at Cadmus. She came to him and knelt.

"I'm sorry, Cadmus, my gawds, I'm so sorry." More tears.

If ever a woman needed to be held, this was the one, and this was the time for it. He wanted to be held as well. If he could just unbreak his neck everything would be perfect.

Then Terrin came into view. He looked shrunken, and he'd not been all that tall to begin with; his hair had gone white, and there was some problem with his face, which was deathly pale and drawn.

"Gawdammit," he muttered, scowling. "Just take a broomstick to my ass and get it over with, why don't you?"

Cadmus had no idea what he was on about, but reasonably certain the suggestion was not directed at himself or Filima. Cadmus felt Terrin's hands on his temples.

"You'll kill him!" Filima cried.

"Dearest," he snarled, "back off. I know what I'm doing."

Terrin straightened Cadmus's head out. Rather civilized of him, but he really should get himself and Filima clear of this wherever-it-is place. Botello might have friends here—unlikely, but possible—and could return any moment.

Then Cadmus heard a crack in his neck almost as

sickening as the first and feeling flooded over him.
Agonizing feeling. "Ow! Ahh!"

"Hang on," Terrin said. He shut his eyes.

A flash of heat and the pain went away.

It was *that* quick.

Cadmus cautiously checked things out. Arms, legs, they
seemed to be working now . . . he didn't even feel bruised
from the long fall. He slowly sat up. Filima had a hand
to her mouth, staring wide-eyed.

"Are you . . . ? Oh, Cadmus!" She threw herself at him.
He gladly caught her. Well, it was worth getting killed
if *this* was the result. She was sobbing and trying to talk
and apologize all at once. So this was what elation was
about. It was quite rippingly nice. He held her and
murmured manly endearments and before he knew what
either of them was about he was kissing her, really *kissing* her. And she was kissing back. Perhaps it was only
the product of a ghastly situation, but he took what she
cared to give and was grateful.

"For crying out loud," snapped Terrin. "You two get
a room!"

This was followed by a soft thud. Cadmus remembered
where they were and pulled away for a look. Terrin lay
very still on the ground, a pile of rags with white hair.

"Oh, no," said Filima. She and Cadmus broke off at
once and went to him. Cadmus felt Terrin's chest for a
heartbeat.

"He's alive, but it's going very fast," he said. "That's
not good, is it? What's wrong with him? Why is he so
old?"

She shook her head. "He may have had an illusion on
himself or . . . I—I think he used up the last of his magic
to heal you."

Cadmus didn't know what to say. No one had *ever* been
that nice to him before. "Do you think magic might
restore him?"

"It couldn't hurt. I've exhausted mine from fighting off Botello."

"And a smashing job you did of it, too." He was all admiration. "The problem is, we're in Hell, I think. Can't expect to find the stuff lying about like windfalls in an orchard."

Terrin moved his lips; they leaned close to hear him whisper, "River."

"The Hell-river?" asked Filima. "He must want its magical energy."

Cadmus shook his head. "But it drains away magic."

"Maybe it's different on this plane. We have to find it, get him there."

For the first time Cadmus paid attention to the landscape. Not terribly enthralling: flat, lots of sere red dust, rocks, lowering dark sky, very close to the bits he'd seen through Myhr's eyes when they'd been psychically linked. That had been an interesting experience. Cadmus concentrated, tried to find some hint of energy with his other senses, but nothing surfaced. He gave up with a shrug.

"Where's Velma?" he asked.

"She got pulled clear of the vortex by your man."

"Hope she's all right. That was very above and beyond of him. I shall have to give him a promotion or something when we get back."

Filima's mouth twisted, and a touch of her old manner with him returned. "Cadmus! We're in Hell! No one gets out of Hell!"

He waved the notion away. Must keep up her spirits. "Nonsense. We'll just have a look around, find someone in charge, and explain it all. I'm sure we can sort it out. We don't belong here. Even if we are dead, we don't belong."

"But I don't want to talk to anyone in charge! Not of this place!"

"You've an excellent point, well-taken. They're likely

to be a very rum lot. We'll just consult some other personage. Perhaps if we find the Gate Myhr went under we can turn up an Outer Guardian or two who might lend us a hand. We can look that river up while we're at it."

At the mention of Otherside help of a benevolent type, Filima calmed down considerably. "Did you see what Myhr saw?"

"A little of it, in flashes. Sort of like that parlor game where you look at a drawing for an instant, then have to describe as much of it as you can. We'll keep an eye out for demons and scout for the gully. They seemed reluctant to follow him there. Let's go, then!" He stood tall, relishing his renewed strength, and picked up Terrin, settling him over one shoulder like a bag of grain. One thing about him being so wasted away, he was very light.

Filima paused and found a couple of hefty rocks. "In case Botello comes back," she explained.

"Good thinking. I must say you dealt with him *very* roundly."

"You played picture parlor games growing up. I practiced 'bird-through-the-window' at the circus."

"Really? You must tell me *all* about it. . . ."

His head and arms hanging down Cadmus's broad back, Terrin emitted a heartfelt groan of pain.

Back in the Succubus Chamber

I surprised me, myself, and I in a major way. I would never have thought anyone capable of doing it with so many women, so many times, so close together, but it happened: I actually lost count. This was *way* beyond what I expected even with the advantage of cat genes floating around my cells.

Of course, being dead might have had an influence on things. It's very freeing. Alive, I might not have been too eager to jump the bones of a bunch of succubae, but

dead, the horns and tails and eye-straining color and all
the rest just made them that much cuter to me. I honestly couldn't tell one from another, but that didn't seem
to bother them.

But there came a point, finally, and I don't know how
many hours later, when I had enough and wanted a break.
They then insisted on making absolutely sure that I was
completely tired out, which was very fun, but afterwards
I dozed for real and nothing they could do would wake
me. They eventually gave up and followed suit. We lay
sprawled over each other like a pile of gerbils.

The last time I'd slept had been the upper room at
Clem's Place, which seemed ages ago. I slipped off easily now, into the best, most restful snooze I'd ever
enjoyed. I was aware of it, strangely conscious of being
asleep and relishing every moment. It came to an end
much too soon. There was some annoying dude snoring
away like a slow buzz saw, and he woke me up.

Squinting and grumpy, I looked around for him, but
the chamber was empty, as in being completely gone. No
glowing orange demon lesbian babes looking to be con-
verted to the straight life for a little while, no soft, squashy
bed for a floor. The brassy blue limbo was back, my sight
limited to a couple yards in any direction, all of them the
same.

"Not again." I said aloud, feeling disappointed. My
voice still sounded flat, kind of like the snoring. I began
to realize I'd wakened myself. I was on featureless blue
ground surrounded by my discarded clothes. "Yo! Girls!
Wanna go for seconds? Come and get me, ready or not!"

No reply. I wondered if they'd run true to the rumors
I'd heard, and instead of spending hours with them my
whole experience had been just minutes in duration, like
a dream. Maybe only seconds. Dream encounters were
tricky things when it came to time.

"Hallo? I say, anyone there?"

Shock time. It was a man's voice calling out from not too far away. I hoped he wasn't an incubus. I scrambled to my feet and hastily grabbed for clothes.

"Hallo?" he said. "Speak again please. It's rather hard to navigate in this fog."

He sounded closer. I had my pants on, though, and made a start on my socks and boots. "I'm over here. Who are you?"

A man's form emerged out of the blueness. He was a little taller than me, even features, dark hair, wearing an old brown tunic and a long, heavy robe. His eyes were closed.

"It's okay, I'm decent," I told him.

"Eh?"

"You can open your eyes."

"Oh, I forgot." He blinked benignly. "I see more with them shut, you know."

No, I didn't. I flared my lip whiskers and wondered if he'd cracked under pressure. "Are you Overduke Anton?"

"I used to be."

Fair enough, considering what he'd been through, being body-napped and all. He gave me a thorough study as I finished dressing. Most people do the curious stare routine and ask questions. Not this dude.

"I had a vision about you," he said, as though commenting about the weather. "Lord Cadmus was in it. And Lord Botello. You wouldn't happen to know where either of them might be, do you?"

"Left Cadmus in the Blue Room at Darmo House. Don't know about Botello. Your girlfriend's looking for you."

His face eased into a relieved smile. "Velma's all right?"

"Last I saw, she was." Gawd knows what had happened since. "We were trying to find you. They sent me to Hell, but my astral thread got cut, so I'm kind of dead . . . is this making any sense to you?"

"Oh, bags of it, my dear fellow. I should inform you that you're not dead, just bodily displaced."

"I'm. Not. Dead?"

"You're disappointed?"

"Well, I was just getting used to the idea."

"You may have to again if we can't take ourselves back to the Reality plane. If you stay here too much longer death could become a permanent condition for you."

Bummer. I'd have to find a way home. Quick. "Can you get me back?"

"I don't know."

Double bummer. "What about the Hell-river? Any way you can fix that mess? I got a friend who really needs you to do that for him."

"As a matter of fact, I've an idea to try, but we must locate Cadmus and Botello."

"They're in the Reality plane."

He closed his eyes a moment. "No, they aren't. Not any more."

"Where are they?" Was he telepathic?

"Damn, but they have put a wedge in the works. Unless it was meant to happen. There's so many variables, and they're all open to interpretation . . . or misinterpretation."

"Hah?"

Eyes open. "Not to worry. What's your name, sir?"

"Myhr. Rhymes with *purr*—"

He chuckled. "How fitting. Well, Myhr, would you mind very much lending me a hand before the world ends? There's a good fellow."

He walked off. Eyes shut again.

He *had* cracked. And I was catching it. I went after him.

Darmo House

Debreban looked down at Myhr's body, mourning with vast regret. What a rotten waste. What a rotten situation.

If he'd only been able to stop Botello or even delayed him for a few seconds, it would have made a world of difference.

Literally.

Shankey, who had taken the catastrophic news rather well, shook his head. "Wonder why he didn't get dragged in with the others?"

Velma shrugged, looking very miserable. "Maybe because his astral self was already there? I dunno. But the rest went in, whoosh. If Drebbie here hadn't grabbed me I'd have gone too."

Debreban winced at the inaccurate diminutive, but kept quiet. It was better than being called "Debbrie."

"Metaphysical things," she continued. "Who can understand that kind of stuff? Poor Anton's got some company at least. Maybe they can all hook up together on the Otherside and figure something out."

"If Lord Botello doesn't kill them," Debreban added cheerlessly. *Or if they're not all dead from the storm.* "What do we do now?"

Shankey went over to the discarded pavilion and pulled a length of black velvet from the pile. They caught onto his intent and helped him straighten the fabric, then solemnly draped it over the body.

"We say a prayer for the dead," he announced. "Then we find Lord Perdle and tell him what's going on."

"Maybe . . ." said Velma, "maybe we could try a séance ourselves. Just to see if anyone's there."

"Won't that be dangerous?" Debreban didn't care to further involve himself with such dark doings.

Shankey nodded, but seemed thoughtful. "Yeah. But if the world's gonna end soon like Terrin told me, what have we got to lose?"

"No, I don't think we should. We need to go to Lord Perdle, and then help with the fire." Debreban went to one of the narrow windows. The glow in the distance hadn't grown, but neither had it shrunk. Perhaps they'd gotten it under control and confined. Few places in Rumpock were far from the river, and if the Watch had the pumps going in time . . . and, "What the hell is *that?*"

"What's wrong?" Shankey came up.

Debreban pointed. "Do you see anything?"

Velma joined them. "Uh-oh. That's bad, right?"

The city appeared to be flooded with an undulating black fog through all her streets and ways. It bumped and washed against the gates of Darmo House like an impatient tide.

"Oh, yeah, that's bad," said Shankey. "That's what all the Talents have been in a twist over. We don't have Talent, so we should *not* be able to see it. I think something really awful has happened on the Otherside."

"Séance anyone?" suggested Velma.

CHAPTER NINETEEN

In Hell

"Shouldn't we be seeing some demons about now?" Filima asked.

"Let's be glad that we haven't." Cadmus had quite enough on his plate; he didn't care to be dealing with demons just yet, thank you very much.

"But they should be all over the place. If they're not, then where did they go?"

Cadmus was reluctant to voice the idea that Botello had rounded them up and would soon descend in a surprise attack. And for that matter where *had* Botello taken himself? There wasn't a surfeit of cover around here; a few scraggly, thorny growths that might loosely be described as trees was the limit of the scenery, along with some rocks.

"Party," mumbled Terrin behind him.

"What's that?" asked Velma.

"They gonna party."

"What do you mean?"

"Wha'dya think? Get me to th' dam' river. An' tell Godzilla boy t' stop bumpin' me so much!"

"Cadmus, we have to hurry!"

"Right-oh!" he said, and began to trot.

In Limbo

"Hey!" I said. "Check it out! My sword and the crystal!" I darted to one side and snagged them from where they lay on the flat blue ground, none the worse for wear, not even scratched.

Anton kept walking. "I'd wondered whose those were," he said. His eyes were still shut. "They skittered toward me in some strong wind that came through. Stopped right at my feet just a few minutes ago."

Minutes? So all that action with the succubae and my long nap had been a time-compressed dream? No way, no way. I had to have been in a space opera-style time warp or pocket or whatever they called those things. It had *happened,* and I was walking funny to prove it. "Why didn't you pick them up?"

"They weren't mine. Besides, I sensed the sword had some cold iron in it and might not be good for me to handle. Disrupts one's Talent, you know. I'm out of magic now as it is. Crystals are even trickier. Never know what energies are stored in the pesky things. Best to leave them lay until one's been properly introduced."

"Is it going to be a problem for you if I hang on to them?"

"Don't think so; just avoid whacking me with either one and we should get along fine."

I looked over the crystal for any sign of light. It had a normal weight now. "Myhr to *Enterprise,* come in. Time to beam me up. Terrin? You out there, dude? Hello?" No answering voice popped into my head.

"Wants to be charged up again," said Anton.

"I told Terrin it needed new batteries." I shoved it in a pocket and got a solid grip on the sword. Didn't know what good it'd do me at the moment, but I felt better having it along.

"Terrin's your wizard friend?"

"Yeah. He was anchoring my astral body. The line snapped, and I don't know why. I think Botello might have interrupted the circle."

"Yes, that would explain some of the things I've seen and sensed. Is Terrin a short fellow with white hair?"

Jeez, I was walking with Anton-Wan Kenobi. "Last time I saw. This magic drain did stuff to him, messed him up. You can see him?"

"I've caught a glimpse or two. He's on this Side. Over in the Hell plane."

I snorted. "That's practically his home turf. Probably having a party."

"Don't think so. Cadmus is carrying him."

My guts made a swoop. "He's not dead, is he?"

"No, Filima's talking to him, but he doesn't look at all well."

"She's here, too? Who else?"

Anton shook his head. "Sorry. Just brief pictures of them. But we must move more quickly."

So we picked up the pace. "How is it you can see like that?"

"It's my Gift. Been rather a bother, but turning out to be useful here. In the Reality plane the visions come through clear, but are not always specific in their meanings. The Powers That Be have to limit our Otherside knowledge or it throws off the balance. They sent me some warnings, but no explanations. Best they could do, I fear."

He was sounding like Terrin, but more refined in his language. "You don't go running around the Reality plane like that, do you? With your eyes shut?"

"Oh, certainly not. The rules are a tad different on this side. I've been shown and told some interesting things, not all of them good."

"Like what?"

"Hard to explain."

"Can you tell me about the Hell-river?"

"It started with Botello."

"He invented it?"

"Goodness, no, but his magical experiments caused something of a metaphysical earthquake, which brought it flowing into the Reality plane when the veils are thinnest, at night. The Overlords in the Hell plane were naturally upset at first, then saw it as a means to escape."

"Into the Reality plane?"

"Into any plane. You've seen their place—would you want to spend eternity there?"

Good point. "Can't these Powers keep them in?"

"That's what the Hell-river's for, serves as a boundary between the planes. It holds a store of magical energy, which is what confines the demons. They can't use magic themselves, but are very familiar with it, like a horse with a bridle. They're always eager to manipulate people like Botello into serving their ends while pretending themselves to serve. He has ambition, a weakness they exploited, but he has always been a trifle short on imagination. Tends to dismiss the obvious."

"Which was?"

"That he just wasn't up to the task. Thought himself special. Stupid bugger. What he's managed to do is botch up the balance. One living being thrown into Hell the wrong way—which is what happened with Botello—is what upset things. It made quite a stir, I can tell you. Brought him no end of attention. The Powers are very specific about protocol. The *only* way you are supposed to get into Hell is through the proper channels. You have to die, go through a bit of processing with the Powers, and if you're really deserving punishment, off you fly through the Gate."

Who would have thought line-breaking could be taken so seriously? On the other hand, who was that eager to break into Hell? "Why didn't the Powers just get him out?"

"They didn't know he was there. The Inner Overlords were hiding him, hoping he could do something to help them escape using the river. Normally it flows in a circle. Any being who tries to cross it is brought right back again. But suddenly the Hell-river vanished from Hell, an unthinkable disaster, and any unshielded Talents in the Reality plane unfortunate enough to be in its path were sucked in. It has quite a store of magical energy from them. That's upset things, too."

"They all died?"

"Not as such."

"Bodily displaced?"

"Close enough. Only there were no bodies left behind. The holes made when they vanished just knitted up, memories were adjusted. The Powers had a hand in that, an emergency measure to keep people from a panic. The missing Talents are imprisoned in the Hell-river, and it wants correcting."

"Would that leave the astral plane empty, too?"

"Look for yourself," he said, gesturing at the blue limbo around us. "Bloody boring, isn't it? The Powers shut everything down so they could better spot any demons who might get through."

No wonder those succubae had been so lonely.

"Now the river flows nightly in the Reality plane. So far, beings in the river when it vanishes from Hell are left behind when it shifts course, but that's about to change. Several more living souls have been pulled into Hell—with their bodies—and *that* has created a link to the Reality plane. Very shortly the Hell-river is going to shift course and be flowing in both directions at once. Then the demons will be able to escape. Well, it's just not the done thing."

"No, of course not," I said faintly.

"So we're going to find Botello, get me back into my proper body, and try to put things right again."

"What about the overlords?" Who and whatever *they* were. "What about the demons?"

"I'm sure you can take care of them."

It was news to me. "Huh?"

"Your sword—"

"Is borrowed! I'm a lover, not a fighter. I didn't do too well on that side of the Gate. One of those demons nearly got me."

"But you fought it off."

"I gave it a paper cut, but nothing that would stop it. That thing was *huge*." I anticipated that overlords were even bigger and meaner.

"How huge?"

"Like a bulldozer."

"What's that?"

"Okay, like a small building. A tall, small building. With arms and teeth."

He smiled. "When it's time I'm sure you'll be up to the task."

"Wish I had your confidence about it."

"You will."

"Hah?"

"Remember where you are. Desire for something can make it occur."

"Really?" News to me.

"Your desires will affect the objects and beings already here, or rather there. When we get to the Gate you'll see. The demons do it all the time, but not for anything pleasant. They're not very smart. Cunning, but not smart."

"Why didn't Terrin tell me that?"

Anton shrugged. "He might not have known. You two aren't from around here are you?"

"You could say that and then some."

"Ah. Likely used to different rules. They change from world to world, you know."

He was spooking me. Seemed to know a lot more than he should. I wanted to find out just how much, but had to focus on the current situation. "How do I do this?"

"Just think of what you want, but it has to be based in this side. You won't materialize a cup of tea, because that's not here."

"Work with what's at hand?"

"Yes."

"Why haven't you done any of that to get out?"

"Because I'm in the wrong body, and escaping is a bit more complex. That's why Botello couldn't escape. Well, here's the Gate. Gird up."

On the Other Side of the Gate

"Looks like Botello's run afoul of the chaps here," said Cadmus.

Behind the questionable cover of a tree, he and Filima watched some rather tense proceedings going on close to the great Gate. A hair-raising and stomach-churning collection of terrifically ugly creatures—demons—were gathered there, the lot of them focused on the interplay between one of their own and Botello. He was presently engulfed in the grasp of that creature, his legs dangling some ten feet from the ground. He appeared to be doing a lot of fast talking.

"He does seem to be in trouble," agreed Filima.

Terrin, lying on his back next to her and apparently asleep or passed out, offered no comment. They were only yards from the empty riverbed, but the space in between was crowded with demons. To get to it, they would have to backtrack a goodly distance, which was not practical at the moment.

"Hope they don't hurt him. For Lord Anton's sake," she added.

"It doesn't look good. They seem none too pleased. I just wish those buggers would shift themselves." Cadmus nodded toward the ones blocking the way to the gully.

As though reading his mind, the demons began to move closer to the Gate, clearing a path.

"I say, that's luck. Let's go while we can. Keep low and quiet." He hoisted Terrin over his shoulder, and they hurried across the open ground.

Botello struggled hard to breathe normally, difficult to do while being held so tight. Maybe he should have taken his chances and stayed close to Filima. He'd removed Cadmus as a threat, and the odd-looking short fellow wasn't strong enough to swat flies. Filima might have proved useful as an offering or at least as an indication of Botello's intent to honor his agreement with the overlords.

"I tell you again, I have brought sacrifices to you," he wheezed. "They are back near where you found me."

"The Gate," said the overlord. "Open it."

"I can't without them." There, a flat lie, but it might buy him time to think of something better.

"Then bring back the river."

"Free me. I can't do anything like this."

"You will escape."

"How can I? I don't know how I got free before."

"Lie," stated the demon.

Botello cried out as a blast of heat washed through him. Not the merely uncomfortable warmth of a summer day, but a real fire roasting his every nerve. His cry rose and extended into a prolonged scream until he ran out of air. He twitched and trembled, trying to struggle away from the agony, then it left him as suddenly as it had come. Panting, he saw his flesh was unseared. If that had been an illusion of pain what would it be like if they began torturing him in earnest?

Best not to find out.

"No lies," the demon said. "Open the Gate or bring back the river."

"All right." He was too weary and frightened to think. Just agree and hope to find an opportunity to . . . and there it was.

Staring down past the demon Botello spotted them making their way toward the riverbed. Filima and the others. How had Cadmus recovered from a broken neck? No matter.

He pointed. "I need them. I told you I brought sacrifices."

Almost as one, the demons turned to look.

"That's torn it," said Cadmus. "Run!" He urged Filima ahead of him. She sprinted like a deer. He strove to keep up and was only a pace behind when she scrabbled down the edge of the bank into the wide, shallow gully.

"Now what?" she asked, still moving.

"Go toward the Gate."

"They'll cut in front of us."

"Then cross to the other side. I don't see any of them there."

"Bad idea," mumbled Terrin unexpectedly.

"Then what do we do?" Cadmus demanded.

"Just put me down and stand back. Something heavy's about to break."

"What's broken?" Cadmus eased Terrin onto the dry red dust, then stood off, fidgeting, wanting to go after Filima.

He sprawled spread-eagled, laughing like a rusty gate. "Just watch."

Cadmus started to object, then speech left him. He stared around in disbelief. Filima gave a sharp gasp of surprise. She scampered back to him and grabbed his arm. That was nice.

Where Terrin's body touched, where their feet touched, thick black fog began to ooze forth from the ground.

"Party time!" crowed Terrin.

Anton and I crouched under the Gate, peering out at the riverbed. The black fog was coming back, swirling up around Terrin, Cadmus, and Filima. Their body language was eloquent; except for Terrin, who just lay there, they were clearly alarmed. "Is that good or bad?" I asked.

"Yes," he said. "Absolutely."

Well, what did I expect from a man with his eyes closed all the time? "So what next?"

"Let's go get my body back." He started forward. I caught him.

"Have you noticed there's a demon convention out there?"

"I believe they'll be rather too busy for the next few minutes. Let's take advantage of it."

He smiled and walked unafraid into the towering crowd. I followed and profoundly wished us both invisible. No way to tell if it worked or not, but the monsters did seem to have their attention focused downriver, even the one who had Botello in its hand. Claw. Whatever.

I kept close to Anton, my sword ready. Maybe my wish was working. None of them looked at us, and we got close to Botello. The demon holding him was growling.

"I told you," said Botello. "Now release me so I can finish the working."

Another growl, but it set him down. The instant he was clear he started toward the Gate.

And what a look he had on his face when he saw *us*.

Anton smiled. "Hallo, Botello. You have something

belonging to me. Be so kind as to return it. No questions asked."

Botello, a big blond guy, briefly showed teeth, then ducked behind a demon. He was still trying to get to the Gate. Anton took off after him, leaving me flat-footed in a forest of demons. A couple of them noticed me, meaning I wasn't invisible after all, but that was it. They and the rest began to file toward the riverbed and its rising fog. The roars and growls shaking the air were anticipatory. They were smacking their chops and making the underworld equivalent of yummy noises.

"Slow up," I whispered aloud, wishing for that to happen. Some of them heard and looked back, but kept going.

Not good, not good. I was supposed to use what was at hand, so what was here? Rocks. Lots of those. Maybe if they formed themselves into a really high wall between the demons and the fog . . .

Chunks of red stone rolled in front of the demons, formed a line, and began stacking up so fast that they seemed to grow. More rocks rained down out of nowhere, locking themselves into place. The wall shot up, ten feet, then twenty, then fifty, blotting out a wide section of the lowering sky.

Ohhhh, man, it was soo coool.

The demons stopped and stared at it, studying the situation. I turned to check on Anton. He and Botello were in a dead heat for the gap under the Gate. Botello made a dive, but came up short. Anton landed on him, and they rolled around trading punches. That must have been pretty weird for them, each hitting his own body. Talk about abusing oneself.

Crash. Rumble.

My brilliant wall came tumbling down. Demons weren't just pounding their way through, they seemed to be causing the stones to fly every which way. They must have been doing the wishing thing as well, and were likely a lot better and faster at it, having had more practice. I dropped to avoid some red missiles shooting my way and imagined them slamming back to whoever threw them. The rocks stopped in midair and reversed. No way to see where they hit, but bear-growls of annoyance boomed soon after.

Dust, there was plenty of that lying around. A sandstorm might slow them. The instant I thought it, it roared up, but I overdid things, and was myself caught in the blast. Half-blind, I retreated, staggering to the Gate, which was clear of the mess.

Anton was barely holding his own, his face bloody. Botello had the larger body, and didn't seem to care what kind of damage he inflicted on his former residence. Rubbing grit from my eyes, I waded in to help, which consisted of poking Botello with my sword to get his attention.

He let out with an unhappy yelp, then squinted at me. "What are you?"

"The name's Myhr." He could figure out for himself what it rhymed with; I was too stressed to be friendly. "You gonna swap with Anton or do I have to invent shishkebab with you?"

He caught the intent, even if the words were confusing, and sneered. "You can't force me out. Not without killing this body."

My guess was he hadn't heard of *The Exorcist*, and that Anton had an ace up his sleeve. "Okay, you win, on your feet so we can leave." Another jab with the sword point convinced him to cooperate for the moment. Anton got up and twisted Botello's arms behind him.

"You okay?" I asked.

"River," he puffed, breathless through his bloody mask.

My sandstorm was gone. Some joker had made it rain, not the cotton-candy stuff I'd encountered when I first arrived, but a harsh, blatting downpour with drops the size of marbles. They hit about as hard, too, turning the sand into muddy soup. The demons plodded easily through it, like tanks with legs.

Beyond them the Hell-river had swollen considerably.

"Is it flowing in both directions?" I wanted to know.

"Unfortunately, yes." Anton's eyes were open now and on the haunted side. "You need to remove those creatures from our path."

"How?"

"Just imagine them over there someplace." He made a wave toward the vague distance.

"I can do that?"

"If you visualize it. Hurry!"

So I visualized all the demons a mile away in the middle of a sandstorm, encircled by a wall. Damned if it didn't happen.

Man, if I could do this kind of thing on the Reality plane . . .

"Move!" said Anton.

I shoved my sword into my belt and helped him push the reluctant Botello forward. There wasn't much ground to cover, but the demons would be back quick enough once they'd figured out a thing or three.

The black fog was up to our shins where we entered it. Strangely, Botello stopped struggling, was even eager to go faster. My instincts didn't like that much, but I couldn't think what to do about it. I was a little busy trying to come up with demon-delaying tactics, adding in a good old Texas-style twister to keep them busy. It sure made for one hell of a roar, even in this place.

Cadmus and Filima were in the black stuff up to their waists, and I couldn't see Terrin at all, but where he had last been the fog bounded up like a smoky fountain.

"Lord Anton?" Cadmus called. "I'm terribly sorry about that business after dinner, but—ow!"

Filima had given him a light swat on the arm. "Later!"

"Yes," Anton agreed. "Later. Do come over and lend Myhr a hand, there's a good fellow."

Cadmus lurched toward us, as though wading. "It's gotten rather thick. Very odd."

It didn't feel thick to me. Must have been a magic thing. They all had Talent and were floundering; I was immune. "Where's Terrin?"

"Underneath. Refused to come out. He *likes* it."

Botello suddenly shook free. He was a big guy and pretty determined. "What?" He rounded on me. "You're *not* the wizard?"

"Only because there's no money in it."

Boy, did he look pissed. "Where is he? Taking *my* power?"

"Heads up, Cadmus, megalomaniacal episode coming through."

"Grab him!" Anton yelled.

We grabbed him. Cadmus was full of muscles, and I had a feline edge that made me strong for my size. We each had an arm, but it was even money how long we could hang on. "Now what?"

"Push him under!"

We did that too. Botello didn't fight us, which was alarming. He didn't fight us for the longest time, like maybe a minute, then began thrashing.

"What's going on?" I asked.

Anton had moved off to one side. "The magic's too much for him to absorb."

"We're feeding him magic?" That seemed a remarkably bad idea. So bad that Cadmus and I let Botello struggle to the surface. He wheezed and choked just like it had been water.

"You're drowning him in it," said Anton. "Put him back under."

"But won't that kill your body?"

"It will kill Botello. That's more important than anything else."

"You . . . can't!" Botello objected.

"I must. You're the one who's upset the balance. Better you die than those poor people back on the Reality plane."

"You'll die, too! What you're in is all that's left of me! You'll remain here!"

Anton shrugged. "I'm willing to make that sacrifice to save them. Part and parcel of being an overduke, you know. Kill him."

"But Lord Anton . . ." Cadmus was horrified.

"Just do it, Cadmus. Be quick. I don't want my body to needlessly suffer."

This I didn't like, but I went along with Cadmus and shoved Botello under. Responsibility can be a bitch. He fought us, a last-ditch madman's effort, but was losing momentum.

Terrin surfaced. Literally. He bobbed up from the fog like a submarine, one with a big grin painted on the bow. He looked better. His hair had gone back to its normal red, and the ruddiness had returned to his skin, which had lost a good century or so of wrinkling.

"Hey," I said. "How you doing?"

"I'm cool. Lot of great stuff floating around here. You should try it."

"No, thanks."

"Check this out." He pointed to his forehead. He had horns. "Ain't they cool? I may keep 'em!"

"Terrin, I'm a little busy here. . . ." The sight of me and Cadmus trying to drown a man in magic fog didn't seem worthy of comment from him.

"No prob."

"And there's a bunch of demons about to do a tsunami on our ass." I'd noticed the roar of my tornado had ceased, replaced by other roars. And I thought they'd been annoyed earlier.

"No prob."

"Anton said if you visualize—"

"Oh, hush, I can fix it."

Since he was back to being his old confident-to-the-point-of-being-snotty self, it was safe to assume he *could* fix things and put my whole attention on Botello. It was really way past awful holding a man down, waiting for him to die. I'd seen something like it in a Hitchcock movie that had made me squirm. This was real, though, and I was an active participant. Cadmus looked the way I felt, but his gaze was on Anton, not the horror at hand.

Anton swiped blood from his eyes and watched, his face solemn, sad, and so weary it hurt to see. I felt terrible for him, and hoped he could slip back under the Gate when it was over. He shouldn't have to stay in Hell, not after this.

Botello had pretty much spent himself. His desperate bucking subsided to an infrequent, reflexive twitch. Not long now.

Wading over, Anton gave a nod. "That should do it."

We lifted Botello clear of the fog. He drooped like a dead man, and seemed heavier than he should be. We dragged him to the riverbank and laid him out.

Anton came forward and took Botello by one hand. Nothing happened for a moment, then I glimpsed a faint rippling between them.

"What was that?"

No answer. Anton's eyes rolled up, and he keeled over like he'd been shot. Cadmus caught him and hauled him over next to Botello. Filima cautiously approached, not eager to get close to either of them, but staring hard.

"I think he's done it," she said. "The auras have changed. Can you tell?"

Cadmus and I both tried. I wasn't sure what was there, but some kind of swap had taken place between them. He shook Botello. "My Lord Anton? Are you there?"

He got a groan in response. The man's blue eyes fluttered open, and he looked around, puzzled. He raised one arm, studied it, than let it drop. "Blind as a bat again. Thank gawds."

"Lord Anton?"

"Yes, I'm here. I managed to get back. I think." With a small spurt of energy, he sat up, undid his trousers, and looked inside. He gave a great sigh of relief. "Thanks gawds," he said, with much more fervor, then noticed Filima gaping at him. "Please pretend you didn't see that, thank you." He did himself up again, and with Cadmus helping, found his feet.

"Are you all right, Lord Anton?" Cadmus sure liked saying that name.

"As well as can be expected. Would you mind very much removing him completely from the river? There's a good fellow." He slogged up the bank himself while Cadmus and I hauled what was left of Botello clear.

"He's not dead," I told them.

Anton wasn't surprised. "There's no death in Hell. I rather hoped he might not know that. However, it's time we left. None if us belong here, even your friend."

Terrin was farther up the bank. He turned toward us once, flashing one of his shit-eating grins.

Uh-oh. What's going on?

I joined him. So did the others.

"Wha'd'ya think?" He gestured proudly at the expanse of Hell within our view. Gone was my high wall, sandstorm, tornado, the works. In place of the dark red dust and rock was a vast, unbroken plain of white, right out of Antarctica. It was dim and dreary, but unmistakable. Silent, sober, and still. Every single one of the demons was frozen solid in place, in mid-move. Ice and snow covered them completely, their growls caught solid in their throats.

"Cooo-oool," I said, meaning its every sense. My breath hung in the shivery air.

Terrin smirked and snickered. "I've always *wanted* to do that!"

"I say," said Cadmus, "that's rippingly original. Who would have thought it?"

He was serious, too.

"It won't last." I pointed to one of the bigger demons, who was beginning to crack free of his subzero prison. "Anton, If you've got a way outta here I suggest we take it."

He smiled. It came off better with him looking out behind his face instead of Botello. "Might be a bit tricky but I think we can manage with your help."

My help? What was I supposed to do?

"Just hold still. Everyone form a circle around Myhr, one hand on the shoulder next to you, the other on him."

What was this, a square dance or a really kinky variation of my time with the succubae? They did as Anton instructed.

"Now everyone visualize being back on the Reality plane again. Four went out, four will return."

What about me? Had I turned into chopped liver and not noticed?

Nothing happened while the four of them focused, which was worry-making. A few more of the demons struggled free of their ice and were lumbering our way. I made more ice appear under their feet. They slipped and fell on their asses, but recovered quick. Still seated, they started sliding toward us: screaming, out-of-control, toothy bobsleds.

Oh, shit.

"You guys think harder, okay?" I said. "And snap it up."

"Chill, Myhr," said Terrin. He sounded tense.

I glimpsed a last vision of the demons on a juggernaut path straight toward us and braced for a killing impact . . . then something happened. It wasn't too much different from Terrin's travel spell; maybe he even put a chunk of that energy into Anton's mojo. The ground seemed to drop away, sending me plummeting, yet not feeling the gravity. It was like falling *up*. Their faces whisked around me in a top-speed blur, made me dizzy, so I shut my eyes.

The next bad thing was my sudden weight-gain. I felt like I'd put on tons of lead. It turned the falling up into a real fall, switching too fast for me to work into a real panic. Before I got even halfway through the process I landed—*whump*.

My breath was knocked so far out I thought I'd never get it back. This wasn't a struggle, but a major war to get air inside. It didn't help that there was something heavy on my face. I wrestled it off, my eyes bulging, mouth open.

Standing over me, their faces stricken, were Shankey, Debreban, and Velma. They held hands as though playing an overgrown ring-around-the-rosie game.

Shankey spoke first, looking at Velma. "Is that supposed to happen?"

She shrugged. "I dunno. I've never done a séance before." She peered hard at me. "Are you dead or what?"

"Uhhh," I gasped. Then wheezed. Then coughed. Then lay flat, resting until my lungs got used to the idea of going back to work again. The leaden feeling gradually passed; I was able to sort myself out. I was in the blue room, on the floor, swathed in black velvet. This was considerably better than the last place.

"Where are the others?" asked Velma. "Are they alive?"

"Uhhh." I tried to make it sound positive.

But her answer came whirling in on its own. They all ducked and shielded against a prolonged gust of wind tearing through the room from nowhere. The velvet whipped from me, and made a complete circuit before wrapping around a pillar like a flag, its ends snapping.

Then the bound-from-Hell express dumped them,

one-by-one, in various undignified heaps: Filima, Cadmus, Anton. Terrin, more used to that kind of travel, landed on his feet.

It looked like everyone would be awhile sorting themselves out and playing catch-up. Velma, once she ascertained that Anton was back to himself again, got real happy and affectionate. Cadmus swept Filima up in a really good face-hugger kiss—when did *that* happen?—and she didn't fight him on it. I chose to avoid the whole Q and A session, trudging to the windows for more air. Man, I was tired. Terrin came over and plopped down next to me.

"Check it out," he said, gesturing at the view. "The fog's gone."

"It better be," I muttered, not bothering to turn around. "I'm *not* going through *that* again."

He felt his forehead. The horns were still there.

"Rad souvenir," I said. "Keeping them?"

"Of course."

"Be hard wearing a hat."

He blew that off with a snort. "How much you think we'll get for this one?"

"For saving the world? A lot. A couple of really big diamonds, at least."

"Rubies are better."

"Whatever, so long as it gets us home or to a place with an astral map, indoor plumbing and decent toilet paper. I assume we helped save the world. Is the astral plane back to normal? Magic energy restored?"

"Yeah, sure. No probs there. The balances are recovering themselves."

"What about all those magicians and the rest who vanished?"

He closed his eyes, humming to himself, but without making any noise. "They've all returned where they belong. Metaphysically, this world's the way it should be. Even Botello."

"You got news on him?"

"Absorbed a flash on the trip out. He's no longer on the event horizon."

"Still in Hell?"

"Naw. He was sucked out feetfirst in another direction. I figure he's got some explaining to do to the Powers That Be. Glad I'm not him, they'll prolly send him back as a dung beetle."

A humongous thunderclap exploded right over the house, making it shake under us. That interrupted conversation for a minute. The others drifted over to the window as the sky opened up. Veils of water poured down on Rumpock. That would fix the fire. I started to ask Terrin if he'd done a magical good deed, but he was on his way out, stretching mightily.

"Later," he called, not looking to see if we noticed his departure.

That rat. He left me stuck in the middle of a rush of hero-worship from all sides. I wanted a nap.

I eventually got it, sometime well after dawn.

Overduke Anton had to leave to take care of the business with the fire and to make a start on restoration. Velma went with him to help out, and eventually Cadmus and Filima joined them. Shankey and Debreban hung with me, and we had an early breakfast in the kitchen. Shankey's girlfriend, the cook, turned out to be an easy-on-the-eye surprise. We scarfed cold pizza while she got the fires going for the morning meal, and I told them some of the stuff I'd seen on the Otherside.

A messenger in black-and-silver livery turned up with a note from Anton. He was also looking for the ducal guardsmen Botello had used, but they weren't to be found. We all kept quiet until the guy left. Shankey read the note.

The fire damage was bad, but not too catastrophic. They lost the bell tower and an inn got scorched up pretty bad, nothing that couldn't be patched over in time for the Mid-Summer Festival. Terrin and I were cordially invited to be special guests of honor at that event and in the meantime were welcome to enjoy the overduke's hospitality at his palace. A formal note would follow.

I had a bad feeling that smoked inn might have been Clem's Place. If so, then I'd see about doing him a few benefit concerts, then slip him the recipe for pizza so he could have the first franchise.

But later. Wining and dining could wait.

I convinced Shankey and Debreban of the necessity of my beauty sleep and went upstairs. The big empty bed in my room looked like paradise. It felt even better. I shucked out of my clothes and dropped face-first into the pillows, so out of it I didn't care if I ever came back.

But no rest for the wicked.

Snuggling into the sheets with lip-smacking delight, I was on the edge of drifting off. Thought I had drifted off. But I became aware of another presence close by. I caught no sense of danger from it. Quite the contrary.

After a little fuzzy reflection, I concluded I really was asleep, but dreaming. Dreams take you to all kinds of places, especially on the astral plane if you're so inclined. I'd never been there before that I could recall, but you can't go to Hell and back without having to endure a few major psychic changes.

I cracked open an astral eyeball. Reclining next to me on the bed was a succubus. She lapped her long tongue on my nose, tickling it. Her tail ran slowly up one of my legs. She had the biggest grin.

"Well, *hi* there, you sweetie-tweetie-piddie pie! How's my favorite virgin this fine day?"

Ohh, mama!